"Time and again Pamela Morsi reaches into her heart to find the way into ours. She explores the depths of emotions with a sweetness and sense of humor that brings a welcome breath of fresh air to the genre."
–*Romantic Times*
D0734078

The Taste of Love

His face was only inches from her own. She gazed into the eyes that had become so familiar, the eyes that she so admired.

"Kiss me," he whispered so softly that perhaps he hoped that she would not hear.

She angled her head and brought her mouth down upon his own. They could share a kiss. The contact, sweet and sensual, swept her away. It was just a kiss, she told herself. Just one kiss. There was nothing too dangerous about it. One kiss, but it was like a hundred kisses, a thousand, as his warm lips lingered upon hers, toying and testing and teaching. A month ago one kiss had gotten them married. Today it made them instantaneously intimate. There was no shyness in either of them. They wanted the touch, the taste of each other. They wanted the incredible closeness of it.

"Morsi is best known for the sweet charm of her novels. . . . Awfully good."

—*Publishers Weekly* on *Sealed with a Kiss*

"Pamela Morsi writes with laughter, tenderness, and most of all, joy."

—*Romantic Times*

"I've read all her books and loved every word."

—Jude Deveraux

HarperChoice

Sweetwood Bride

PAMELA MORSI

HarperPaperbacks
A Division of HarperCollins*Publishers*

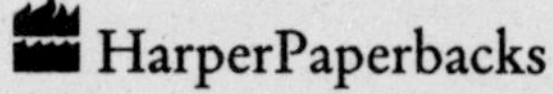

A Division of HarperCollins*Publishers*
10 East 53rd Street, New York, NY 10022-5299

ISBN 0-06-101365-X

First printing: July 1999

Printed in the United States of America

❖ 10 9 8 7 6 5 4 3 2 1

For my talented and helpful assistant, Merrily,
for making my life so much easier

And for my fellow Bandidas Laura Bradley,
Jo-Ann Power, and Evelyn Rogers
for making my life so much fun

Sweetwood Bride

I

THEY'D come for him a little after noon. He'd been boiling with sweat and hitched to the back end of a plow. Company was as welcome as a cool dipper of water, and he'd greeted the men with a smile. It hadn't taken long for it to fade. He had been completely dumbfounded by the accusation. It was all a mistake, he'd assured them hurriedly.

Mosco Collier had never been guilty of a crime in his life. He'd never said a word untrue, never cheated in a poker game, never borrowed a chicken from a coop he did not own. Any wild, rebellious streak of youth had been sweated out of him by hard labor tilling rocky ground and shouldering a man's responsibilities on a boy's young shoulders. His whole life had been lived on the straight and narrow.

Nonetheless, he stood accused. He was innocent, yet he was found to be guilty. His punishment, it was determined, would be a life sentence.

Condemning eyes surrounded him. As he stood in the meetinghouse doorway, the words were read aloud.

". . . for better, for worse, in sickness and in health, as long as you both shall live?"

Moss hesitated only a moment as he stood on the

pine plank steps. Through his thin summer work shirt he could feel the cool metal of a shotgun barrel between his shoulder blades.

"I do," he replied.

Moss glanced at the young woman at his left.

"And do you, Eula Orlean Toby, take this man to be your lawful wedded husband," the preacher continued, "to . . ."

Moss glared at her. The conniving little Jezebel looked extremely pleased with herself. It was her word against his. And what kind of woman would lie about being dishonored?

The kind to whom Moss was about to be married.

Couldn't they see she was lying? It was very obvious to Moss. Her tone was strangely high-pitched. She was talking very fast. And she was unable to look him in the eye. She was not a very good liar, yet everyone believed her.

"By the power vested in me by our Father in heaven and the state of Tennessee, I pronounce you man and wife."

There was a collective sigh of relief. The shotgun was lowered from Moss's back.

He turned to look at the face of the woman he married, or rather to stare at the freckles upon her face, which covered it completely. How could he have thought her pretty? That day by Flat Rock Falls, he'd actually thought her pretty. She'd been all golden hair and sweet innocence. That innocence had proved to be a mercenary ploy, and her hair . . . her hair was just stringy blonde.

"You may kiss the bride," Preacher Thompson told him.

"No thanks," he replied. "That's what got me into this mess in the first place."

He turned to face the half dozen other men crowded around the church steps to see justice done. They were subdued, satisfied, and self-righteous. They were not strangers. These men were his friends, his neighbors, his occasional drinking companions, and his hunting partners. Moss glared at them, openly furious that they believed Eulie and thought so little of him.

They accepted the story that he'd played fast and loose with a fresh young gal, laid with her out in the open woods, and then refused to offer for her. A man who'd do such a thing was too worthless to waste plugging with buckshot. That is what Moss had always believed. And that is what these men believed of him.

The female was standing beside him now. Moss didn't even glance at her, but he saw that everyone else was looking in her direction.

"We wish you happy, Mrs. Collier," Enoch Pierce said to her formally.

It had been Enoch who'd held his shotgun between Moss's shoulder blades. Obviously, *Moss's* happiness had not been Enoch's concern. Moss pushed through the crowd angrily, unable to speak, unwilling to display the anger that he felt. If these men could believe the worst of him, well, then so be it. He'd never give them a thought once he was far away. Once he was on his own in the West at last.

"Thank you, sir," he heard his new wife answer behind him. "We appreciate your good wishes."

Good wishes! Moss was seething inside. The whole

lot of them had wished him into a hell on earth. How would he ever get West with some no-account woman at his side?

Moss stormed across the clearing in front of the meetinghouse and grabbed up the dragging reins of his rust-colored gelding.

Red Tex was the finest saddle horse ever seen in these parts. And like a fine mount anywhere, Red Tex easily picked up on the temperament of his rider. He'd stood through the whole ceremony, calmly munching a tall bunch of fresh spring grass. Now, with an angry Moss beside him, he was skittish and alert.

It was one bit of extravagant luxury for a plowing man to own a fine riding animal. But Moss was willing to endure the criticism of his neighbors in exchange for the pure pleasure of sitting tall and proud in the saddle. And a man headed west needed a good horse. Moss Collier, in his most fervent plans and dreams, was headed west.

He mounted with an urgency born of the need to be away from this place, these people, the embarrassment of being judged as a liar and seducer, the humiliation of being forced against his will to take a wife. He wanted to be in the saddle, racing into the wind. He wanted to leave all this behind him. Red Tex sidestepped nervously, his head high and taut, his ears twitching to the side expectantly.

"Ransom," Moss heard his new bride say to her younger brother, "you gather up Clara and the twins. I can stop by and get Little Minnie on the way to Mr. Collier's farm."

Moss reined the horse in tightly and turned to stare at the woman in disbelief. He was not alone. Every man among them was equally dumbstruck by her words. The silence in the little hillside clearing of the Sweetwood was broken only by the rustle of breeze through the oaks and elms and the muted barking of gray squirrels.

The old preacher gave Moss an anxious glance and then spoke softly to the stringy-haired blonde gal.

"Perhaps you needn't take your whole family with you today, Eulie," he suggested urgently. "It is your honeymoon, after all, and–"

"How much family you got?" Moss asked her coldly, not caring if he interrupted the preacher's calm advice.

He hardly knew the woman, this Jezebel that was his bride, but he vaguely recalled having heard it said that Virgil Toby had left this world with nothing to call his own except a passel of children.

"I've got five youngers," Eulie answered him, her chin lifted in pride as if it were some personal accomplishment. "My brother here and four sisters."

Moss's eyes widened and his jaw dropped in shock.

"Five!" He was incredulous. "Five new mouths to feed. Six, counting your own."

The shouted words made the big horse uneasy. He pranced with agitation, and the men around him, unaccustomed to such a high-strung animal, moved back, giving him a wide berth.

Yeoman Browning, one of Moss's most frequent hunting companions, was the first to speak up. He was a quiet, fair fellow, and Moss had often relied upon his judgment. At the current time he, at least, had the good grace to appear ill at ease.

"The boy is pretty near growed," he assured Moss

quickly. “He must be ten or twelve year at least.”

“I’m thirteen,” the boy spoke up, his chin raised in challenge. “But I work as hard as a man. Ask Mr. Leight, he’ll tell you the same.”

Moss glanced assessingly at the boy, who favored his sister, he supposed. They both had that wan, stringy blond look. He appeared to be tall enough and strong enough to do a bit of work. But he was still just a boy, and one that seemed to have a chip on his shoulder and an inflated idea of his own value.

Yeoman nodded hopefully. “The boy can be a help to you, Moss. And the girls . . .” he hesitated momentarily. “They’ll . . . be good company for your wife.”

Moss felt the anger flash through him once more. He dismissed Browning’s suggestion and the proud young boy in the same condescending gesture. These men were expecting him to feed and clothe six more people on a rough piece of rocky hill that could hardly support him and his old uncle alone.

“Maybe it’s best if you wait a while, Eulie,” the preacher said once more. “You can get settled in and—”

“Bring the whole dadblamed lot of ’em.”

Moss directed his words angrily to his new young bride. “If they are coming to starve at my house, they may as well start today.”

Eulie smiled pleasantly and turned to squeeze her brother’s arm in obvious delight. Her cheerfulness in the face of Moss’s bad temper was jarring.

For his part, young Ransom didn’t appear nearly as elated by the words as his sister.

Preacher Thompson stepped up next to Red Tex and patted the horse’s withers with an aged, gnarled hand, settling him down before gazing up at his rider.

The preacher's voice was no longer stern and strident, as it had been before the wedding. His tone was now conciliatory.

"It's a big bunch to take on," he admitted to Moss quietly. "It may well taste a hard and bitter cup today, son. But I promise you'll feel differently about this and her and everything after that baby comes."

"I told you, they ain't no baby coming," Moss answered between clenched teeth.

The preacher's gray brow furrowed and he tutted in disapproval. "You're married to her already. It makes no sense to persist in denials."

Moss jerked at the reins, pulling his horse back away from the man. He wanted to be away from this place, away from these people, away, so far away. That's all he'd ever really wanted, to get away. Now the dream seemed further in the distance than ever before.

"Get your whole family," he ordered Eulie angrily. "And have them out to the farm by suppertime. I got plowing to do this afternoon."

His young bride was still smiling, still happy. She must be feebleminded, he thought unkindly.

Moss dug his heels in the horse's flanks. Yeoman called out to him.

"Ain't you going to give the gal a ride back to your place?"

Eulie was still standing there, smiling as if this were a truly happy wedding day. That sweet, innocent smile—it was the same one she used when she was lying through her teeth.

"Red Tex don't ride double," Moss snarled back determinedly. "And she's plenty used to walking."

* * *

It was, without a doubt, the most conniving, low-life, sidewinder trick ever played on a man. Eulie was not proud of it. But it was for a good cause, and at least it had worked. By nightfall her entire family would be safe and cared for under one roof.

Of course, the husband-man was in a near bleeding choler about it. But it was best for him, too, she assured herself. Every fellow needed a wife, and Moss Collier had nobody. Eulie might not be the best candidate for wife in the Sweetwood, but she was absolutely certain that she was better than nobody.

She grinned at the uncomfortable men standing all around her. Moss Collier's anger was embarrassing. And her own cheerfulness seemed to disconcert them even more. Eulie didn't want to ride the husband-man's big horse anyway. She much preferred to walk out to the farm with her brother and sisters. And she flatly refused to worry about the future or take offense at anything that was said.

A woman's wedding day was supposed to be the happiest day of her life. If this was the happiest she was ever going to be, Eulie was determined to enjoy it.

She was Mrs. Moss Collier. Now and for all time. She'd just vowed it before God. And she had no intention of taking such a thing lightly. He was her husband-man till death to part.

She suspected that she'd known of Moss Collier most of her life. But he had come to her attention for the first time one Sunday morning last winter outside the meetinghouse. Not that Moss Collier had been attending the service. He avoided the monthly preaching with a regularity dependable as sunrise. But Eulie had spied him riding by tall in the saddle on his big red horse. He never hesitated on his way, but he tipped his broad-brimmed wool hat sort of vaguely in the direction of the churchgoers. His hair was the thickest, blackest, shiniest hair that she'd ever seen on a man. His face was weathered and determinedly strong-jawed, but somehow handsome in its own way. Eulie had felt almost a shiver at the sight of him.

"Who's that fellow on the horse?" she'd asked Mrs. Browning.

"Why, that's Mosco Collier," the old woman had answered. "From up on Barnes Ridge. You know him."

Eulie thought that vaguely she did, but she'd never given him quite a look before.

"Has he got a woman?" she asked.

"No, and more's the pity," Mrs. Browning answered. "He lives with his old uncle that was injured in the war. The man is a hermit, and Moss has taken care of him since he was little more than a boy himself. A fine, good fellow he is and a good friend to my son."

Whether it was his good looks or Mrs. Browning's high opinion, Eulie knew right then and there that when looking for a husband-man, she wouldn't do much better than Moss Collier.

She glanced at the guilty-looking men standing around her. Shifting from one foot to another, they were embarrassed on her behalf and uncomfortable with what they knew of her most intimate life.

Eulie grinned broadly at them and tossed a hank of tow-colored hair back over her shoulder. The sun was shining, the breeze was warm, spring was in the air, and she was a married woman.

Preacher Thompson patted her hand, looking worried.

"You don't have to go out there to his farm if you're afraid," he said.

Eulie gazed at him, incredulous.

"Afraid? Why would I be afraid?"

The husband-man was angry for certain. But Eulie was not in the least afraid of him. She considered herself a pretty good judge of the basic decency of people. And Moss Collier, mad as he could be, was basically a pretty decent man.

In truth she was excited to go, anxious to start her new life. She'd sneaked up to his cabin a couple of weeks ago and had a good look around. It wasn't the most prosperous place on the mountain, but it was bigger than she had hoped. The wall timbers looked sturdy, and the roof was in good repair. A couple of the outbuildings were pretty disreputable, but nothing that couldn't be patched together with a half dozen board feet and a hard day's effort.

The preacher glanced around at the other men and then spoke to Eulie more quietly, as if he preferred that others didn't hear.

"He's your husband now, Eulie," he said. "What's between you two is none of our concern." He hesitated thoughtfully. "If . . . if he beats you, you can come back to the parsonage. In your condition, Mrs. Thompson and I wouldn't hesitate to take you in."

Her eyes widened. The preacher thought Moss Collier might beat her. She had never even considered that. Although she did suppose she knew the fellow might be some put out with her. Most fellows seemed to want to choose their own wife. But Moss Collier was pretty old not to have gotten around to choosing. He looked easily twenty-five years of age and nary a potential bride in sight. It might even be said that Eulie had done the man a favor.

Of course the husband-man himself might not see it that way. And he might well be the kind of man who impressed his opinion upon his nearest with the aid of a strap or a switch. Eulie wasn't really used to such. Pa had taken a razor strop to Ransom a time or two for sassing him. Her brother had a fresh mouth and an argumentative nature. It was a father's duty to try to teach his son respect. But Pa had never been in a temper about it. He'd done it as if it were a distasteful chore that he hated more than Rans did.

Eulie supposed telling a lie that forced Moss Collier to marry up with her might well be a beating offense. If it was her due punishment, she'd take it, but she wasn't about to allow nobody, not even a husband-man, to make a rug of her for his own comfort.

"Don't worry about me, Preacher," she assured him. "My family and me, we'll be just fine. Eulie Toby takes care of her own."

Her confidence was unshakable. The old preacher didn't look so certain.

"You're Eulie Collier now," he pointed out.

A change of name wouldn't make any difference.

With a spring in her step, Eulie began gathering up her things and her family. There was very little of the former and a lot of the latter. She'd left the Knox homestead that morning with all her worldly possessions tied into a ten-pound poke. The weather had looked sunny and bright and she'd determined that it was a perfect day for a wedding, so it might as well be hers. With yesterday being Preaching Sunday, she knew that the pastor of the Sweetwood congregation was still at home. He'd be setting off tomorrow to ride his circuit. If she didn't get married today, she'd have to wait a whole month. She simply decided that sooner was better than later.

Smiling and cheerful, with her brother at her side, Eulie began making her way up the path toward Moss Collier's place on the high ridge above the falls. She was as familiar with these narrow mountain trails as the back side of her own hand. Eulie had lived her whole life within the shadow of the tall, tree-covered peaks. It was where she was from and all she knew. It was all her mother and father knew. It was where the Toby family had lived out their lives for half a dozen generations. And Eulie was going to see that they survived here for a dozen more.

At her side, her brother was silent until they were out of hearing range of the men at the meetinghouse.

"I don't like him, Eulie," her brother declared. "No way, no how, I just don't like him."

She gave her ill-tempered sibling a dismissing glance of unconcern. "Oh, Rans, you don't like anybody," she reminded him.

Ransom didn't argue the fact, but he still didn't look pleased.

"I don't know why you have to up and marry some fellow anyway," he countered.

"I explained all that to you," Eulie said. "It was the only way that we could all be together. Nobody in the Sweetwood is going to let a family of women and children sharecrop for them. And you ain't big enough to do it on your own. If we are ever going to have our own place again, one of us gals has to marry some land."

"Then you should have let Clara do it," Rans told

her. "Mr. Leight's a fine fellow. I wouldn't have no caution about him joining the family."

Eulie turned to look her brother in the eye. His bowl-cut blond hair was not as clean as it could have been, and his face was in need of a good scrubbing as well, though it was difficult to tell how much was dirt stains and how much freckles.

"Clara is not marrying that old Bug," Eulie stated adamantly. "I don't know where you'd get such an idea."

"From them," Rans answered. "You ain't seen them together, Eulie. I told you, they're plumb lovestruck with each other."

Eulie snorted in disapproval. "Well, sure enough he'd be lovestruck with her. Clara's the sweetest, kindest, prettiest girl in the Sweetwood and I ain't just saying that 'cause she's my sister. But him . . ."

Eulie screwed up her face in an expression of distaste.

"They don't call him Bug 'cause he's got a pig-face."

"It ain't his fault, Eulie. The doctor down at McComb says he's got some kind of glandular complaint," Rans told her, not for the first time. "That's what makes his eyes bulge out like that."

"Well, my sister ain't marrying nobody that's got no glandular complaint, especially not one what looks like a click beetle."

"Well, ain't you just the belle of the valley," Ransom sneered. "You're not so dadblamed pretty yourself that you need to be carrying on about the shortcomings of others. Looks ain't everything."

"And looks ain't everything the man's doing without," she countered. "Bug is as dull as a widow's ax and easily half as smart."

"I don't care what you say, I'd still rather have him for a brother-in-law over a fellow who acts like he ain't got no use for you nor none of your kin," Rans told her.

Eulie waved his words away.

"Moss Collier'll suit us just fine," she assured him. "He just ain't got used to the idea of marrying and starting a family."

"The way I heared it, he done started one already," Rans answered.

When Eulie didn't answer, he stopped abruptly in his tracks and stared at her in disbelief.

"Good Lord save us all!" he said under his breath. "You lied about it, didn't you."

Eulie hushed him with her hand and glanced around guiltily.

"It ain't no big catastrophe," she assured him in a whisper. "Moss was sure to come around sooner or later. A little tall tale just had it happening more speedy than was perfectly natural."

Rans had covered his face with his hands and was shaking his head in disbelief.

"No wonder he continued to deny it all, even after it was certain they was going to insist he marry up," Rans said.

"He'll just get used to the idea of all of us and he'll be settled and resigned to it," Eulie said with certainty.

"Lord, he'll probably kill us all in our beds and feel right and justified," Rans moaned.

"The man needs a wife, clear and simple," Eulie declared. "It ain't like I cain't do the job."

"Oh, my God," Rans whispered under his breath. "Oh, my God almighty."

"Quit taking the Lord's name in vain!" Eulie scolded.

"Don't be reproving me, Eulie Toby," Rans snapped. "You've done told the biggest lie ever heard in the Sweetwood."

"It ain't all that big a lie," she said. "He did kiss me."

"He kissed you."

"Yes, he done kissed me," Eulie said. "I made myself all pretty and then sort of chanced upon him. He kissed me of his own free will, so it ain't totally a lie."

"Kissing ain't getting a baby," Rans told her. "If you had it in your head to tell such a tale, you should have at least a let him have a shag so he could wonder."

"A shag?"

Rans stared at her incredulously.

"You don't even know what it is, do you?"

Eulie was silent.

"You're so dadblamed ignorant, you don't even know where babies come from."

"I do, too," Eulie shot back. "I just didn't know what you call it."

Rans continued to shake his head. "We'll be murdered in our beds."

"Just stop that foolish talk," Eulie said. "I don't want to hear another word about it."

"Eulie, this ain't going to work," Rans told her quietly.

"It already has," she answered. "Now it's getting late and it's a long way up the mountain. You best be getting the youngers. I want to get Little Minnie and still have time to fix the husband-man a good meal."

"A plate full of hot food ain't going to fix this," Rans warned.

"Just stop your worrying," she said. "Everything is going to be just fine."

As Eulie watched her brother take the ridge row path, she wondered if she believed the words herself. But she raised her chin and headed her own way, determined. Eulie had learned most of life's lessons at her mother's knee. And if there was anything that her mother had been certain about, it was that the more distasteful the job, the quicker it had to be faced. In the last few years, Eulie had been forced to face more distasteful jobs than she cared to think about.

Her mother, a strong, hearty woman who had always seemed capable of overcoming even the most daunting of life's obstacles, had succumbed to childbed fever only a week after the birth of Little Minnie. Her death had been more than a husband's grief for Virgil Toby. A sickly, often listless daydreamer, he'd counted on his wife both to do most of the work and to raise his children. His death last year was as much from simply giving up as it was from the weak, rheumatic heart he'd lived with from childhood.

At age seventeen, Eulie had found herself to be in possession of very little and the head of a large household. Clara had been able to take on most of the childcare duties of Little Minnie. Ransom, though prone to complaint and quick to take umbrage, was a very hard worker. And the twins were as biddable as two children could be. But it had not been enough to keep the family together. Within months they had all been farmed out, living at different places.

The twins had gone to live with Mrs. Patchel. The old widow, known as Miz Patch, was the finest weaver and tatter around. Lately she was bothered with aching bones, and she'd been eager to provide a home for the two nine-year-olds who could thread the loom and do needlework from daylight till dark.

Little Minnie stayed with the Pierce family. It was Enoch Pierce's land that Virgil Toby had been sharecropping. The bond between landlord and sharecropper was usually tenuous, requiring only an occasional conversation and an annual payment. But the Pierces had taken an active interest in the Toby children after their mother's death. Enoch checked on them daily and often brought meat and game for the table. His wife, Judith, had been equally kind and dependable. She had taken quite a shine to Little Minnie. Evicting the Tobys had been a necessary cruelty. It was made more palatable to the Pierces by their taking the youngest to be raised in their home.

Farmer Leight had hired on Ransom to help him. Bug seemed to be one of the few people in the world to get along well with Rans. When the farmer later offered room and board for Clara to cook and clean for him, it seemed an ideal situation. It might have stayed that way if the fellow hadn't cast his bulging insect eyes upon Eulie's sister.

But that was all in the past now. Eulie was married fair and square to Moss Collier. She'd have her whole family together again under one roof.

Unwillingly her thoughts drifted to what Rans had called shagging. She'd been raised outside for the most part and was not totally ignorant of the ways of procreation. Of course, she'd never been allowed anywhere near the pens when the hogs were bred, but she'd seen birds and squirrels pairing up.

Eulie swallowed a little unhappily. It didn't look like anything she'd personally like to do. Downright embarrassing, she thought. Still, she supposed that now that she was married she'd have to let the husband-man shag a time or two. But if Moss Collier thought she'd be allowing that every spring like some barnyard animal, she'd simply have to dissuade him of the notion.

And if her brother Rans thought she was going to allow herself to be worried and anxious on the happiest day of her life, well, he was just as cross-hinged as a two-headed pup.

2

Moss didn't return to his plowing. When he got back to the field, he'd hitched up the jenny. The dependable little she-mule was right, ready, and agreeable to pull, but when Moss stared at that rocky ground and thought about those extra six mouths to feed, he just got so mad all over again that he didn't work a lick. He walked up and down the half-turned rows cursing a blue streak and wishing his new bride into perdition.

She was going to be sorry. Eulie Toby and her whole worthless, hungry family were going to be sorry. With them like a millstone around his neck, why, he might never get West. And if he didn't, they'd be sorry. The whole sorry lot of them would be sorry.

He went over the events of the morning again and again. Even knowing what had come to pass, he still suffered from disbelief. How could a slip of a stringy-haired gal just walk up to the preacher and declare herself dishonored and point to him as the guilty party? It was as if his ability to resist temptation meant nothing.

He remembered that afternoon at the falls with vivid clarity. He'd been out with his old hound running a fox to ground when he'd happened upon her. Sitting on the big rock, she was dangling one foot into the water while she combed through her damp hair. Her unexpected appearance momentarily startled him. And the sight of her bare leg hastily covered by her skirt was equally disconcerting. All flushed and clean from bathing, her body was outlined with exquisite accuracy by her thin cotton clothes. His imagination had taunted him. What if he'd arrived only moments earlier? What if he had caught her wet and naked in the frothing water? The fantasy had him immediately aroused. The reality of the feminine charms within his reach was a lusty provocation.

"Morning," he'd said, politely doffing his hat.

"A good morning to you, too, sir," she'd answered. Her smile was broad and welcoming, all plump pink lips and pearly white teeth.

The old hound quit his tracking and hurried, tail a-wagging, to her side. She immediately began to scratch him behind the ears.

"What's the dog's name?" she asked.

Moss shrugged. "I just call him Old Hound."

She laughed at his words. It was a warm, enticing sound.

"Well, hello there, Old Hound," she said to the animal and commenced talking baby talk to him in a pouty-mouth fashion.

As Moss watched her hugging and snuggling against the dog's neck, prickles of excitement skittered upon his skin like lightning. If she had that much affection for an old hound, how much love might she have for a man?

She spoke to him with words so soft they could not be heard over the rumble of water cascading down the river over great flat boulders.

"What did you say?" he asked her.

She raised her hand to him and he helped her off of her rocky perch. Stepping up within arm's length of him, she smelled fresh and sweet. She gazed up at him with eyes of awed anticipation and innocence.

"I'll have to get closer to hear you," she replied.

Moss wondered if she could hear the pounding of his heart. It was certainly sounding loud enough in his own ears.

"I hope you don't mind me washing in your falls," she said.

He nodded mutely, unable to reply.

"I guess I wasn't really in your falls," she continued. "I was sitting there on that rock next to the falls. It's on the creek side. Nobody owns the creek."

"No . . . nobody owns the river, or the falls, neither," he assured her. "It just is smack-dab in the middle of my acreage."

He didn't want to talk about farmland. He didn't want to talk about anything. She was there, so close to him. He didn't want to talk at all.

"You're looking right pretty, and real welcome," he said.

She blushed and lowered her chin before glancing up at him beneath demure lashes. She seemed to be such a cheerful, happy person, it was difficult to look at her without smiling. It was like sunshine bubbled up inside her bursting to get out.

"My name's Eulie," she said. "Miss Eulie Toby. Thank you for allowing me to wash in your water."

The reminder that she was so recently naked teased him, and Moss felt a near-irresistible desire to do likewise. He raised a questioning eyebrow.

"Do you mean that you don't intend to pay?"

"Pay?"

"Why yes, Miss Eulie," he said. "Don't tell me you are unaware of a tariff on the use of Flat Rock Falls for bathing."

"A tariff?" She looked genuinely concerned. "How much is the tariff?"

Moss smiled at her.

"Well, it depends," he answered. "For somebody's old stray milk cow, I usually charge a bucket of sweet cream skimmed from the top. For a noisy old goose, I might roast her offspring for Sunday dinner. Now a pretty little gal like you—well, I suspect a kiss might seem a fair enough trade."

He'd half expected her to huff up and give him what for. That's what nice females had a tendency toward, he was certain. But she didn't do that at all. She raised her head and pursed her lips, closing her eyes in expectation.

Moss had looked at that upturned mouth for a very long moment. He'd been careful to avoid the young gals of the Sweetwood. They were looking for mates. He'd made certain that he was always looking in the other direction. Best not to catch the eye of a maiden who was marriage-minded. As he gazed down at the slim young woman with the pretty blonde hair and the puckered little mouth, his resolve faltered. One kiss wouldn't hurt anything, he assured himself.

One kiss had ruined his life. He should have just walked away. While she had her eyes closed he should have turned his back on her and run as if his life depended upon it. Because in a way it did.

Moss gave a whispered curse under his breath.

She'd trapped him. She'd lied about him and trapped him like some fool rabbit in a snare. If he had any sense at all he'd take off running now. It still wasn't too late. He could just walk out on the whole lot of them. Leave them high and dry and head out west on his own. That's what they deserved. That's what *she* deserved.

In his fury, Moss eyed the big sandstone boulder that he'd been plowing around all his life. It graced the center of his cornfield, ever unmovable, ever in the way. Today that rock looked even larger than it had before.

Frustrated, he kicked it, then howled in pain at the ungiving reception it had offered his foot. He'd acted the fool and now he was suffering for it.

Limping, he unhitched the mule back from the turning plow, which he left standing in the field. He gathered up the leading strings on Red Tex and led the animals down the mountain toward his place. He still felt shame at his public humiliation and anger at the conniving Jezebel. Those emotions, however, were overridden by an incredible gnawing sense of disappointment that was so sharp he could nearly vomit. He was tied now. Tied with the bonds of matrimony. Tied to that woman and her kin. Tied to this place, once again.

As a boy it had looked so easy. All he had to do to get away was grow up. And growing up happened without even trying. He'd grow up and he'd move away. He'd leave behind the hardscrabble life that made men tired and old. Break free of the restraints and constriction of mountain ways. Declare his freedom from the land that held him prisoner.

But he'd learned that growing up could be different than a man thought. He'd learned that as he leaned tearful over his fevered mother's deathbed.

"Promise me you'll take care of Jeptha," she'd whispered. "He ain't going to have nobody but you. You got to promise to care for him all his life."

"I promise, Ma," he'd whispered. "I promise to take care of Uncle Jeptha. Now you promise to get better. You promise to get well, Ma."

She hadn't made the vow she couldn't keep. They'd lowered her into cold Tennessee ground less than a week later.

He hadn't worried much about Uncle Jeptha. Jeptha was old and sick, ruined from the war and not long for this world. That's what young Moss had thought. Ten years later, his uncle was exactly the same as he had always been. He seemed not older, nor sicker, nor any more eager to meet his maker.

Not that Moss wanted him dead. That was not it at all. The old man was family, his only family. And he would always keep his mother's dying wish. Still, Uncle Jeptha stood in the way of his leaving. And Moss couldn't quite help but resent that.

But now it wasn't just him. Now it was all of them. Stringy-haired Eulie and her five youngers would forever be a rock he couldn't move, one he'd spend the rest of his life plowing around. Moss cursed once more, while only Red Tex and the old jenny could hear him.

He made his way down, around, and up once more to the homestead. The earth smelled of spring, fertile with forest duff and green moss. In the distance, a lark sang in the meadow. Closer, a big grasshopper whirred in the tall grass.

The cornfield was almost within shouting range of

the house, but the rocky ridge paths that skirted the water's edge made the traveling route from one point to the other three times the distance. The high land next to the river was surrounded by dense woods and reed-thick backwash marshes. The cold, clear water bred fish and fowl in abundance. That had apparently held a keen attraction to his mother's ancestor, the old Scotsman, who had settled upon the land over a hundred years ago.

Glancing around the homestead where five generations of his family had been born, Moss thought about the old Scotsman. He had *chosen* this place to live. All Moss's life, he'd craved the same opportunity, to choose his own place to make his own mark. The last thing that he'd wanted was simply to live out some destiny that had been forced upon him. A destiny some lying Jezebel had forced upon him.

The barn, like the rest of the buildings on his place, had been constructed before the war. Aged and sagging now, it could hardly manage to keep the weather out. The pens and split-rail enclosures were weak and rotted. Red Tex and the mule stayed within their confinement only by force of habit.

Moss had not spent money or time on a new barn or new fences. He was leaving this place. He was leaving it all behind. He was going west. As he awaited his opportunity, he neglected his farm. Only the essential tasks were accomplished; all his profits were hoarded and stored.

Moss unhitched the mule and casually surveyed his surroundings. They did not look like fields and farm capable of supporting eight people. They looked poor. They were poor. The sack of coin stowed away in the strongbox beneath his bed notwithstanding, the place was kept no better than a sharecropper's hovel.

He shook his head. He would have thought that a scheming Jezebel determined to force a man to marry her would have at least picked a fellow who appeared prosperous. Of course, maybe this dreary place seemed familiar. Certainly the poor, rocky scratches that her father had farmed looked no better. He recalled with some displeasure how cheerful and pleased she was at the wedding. Perhaps the woman was just not quite right in the head. That would explain a lot.

Moss snorted in disgust. That would just top it all, he decided. Not only was he saddled with a woman he didn't know and her whole hungry family, she was probably teched to boot.

When he finished with the mule, Moss rubbed down Red Tex carefully and adoringly. The big red horse was the living symbol of all that Moss wanted and all that he dreamed about. He was a Texas horse, bred for wide plains and working cattle. He was tangible proof of the commitment to go west. Moss loved him.

The horse had been run hard that day, hard enough to lather. And then he'd been left to stand while Moss had cursed and kicked rocks. He deserved a bit of attention and some good treatment. It sure wasn't the horse's fault that that no-account lying woman had slithered in and ruined his life. Lingering over the task, he thought once more of his lawfully wedded wife, and it drew his mouth into one thin line of displeasure. He thought of her damp clothes against her body. He thought of her arms so lovingly wrapped around his old hunting dog. Grimly, he thought of the matrimonial trap he had fallen into.

"If she's so dang fond of that old hound, maybe I'll

have her sleep under the porch with him," he boasted to Red Tex unkindly.

Once the horse was clean and relaxed, Moss gave him a bucket full of oats and headed for the cabin. He had to give Uncle Jeptha the news, though he dreaded it like the plague. He didn't want to talk about what had happened. He didn't want to have to explain himself to anyone. But the subject couldn't be avoided. She and her family would be showing up before supper. Moss couldn't just allow them to arrive unexpected. He had to tell Uncle Jeptha. And he wasn't at all sure how the old man would take it. Moss had been shackled to this land all his life, but it was, after all, Jeptha's farm.

This homeplace, the double cabin that had been sitting on the flat of this ridge since the old Scotsman built it, was two windowless rooms with a wide porch running the total length of the front and side. The kitchen and smokehouse were separate, a stone's throw away. That building had burned once and was rebuilt, though the fireplace, blackened both outside and in, bore witness to the ferocity of the blaze. Moss had laid brown river rock chiseled flat and even as paving for a walkway easy to traverse and free of spring mud. But the safe distance from the cooking fire could seem a lengthy trip on a cold winter morning.

The double cabin had a small fireplace of its own that was used only in the very frostiest weather. He and Uncle Jeptha didn't require a lot of space, so they lived in one room and used the other for storage. The two men were satisfied with the arrangement and it saved them from the need to replace the leaky roof on the grain shed.

Moss deduced with annoying certainty that with the

place about to be filled to the rafters with unwanted children, he'd be repairing those shake shingles atop the shed very soon.

With spring already nearly upon them, Moss had removed the front door and replaced it with a frame-stretched wire screen. It would keep the worst of the pests and insects out of the place and offer a bit of ventilation to the windowless building.

He stepped up onto the porch and, without bothering to open the screen, hollered out to the cabin's occupant.

"Uncle Jeptha!"

There was a slight screech of wood and sound of wheels turning on white pine floor.

"Did those men find ye?" the old man called back. "They's a whole passel of them looking for ye. I said you were up at the cornfield."

"They found me," Moss answered quietly.

"What'd they want?" his uncle asked. "They looked as sober and determined as a lynch mob."

"You've got the right of that," Moss answered.

"What'd they want?"

"They wanted me to go down to the meetinghouse with them," he said.

"The meetinghouse? In the middle of the week? What for?"

"To get married," Moss answered.

A moment of complete silence followed his words, and then the scrape of wheels against wood was heard once more as Uncle Jeptha propelled himself to the doorway.

"To get married!" the old man exclaimed with disbelief.

The subject was so abhorrent, Moss could hardly meet the man's eye.

"I married Eulie Toby this afternoon," he said simply. "She and her younger brother and sisters ought to be here by suppertime."

Uncle Jeptha stared at him in disbelief as he ran a worried hand through his waist-length steel gray hair and then pulled thoughtfully upon the long white whiskers that hung nearly to his belly.

"You done married her?" His voice was incredulous. "I didn't know you'd even been courting her."

"I ain't courted her," Moss answered.

It was on the tip of his tongue to declare that he never *would* have courted her. He wanted to denounce her as a scheming, bald-faced liar. He wanted to declare his innocence in the whole shameful, sordid story. But she was his woman now, for better or worse, and a man who spoke ill of his wife was as low-crawling as Eden's serpent.

"I ain't courted her, but I married her," he said simply.

Uncle Jeptha's brow furrowed in concern. His words were only a little above a whisper.

"I take it the men this morning were thinking the gal had a grievance against you."

Moss shrugged. He was tired of denials. He was tired of explanations.

"I married her," he said simply. "She's on her way up the mountain with her kin. You'd best be expecting strangers come to live here."

"They're all coming to live here?" Jeptha asked. "They're all to come here, for permanent?"

Moss nodded.

"Four young gals, one near enough to marrying age, but the rest still children," he said. "The boy's about half-growed, but considers himself more so."

"Here? Here in my cabin?" Jeptha's expression was mutinous. "They cain't come here to live in *my* cabin."

Moss raised an eyebrow and gave the old man a long look. "She's my wife and they're my wife's kin."

"I'm your kin," Jeptha proclaimed. "This is my farm. I don't see people and I don't like strangers. You cain't just bring in a bunch of strangers I don't know and make me live with them."

"Would you have me turn them out?" Moss asked. "We're all just going to live here together. It will all be fine, I'm sure of it."

Moss didn't even believe his own words as he said them.

"It's my place, you cain't just bring a passel of children to live here," Jeptha insisted.

"It's where I live," Moss told him. "It's where I work. I've got a perfect right to bring a wife into this cabin. A wife, and her kin, and even a one-eyed possum if that's what I've set my mind to. You're my uncle and I like and respect you, but I've worked this farm like it was my own since I was a boy. I got some say about the place, too."

Jeptha's expression became steely and determined.

"There ain't no room here for a new family," he said with certainty. "Children take up a lot of space and there just ain't none."

"We'll empty out all that storage," Moss told him. "I'll put a new roof on the shed and we can move the barrels and grain out there."

The old man snorted, disgruntled. "It'd be better to put the noisy children out in that shed."

"Uncle Jeptha . . ."

"Is that her coming?" the old man asked, looking beyond Moss to the ridge path.

Moss turned in that direction. It was her, all right. Her and one of her sisters. The little one was done up very fine in a pretty and serviceable calico, long blonde curls hanging down to her shoulders. His wife didn't look half so well. Her gray homespun had seen far better days, and her stringy hair was flying around her face like a loose dishmop. She was a bit too tall, a bit too thin—a bit too much married to him.

Suddenly looking at her, Moss felt too tired to even argue with Uncle Jeptha. He didn't want the girl or her family here any more than the old man did. She'd ruined his life, but there was not a thing he could think to do about it. With a sigh of resignation he leaned his shoulder against the porch pillar and watched them approach the cabin.

His new bride had a ten-pound poke tied to a stick balanced upon her shoulder. The younger girl carried a small handsome carpetbag. When she spied Moss watching her, the little one was brought up short in hesitation.

His wife glanced up and saw him and she actually smiled as she urged her sister forward. She was, it seemed, still as cheerful and pleased to be wed as she'd been this morning.

The screen door slammed open against its hinges, and his uncle wheeled himself out onto the porch to get a better look at the new arrivals, the ones who were taking over his house, the ones who were invading his private sanctuary. He was red-faced and angry, his teeth clenched.

The little girl caught sight of Uncle Jeptha and gasped.

"Look, Eulie!" she hollered out pointing at him. "That man ain't got no legs!"

At that moment, that precise moment when she was hoping to make a fine impression on her new husband and his family, Eulie Toby, who had never once raised a hand to any of her siblings, could have gladly cut a peach tree limb and switched Little Minnie's legs to blisters.

She had hurried to the Pierces' home with a spring to her step, grateful that at last she could bring her family together. There had been some uncomfortable moments. She'd been forced to tell that outrageous lie to the preacher. Moss Collier had publicly denied her. She'd been married with the groom under threat of a shotgun. Her husband-man showed every evidence of hating the sight of her. And now practically all the men on the mountain believed her to be a young woman of assailable virtue. But it was all going to turn out fine. Of course it would. She would make sure that it would. It just had to.

Rather than being delighted and thrilled at the news that the Toby family would all be together once more, Little Minnie, dressed like a doll in one of the many new dresses Mrs. Pierce had bought her, turned stubborn and set up a pout.

She didn't want to go live up on the mountain. The Pierce house had wooden floors with soft rugs. Minnie had her own room that she didn't have to share with anyone. And Mrs. Pierce let her eat biscuits and honey whenever she wanted.

"I don't want to be one of those nasty Toby children," she complained.

If her sister's childish whining hadn't been annoying enough, Mrs. Pierce had taken to sniveling even before Eulie got there. Apparently Mr. Pierce had hurried home with the news, and his wife had immediately begun to blubber. Her sister was a sure-enough cutie, Eulie couldn't deny, but who would have thought that after only a few short months the childless Mrs. Pierce would grow so attached to the girl?

Eulie tried unsuccessfully to cheer the woman up. But there was simply no cheering. Judith Pierce sobbed uncontrollably and clung to Little Minnie as if she would never see the child again. Eulie explained repeatedly that they would just be going as far as Barnes Ridge and they would attend services at the meetinghouse every month. But even that didn't seem to comfort the woman.

They'd left Judith in tears. And Little Minnie complained every step up to Barnes Ridge. Eulie had managed to keep her determined good temper with difficulty. However, when she looked up and saw Moss Collier on his porch, obviously waiting and watching for her, she was heartened.

He was still wearing his wedding clothes. Of course, he hadn't really been dressed for a wedding. But the sturdy brown ducking trousers fit him well, and the leather galluses that held them up looked handsome enough against the plain cloth buttonless overshirt he wore.

He was really a very nice-looking man—tall and sturdy, with a broad, powerful back and shoulders and all that thick black hair. And if his gentle kiss was indication of anything, he could be tender, No, it was not going to be any big sacrifice for Eulie to ease his sad loneliness. And once Moss Collier saw how pleasant her family could be, he'd forget all his anger over the dirty trick she'd played on him. She was sure of it.

"Look, Eulie!" her sister hollered out, pointing toward the cabin doorway. "That man ain't got no legs!"

Eulie looked up, stunned and horrified. She knew, of course, that Moss Collier's old uncle was a war veteran who'd lost his limbs in battle. But she had never seen the man so much as darken the church door. He was a hermit. He never left the Collier farm, and Eulie supposed that she thought him a poor suffering saint who never left his bed. But here he was on the front porch, sitting in a low wheeled cart and looking decidedly unfriendly.

Little Minnie clutched her leg tightly, fearful.

"He's just a man," Eulie assured her, trying to pry the child loose from her so that she could walk. "He's my husband-man's uncle. I guess that makes him our uncle as well."

"Ain't no legless man a relative to me," Minnie whispered with certainty.

Eulie continued to half lead, half drag her sister forward. This was their new home, and these men were their new family. It was important to make a good impression. Unfortunately, Little Minnie was disinclined to make an effort. And neither of the men appeared particularly welcoming.

The husband-man leaned against the porch post in a posture that should have indicated indolence. But Eulie could see that even in the relaxed pose he was rigid with anger.

"Howdy!" she said, smiling as if nothing had happened.

Neither man bothered to respond. At the foot of the step, Eulie released her sister, and the little girl immediately hid behind her.

"Howdy," Eulie said again. This time she directed her words to the man in the cart and extended her hand. He was pale and scraggly and appeared to be dirty and amazingly unkempt.

"I'm Eulie Toby, I—" She stopped herself midsentence, shook her head and giggled. "I mean, I'm Eulie *Collier.*"

She shot a quick smile toward Moss. His expression was so grim she turned immediately back to the older man.

"You must be Mr. Collier's uncle. It's so nice to meet you."

"Jeptha Barnes," the old man responded as he accepted her handshake without enthusiasm.

"This is my sister Minnie," she said, trying unsuccessfully to pull the child to her side. "She's just a child."

It was an explanation as well as an excuse. Children couldn't be expected to know that pointing out a man's missing legs did not fall into the realm of good manners. In truth, Eulie thought that Little Minnie was old enough to know better, but it was not the time to go into that now.

"Where's the rest of them?" Moss asked her.

"Oh, they're coming," Eulie assured him. "Rans went to round up the twins and my sister Clara. I thought Minnie and I had better hurry up so I'd be here in time to start supper."

Moss eyed her unpleasantly. "We've been cooking for ourselves a long time," he said.

She nodded. "Of course, but we couldn't expect you to cook for us," she said.

His tone was cynical. "I don't know why not—you're all expecting to eat my food."

It was not a kind thing to say, and Eulie blushed with embarrassment. He was plainly still angry. Of course, it had only been a few hours since the wedding, so she supposed she couldn't exactly accuse him of holding a grudge. Still, Eulie was quite ready for him to simply get over it. They were married now, and she was ready to live happily ever after. She guessed that it might take him a while to come around to that way of thinking. But she was sure that he would.

"I'm a really fine cook," she informed him, not even attempting to hide her pride. "I've been hired out over at the Knox place and them younguns of theirs quite prefer my vittles to the ones their own mama fixes."

Moss Collier shrugged.

"We eat real plain here," he told her. "Bread and gravy, potatoes and corn. Spring vegetables when we got them."

"And that's exactly what I like to cook," she said. "Plain food, but better than you've ever tasted."

The husband-man did not appear awestruck at his good fortune.

"Have you put in your garden yet?" she asked him. "I'm a wonderful gardener. Best on the mountain, iffen I do say so myself. You give me a little plot of land, tired and poor as you please, and I'll grow you food till all your stores and cellars are full to bursting."

He still didn't look all that impressed.

"Garden plot is on the other side of the kitchen," he said, indicating the nearby building. "I put down some, but with all your brood come a-begging we'll need more than twice that measure at least."

Eulie disliked the inference of her family as beggars, but she swallowed down the insult as if it were a joke.

"Yes, sir, there's a full mess of us Tobys, all right," she said, chuckling. "But we're a hardworking family, used to pulling our own weight. We won't never be no burden to you."

The husband-man's expression was incredulous, as if her words were completely beyond belief and he was primed to say so. But he glanced down toward the old man and perhaps for his sake held his peace.

He relinquished his position against the porch post and turned toward the front of the cabin.

Seeing it close up for the first time, Eulie was elated that even in its very worn, weathered state, the chinking was in good condition and it appeared snug and tight. The old man in his little cart blocked the doorway so she couldn't so much as get a glimpse inside. But she was not discouraged. She could make a home out of a prairie dog tunnel as long as her family would be all together.

"We'll have to crowd here in the south section of the cabin for now," the husband-man told her. "Once I get a new roof on the shed we can move the grain in there and you-all can have the north space."

Eulie nodded. It was on the tip of her tongue to tell him that she and her youngers would be happy to put on the new roof. But their only experience in such was some poorly done patching that was essential just for keeping the rain out.

"It will be kind of close for a while," he said. "But it will only be temporary."

"We don't take up much room," she assured him. "And it's kind of family-like to be all bunched up together."

He met her good humor with stark stoniness. Glancing toward the old man for a moment, he turned his attention to her, his eyes boring into her, his tone of voice stern.

"Uncle Jeptha ain't used to children and don't feel well enough to tend them."

Eulie turned to Uncle Jeptha, intent on assuring him that he was just going to love her younger brother and sisters. The old man's expression was so slit-eyed and cold, it caught her up short. Indeed, he did not appear to be a man interested in the care of children or even in their existence.

"Keep your youngers out of his way," the husbandman added.

Eulie couldn't imagine how that would be possible in such a small place, but she indicated agreement anyway.

"They are all well-behaved and easygoing," Eulie boasted optimistically. "I'm sure we're all going to get along just fine."

Moss Collier looked as if he'd just eaten something extremely disagreeable.

"Is that them coming?" Uncle Jeptha asked.

Eulie turned to see Clara, Rans, and the twins coming up the path. Clara was pretty as a picture, even from this distance. And the twins were neat and well groomed, as always, and looked like they'd grown a couple of inches since the last time she'd seen them.

Rans was dragging a flat skid behind him with all their possessions loaded upon it. Eulie was momentarily grateful for Clara's stow-it-all, hoarding ways. The wheelless pull might be piled high with all the useless things her sister couldn't part with, but at least it didn't look as if Eulie's family was coming to Barnes Ridge empty-handed.

"Look how full that skid is," Eulie pointed out to the husband-man. "My brother must be about as strong as any young fellow on the mountain to be able to drag it up here that way."

At that very moment, Rans apparently complained to his sisters, and Eulie watched as Clara grabbed up one of the ropes to help him with the task.

Eulie swallowed the bad taste in her mouth.

"'Course, my sisters are nearly as strong as boys themselves," she added.

Moss Collier said nothing. He didn't even look in her direction.

Uncomfortable in the less-than-happy silence, Eulie tried to involve Little Minnie in conversation.

"Here comes your brother and sisters," she said, trying to get the child to loosen her grip on the back of Eulie's skirt.

The child showed no interest.

"I don't suspect you've seen all of us together in some time."

"I don't like them nasty Toby children," her sister said. But she peeked out from behind Eulie at last. While Minnie was uninterested in the arrival of her siblings, she seemed morbidly curious about Uncle Jeptha. She even screwed up her courage to question the old man.

"How'd you come to have no legs?" she asked, her chin raised in courageous defiance.

Jeptha's eyes narrowed in anger and he glared at her.

"The bogeyman come and chewed them off, and if you don't leave me be, he'll come and chew yours off, too!"

Little Minnie began screaming.

3

BABY-MAKING was not the only thing that Moss Collier's new bride could lie about, he decided. She'd stood at his porch and proclaimed herself a good cook and described her brother and sisters as easy to get along with. It was perfectly obvious within hours of their arrival that neither pronouncement was true.

The eight of them crowded around the tiny square table in the far side of the kitchen building. There were only two chairs; Moss and Jeptha had never required more. So the children were forced to eat standing up, and plates were squeezed into every inch of space.

Supper consisted of hocks burnt black on the outside and not even warm in the middle. And cornbread, minus the leavening, that lay thick at the bottom of the pan and could have been better utilized as a cultivating disk. Even the old hound waiting expectantly in the doorway wouldn't have anything to do with the bread, though he certainly got his share of the blackened hocks.

Moss would not have described the meal as a pleasant occasion. The youngers, as his bride called them, were hateful, backbiting, and filled with complaint. The little one set up to screaming again every time

Uncle Jeptha so much as glanced up from his plate.

"I'm unaccustomed to your kitchen," Eulie explained sheepishly about the food she set down in the plate before him. "Once I get more used to it, things will be better."

Moss couldn't imagine how cooking on one fireplace could be much different than any other. But he picked at the inedible offering and held his peace. He'd already decided that he was not going to spar with her in front of Uncle Jeptha or the children. That was not the way he would exact his revenge. He intended to see that she suffered, all right. His deceitful young bride was going to learn to be sorry for the day she was born. But she was his wife, for better or worse. Her lying trickery was between them alone and he was not about to have the whole family involved in it.

Besides, he didn't need to offer any complaints of his own this evening. Her brother and sisters seemed to have taken on the task with a vengeance.

"I don't eat hocks and side meat anymore," Minnie explained. "Mrs. Pierce says that there should always be a bit of ham for a pretty little girl like me."

"Pretty is as pretty does," Clara corrected the child gently.

"Well, there ain't a dang thing pretty about burnt pork," Ransom pointed out, plopping the unappetizing meat back onto his plate.

"Don't you be cursing at this table!" Eulie scolded him a little more harshly than was required.

"'Dang' ain't cursing," the boy answered with a surly sneer. "And I ain't even at the dadblamed table. I'm having to stand in the middle of the room."

The twin girls were equally unhappy, though they

at least had better manners about it than their brother.

"Miz Patch can cook up hocks to melt in your mouth," one said.

The other nodded her identical head in identical agreement. "And her cornbread is near as light as biscuits," she added.

Even Clara, the mature and attractive older girl, couldn't keep the wistfulness out of her voice.

"I had a big kettle of mixed greens and fat back simmering at the fire since after breakfast," she said. "I suspect Mr. Leight is eating mighty fine this evening."

The children sighed wistfully at the thought. Moss's own mouth was watering.

"But he's not as happy as us," Eulie pointed out with a broad smile and complete conviction. "He's eating all by himself, and we are a family, all together for supper."

Moss failed to see the advantage, and from the looks on the faces of those around him, he was not alone.

Uncle Jeptha snorted with disagreement.

Eulie appeared undeterred in her enthusiasm. Determined in her cheerfulness, she picked at the unappetizing dinner long after the rest of them had given up.

Moss watched his new bride in wonder. She was apparently undaunted by his most unfriendly welcome and his stern demeanor. She continued to flit about the kitchen as if everything were perfectly fine and they were all living happily ever after.

There was nothing happy about the way he was feeling. And it was clear that he was not the only one who felt that way. He took stock of her siblings more critically.

Clara was pretty. Much more so than his new bride. Her hair, which was bound neatly into a bun at the nape of her neck, had more golden hues among the wheat color. Even in her sacklike work dress she showed ample evidence of a fine figure. And her face was positively heart-shaped with a pair of large, luminous blue eyes as her most memorable feature.

The boy, upon close observation, appeared exceptionally strong and sturdy for his age and size—evidence, no doubt, that he was very familiar with hard work and long days. His tow-colored hair was bowl-cut and ill kept, and the sprinkling of freckles across his nose did nothing for his surly expression.

The twins had yet to be sorted out in his mind. Nora May and Cora Fay were their names, though which was which, Moss still was uncertain. They were identical girls, tall for their age and pleasingly soft-spoken. Their hair hung in long braids down the middle of their backs. The only way to tell them apart, they had informed him, was the mole on the right cheek of . . . on the right cheek of one of them. From his seat at the table, Moss found the mole easily enough, but he couldn't remember which twin it belonged to.

The two had an uncanny way of simply glancing at each other without word and somehow communicating. Moss watched this nonconversation with a strong sense of wonder.

Little Minnie was the baby of the family. Typically, that position had led to her becoming somewhat spoiled. And she was fast approaching the age when brattiness stopped being cute and commenced becoming annoying.

Minnie showed every potential of one day being as

pretty as her sister Clara, but Moss was fairly certain that she would never have the older girl's pleasing temperament. There was a high-pitched undertone to her voice as if she were forever whining with every word she spoke.

All in all, they were not bad children. Moss looked them over with some sense of admiration. To have been raised catch-as-catch-can on the mountain, they had not turned out so badly.

Now, of course, they were Moss's responsibility. And the memory of that made a bitterness well up in his throat that he tasted unpleasantly. His deceitful, lying bride had forced these hungry mouths upon his good nature. And he was not about to forgive or forget the injury done him.

But with his own stomach still rumbling at the end of the meal, Moss took pity on the innocent youngers. He was not a man to send five children to bed hungry, even if they were the siblings of his lying bride.

Moss got up from his chair. The boy, Ransom, immediately sat down where he had been. Moss glanced back at him. The young fellow's defiant, upraised chin almost dared him to comment. Moss didn't even bother.

In the far corner of the room, stacked upon open shelves, was his supply of airtights. The store-bought canned goods were expensive and rarely utilized for an ordinary meal. Moss plundered through until he found a can of peaches.

He carried it over to the table. The children were hushed in expectation. Moss dug his Barlow knife out of his pocket and set the point at the very edge of the can's lip. Using the heel of his hand as a hammer, he punched through the tin and then moved the knife tip, repeating the gesture until he had cut the top off completely. He set it aside and, utilizing both his thumb and the knife blade, he routed out the top quarter section of peach and laid it without fanfare in the center of Uncle Jeptha's dish.

He dug into the can once more and fished out another piece. He glanced at the faces around the table before settling on the little one with the fine dress and the carefully tended curls.

"Hand me your plate," he said to Little Minnie.

The child complied eagerly, never taking her eyes off the dull yellow fruit swimming in sugary nectar.

He served the twins next and then Clara, as silence gave way to the excitement of a special treat.

Ransom looked steely-eyed and mutinous, as if he fully expected to be passed over and had no intention of suffering in silence. Moss doled out a peach quarter for the boy. The fellow seemed momentarily disappointed. Almost, it seemed, he would have preferred a fight to the fruit. But only almost. After a brief hesitation, he dug into the sweet fare with as much enthusiasm as his sisters.

As Moss fished out the next section he saw that it was the very last. One piece of peach for two people. Himself and his bride. Everything that he knew, everything he had been taught about duty and charity and honor extolled him to sacrifice his own needs. To give the last to the young woman who had so gamely provided the most inedible meal in his experience. The woman who had publicly humiliated him with her lies and had ruined what was left of his chances to get off of this mountain and out West where he belonged.

Moss plopped the last peach into his own plate, black-hearted and unmoved. He handed the can to Eulie. It was empty except for a jigger or more of nectar in the bottom.

"You can have the juice," he said simply.

Eulie smiled at him broadly as if he'd done her a great honor.

"My favorite part," she told him.

Eulie lingered over her peach nectar, savoring the inestimable pleasure of having her family together once more. Of course, it hadn't been a perfect dinner. She had been near to shame over the unpleasant outcome of her cooking. The hocks were the worst effort she could recall. And it had been a coon's age since she'd forgotten an ingredient so necessary to cornbread as baking powders.

Her youngers had been out of sorts and complaining. You'd have thought they'd never had to take their dinner standing up. And the husband-man was still looking like he could spit nails and would gladly use them to pin her ears back.

Eulie drank the last drop of peach nectar from the can. The sharp, metallic taste of tin nearly overpowered the sweetness of the peaches. The children had begun to horse around the room and play. It was time that she commenced clearing the meal. Still she lingered.

She had thought he was going to give her the last peach. Just for an instant, a brief, blissful instant, she had thought it. Of course he should take it for himself. They were his peaches, after all. And sharing them with the youngers was a kind, decent thing to do. She wasn't wrong about him. He was going to be good to her. He was going to be good to the youngers. And they were going to be good to him, she vowed. She would see that they were all good to him.

"Here! Stop that, bring that back!"

It was Uncle Jeptha's voice raised in anger. Eulie glanced up to see that Ransom and the twins had appropriated the old man's cart and were intent upon taking rides in it across the length of the kitchen.

"Get out of my cart and bring it back to me this instant."

Eulie hurried to her feet. The strident command had worked with the twins, who were obliging and quick to obey. It was just the tone, however, that was guaranteed to set Ransom's teeth on edge and get his back up. He did not like being told what to do.

She saw her brother draw himself to full height, hold his arm out to stop the progress of the twins and set his jaw mutinously. Eulie wished herself across the room to put her hand over his mouth to stop his words. But she could not.

"You want it, you old cripple," he spewed out, "then you come and get it."

The instantaneous silence in the room was as thick as spring fog in the valley. It was followed by such an inhuman cry of rage and impotence that Eulie feared the old man might throw himself upon the floor and drag himself across the room on his hands to get at Rans.

Such action was unnecessary. The husband-man took two steps and was by his side. He grabbed her brother by the nape of the neck and jerked him off his feet. Moss Collier tossed him toward the door, where he easily regained his balance.

"You'd best keep a respectful tongue in your mouth around this place," Moss told him. "Now get up to the cabin before I get a mind to take a strap to you."

"Ain't nobody taking a strap to me," Rans shot back. "I'm leaving."

With that he was out the door and heading down the path at a run, as if he thought somebody would actually follow him.

In the uncomfortable moments after his departure, the twins rolled the cart back over to its position just at the left side the old man's chair.

"Sorry, Uncle Jeptha," Cora Fay told him sweetly.

"I ain't your Uncle Jeptha," the old man answered, his voice still rough with anger and frustration.

"We didn't mean no harm," Nora May assured him. "We was just playing."

"It ain't no plaything," Jeptha insisted. "And it's mine. I don't want not one of you to touch it. Don't even touch it."

He glared meaningfully at each of the children in turn. They all lowered their heads in shame, except for Minnie, who commenced screaming like the demons of hell were after her once more.

"For lawdy sakes, cain't you shut that child up?" the husband-man asked Eulie impatiently.

"Hush, Minnie, there's no need in carrying on so."

The little girl modulated her tone but continued to make an unappealing amount of noise.

The old man's face was dark with fury. Grasping the right edge of his chair with both hands, Jeptha rolled over onto his stomach and lowered himself into the cart. With one of the wooden blocks in each hand he easily negotiated the turn and headed out the doorway. To Eulie's surprise, the twins followed in his wake, apparently determined to be of some sort of assistance to the silent, angry amputee.

"Do you want Minnie and me to help you clear the table?" Clara asked.

"No," Eulie assured her quickly. "I can do it."

Clara nodded and then shot an anxious look toward the husband-man, who was standing thoughtfully hands upon hips and looking a little bit dangerous.

"Come on," Clara said to Minnie. "And stop all that fussing foolishness."

"He said the bogeyman was going to chew off my legs," the child complained.

"There is no such thing, so hush up about it," Clara told her in a plaintive whisper.

As the two hastily quit the room, Eulie became a little bit uneasy. It was good and well to know that you did the right thing and that it would all work out for the best, but it was an entirely different case to explain that to anyone. Especially anyone very tall and broad-shouldered and scowling unpleasantly.

Eulie rose to her feet and began gathering the plates from the table. She'd left a dishpan of washing water warming in a small tub on the hearth. She carried the pile of dirty dishes there and slipped them in to soak beneath the brown lye soap that scummed the top of the water.

She had thought to lift the dishpan to the table and wash and dry the dishes there. But the husband-man was standing near the table, and Eulie thought the more distance kept between the two of them the better. She found her soapy scrub rag and knelt beside the hearth. She concentrated upon her task, but still felt his eyes upon her. He was watching her every move. Evaluating and judging her. And Eulie feared she was not showing at her best. Deliberately she kept her back straight and her face serene as she tried to keep from dropping any of the slippery plates and utensils in her grasp. The skillet in which she'd cooked the hocks was burnt black on the bottom and desperately needed a good sand scrubbing. Carrying it outside for sand, however would involve walking past the husband-man. And just now she was hoping that he would grow tired of his perusal of her and simply quit the place on his own.

Unfortunately, he did not.

She finally had to give up on the hock skillet.

"I'll let that one soak overnight," she told him as she rose to her feet.

She'd managed to slosh a good deal of water upon her dress and thought belatedly of her sturdy apron still stowed in her carrying poke. The bachelor kitchen sported no such luxuries.

With the soapy rag, she washed down the cabinets and the shelves, taking as much time as the task could possibly afford. Finally, with no choice left, she made her way to the table and began scouring it with enough energy to strip off the pine tar.

"Should somebody be out looking for your brother?"

It was the first words he had spoken. Eulie took heart that they were not ones of anger, but of familial concern.

"Oh, he runs off like that all the time," she told him. "He'll walk a mile or two cooling off, then he'll realize that he ain't got no needments nor money and nowhere to go. That'll have him back here in an hour or so."

The husband-man nodded.

"He has a temper with a hair trigger," she said. Immediately Eulie wished she could call back the words. She didn't want the husband-man thinking ill of her brother. "But Ransom is a hard worker and very dependable."

Moss Collier raised an eyebrow at her skeptically.

"He's a fine fellow," she insisted. "I'm proud of him always. He just . . . well he just has a tendency to take umbrage at . . . being told what to do."

The husband-man folded his arms across his chest and sighed with resignation.

"Once he gets to know you better, you won't have no trouble with him. And that's the truth," Eulie said.

"The truth?" The husband-man's voice was deep and gruff, his tone heavy with sarcasm. "I wouldn't be looking to a woman like you to be telling the truth."

Eulie felt the heat of embarrassment staining her cheeks. She ignored his words and hurriedly rinsed the soapy rag before hanging it upon the chair back to dry.

"I'd best see about getting my youngers to bed," she told him.

She made a move for the door, but he was there first standing on the threshold with one arm across the frame blocking her path.

Eulie stopped in her tracks and looked up at him. He would never hurt her, she assured herself. She would never be afraid of him. Still, his tight-jawed countenance was daunting. It was one thing to assure herself that everything was going to work out for the best. It was quite another to keep smiling as she stood here with him glaring down at her.

"Let me pass, Mr. Collier," she said with as much pleasantness as she could muster. "It's near to dark and the children won't know where to lay a pallet."

"Why did you do it?" he asked quietly. His expression was both inquisitive and intense. "Why did you do this to me?"

Eulie hadn't planned a speech. She hadn't even thought up a good explanation. Secretly she'd hoped that he would merely accept his good fortune and be content to live happily ever after. Apparently he wasn't going to make it that easy for her.

She considered concocting a big lie. Lying was not something that came naturally to her, but she was getting better at it. Perhaps she could tell him that the old soothsayer on Button Creek had warned her that she must marry a dark-haired man before the next full moon. Or maybe she could insist that she hadn't lied and that she wasn't at all sure that a woman didn't get a baby on the way when a man kissed her. At the very least she could try to convince him that she was madly in love with him and that she couldn't bear to live another day without him.

Eulie looked right into the husband-man's narrowed brown eyes and told him the absolute truth.

"I needed my family back together," she said. "I needed a place for all of us." She halted nervously, swallowing a bit of anguish. It was the truth and it was not so terrible a thing; still, it sounded conniving and selfish when spoken aloud. "You have a pretty good-sized place here," she continued. "And I figured you were lonely."

"Lonely!" He spit the word out as if it tasted badly. "What in the dipfoot devil would make you think I am lonely?"

Eulie blanched slightly at the level of mockery in his tone. "Don't curse at me," she scolded.

"'Dipfoot devil' is not cursing."

"Well, it's almost cursing, and I don't approve of it a bit."

"You don't approve . . ." His brow furrowed with disbelief.

Eulie didn't give him a chance to say more. She ducked under his arm and scurried through the door and up the path. When a husband-man gets into a temper, she decided, it was best just to quit the area.

"Wait just a dadblamed minute!" she heard him calling after her.

The words didn't even make Eulie hesitate. She had no more explanation to make and she wasn't about to stand around allowing a fellow to curse at her.

She hurriedly made her way around the cabin and onto the porch. But any thought she might have had of determinedly keeping peace and avoiding conflict drifted further from possibility as she heard the voice of her youngest sister whining plaintively.

"I can't sleep on no hard floor pallet or with nobody else. I'm used to my own bed now."

"This bed had been mine for twenty-five years," Uncle Jeptha said, his voice far too stubborn to broach any disagreement. "I ain't about to give it up to any passel of sniveling youngers."

"If somebody has to sleep down there," Little Minnie insisted, "then it ought to be you rather than me. With no legs, you're a lot closer to it anyhow."

Eulie stepped into the cabin to find her youngest sister standing obstinately in the middle of the room, her bottom lip protruding. Her irrational fear of Uncle

Jeptha had apparently been conquered by her selfish nature.

"Of course, we would never put you out of your bed, Uncle Jeptha," Eulie assured the old man hastily.

Minnie turned to her wide-eyed and furious.

"I ain't sleeping with Clara or the twins," she said. "Mrs. Pierce let me have my own bed and I ain't going back to sleeping with my sisters."

"Then you'll have to make a pallet on the floor," Eulie told her. "It won't be like the sharecropper's shack we lived in. Look at these floors, Minnie. Such nice soft pine, they'll sleep as fine as any feather bed anywhere."

"No they won't. It's still sleeping on the floor," she said. "A pretty little girl like me shouldn't have to sleep on no floor."

"And you won't have to."

The words were spoken behind her. Eulie turned to see the husband-man in the doorway. His tone was neither friendly nor conciliatory. Minnie apparently didn't notice and smiled delightedly.

"You can stand up in the middle of the room, or sleep in that old rocking chair, whichever suits you better than a floor pallet."

The little girl's expression turned immediately from delight to dismay.

"He cain't tell me where to sleep," she insisted, looking at her oldest sister for corroboration.

Eulie wasn't given a chance to intervene.

"Oh yes I can, young lady," the husband-man insisted. "This is my uncle's house and it runs by our rules. We'll decide who will sleep in it and where they'll sleep."

Minnie made a tiny sound of piteous displeasure and looked again to Eulie to dispute his words.

What could she say? It was the man's house.

Moss Collier's tone became more quiet as he made his pronouncements.

"Uncle Jeptha will sleep in his own bed, as usual," he said. "Miss Clara may sleep in mine. You twins make yourself a place out of the way in the corner there. And you, Little Minnie—and your brother, when he gets back—may stand, rock, or take to the floor as is your pleasure."

Minnie's lip was back in much evidence, but with none to gainsay him there was little that she could do.

Eulie gave the little girl a hopeful smile and tried to cheer her.

"You can have my place sleeping with Clara," she told her.

"Oh no," the husband-man said.

Eulie turned to him. Surely he'd seen that he had won and there was no call to belabor the point.

"She's learned her lesson," Eulie told him. "And really I don't mind the floor. I can sleep anywhere."

"You mistake me, Mrs. Collier," the husband-man said, stepping forward and unexpectedly wrapping a thick muscular arm around Eulie's waist. "My new bride will naturally sleep with me."

4

Moss didn't know why he'd said it. Why he'd even thought it. He suspected it was because he had even fewer brains than the grasping, conniving female who now shared his name. The woman might have been able to force him into taking her as wife, but no one could force a man to take a woman to bed.

This fact being what it was, no explanation could be found for why, after seeing his uncle and her sisters to bed, he led the woman back down the path to the privacy of the kitchen.

Beside him she walked with obvious hesitation. His grip upon her arm was not forceful, but he had to consistently pull her along. The blankets slung over his shoulder left no secret of his intent. She should plainly understand what he was up to, even if he was a bit unsure of it himself.

Moss glanced over at his new bride. In the sparse silvery light of a crescent moon, she appeared nervous and pale. He was grateful, at least, that he'd finally wiped that ever-cheerful grin off her face.

That's all he wanted, he reminded himself. He wanted to scare the wits out of her. She'd soon learn to be sorry for what she did to him. He would not be so foolish as to bed and breed the woman. That would serve her purposes far more than his own. As soon as her belly began to swell, every man on the mountain would nod his head in self-righteous certainty that in forcing the marriage, they had done what was just. Moss wanted the satisfaction of being vindicated. He wanted all of them to know that they had been wrong. He wanted them to see that she had lied.

So if he was only going to affright her and make a bluff, why was his heart pounding like he'd run up a ridge row? Why was his fevered skin chilled by the coolness of the evening breeze?

The doorway stood wide open. Moss stepped across the threshold first. She dug in her heels, reluctant to take the final step. He gazed at her with feigned curiosity. In the faint light of the moon he could see her chin trembled, as if she was near tears.

Good, he thought to himself. He wanted her to cry, to beg, to plead for mercy.

"Oh, I almost forgot," he said, dropping the blankets just inside the door. "I'm supposed to carry you inside."

Her startled expression was purely priceless. Moss stepped toward her, but did not wrap his arms around her back and knees and pull her to his chest. Instead he bent to grasp her about midthigh and flung her across his shoulder like a sack of meal.

The sound she made could have been protest or surprise. Moss didn't know or care which. He carried her into the empty silence of the kitchen. The coals from the banked fire glowed red in the darkness but offered little light for him to see by. She was wiggling a bit as if trying to get free of him but was apparently too overcome with astonishment to put up much of a fight.

Moss turned a full circle inside the dimly lit building before deciding the perfect place to put her down. He walked up to the edge of the table and bent forward at the waist until the woman lay with her back against the scuffed, soap-scrubbed wood.

He did not immediately move away, but leaned over her there. His elbows on either side of her shoulders, he straddled her knees, entrapping Eulie beneath him.

He would frighten her with his nearness, Moss told himself. He would scare her with the coarse nature of his sexuality. She'd be begging forgiveness quick enough. Pleading for mercy, no doubt. Sorry she'd ever schemed him into her wicked little web.

Moss lay over her in the darkness. His chest to her bosom, he pressed her back against the hardness of the table. Her flesh was soft, yielding, more rounded than he would have suspected. He inhaled the sweet, fresh feminine scent of her and enjoyed it more than he should have.

His past experience with women had been raw and ribald and infrequent, more transaction than tryst. Those women smelled of cheap perfume and cheaper whiskey. This woman exuded fragrance that could never be priced. The wholesomeness of it was alluring, enticing. Moss could feel his own heart pounding against the softness of her breast.

He felt the gentle flutter of her breath upon his cheek and realized how close her mouth was to his own.

He could kiss her. He could kiss her now within the cloak of inky blackness of the unlit kitchen. He could kiss her as he had wanted to that day by the creek. Not with the halting, hesitant respect he had shown, but with the full force of his most carnal nature. And there was nothing she could do to stop him. Nothing she would do to stop him. It was his right. He was her husband. Lustily he opened his mouth above her lips.

"Don't you think it's too dark in here?" she said.

He stopped short. "What?"

"Don't you think that it's way too dark in here?" she repeated. "I cain't even see what's right in front of my face."

"I'm right in front of your face," Moss answered, only inches above her.

"Well, it could be you, or somebody else," she told him. "I cain't see nary a thing."

Nonplussed, Moss straightened up. "Someone else?" he muttered.

"Well, it could have been someone else," Eulie continued. "I'm no forest creature what can see things in the night and all. Don't you have no candles?"

"What?"

"Don't you have no candles?" she asked again. "Iffen you don't, well, I can make you some. Just some alum, tallow, and cotton cord, and a bit of wax myrtle goes good when it's prime. Melt it down and pour it in the molds. Have you got molds? If you don't, I can dip them. My mama taught me to make dip candles. I ain't done it in a while, but I still can. I make some of the best tallow candles on the mountain, even if I do say so myself. They don't hardly smoke none at all."

Moss was tempted to put his hand over the woman's mouth.

He walked over to the kindling box and pilfered

through it until he found a good-sized pine knot. He laid it on the fireplace hearth and stirred the fire momentarily before he speared it with the poker. He held the pine knot in the red hot coals for a minute or two until it flamed to light. The strong scent of scorching resin filled the room.

"Can you see good enough now?" he asked her.

She was sitting up on the table, still wide-eyed but smiling at him sweetly as if she weren't the most exasperating woman on the face of the earth.

"Much better," she answered.

Moss banged the pine knot into the heavy firebowl on the mantel. Its shiny tin reflector threw the light back into the room, bathing every corner with a bright yellow glow.

His stringy-haired bride continued to chatter, explaining to him the advantages of candles, as if she were the wisdom of the Good Book itself and he a know-nothing oaf.

"And candles last a lot longer than pine knots," she said, barely pausing to take a breath.

"I don't think we're going to need all that much time tonight," Moss interrupted. "Take off your dress."

That shut her up.

She sat on the table with her mouth open, but silent at last.

Moss folded his arms over his chest and leaned cross-legged against the chimney rock to watch her. She didn't make a move.

"Take off your dress," he repeated. "You wanted to be my bride, didn't you? Well, you may be ignorant of a lot of things. But surely you know that to be a perfectly reasonable husbandly request."

He watched her hands flutter nervously at the front fastenings of her bodice, but she made no move to undo them.

"Are . . . are you going to shag me?" she asked in a wary whisper.

The coarse term from her lips had Moss standing up straight in shock.

"Where'd you hear such a word as that?" he asked her.

"I heard it," she answered, her chin raised bravely. "I know what it is. I don't know what else you call it."

"Well, decent women sure call it something else," Moss told her. "I don't want to hear things like that from you."

His scolding tone actually seemed to please her. But then, Moss figured he shouldn't be surprised. The woman made no sense at all.

"What do you want me to call it?" she asked him.

Completely at a loss, he had no answer.

"You don't need to call it anything," he answered.

"Well, I sure need to call it something."

"Just . . . just call it obeying your husband," he said finally.

She nodded. "Are you going to . . . have me obey my husband?"

It was truly annoying. The woman didn't show nearly enough fear to suit him.

"Just take off your dress," he ordered.

Nervously her hands went to her throat and she clumsily began to undo the fasteners of her bodice.

Moss watched as his throat became dry. *Are you going to shag me?* He could hear her bawdy question again and again in his mind. He no longer knew the answer.

She removed the bodice completely and scooted off the table. Carefully she hung it on the ladderback of the chair, as calmly as if she were unaware that thin material of her josey chemise barely covered her, leaving exposed the length of her arms and the enticing flesh between the curve of her throat and the swell of her breast.

She was thin, he noted, though her arms and shoulders appeared more muscled than emaciated. His new bride obviously worked too hard and ate too little. Beneath the worn thin fabric of her josey, there was more than a hint of a shapely rounded bosom.

"You'll not regret that you married me," she was telling him.

He heard the words as if they came from a great distance, the sound nearly drowned out by the pounding of his own pulse.

"Me and my youngers, we're all hard workers," she said. "We can fix this place up, care for your uncle, and give your life a bit of ease. A man is bound to marry anyway. You might as well do it where he makes a fine bargain and brings a family together at the same time."

Moss was hardly listening. He was watching the rise and fall of her not-inconsequential bosom beneath the gauzy covering.

Her fingers went to slip the knot on the ties of her skirt. Her movements were practical and no-nonsense. But Moss could see that her hands were shaking. The circle of worn calico dropped to the floor and she stepped out of it. Her josey came to just above her knees, and as she bent to retrieve the pile of discarded calico, Moss got an expansive glance at the back of a pair of bare thighs, no evidence of pantaloons within sight.

"Don't you wear no drawers?" he asked her.

Her hand went protectively to the tail of her chemise. Her face was bright red with embarrassment.

"It's . . . it's a waste of good muslin," she answered defensively. "If a woman keeps her skirts long and stays out of the wind, why, there's no purpose for them at all."

Her adamant declaration hinted at defensiveness.

"The old grandmas never seen fit to wear them," she said. "And what's good enough for grandma is good enough for me."

Moss could hardly argue with that. And at the present moment, the usefulness of such a garment was inconceivable.

"You'll find that I'm a thrifty wife as well as hardworking," she assured him. "I won't be pestering you for pretties or gewgaws or fancy raiment of any kind."

There was nothing fancy about the raiment in which she was currently clothed. As his bride stood next to the table, he could see that the much-washed josey was thin, gray, and worn. It revealed as well as it concealed.

He covered the distance between them in haste, no longer even attempting to deceive himself about his own arousal. He could shag her once, he told himself. He'd always heard that a woman never got with child the first time. He could shag her once and enjoy himself. That was fair enough. She did trap him into marriage. She deserved it. And she was his wife, anyway. In truth, she wouldn't legally be his wife if he didn't. So in a way, it was his beholden duty to her to do it.

The width of the kitchen was only a few paces, but he was inexplicably out of breath when he reached her side. His instinct was simply to press her against the wall, spread her legs apart and bury himself inside her. Moss clamped down on that reflex and solaced himself with the idea of touching her.

His palms were sweating, and he wiped them upon his trousers before raising his hand to the narrow sleeve of the undergarment. Slowly he pulled it down, exposing inch by inch the pale flesh beneath it.

He glanced up into her wide, frightened eyes, but she could not hold his gaze. There were more amazing things to look at. The soft secrets of her womanly bosom was being unveiled before him, and the sight captured every fiber of his attention. Down, down the fabric came, displaying in the warm yellow glow of light an unexpected abundance of flesh.

Standing stiff as a board and, staring straight, she began once more to chatter like an old game hen.

"I'm not used to anything high-step of any kind. I told you I'm hardworking, but I'm also easygoing and thrifty. I'm very thrifty."

The josey seemed to catch upon her upraised nipple as if reluctant to reveal her to him. Moss tugged slightly and down it came, uncovering her right breast. The firm, feminine mound was topped with a dark pink bud as thick and tempting as a brambleberry. A minute earlier he had been panting audibly; now it seemed he could not breathe at all. The silence was broken by a strange, almost whimpering sound from her throat.

He looked up at her face. She held her chin bravely high, but her lower lip was trembling.

"Did I tell you I can pull a plow?" she asked. "When Daddy didn't have no mule, it was me and Rans what pulled his plow."

Moss eased down the other sleeve, baring her completely to the waist. He swallowed. His body was screaming to touch her. He held himself frozen, as if reaching out for her might unleash passions he could never control.

The woman stood unflinching before him. But his hesitation apparently increased her anxiety.

"I know I'm too bony," she told him defensively. "But my teats are good-sized for a thin girl."

They were indeed. Moss was far beyond commenting on the fact.

Finally, keeping a tight rein upon the desires that urged him, he reached out to touch her. One sun-browned, work-callused finger caressed the rosy peak that protruded so prettily in the cool night air.

"Oh my!" She gasped sharply. "That feels very strange."

He spread his palm upon her skin and held the full breast in his hand.

"I never imagined that it felt like . . . like this to be touched."

He brought his other hand to grasp her other breast.

"It's as if . . . as if my whole body is connected to this one place."

Would the woman never shut up?

"I don't think I—"

Moss angled his head and brought his lips down upon her own, effectively silencing her at last. The taste of her stirred his memory. She was sweet, almost treacly like she'd been sampling honeysuckle. Tonight he knew it to be her own special seductive savor. He reveled in it, sucking indulgently at her mouth as he stroked and fondled her naked bosom.

She made tiny, pleased and pleading noises at the back of her throat that coaxed him onward eagerly to the edge of his control.

He was hard now, hard and desperate to press her against him. He loosed her breasts to grasp her buttocks and urge her tightly to the ache in the front of his trousers.

He moaned at the contact. It was everything. It was not nearly enough.

He squeezed and handled her backside pleasurably for several moments before recalling with enthusiasm what little impediment her thin josey was to him. He jerked the hem of the singular undergarment out of his way, and immediately his hands encountered her bare flesh. The smooth, delicate skin covering a firm, rounded derriere was far too great a temptation to resist. He didn't even try. Exploring with urgency, he clasped and caressed and cosseted. His huge hands could cover her completely. It made him feel powerful, masculine, conquering.

He needed more. His only thought, if thought it was and not instinct, was to be inside her.

Ending the kiss with a hasty reluctance, he circled her waist sat her once more on the edge of the kitchen table. He grasped her knees and parted them, stepping in close between her thighs. The scent of her arousal spurred him forward. He wanted her. He wanted all of her. And he wanted it all now.

He lowered his head to her bosom. The nipples were hardened and thrust out before him as if pleading for his attention. His tongue snaked out and swiped at the right one.

"Oh! Oh! That's . . . oh, that's . . ."

She was talking again. Somehow it no longer bothered him.

He nuzzled against her and sucked at her breasts, voracious in appetite. He soothed and massaged the smooth straightness of her back, following the trail of her spine from between her shoulder blades to the narrowness of her waist and beyond.

She buried her hands in his hair, stroking him and holding him against her. There was no need. He wasn't moving away. And the touch of her fingers only excited him further.

Her heels dug into the back of his thighs urging him forward. And he was ready. The furies of nature set course for his destination. He wanted to be inside her.

"Um yes . . . oh yes, that . . . oh . . ."

Her words no longer had sense or pattern. They spoke to him with amazing clarity.

Moss released his hold upon her just long enough to jerk the galluses from his shoulders and allowed them to dangle near his knees. He clasped her waist again, not able to bear the loss of contact for more than an instant.

He stood at full height once more, reluctant to leave the warmth of her bosom but eager to taste her lips again. She met his mouth, her own open, willing. She wrapped her arms around his neck, giving as he got.

The hot, sweet flavor of her fired him beyond caution.

Moss reached for the buttons of his trousers. Beneath them, his erection strained and ached and pulsed with need.

"Eulie, you in there?"

The words crashed in upon the tiny, fog-lit world of two people with the effect of dousing cold water on a pair of hounds.

"Rans!" Her voice was almost a squeak.

Moss glanced toward the door. The boy stood there, slack-jawed and staring.

Contrary reactions swept through Moss. He wanted to chase the boy away. He wanted to protect the modesty of the woman in his arms.

Instinctively, he chose the latter, moving closer to shield her body from the sight of the intruder.

"Get out of here!" he yelled furiously.

"I was just . . ." her brother began, flustered. "I come back and saw the light and–"

"Get out of here!"

The boy fled. And with him went every drop of mutual passion.

Moss looked at the woman in his arms. Embarrassed, she had covered her bosom with an arm and was trying to pull down the hem of her josey to cover her nakedness.

He released her immediately and turned his back to her.

"Beg your pardon, ma'am," he said.

5

THE sounds of a raucous fiddle filled the mountain clearing lit by the glow of a dozen torches. He stood in the middle of the shouting cheering circle.

Shuffle, slap, heel, stomp. Shuffle, slap, heel, stomp. Stomp, kick. Stomp, kick.

He glanced over at his rival. Pomper Dickson was a sleek-limbed and graceful dancer, but now he was sweating profusely and tiring badly. Pomper would not beat him tonight. He was going to win this competition. He was going to win the right, once and for all, to claim himself finest jigger on the mountain.

"Look at him," a young voice whispered. "He's twitching."

It was strange how he could hear the small voice over the whine of the fiddle and the noise of the crowd.

He ignored it. He kept dancing.

Pomper was slowing, slowing so that he could hardly keep the rhythm, and all his fancy steps were gone.

He jigged on. He held his upper body straight and rigid while his feet flew against the packed dirt beneath him.

Shuffle, slap, heel, stomp. Shuffle, slap, heel, stomp. Stomp, kick. Stomp, kick.

He glanced over as Pomper stopped abruptly, dropping to his knees in exhaustion, trying to catch his breath.

He had won it. He had truly won it. The knowledge swept through him like a new burst of energy and he twirled and stomped with renewed enthusiasm. He was the one. The finest jigger on the mountain.

"Don't touch him," a voice warned breathily.

There was no one close enough to touch him.

He jigged on, allowing his gaze to search through the faces in the crowd. They were there. They were all cheering for him.

There was Myrtle with her strawberry blonde curls, and luscious little Garda June. He spied Dora Dickson, Pomper's dark-eyed sister. And, of course, there was Sary. His sassy Sary. Her smile shining like a new copper penny.

He should get that girl alone some time and kiss her. Lord knows, he'd always wanted to kiss her. Maybe tonight. Tonight, with the taste of victory on his lips. Maybe tonight he would kiss her.

With high step and full jig he danced over in her direction. She was smiling at him. His sassy Sary was smiling at him, and it was a smile a man could never forget.

The ground exploded in front of him. Pain ripped through him like fire and he was falling, falling, falling.

"Sary!" he screamed as he hit the ground with a thud.

He was dead.

No, no—he wasn't dead. He opened his eyes. He was alive. Thank God he was alive. He was alive, and he had to find Sary.

He raised himself slightly on one elbow. The pain shot through him, searing him like fire. He grimaced, but he was grateful. He was alive. Thank God, he was alive.

Just a few feet away from him a bloody, severed limb lay in the dew-soaked grass, steam still rising from its torn opening as the body warmth inside escaped into the cool air of a Virginia spring morning.

He felt the bile rise to his throat and thought he might vomit. He thought of the leg's owner. Poor bastard, poor unlucky bastard. He hoped the man was dead. Better dead than to live life as a cripple.

It was then that he recognized the boot.

"No!"

As Jeptha screamed the word, he sat bolt upright. His cry was echoed by the swarm of children around him surrounding his bed who gazed at him wide-eyed and cowered away.

"What are you doing?" he asked through labored breathing. His heart was pounding, and he was covered with sweat.

"We weren't doing nothing," the boy, Rans, insisted defensively.

"Your bed was squeaking, and it woke us all up," one of the twins explained.

"We didn't mean to bother you," the other one assured him. "We thought you might be sick or something."

He had had another one of his nightmares. Another of the frightful visions that had plagued his sleep for twenty years. He had seen it all again, lived it all again. The ground exploding, the scream, the pain, the severed leg wearing his boot. Was once not enough to live through such a moment? In his restless sleep, Jeptha had lived through it now perhaps a thousand times.

"We all have bad dreams from time to time," the older girl, Clara, said.

"You was twitching," the spoiled little brat girl told him accusingly. "Twitching like you was running or . . . or . . ."

Dancing. Jeptha thought the word but did not utter it. He'd imagined himself dancing at the spring social. He had seen himself once more as he had been, young and strong and whole.

"Get away from me, all of you," he yelled angrily at them. "And leave me be."

They scurried back from him as if he were a rabid dog. Jeptha supposed that he knew how one felt. He ruminated unkindly upon why his nephew had married a woman with a whole passel of children in tow. He didn't want to see anyone. He didn't want to know anyone. It had been better than twenty years since he'd had more than a word or two to say to anyone but Moss. How in the devil was he suppose to continue his life with a half dozen noisy, nosy children romping around the cabin?

He reached for his shirt and pants hanging upon the bedpost. The former he pulled over his head without ceremony. The latter he dragged beneath the covers, managing to struggle into them inexpertly from a lying-down position. The gentlemanly behavior was not as much modesty as it was defense. The uneven stumps of his legs were a sight he could barely look upon himself without recoil. He would not inflict upon himself the horror and pity of onlookers.

The ripped stump on the right was the one lost to the cannon shot. It was the longer of the two; badly sewn, it was jagged and lumpy just above the knee, part of the useless joint still inside. The left stump was infinitely neater. Cut cleanly at midthigh with a surgeon's saw, it was carefully covered over with a flap of skin and stitched with the capable competence of a physician who did a dozen amputations per day.

The front of his short trousers buttoned, he was clothed and ready to start the morning. He had long since given up such civil niceties as washing and shaving. Under no circumstances would he bathe naked in the creek as Moss did. And he was far to proud to ask his nephew to carry water to fill a tub in the cabin for him. He swiped off with a rag from time to time, frequently enough to keep the lice at bay. And he just allowed his beard to grow as it would. He didn't see anybody and nobody ever saw him. There was no purpose in his life for dandifying. There was no purpose in his life at all.

Grasping the headboard for balance, Jeptha leaned over and felt beneath the bed until he found his cart. His movements were slower and more deliberate than usual. Carelessness had caused more than one tumble onto the floor. He didn't relish the bruises at any time, but now that he no longer had his privacy, pride was at issue as well.

He slid down the side of the bed onto the cart without much trouble. He glanced up at the children. None were looking directly at him, but he felt their surreptitious gaze. They were curious and could hardly be blamed for that, he reminded himself. The whole world seemed to be drawn to the sight. The young were just honest enough to be unable to hide the morbid fascination.

Jeptha understood that. He'd been a boy once himself. A curious, cheerful, adventuresome boy, full of hopes and aspiration, though he tried not to remember it.

The dreams were the worst. In the dreams it was often as it had been last night. He was Jigging Jeptha Barnes once more. Young and full of life. A delight to the ladies' eyes, not an abhorrence they couldn't take their gaze from.

Jeptha picked up his "oars," the two little blocks of wood that he used to propel himself forward. Forward, into another sunrise, another day, another eternity of hell on earth.

He hadn't thought that he would live. In the field hospital, when they'd cut off his other leg, putrid with gangrene, he hadn't even offered an argument. He hadn't believed that he would live.

Why should he live? Neither of his brothers had. Nils had been cut down by a blunted saber at Antietam. And young Zackary, just fourteen, had been blown to bits by a canon shot at Piney Ridge. DeWitt Collier, his sister's husband, had fallen at Gettysburg before ever getting a glimpse of his baby boy. Claude Pusser and Madison Pierce. Judd Browning and Tom Leight. Even his old rival, Pomper Dickson—they were all long since dead. People said that they were lucky the war had never come to the Sweetwood. Seemed that it couldn't have got much closer than touching every family.

Jeptha had come home in the back of a wagon, willing himself to live long enough to be buried on his own home ground. His days were numbered; the doctors had said so and he was certain it was true. Now, after twenty-two years, the number seemed an infinitely larger one than he had ever counted.

The children began filing out of the room, apparently intent upon getting breakfast.

"Don't go down to the kitchen," he ordered gruffly.

The little group turned to look at him as if he'd suddenly grown legs.

"Why not?" Clara asked with sincere innocence.

"We're all washed," one twin said.

"And dressed," finished the other.

"I'm hungry," young Minnie declared, her tone typically whining.

"I do as I see fit, old man," Rans declared.

Jeptha wanted to knock their youthful heads together. But it wouldn't give them one bit more of understanding. Time would soon enough teach them the ways of the world.

He didn't answer, but rolled his cart past them, over to the doorway. From the corner of the porch, in the faint gray light of daybreak, he could see the little kitchen building.

It was the morning after his nephew's wedding night. Unlike the children, he was quite aware of that significance. He wasn't about to go busting in upon a couple's privacy. Or to let the young ones do it either.

They had followed him out on the porch and were now also staring with curiosity at the little building.

"Ain't none stirring down that way," he said.

"How strange," Clara said. "Eulie is always the first one up."

"Look," a twin said. "There's no smoke coming from the chimney."

"If she ain't even got a fire going," her sister concluded. "When will we ever eat?"

"I'm hungry," the youngest complained.

"Oh, shut your mouths!" the boy ordered. "If you weren't all so blame dadblamed ignorant you'd know they just got married yesterday."

The girls looked at him blankly.

"We do know they got married yesterday," Clara said. "What does that have to do with . . ." The pretty young woman's eyes widened in horror and her cheeks were suddenly stained bright red. "You don't think . . ."

She glanced down at the strangely quiet kitchen and then at Jeptha. He deliberately refused to look her in the eye. With a gasp of horrified embarrassment, she turned and rushed into the cabin.

The other girls watched her departure with puzzled confusion.

"What's wrong with her?" one twin asked.

"She sure got blushed and befuddled over something," the other declared.

"Clara's just realized that a new married pair would have spent their night shagging," Rans explained, his tone condescending and worldly wise.

"Shagging?" The twins had obviously never heard the term.

"What's shagging?" Little Minnie asked.

"That's not a proper word to be speaking to young girls," Jeptha told the boy sternly.

Rans gave Jeptha a cursory glance, his gaze lingering on the wheeled cart. Deliberately he ignored the older man's advice.

"I don't know how gals can live as long as they do and know nothing about how things is," Rans commented with superior sarcasm. "Shagging is how men and women is just like the animals," he began.

"I don't think it's your place to be explaining things to your little sisters," Jeptha interrupted. "Eulie should do that, or perhaps Clara. They are both older and female."

The boy bristled.

"They's my sisters," Rans answered, his voice full of challenge. "I'm the man of my family. I can tell them whatever I want."

"Well, I'm telling you to keep your knowledge to yourself," Jeptha warned.

"And what are you going to do about it, old man?"

Jeptha gave Rans a long, narrow-eyed look.

The boy relaxed, apparently accepting the silence as impotence. He was completely unconcerned, nearly grinning. But he'd made the mistake of standing too close. Like a flash, Jeptha reached out and grabbed him by the flesh of his collarbone.

The girls gasped and stepped back. Rans, succumbing to the pressure at his neck, dropped to his knees beside the cripple cart. Moderating his grip, but keeping it steady, Jeptha eyeballed the youngster.

Having used his hands and arms to propel himself through life for more than twenty years, he was extremely strong. He could have snapped the boy's neck like a chicken bone. But Jeptha was careful not to hurt him. He was simply trying to get the young fellow's attention.

"Your sisters," he said quietly, "will all grow up and learn the ways of men and women soon enough. As man of the family, it's your job to keep them sheltered from that knowledge till they're done with childhood."

Rans glared at the man in mingled humiliation and disbelief, as if it were impossible that he could be held as securely as a chained prisoner by one crippled man at arm's length.

Jeptha's tone was soft, almost conciliatory. Now that he had the youngster in his power, it was possible to see him as simply an orphan boy with no parental guidance. A strange tug pulled at Jeptha's heart. He could recall what it was like to be young and cocky and oh, so very sure of oneself. He didn't envy the young Rans even a bit.

"An important part of being a man," he told the boy, "is knowing when to speak and when to keep your silence. It's a hard lesson to learn. But I think you can start here today."

Jeptha could see that the boy's skin beneath his grip was completely white and bloodless.

"Are you ready to start practicing that lesson?" Jeptha asked him.

The boy didn't immediately answer. He didn't want to give in. He didn't want to be bested. Jeptha understood that. Nobody liked it. But it was a thing a man had to learn to take with grace.

"Are you ready?" Jeptha asked again.

"Yes!" the boy ground out painfully.

Jeptha released his grip immediately and Rans stumbled backward before coming to his feet once more. His expression was one of fury, but along with it was a wariness that Jeptha knew was the beginning of youthful respect.

"Why don't you girls start gathering up what eggs you can find," Jeptha told the wide-eyed sisters watching. "Those chickens roost in nearly every low branch, so you've got to do a good bit of looking."

Little Minnie puffed out her lower lip in a manner that was beginning to inordinately annoy Jeptha.

"I don't never gather eggs from tree roosts," she said. "I'm not like those nasty Toby children. Mrs. Pierce has got a henhouse, and her chickens lay all their eggs in there."

"Well, that would certainly take all the trick out of finding them," Jeptha told her. "And there wouldn't be a bit of glory in being the one to find the most."

"I can find the most," Minnie declared with complete assurance.

"Not if we get to them first," one of her sisters said as she and her twin hurried off the porch.

"No fair!" Minnie claimed as she raced after them.

Silently, Rans turned to follow.

"Let the girls gather the eggs," Jeptha said.

The boy turned back toward him.

"Moss does it mostly around here, but it's kind of a woman chore," he said. "Why don't you go take care of the stock. I wouldn't want one of them little girls around that big horse, he's pretty dangerous."

The words were offered with no warning of their own and no obvious boon. But the boy accepted Jeptha's unspoken confidence like a cool salve on a hot, raw wound.

"Sure, I'll take care of the stock," Rans said, his chin rising proudly once more. "Wouldn't want one of the girls to get hurt."

Jeptha watched the boy walk toward the barn and wondered. Had he himself ever been like that? No, he was sure he had not. As a youngster, Jeptha had been happy, well-fed, certain, and sure. His own childhood had been one of a boy wrapped in cotton batting.

But Moss had been like this boy, he realized. Moss had been burdened but unbeaten, old before his time. A boy with all a man's troubles but none of a man's respect. Moss had been just like that.

Jeptha glanced toward the kitchen building and pressed his lips together, making a note of worry. He sure hoped that Moss had had time to overcome it.

6

EULIE awakened slowly, her muscles cramped, not particularly rested. Her makeshift pallet on the kitchen floor was no harder than her typical sleeping arrangements, but she had lain awake through much of the night. She wasn't sure which was worse: the thrilling feelings that had been sparked within her or the untimely interruption that had brought them to a halt.

Yawning, she ran a careless hand through her wild hair as she sat up and surveyed her surroundings. Her husband-man was stretched out asleep in two chairs. The one he sat in was rocked backward, only the rear legs making contact with the floor. At a long-limbed distance away, his bare feet were in another. His galluses, removed from his shoulders, hung down, scraping the floor on either side of him. His arms were folded across his chest in an almost belligerent manner, uncharacteristic of a sleeping man. And his head drooped near his shoulder at an unnatural angle, certain to give him a crick in his neck. She had no idea why he hadn't joined her on the pallet. It was the height of foolishness to attempt sleeping sitting up when she was perfectly willing to share her bedroll.

The rickety ladderbacks were never meant for any kind of comfort at all.

Eulie smiled at the sight of him. He didn't seem nearly as strange and unfathomable this morning as he had last night. One long dark forelock hung over his eyes, making him appear boyish and vulnerable. He had not been at all that way when he touched her. There had been nothing hesitant or uncertain. Moss Collier was a man who knew what he wanted. And last night he had wanted her.

Eulie had loved the wonderful kisses and the touch of his hands. She had not imagined that it would be as pleasant and as exciting as it had been. The naked part had been a little embarrassing; she had certainly never allowed anyone to see her completely without attire. But the look in his eyes when he had gazed at her had undone much of her natural modesty. She would have been content to allow him to look his fill. Unfortunately, their time together had been brought to an unexpected halt.

Eulie rose up on her knees and retrieved her clothing, piled so neatly next to her sleeping place. She had been embarrassed that he'd discovered that she didn't wear drawers. Her frugal justification was almost as humiliating as the truth. The Toby family had lived directly off the land. And what little grain they put up, they milled by hand. Flour sacks were few and far between. Without a quantity of material, it was impossible to provide sufficient amount of clothing for four females. As the eldest, Eulie believed that if anyone must do without, it should be her. However, she would have wished that the husband-man hadn't found out about it.

But he hadn't seemed to care. It was almost as if he believed her excuse. She was grateful for that, at least. And he had been so gentle, so loving.

After the appearance of Rans, however, everything had changed. The husband-man had ordered her to right her clothes and make her bed.

He'd acted almost angry with her, as if it weren't he himself who started all the kissing and cooing. She would have been fine sleeping with Clara, Eulie declared silently, with only a twinge at her dishonesty. Under no circumstances would she have wanted to miss being in his arms last night.

Surreptitiously, not wanting to wake him, Eulie eased herself off the pallet. Moving with slow, deliberate movements, determined to remain quiet, she stood and straightened her dress, combing her fingers through her hair.

She carefully folded up her pallet and began tiptoeing to the door. His double chair perch was right in the doorway, and Eulie would have to get up very close to him in order to go around. She had not had a good deal of experience with this skill. More often than not she had to holler, bribe, and threaten her brother and sisters awake. But she didn't want to face Moss Collier quite yet. She could make her way down to the water, take care of her necessary, and wash up a bit and do her hair before the husband-man saw her again in the clear light of day.

She picked up her skirts to keep them safely out of the way. He continued to sleep on, undisturbed. Eulie became confident that she could slip past him. He would start his day with the smell of the finest coffee brewed on the mountain. He'd open his eyes to see his clean and tidy wife hard at work next to the fire. And before he had a chance to say more than "A good morning to you," she would set before him a fine plate of side meat with a half dozen eggs fried to perfection. How lucky he would think himself to be a married man.

She was right up beside his chair. Whether he had chosen this place just in front of the door for her protection or to catch the cool night breeze, it was now necessary to ease herself around him, only inches away. She was in the process of doing just that when she grasped the doorjamb for balance and the timber creaked loudly. Eulie smothered a gasp and stood frozen, still, waiting, watching him, not breathing, less than an arm's length away from him. He made a slight snorting sound, moving his head slightly, then once more he quieted. The rhythm of his breathing was once again the only sound in the room. Slowly Eulie let out her breath and relaxed. If that didn't wake him, she thought, then nothing would.

She turned again to the doorway, her mind once more upon a neat, clean bride, fine coffee, and a hearty breakfast.

Her foot caught in one of the galluses hanging at his side. She had no chance to untangle herself before she realized that she was falling. She dropped the hem of her skirts and hastily reached out for something to steady her. Her choice was an unfortunate one. She grabbed the back of the chair where his feet were. It broke her fall all right, but not before rocking precariously, tossing off his feet and causing the chair he sat in, balanced on its back legs, to fall to the floor with a loud clatter.

The sound of the back of his head hitting the dirt floor was not pleasant. Neither was the oath that sprang from his lips.

Eulie took a deep, determined breath.

"Good morning," she said very cheerfully.

He had rolled out of his chair and sat crossed-legged, looking up toward her with near murder in his eyes.

"What in all unholy hell is going on?" he demanded.

"You mustn't curse," she reproved him firmly. "I was just stepping outside, but I'll be back in no time to fix you some of the finest coffee that you've ever tasted."

"I can make my own damn coffee," he answered. "And it's my house. I can curse a blue streak if it suits my temper. Right now it suits my temper. What were you trying to do to me?"

"I was just trying to get by," she told him. "I was trying to get by and I tripped upon your galluses."

The husband-man was apparently plagued with morning bad tempers. Eulie's chance of pleasing him was no better than a grasshopper's in the chicken yard.

She didn't stay around to even try. Hurrying outside she made her way past the small fenced garden and through the wooded path down toward the river. Her heart was pounding, but she refused to allow herself to be disconcerted. He was awake. That was the purpose of morning, after all. She was sorry about his head, but accidents sometimes happen, they were nobody's fault.

And as for her dream of being cleaned and combed when he opened his eyes, well, it was undoubtedly best to start out seeing each other in the morning exactly as they were prone to look. She was a bit untidy and he was somewhat out of sorts. It was best for them to know that now, in order to begin their lives together in a more honest fashion. There had been more than their share of deceit in this marriage already.

She glanced up at the cabin and was delighted to see that the youngers were already up and dressed and busy gathering eggs. Eulie made a little sigh of grateful relief. Today should be a better day than yesterday, at least, she assured herself. They would all be able to prove to him how well they could get along and how hard they could work and before you could say "weevils in the flour," the husband-man would be thanking good fortune for bringing his new wife this way.

The river was clear and flowing smooth this morning. Only the tiniest bit of breeze fluttered little waves across the top of the water. A turtle or two could be seen here and there, only their heads raised above the surface. A fat mamma duck noisily herded her little ducklings in for a morning swim. The croak of frogs and the occasional splash of fin or feather were the softer sounds of morning. In the distance a cranky old gander honked with displeasure over something that clearly didn't suit him.

To the east, the sky above the water was as colorful and pretty as a meadow full of wildflowers. The bright yellow sun shone through billowy pink clouds in a background of deepest blue. It was truly something beautiful, and she could hardly look away.

Eulie liked the river, she decided. This was one of the widest, slowest running stretches of it. It broadened here, becoming almost lakelike, and then narrowed dramatically to pass over the falls just downstream. Clearly it was a grand benefit to have so much water on such high land. But she was stirred by the beauty of it as well as she washed herself and tidied her hair.

Eulie was glad that she had married him. He might be prone to gruffness, but she was certain there was goodness in him. He had shared his peaches. He had shared his cabin. And last night, he had shared kisses too sweet to be imagined.

Not for one moment did Eulie even suggest to herself that she hadn't liked it. She had been enjoying herself quite nicely, in fact, before her brother's untimely interruption. She wished that it could have gone on. Then at least that part of it, the obeying-her-husband part, would be over with. It would be good simply to have it over with.

She didn't expect anything really terrible. Oh, she'd heard women talk about the horror of the wedding night with veiled mentions of pain and blood. But she knew it would be nothing like that. Women wouldn't be so eager to get married if it were such a frightful ordeal. And some people, Eulie knew, just looked at everything as if they expected it to turn out badly. She could never understand those people.

For Eulie, the world was a wonderful place where, if they just put their hearts and minds to it, people could always find good reasons to be happy. It didn't matter where you lived or what you had; it was deliberately embracing your happenstance and finding what was best about it, that made you content.

At that moment, the husband-man stepped out of the trees behind her. He seemed very large and powerful and didn't appear to be in the best of moods as he forcefully set a small bucket beside her.

"Good morning to you," she said sweetly.

"Were you thinking to wash without a towel and soap?" he asked her.

Both items were sitting in the pail that he brought her.

"Oh, how thoughtful you are!" she told him.

He blushed as if he was embarrassed. Her praise seemed to worsen his already grumpy mood.

"I didn't ask for a wife and family, but if I'm going to have to have one, I insist that they at least be clean," he said unkindly.

Eulie allowed the insult to pass as if it were never said. She had lied about him, she reminded herself. And he had shared his peaches with the children.

"I was just looking at the beauty of the morning. The river and the ducks and . . . and look at that sky, all pink and blue." She pointed toward the eastern horizon. "Have you ever seen anything more pleasing to the eye?"

He surveyed the loveliness that had so warmed her and made a disgusted sound in his throat.

"Looks like it's going to rain," he replied unhappily. "I wanted to get some things straightened out between us this morning, but I'll need to get the rest of the plowing done right away."

Eulie glanced up at him, almost disbelieving. They had both gazed at the same sunrise. All he saw was that it looked like rain? Could the husband-man not appreciate what was in front of him?

"Your place is as pretty as any on the mountain," she told him, hoping to lighten his mood.

"Pretty? It's pretty all right, a pretty prison." He nearly snarled his words.

"A prison?" Eulie was completely taken aback.

He turned to look her directly in the eyes, his brow furrowed with plain displeasure and accusation.

"All I've ever wanted was to get away from this place," he said. "Now with you and your youngers I probably never will. And don't you think that I will ever let you forget it."

She was stunned to silence.

"If you're thinking to soften me up with sweet words and kissing, don't waste your time," he continued. "I done kissed plenty of women and it don't mean a dadblamed thing to me. And I'm not about to get you with a baby in your belly, so that all the lies you told about me will come true."

"I . . . it was you that kissed me," she defended herself.

"Well don't expect to have it happening again," he told her. "Get done here and get back to the kitchen. Those ill-bred youngers of yours will be whining for feed any minute. Coffee's brewing in the coals."

"All right," she said.

"The preacher says you're my wife and helpmate," he told her. "Well, you will danged well help, but don't expect to mate."

He stomped off in obvious fury. Eulie could only watch him go, shocked and speechless.

As far as Ransom Toby could tell, his sister's happily-ever-after plans were not working out all that well. But then, he hadn't expected much. He never expected much from anything. His father used to say that when the Good Lord was handing out temperament, Eulie had gotten all the sunshine and Rans nothing but rain.

He guessed that it was true, at least partly. But he

figured that if something could just go right for him once in a while, then he would appreciate life maybe a whole lot better.

He had appreciated life pretty good at Mr. Leight's place. Mr. Leight didn't talk down to him, like he was nothing but a boy. Mr. Leight appreciated all the hard work that he did.

Moss Collier didn't appreciate him at all.

Rans had agreed to tend the big red horse like the old legless man had told him. And he was doing a pretty dadblamed good job, he thought. The animal was big and half-spooky, and Rans was not that familiar with saddle horses of any kind. But he'd gone into the barn and warily measured out some hay as the disdainful brute watched him.

The barn was a small building, one side used exclusively for hay storage. The stalls were constructed beneath a south overhang, protected from bad weather on three sides. The animals were free to wander in the fenced corral that adjoined the area.

Rans didn't mind the jenny at all. He had worked with mules since he was old enough to hold a stick and knew them to be disagreeable and stubborn.

The Texas saddle pony, however, didn't give any hints as to what he was thinking. He might be as placid as pie or ready to take a hunk of flesh out of Rans's shoulder. There had never been such a fine horse in these mountains, and there was no understanding of how high-strung he was.

Rans screwed up his courage and tended the animal. If his hands trembled slightly as he laid the hay out in the trough, nobody would ever know. And if he had winced and caught his breath when the big horse nervously sidestepped, he would never have to admit it.

For his valor and perseverance, Rans hadn't expected any thanks or praise. Somehow that sort of thing never came his way. But he hadn't imagined that faultfinding and ingratitude would be his wages.

"What the devil are you doing?"

Moss Collier's voice was not harsh, but Rans thought it accusatory.

"I'm feeding your horse," he answered, immediately defensive.

"You're feeding him," Moss said impatiently. "Have you watered him?"

"I . . . I was going to do that next," Rans insisted.

"You don't water a fine saddle horse *after* a feed," Collier told him. "That'll give even an old plowing nag the colic."

He grabbed the horse's mane and pulled his head away from the feed trough.

"Colic can kill a horse," the man said. "If you don't know anything about the animals, then stay away from them,"

Rans felt the sting of embarrassment stain his cheeks. If Eulie's new husband had said, "You're stupid!" he couldn't have felt more humiliated.

Moss Collier slipped a rope around Red Tex's neck. He opened the gate and led the big horse out. The jenny followed as they made their way down the slope toward the river. Rans trailed after them, his hands in his pockets, silent and angry.

A small trail was worn into the ground near the river where for countless years animals, both wild and domestic, had easily gained access to the water. The horse and mule dipped their heads eagerly to have their fill. Moss Collier stood beside Red Tex, stroking and patting the horse proudly. As if, Rans thought unkindly, drinking water were some kind of special trick only a fine saddle horse could manage.

Rans bent down and perused the ground around him for a few minutes until he found a nice flat round stone. He wiped the dirt from it with his thumb and forefinger testing it for smoothness. It suited him perfectly. He rose to his feet and, with a sideways sling about waist-high, he sent it sailing across the water.

Plop . . . plop . . . plop. Three times it grazed the water before dropping in.

The old jenny didn't even notice. But the big red horse jerked his head up and skittered back away from the water.

"What the devil are you doing?" Collier hollered at him as he moved to quiet the animal.

"Sorry," Rans said, guarding his grin with a mask of innocence.

He felt a good deal better after watching the man's efforts to quiet the spooked horse. When Red Tex was drinking again, Rans sided up next to Collier.

"Most folks just let their animals roam. Then they can get their own grass and water as they need it," he said.

The man didn't even bother to look his way. "*Most folks* don't own any animals as valuable as Red Tex. He gets plenty of spring grass, some cowpeas and shock, and a bucket of oats every day."

Rans tried to hide his surprise. No work animals with which he'd been familiar ever ate so good. On the old place that they'd sharecropped for his father, any oats or cowpeas that they'd managed to harvest would have been next seen in the dinner plates of him and his sisters.

But Rans had already discovered that on Moss Collier's place, a person could live on store-bought canned peaches. That was amazing. Rans had never tasted anything so fine in his life. But he flatly refused to feel beholden about it. Moss Collier had opened up those peaches, he assured himself, because he'd wanted to sweeten up his new bride. It had obviously worked. When he'd wandered back to the place and seen the light in the kitchen, he'd thought his sister was still cleaning.

He'd only gotten one glimpse, but it was surely an eyeful. Moss Collier may not have wanted to marry Eulie, but he'd overcome any contempt for her in a sure-enough hurry.

But that was the way of things, at least as far as Rans had observed. Men would do just about anything to please a pretty girl. Of course, his sister Eulie was not what Rans would describe as a pretty girl. However, he suspected a fellow could never judge fairly concerning his own sister.

As long as she suited Moss Collier, then, Eulie had a chance of making a home here for herself and the girls. Rans was not convinced that a home here would suit him at all.

Once the animals were watered, Collier walked them back up to the corral. Rans followed and watched the man feed the saddle horse and pen him before turning his attention to the jenny.

"You ain't going to work the horse in the fields?"

The man looked up then, his expression disbelieving.

"The mule pulls the plow," he answered, almost angrily. "Red Tex is a saddle animal."

Rans was genuinely curious.

"You mean the horse don't work at all?" he asked.

"He works cattle," Collier answered.

"Cattle?"

Rans was genuinely surprised. The only cattle he was at all familiar with were Jersey milk cows. But he knew enough about the animals to realize that they required open space and acres of grass. Nobody raised cattle on steep, wooded upland farm.

"You've got cattle?" he asked.

"Not yet," Moss Collier replied. There was bitterness in his tone. "Not yet, but someday I will."

Rans in no way understood the man's meaning.

"Well, if I were you," he told Collier in a superior and advisory tone. "I'd get rid of a horse that eats that good and don't work a lick."

It was tried and true advice. Rans knew that nearly every man in the Sweetwood would agree with him.

From his stony expression, Moss Collier apparently did not.

"You don't need to concern yourself with my animals," he said. "I don't suspect you've had that much experience with livestock."

Rans felt as if he'd been slapped. To say he was unfamiliar with animals was to say that Rans was no man at all. Every farmer he'd ever worked for had mules. His father, of course, had never owned any animals. Moss Collier was obviously referring to that. His father had basically never owned anything. The clothes on his back were most likely from charity and the food on his table a gift from his wife and children.

Eulie had always tried to make it out that Virgil Toby was sickly and delicate. That he was troubled and infirm. That was why he didn't work much.

That was true as far as it went, but Rans was very aware that most of his father's sickliness came out of a corn liquor jug. His inability to work was more from pure laziness than a frailty of health. He sent his children out into the fields with hunger still gnawing at their bellies while he lay around the shack sucking up strong drink and whining about not having more. He'd watched his wife work herself into an early grave, and then he'd moaned and wept in grief at losing her.

It was Eulie's contention that their father had pined away for love of his wife. It was Rans's belief that too much whiskey had killed him. And his father's swollen gut and yellow-tinged eyeballs suggested that he was right.

A son could not respect a father like that. And Rans had no respect for Virgil Toby. When he thought about it, and that was more often than was good for him, he thought he despised Virgil Toby. He hated him.

What was so repellent in his father was even more so in himself.

Like father, like son.

That was the old saying. Rans feared that there was truth in it. Even if there was not, he knew that when men looked at him, they didn't see a hardworking, determined young fellow. They saw the boy of that lazy, worthless Virgil Toby. Rans wanted to be treated like a man, he wanted to be treated like his own man.

Moss Collier didn't treat him like a man at all.

After the mistake about the saddle horse, Rans

kept his distance, waiting for a task of which he was more certain.

When Eulie's husband began to harness the jenny, he walked over to help. Mr. Leight always appreciated an extra pair of hands.

"Stand back," Collier told him. "She's liable to kick you."

"I was going to hand you the jackstrap," Rans said.

"Just stay back," he insisted. "This old jenny is a one-man mule for certain."

Rans did move back then, all the way to the fence—not because he was cautious of the mule, but because he was cautious of the man. He leaned in studied indolence against the railing, his eyes narrowed in displeasure. To have his help refused was a slight he could hardly bear. If he was not allowed to pull his weight here, he would have to leave. A horse that didn't work should not be tolerated. And a man that wouldn't work could not be. Rans could never take sustenance from a man's table without earning his share.

Leaving, he knew well, was an easy thing to decide to do but a difficult one to have come to pass. The truth came to him repeatedly when, like last night, he would take off in a fit of anger. There was no real hope of leaving without planning. A man required a poke of needments, victuals for the trip, a sample of coin, and a destination in mind.

Rans had none of these.

He had been so hopeful about Mr. Leight. Bug, as he was called by most in the Sweetwood, was a very patient, thoughtful fellow. He appreciated hard work and knew an able hand when he saw one. It was Leight who first gave Rans hope that a man could indeed be respected for what he did rather than who he was. And Bug's quiet good nature was so unshakable that the worst of Rans's moods bothered him not at all.

Rans worked for room and board, which he was careful and conscientious to earn every day.

When Clara came to cook for them, well, things just got better. Mr. Leight was a bit shy with her at first, seeming a bit uncomfortable about having a woman in the house. And Clara was a little flustered herself, blushing every time the man spoke to her. That day early in the spring when he'd picked a handful of wildflowers by the fence row to "bring some color to the cabin," Clara had become all honey-eyed and sweet-voiced about it.

Rans couldn't have been more pleased. Bug was a fine fellow, and Clara could do no better than a steady, dependable man who obviously adored her and respected her brother.

Unfortunately, Eulie didn't see it that way.

Moss Collier began to lead the jenny out of the enclosure, and Rans followed.

The man turned abruptly and looked at him.

Rans spoke up first.

"You going to plow some before that east rain gets here?"

Collier's brow furrowed as he answered. "That's what I intended."

"It sounds like a good idea," Rans agreed, a bit loftily. "We'd better get at it."

"You haven't even had your breakfast," the man said.

Rans shrugged. "I'll grab a biscuit and meet you in the field."

Collier hesitated, his expression one of rather obvious discomfiture. "Perhaps you'd better stay here and help your sister," he said. "She told me that she'd be trying to expand the garden today."

Rans stood still as a stone. The vegetable garden was women's work. He was being relegated to being no more a hand on this place than one of his sisters.

Without another word, Rans turned and began walking away.

"I got to get out of here," he muttered to himself determinedly. "Some way, somehow, I got to get out of here."

7

EULIE was determined that no one and nothing was going to ruin their first day together as a family on the farm. Not that anyone was going to make it easy for her. Rans was in a bad temper. Minnie was in a pout. The twins kept getting distracted by all the new things around them. And Clara kept looking at her as if she'd grown two heads.

"Are you sure you want to do this today?" Clara asked her. "If you aren't . . . aren't well and need to rest . . ."

"Rest? In the best part of the day?" Eulie couldn't imagine what her sister was thinking about.

The only normal enthusiasm that Eulie encountered was that of Old Hound, who was at her heels every minute and appeared to be delighted that she was here.

Unfortunately, dogs are not particularly adept at gardening.

The vegetable plot was on the south slope near the kitchen, where it easily drained into the river below. It was surrounded by a split-rail fence, which was useless for keeping out rabbits or fowl, but hogs and cattle wouldn't wander through it at least. Greens were already coming out of the ground. It was late to be adding to the planting, and potatoes put down after Easter were considered bad luck. But Eulie was going to add some limas, beets and turnips, a row of salsify, and some okra. She wouldn't waste her time with onion or carrots. Both grew freely in the woods and any seed crop planted was more than likely to cross with its wild cousin and come in spindly and poor.

Eulie was determined to double the area, though the hillside steepened less gradually on the southeast corner. She feared the heavy runoff from that spot would render it mostly useless. Maybe she could build it up and make it a squash or pumpkin hill.

The husband-man had left her brother here to help her, and Eulie saw that as a kindness indeed. He knew she'd need help moving those fence posts, and Rans, who was in another of his bad tempers, took on the job with an angry determination. A worm fence was merely a series of rails in two sizes stacked upon each other at an angle. It required more sweat than skill, but it was the consensus of the mountains that it had to be "horse-high, bull-strong and pig-tight." The biggest job was moving and redigging the ground rails. Rans manfully put himself to the task.

Eulie smiled at the sight of her brother at work. It was pleasing to her in a way that none else could know. Without any indication of his reasoning to anyone, the husband-man had Rans stay back from the plowing. Clearly he was growing fond of her. And the favor was as sweet to her heart as the nectar of canned peaches. Eulie happily anticipated their future together: Mr. and Mrs. Moss Collier of Barnes Ridge Farm.

The youngers would grow up here on this place with

plenty to eat and a dependable roof over their heads. They would be clean every day and their clothes well mended. She would make such a wonderful home that the husband-man would be forever grateful to her. And they would all be so happy together from now on.

The thought cheered her so much that she began to hum as she worked.

Yes, it would be wonderful, perfect. Maybe she could plant a few posies around the porch and they could get a cow. The Tobys would all be together again and there would be big family picnics and celebrations and babies.

That thought stopped her momentarily. The husband-man said there would be no more kisses. There would be no babies. It was probably not right for a wife to wish that her husband was a liar. But at that moment, Eulie hoped that at the very least he was mistaken.

He said he wanted to get away from this place. He called it a prison. Eulie looked around her at the cabin, the outbuildings, and the river all nestled so lovely within the tall woods around them. How could anyone ever bear to leave, let alone wish for it? Eulie shook her head. Surely he did not mean that. Surely he did not truly want to get away.

"Look! Look what we found!" The twins were coming from the tack shed, their hands full of harness.

Minnie got there first, and her curiosity turned immediately to excitement.

"It's for a pony cart!" she cried delightedly. "Mrs. Pierce said I should have a pony cart."

Clara examined it next and shook her head at her younger sister. "It's too small to harness a pony. See, the girth strap is much too short. It must be for a dog or goat."

"Do you think they have a sulky?" Nora May asked.

"We wouldn't be too big to ride in a sulky," Cora Fay assured them both quickly.

"We could strap this on the dog," Rans said, examining the long brown leather lines.

"To the dog?" Cora Fay and Nora May glanced at each other.

"That dog couldn't pull us in a sulky," one said.

"That's because you nasty Toby children are not tiny and precious like me," Minnie told them, more than a hint of taunting in her voice.

Rans looked at his youngest sister with disgusted disapproval. "I hadn't noticed you being tiny and precious," he said. "More like stumpy and annoying."

Minnie immediately began to cry. But rather than sobbing and tears, it was more like screaming and wails.

"For heaven's sake, Minnie!" Clara protested.

"Hush up, right now!" Eulie scolded.

Words had no effect.

"Ignore her," Rans suggested.

It was easier said than done.

"We could use this to harness the dog up to the wheel-hoe," Rans told Eulie. "It would make breaking the new ground a lot easier."

It sounded like a good idea, but Eulie had never heard of such.

"The dog won't know anything about plowing," she said.

"What's to know?" Rans answered loudly, attempting to be heard over his youngest sister's continued lamentation. "Get the plow headed in the right direction and have somebody lead him."

Eulie glanced down at the happy, enthusiastic old hound who was even now sniffing eagerly at the harness, and wondered if they were about to do the poor dog a tremendous disservice.

"Well, they'd be no harm in trying," she conceded as she squatted down, patting her knee and calling the dog to her.

Old Hound sided up eagerly and made no complaint as she attempted to fit the headpiece on his long brown muzzle. The only difficulty proved to be the slobbering tongue that he kept using to lick her. The girth strap around his middle fitted only in the last notch, but they were able to secure it reasonably well. Although obviously made to be attached to some sort of vehicle, the fastenings were quite low and easily joined to the outside portion of the wheel-hoe's axle.

"This is going to work great," her brother assured her. "We'll be able to get this new ground broken in half the time at least."

Her sister, Clara, remained a little skeptical. "The dog won't know the first thing about plowing a straight furrow."

Eulie was oblivious to that concern. The youngers were all delighted and excited. It was the first genuine enthusiasm that had been shown since their arrival at their new home, and Eulie wasn't about to waste it.

"We'll have to try out different hands," she told them. "Since we don't have any idea who will be best able to handle our new plow dog, we'll need to give everyone a chance to drive him."

Little Minnie ceased her caterwauling and began to

clap her hands and squeal with delight. The twins shared a glance of unveiled excitement. Even Rans looked eager. Clara offered her a surreptitious wink in congratulation on the brilliance of her plan.

It would be fun, they could enjoy it together, and whether the dog was truly helpful or not, the pleasure of it would make the work go faster. Beyond the din of the spirited activity around her, Eulie heard the angry dissenting voice.

"Stop that! Stop that right now!"

Glancing up, Eulie saw Uncle Jeptha at the edge of the kitchen stone path. His face was red with fury, and he was shaking his fist at her.

"Get that harness off that dog!" he hollered. "Get it off!"

All around her the youngers had quieted.

"That harness belongs to me, and it ain't for hitching no hound to a plow."

The dog had begun to wag his tail and was tugging to pull himself away, jerking the wheel-hoe in such a way that it nearly came crashing to the ground.

Cora Fay knelt and held the dog's head. Rans gripped the handle and used his foot to press the blade securely into the ground.

"He's going to get us!" Minnie warned with a loud wail.

Eulie had no choice but to see what the old man wanted. He was obviously very angry about something. Undoubtedly, she assured herself, he didn't understand what they were doing and how harmless and inventive it was.

Eulie made her way carefully across the neat little garden rows already sprouting green and through the rickety slat gate. She went up the slope toward the kitchen smiling, hopeful, in the face of the man's undisguised irritation.

"What is it, Uncle Jeptha?" she asked as she approached. "Do you need something?"

The old cripple's eyes were cold with fury. "That goat harness belongs to me. I didn't say you could borrow it. So you tell those children to get it off that dadgummed dog this instant!"

Eulie gave him what she hoped was a serene, reassuring smile and spoke softly.

"You really shouldn't curse, Uncle Jeptha," she said. "It's a bad example in front of the children and a true danger to the purity of your soul."

"Curse!" His voice was incredulous. "Hail, wire and creation, gal, I know words so bad they'd curl your hair, and I ain't said nary a one."

Eulie decided not to argue the point. The old man was narrow-eyed and spoiling for a fight. She was determined not to give him one.

"The children found the harness in the tack room," she told him. "It fits the dog very well and we thought we might get Old Hound to help us with the plowing."

"A dog cain't do plowing!" he assured her adamantly. "And that harness belongs to me. It's not for that."

"What is it for?"

The man seemed momentarily nonplussed before he answered her. "Moss bought it with a goat trained to pull my cart. I was supposed to use it to take me places I wanted to go."

Eulie was puzzled. "You never go anyplace," she said.

"Just so," Uncle Jeptha replied.

A silence ensued where Eulie expected him to explain. The man was almost rigid with anger as he sat straight and tall, chin high and shoulders back in the low, narrow cart.

Now that he was no longer yelling, the children had become distracted. Rans had moved away from the hitched-up dog to take up a roughhouse game of tag with Little Minnie.

Clara was watching them, laughing at the antics as Rans would almost let the little girl catch him and then scurry away just out of reach. The twins apparently decided that they could best be of assistance to Eulie and were running up the slope toward her and Uncle Jeptha.

"You should come help us with the dog," Cora Fay called out to him.

"The little harness fit him just perfectly," Nora May said. "Do you have a sulky somewhere?"

Eulie felt the change in demeanor of the man beside her. He was obviously still very annoyed, but she knew from her own experience how hard it was to maintain a stern countenance in the face of the genuine sweetness of her twin sisters.

The two plopped down on their knees on the ground beside the amputee cart. Their nearness seemed to startle the older man, and Eulie wondered how long it had been since he had been truly close to anyone.

When Uncle Jeptha continued not to speak, Eulie posed a question.

"What happened to the goat?" she asked.

He looked up at her, surprised.

"A goat!" Nora May looked delightedly into the eyes of her twin.

"A goat pulling a sulky would be even better than a dog," Cora Fay agreed.

"There ain't no sulky," Uncle Jeptha told them. "The harness is to pull this cart. And the dang goat, why Moss got rid of it ages ago. It has long since been boiled down to soap."

The children let that reality soak in for a moment but were not deterred by it.

"Old Hound could pull your cart," Cora Fay said.

"He's plenty big enough," her twin agreed.

"That dog ain't been trained to pull nothing," Uncle Jeptha answered with annoyance. "He's a hunting dog."

"Is he a good one?" Eulie asked.

"Well, sure he is," Uncle Jeptha man replied. "Moss wouldn't have nothing less."

"Then if he's smart enough to hunt," Eulie told him, her glance taking in the girls as well. "He's got to be smart enough to pull a plow . . . or a cart."

Uncle Jeptha shook his head. "You'll never get him to pull anything."

Eulie nodded. "That's why we need your help," she said. "You could train him to help."

"Yes! Yes!" the twins agreed. "You could train him."

"Why would I want to do that?" he asked her.

Eulie thought about her answer for a long moment. The twins' eyes were wide with unconditional generosity and innocence that was infinitely more compelling than any words could ever be.

"Why should you help us?" Eulie repeated. "Because we need it and because you can."

At that moment a rabbit took the opportunity to pass through the edge of the woods within sight of the garden. Old Hound howled for the chase and took off after him, overturning the plow he was hitched to and dragging it with sad results across both the untilled ground and the fledgling new plants of the original garden.

Cries of shock and horror erupted from every voice.

"Stop! Stop!" Eulie begged the animal at the top of her lungs.

He did, finally, after scampering beneath the bottom fence rail, only to be brought up short when the plow wedged itself firmly between the posts.

The dog continued to bark and jerk at the harness to which he was attached. They all surveyed the extensive damage in silence. Beans trampled, potatoes uprooted, the garden now had a nasty gash cut right through its center.

Eulie swallowed the lump in her throat. The husband-man would not be pleased with this day's work, either, she thought.

She turned back to Uncle Jeptha and determinedly forced a smile to her lips.

"Well at least now we know for sure that he's strong enough to pull it," she said.

The threatened rain held off until late afternoon. Moss came down from the field, as both he and the mule were soaked. He tended his animal and his wet tack, grateful for the time alone. His stringy-haired bride was nowhere in sight. But her whole eat-him-out-of-hearth-and-home family was up on the porch. He did not look forward to spending the afternoon trapped in close quarters with them.

But that was better than being alone somewhere

with his wife. He'd handled it badly. He knew that. It was important that he talk to her. But he hadn't any idea of what he would say. He'd handled it very badly. First he'd taken her off to the kitchen with him and had been on the verge of consummating their marriage. Then he'd blamed her for the whole thing. Of course, most everything was her fault. But not the kisses. For that stupid error in judgment, he had no one to blame but himself.

He'd hurt her feelings. And he'd done it on purpose, with clear intent. He wanted to punish her, take her down a peg, wipe that cheerful grin off her face once and for all. It was mean and it was beneath him. But he'd done it and he couldn't quite conjure up being sorry.

He hung the oiled lines on their tack room peg and headed for the door. There was no way to avoid his new family indefinitely. From this distance it was hard to see exactly what they were doing. Clara appeared to be sorting seed. The boy was whittling pegs of some sort. The twins were staving willow strips for Uncle Jeptha, who sat weaving a chair seat. Everybody seemed busy except Little Minnie, who was dancing across the porch.

Moss sighed, knowing he'd just have to get used to the worthless bunch. He'd teach himself to tolerate them. People could learn to put up with anything if they sincerely put their minds to it. He'd seen plenty of folks with body lice or a bad tooth who lived just as content as anyone else.

He would have to give up his dream. That was the rub, of course. His dream had been in the front of his mind for most of his life now. It was hard for him to think of a future without it. The whole plan of his life had hinged upon it. Now it seemed that with one fateful falsehood, everything had swung out of control.

He would have to live here on this farm with these people until he drew his last breath. It was with that less-than-serene thought that Moss pulled together the neckline of his shirt and loped from the barn to the cabin porch. His clothes stuck to him clammily and water fell from the brim of his hat in rivulets. But the drenching invigorated him.

He jumped up onto the far east corner beneath the protection of the overhang and shook the excess water off his arms and legs.

He slapped his hat against his thigh twice and straightened the brim before tossing it on a porch peg to dry.

The activity he had spied from the barn had subsided somewhat. The whiny one, Little Minnie, was holding her doll and glaring at him as if he had disturbed her afternoon.

The boy, Ransom, no longer leaned against the porch post as he worked, but stood straight, hands still, in his own way daring Moss to make some comment.

There was a lull in the young Clara's effort as well. She came to her feet and hurried into the house to get him a towel. He was surprised and pleased at her eagerness to see to his comfort. That's how it should be, he reminded himself. He was the one wronged here, and this whole family of young beggars should spend the rest of their lives trying to make it up to him. He was less than delighted when what she came back with was a tattered portion of an old oat bag that he often used in winter as a hearth rug for Old Hound.

"I'm fine," he assured her, demurring to wipe his face on what was undoubtedly a flea-infested cloth. "A little damp never hurt me."

"We're making chairs so all of us can sit at the table," one of the twins told him proudly as she dipped the cut willow strips into the bucket of brine at her side.

"If we can make just one a day," the other piped in. "Not counting Sunday, we'll all be able to sit together for vittles in less than a week."

Uncle Jeptha made no comment, but Moss watched as he wove the soaked strips in a square pattern over a seat frame. His hands moved in a sure and steady rhythm, and with each completed strip he ran his palm across the work, smoothing it with pride.

It had been a long time since Moss had seen the old man so industriously engaged. He worked hard to do his share, of course. But he rarely showed any enthusiasm for his chores. Perhaps he simply enjoyed the task. Chair weaving was not a typical everyday activity.

"Well, I guess we needed the rain," Moss said, by way of conversation to nobody in particular.

"Yes, we sure do," the boy said in a mature manner that was so ill-tuned to his youthful soprano voice. "Rain is mighty welcome this time of year. Even if it does get us all holed up here on the porch."

"Where's . . ." He hesitated, somehow reluctant to use her name. "Where's your sister?"

"Eulie's down at the kitchen," Clara answered. "She said she wanted to put some limas on to boil and get the place straightened up so she could find everything."

Moss nodded, grateful not to have to face her again just yet.

"Did you get much done on your garden?" he asked.

Nobody answered, and Moss glanced around at them curiously. They all appeared somehow almost guilty.

"We . . . we got a good deal accomplished before the rain set in," Clara assured him, but there was a strange uncertainty in her voice.

"We all helped out," one twin said.

"It makes the work go faster," the other added.

Moss nodded agreement and gazed out through the rain to the far side of the kitchen. He could see that the boy had successfully moved the fence posts to a further perimeter and that the soil in the new area had already been turned. He was pleasantly surprised they had managed to get so much done. That surprise turned to puzzlement when he noticed, to his complete amazement, what appeared to be an attempt to dig some kind of ditch right through the middle of the existing planting.

"What in the devil happened to the garden?" he asked.

Nobody said a word.

He asked them again, more forcefully. "What in the blue blazes happened to the garden?"

"It was your dog that done it," Little Minnie told him, her lower lip poked out stubbornly. "It weren't none of us."

Moss tutted at the child in lieu of scolding. "That old hound couldn't a done anything like that," he said with certainty.

"He could with a plow hitched to him," the boy, Rans, answered.

"A plow?"

Uncle Jeptha cleared his throat and commenced the explanation.

"The children borrowed that old goat harness you got for me," he said. "They used it to hitch the plow to the dog. It actually works pretty well. 'Course, the dog did get away that once."

Moss shook his head, not quite sure whether to believe what he was hearing.

"You hitched the dog to the wheel-hoe?"

"It actually worked pretty good," Uncle Jeptha repeated.

Moss gave his uncle an accusing look and then whistled for the dog. Old Hound came crawling out from underneath the porch. He squatted down and petted the dog, running his hands along his back and shoulders checking for gall marks or injury. He found nothing but one fat brown tick inside the dog's ear that he promptly disposed of.

"He seems all right," Moss admitted finally.

"Of course he's all right," a twin said.

"We wouldn't never do anything to hurt an animal," her sister chimed in.

"My hunting hound dog was never meant to pull a plow," he stated firmly. "I don't want to see him doing that."

"Well, he *can* do it," Clara told him. "And he did it very well."

"The stock on a farm need to earn their way same as the people," the boy pointed out.

"Old Hound earns his way out in the woods."

No one could argue that, and didn't.

"What about that big red horse?" Rans asked him.

"Seems to me he does nothing but eat oats. If you trade him in for a cow, we'd have butter and cheese to put on biscuits. And children need to drink milk."

"You want me to trade Red Tex for a milk cow?" he shouted. "That is the finest saddle horse in this corner of Tennessee."

"He is?" The youngster considered that very thoughtfully. "Then perhaps you could get a couple of hogs as well," he said.

"Hogs! I will never get rid of Red Tex," Moss declared adamantly.

The words had barely left his mouth when he realized how foolish they were. Red Tex was part of the dream he was going to have to give up. The horse was his saddle pony, his way out West. A cold chill of disappointment swept through him.

His stringy-haired bride had lied about him, and now all was lost.

Without glancing in either direction, Moss stepped past her brother and sisters on the porch and into the dark confines of the cabin.

Behind him he heard the murmurs and questions.

"Did you see the look on his face?" the boy said. "What made him so upset?"

"He sure sets a fine store by that horse," one of the twins said.

"It is prettier than some old milk cow," the other pointed out.

"What's he up to in the cabin?" Little Minnie whispered.

"Mind your own business," Clara scolded.

The little girl made a noise of distress signaling a soon-to-come dismal wailing.

It never came into being. It was Uncle Jeptha who called for the girl to fetch something to him. The old man was obviously growing accustomed to having the mewling brat around.

Moss walked over to his bed and knelt beside it. From beneath the corner he pulled out a wooden box. Part strongbox, part trunk, he had made it himself from strips of fine walnut, ash, and hemlock culled from the cabin and outbuildings. It was his piece of home and heritage that he meant to take with him on his journey to the rest of the world.

He ran his palm across the flattop lid. He wasn't much of a carver, but he'd etched his name, COLLIER, deeply into the wood, varnished it with pine resin, and shined it to a high gloss. He had been saddened when he'd made it, thinking of how he would feel when all of the people and places here would be in his past. But for years now it had gladdened him when he opened it. It was solid, graspable evidence that someday he was leaving this place. Often it was all he had to hold onto.

Moss unhitched the latch and opened the lid. He gazed with love and longing at the contents inside. The little pamphlet he had sent away for was frayed and tattered from much handling. Carefully he picked it up and read the title aloud: "The Emigrant's Guide to Texas Settlement and the Far West with Maps and Statistical Information Relative to the Same."

He perused the handbook as perhaps he had a million times, plotting his route, weighing his alternatives. He could head down the mountains toward Charleston or Savannah, get a job shipboard, and work his way around Florida and across the Gulf. Or he could go west to the big Mississippi, take the river south to New Orleans, and go by paddle boat across to Galveston harbor. But his preferred plan was to ride Red Tex, continue across Arkansas to the Indian Territory, and follow the south-leading cattle trails into Fort Worth or Abilene.

As Moss stared at the tattered pamphlet, he tried to come to grips with the reality that he was not going to get to go. She had ruined that for him. He would live his life and be buried on this mountain without ever having a chance to see what life was like anywhere else.

He lay the guidebook upon the bed and took out a hefty cotton sack filled with coins. His life savings. He weighed it in his hand, but he had no need to count it. Every extra penny he had ever come upon had gone into the sack, every cash-paying job he could come up with, every hand of poker he'd ever won—twenty-seven dollars and forty-two cents at last count. It was a fortune in cash money meant to give him a good start on a new life in the West. It had no more value to him at this moment than a sack of nails. If he was staying here in Tennessee, not even a fortune could make him happy. He set the money aside.

From the box he withdrew his shiny single-action .44 Frontier. He stroked the shiny blued nickel finish admiringly. He pointed it toward the fireplace and scoped down the sites. It was a fine, expensive side arm. Much better than any man on the mountain had ever owned. Handguns, inappropriate for hunting, were a luxury most Tennessee farmers weren't willing to sacrifice for. But then, they weren't going West, where a side arm was as much a part of a man's gear as his hat and his saddle bags.

The Colt had cost him twelve dollars and was

worth, to his mind, every penny. Like Red Tex, it was purchased for his future. Now he had no future. Just more days, more days just like this one. Working his life away on the only plot of land he'd ever known. And he wasn't even going to have the serenity of silence and solitude. His stringy-haired bride and her whole sorry family were to be a boil on his back forever.

"Whew, lordy! Where'd you get a gun like that 'un?"

Moss looked up, annoyed, to see his wife's brother hurrying across the room toward him.

"That's the prettiest gun I ever seen in my life," Rans said holding his hands out as if expecting Moss to hand it to him.

He gave the boy a dismissing look, irritated at the interruption.

"You've never even seen another like this one," Moss told him. "And you're not likely to."

Abruptly he put it back in the box, followed by the bag of money and the guidebook pamphlet. He shoved the carved wood trunk back under his bed.

"A Frontier .44 ain't no gun for a boy," he said. "I don't want you even so much as looking at it."

The boy paled as if he had slapped him. Then his chin drew up high and his eyes narrowed in fury.

"Butthole!" he screamed.

Turning, he ran out the cabin door, across the porch, and off down the mountain as the rain poured down on him.

8

It was Cora Fay who spotted them first. It was nearly dusk, and the rain had stopped; in the distance she spied a flurry of activity coming sidehill from across the river.

"They's folks coming," she called out to her sister.

Nora May took up the cry.

"They's folks coming!"

Eulie, who'd spent most of the wet afternoon sweeping the kitchen's dirt floor until it was tight and packed as stone and scrubbing down the walls with ashes was in no mood for company. She was hot, sweaty, and dirty-faced and her hair a fright.

But sure enough, when she gazed in the direction that her sisters pointed, below the house on the second rise, there were people coming. And not just a lone neighbor or pair of travelers. It looked like every man, woman and child in the Sweetwood was headed their way.

"Everybody in the cabin," she said anxiously. "We've got to get cleaned up."

Clara hadn't even waited for the order and was already inside, flushing Uncle Jeptha out onto the porch.

"Where's Rans?" Eulie asked.

"He took off in another snit," Little Minnie told her. "And he ain't wandered back yet."

"You twins will have to tote the water, then," Eulie said.

The two hurried quickly to the buckets hanging under the kitchen eaves. They were full of rainwater, and the two girls began dumping it into the covered barrel reserved for drinking. The twins then hurried with the empty buckets in the direction of the river, which would furnish what was needed to wash.

"Little Minnie can help you," Eulie said, reaching inside the kitchen door to grab the smaller scrub pail to hand the youngster.

The child's jaw dropped open in surprise, and then she stuck her lip out stubbornly.

"Mrs. Pierce don't make me tote no water," she said with breathy certainty. "I'm her princess. They's plenty of folks to work better than me."

"You need to watch how you're talking, missy, or I know a princess who'll have a switch taken to the back of her legs," Eulie warned.

"I ain't afraid of you," Little Minnie declared. "If you want me screeching and bawling when company comes, then go ahead and take a switch to me. I ain't toting no water."

To prove her point, she abruptly seated herself on an the old hickory stump that was used to split firewood and gazed up at her older sister defiantly.

Eulie maintained her patience with some difficulty. Her family could certainly be a strain on her good nature.

"All right, Little Minnie," she said quietly. "Don't

tote any water. But those who don't tote it, don't wash with it. With a crowd like the one coming, more likely than not Mr. and Mrs. Pierce are among them. I suspect they'll be surprised to see that in one day their *princess* has turned into a dirty, ill-kept cracker."

Little Minnie didn't answer, but when Eulie held out the scrub pail again, this time she took it.

Eulie hurried up the slope toward the cabin. The husband-man stood on the ground near the edge of the porch holding a flathead adze and talking to Uncle Jeptha.

"Your sister done run me out of my own house," the older man complained to Eulie.

"She's got to wash up," Eulie answered. "We've all got to get washed up."

Moss Collier gave her a hard look.

"I wash regular," he said disdainfully. "That way the sight of a crowd headed my direction don't send me in a panic toward soap and water."

Her family kept themselves as clean as he did—and a good deal cleaner than his Uncle Jeptha. But Eulie refrained from pointing that out. She smiled at him instead.

"I guess we're just excited to see folks," she said. "I guess they're coming for a pounding."

"What?"

Both men spoke simultaneously. Neither looked pleased.

"Well, we did just get married," she pointed out. "It's right and neighborly that folks would want to wish us the best and give us a little something to help get us started."

The expression on the husband-man's face indicated clearly that he was not in any way pleased by the notion of an outpouring of good will.

Eulie suffered a great pang of guilt. These were his friends and neighbors as much as her own. But he didn't want to see them because they thought ill of him.

She glanced over at Uncle Jeptha, whose attention seemed to be upon the distant invaders.

Quietly she addressed her words to Moss alone.

"If you want me to tell them the truth, I will," she told him. "It's right that folks should think I'm a liar, since it is so."

The husband-man looked down at her, but there was no real forgiveness in his eyes.

"Since I have to be married to you anyway, I guess it don't matter that much how it came to pass."

The hardness of his words were hurtful. Eulie looked away, not wanting him to see how easily she could be wounded.

"Here come the girls with the water," she said with determined cheerfulness. "You don't want any of it?"

He hesitated only for a moment.

"Give me a towel and my good shirt," he told her. "And I'll wash down at the river."

She smiled up at him, pleased.

"Do you want a clean shirt, too, Uncle Jeptha?" she asked.

The older man turned back to look at her. There was something in his expression that Eulie thought might be near panic.

"I ain't got no other shirt, nor do I need one," he answered. "I'll be in the barn till every last one of them has been and gone."

His tone was so angry and adamant, Eulie glanced over to the husband-man with concern.

Moss Collier apparently didn't see anything amiss in his kin hiding out from company.

Eulie didn't have time to worry about it now. She helped the girls get the water into the cabin. They hastily hung their bonnets on the peg.

Clara was already stripped down to her petticoats and was bent to the waist brushing a pinch of cornstarch through her long blonde hair to freshen it.

"How far away are they?" she asked anxiously. "How much time do I have?"

"We have time to get everybody washed and dressed, but only just," Eulie answered.

She quickly grabbed up the husband-man's good shirt. A towel was more difficult, but Clara pointed one out to her that was hanging in the mantel corner.

Eulie gave it an unappreciative glance. It looked more like a worn-out, flea-ridden rug than a towel. But she took her sister's word for it and hurried by outside and tossed both hastily in Moss Collier's arms.

She glanced up toward the new arrivals in the distance, to see that they were already near the falls crossing. There would be barely enough time to get the children clean.

"What the devil!" she heard the husband-man call out, but she didn't even stop to reprove him about cursing.

Clara had already poured water in an enameled basin, and she and the younger girls were taking their turns. Eulie hurried to the peg where they had hung their Sunday best.

Eulie had, of course, worn hers yesterday, and Little Minnie had several to choose from. She shook out the matching blue calico dresses that she had made for the twins. Neither girl had shoes, stockings, or a decent petticoat, but at least they would have the confidence of a pair of well-made flour-sack drawers under their clothes.

An argument broke out when Little Minnie tried to keep all the water for herself; surprisingly, it was with Clara.

Eulie hesitated to scold the younger girl, remembering her threat to pitch a fit in front of company.

"Let's get the little ones ready first, Clara," she said. "Then we'll have some time for ourselves."

"You'll have to tend the children," her sister answered. "I have to look my best."

Eulie glanced at her, puzzled. "Whatever for?"

Clara handed her the hairbrush, and unthinkingly Eulie began to run it through the long length of blonde tresses as long and thick as a horsetail.

"Mr. Leight is with them," Clara said in a furtive whisper. "I can recognize him on that gray mule even at that distance."

Eulie rolled her eyes. "Why do you care about him anyway?"

Clara didn't answer.

"You can do a whole lot better," Eulie told her.

"Better than a kind man who owns his own farm and seems to . . . seems to care for me?" Clara was downright indignant. "I'm not sure there is anything better."

Eulie didn't have time to argue about it.

She was too busy inspecting the cleanliness of a

half dozen ears, three necks and more fingernails than she could count. She didn't want to embarrass Moss; she didn't want to make a bad impression. Her family had never had such a fine reputation, and now she'd besmirched both her own name and his with her devious lies. If she ever intended to win back the approval of her neighbors, a clean family and a neat homeplace were absolutely essential.

"They are here! They are here! I can hear people!"

Little Minnie was jumping up and down in her enthusiasm.

In another minute, she, Clara, and the twins were racing out the door. Eulie was still as sweat-stained, dirty, and haggard-looking as the moment she'd walked in.

She jerked her dirty dress over her head and ripped the pins out of her hair. The sound of folks hailing the husband-man, who was apparently standing some distance from the cabin, could be heard clearly.

Eulie washed quickly and nervously, wishing that summer did not require removal of the front door.

She bent toward the enamel basin. Cupping the water in her hands she brought it up to her face.

"Eulie! Folks is here."

She startled at the husband-man's voice. Her eyes were full of water and she jerked backward, attempting to modestly pull down the tail of her josey, the basin spilled, she slipped and landed hard upon her rump on the pine floor.

Moss Collier was standing in the door way, eyeing her curiously.

"You'd better get your dress on and tie up that hair," he told her. "Everybody we ever knew is here and most of them have brought us something."

Eulie didn't have a chance to say a word. An angry voice called out from the doorway.

"What's going on here? I heard a big thump."

Protectively, the husband-man tried to block entrance to the door, but Miz Patch was not so easily kept back. She pushed right past him as if he weren't there. She was a slight woman of middle years. But there was nothing frail or indecisive about her. The widow of Ezra Patchel, Miz Patch, as she was called, was a formidable human being. Like a bantam rooster, her small, delicate beauty disguised a ferocious tenacity and a will of iron. When she said "frog," the whole room would start hopping. She had a soft spot in her heart for Eulie's twin sisters, and her concern extended to the rest of the family.

"What are you doing on that floor?"

Before Eulie had a chance to answer, she turned accusingly to the husband-man.

"Keep those people out of here, Mosco. Cain't you see that your bride is upset?"

Since that was exactly what he'd been trying to do, his expression was clearly puzzled.

Eulie didn't feel upset, she didn't think she was upset. She had no reason to be upset.

Inexplicably, she burst into tears.

"Oh, no." The husband-man's words were almost a groan.

Eulie knew she shouldn't cry. She didn't even want to cry, but somehow she just couldn't stop.

Miz Patch grabbed a quilt off the bed.

"Here, tack this over the door," she told the husband-man. "Tomorrow she can be hanging a curtain. There's got to be some kind of privacy for a family with five females."

Somehow they managed to get the quilt over the door, and then the woman shooed him out.

"You go say your howdy-do to the folks and I'll take care of your Eulie."

And she proceeded to do just that, helping her off the floor and onto the bed.

"Now what's wrong, gal?" she asked.

Her question brought on a new spate of tears, but Eulie bravely tried to answer.

"I had to get the children clean and Clara was no help and I slipped and I burned the hocks on the best day of my life and he fed them peaches and he kissed me, but the dog dragged the plow through the garden and I wore my dress yesterday and I ain't aired it and I don't got no drawers."

The last was almost a wail and Eulie covered her on mouth with her fist.

"There, there now, Eulie," Miz Patch comforted. "We all got days like that and lots of them are right smack-dab in the beginning of our happily-ever-after."

Eulie couldn't get control of herself. The more she tried not to cry aloud, the more the tears came down.

"I just want to be happy," she sobbed. "I just want us all to be happy."

"More than likely it's your nesting nature," Miz Patch told her. "I heard talk coming up here that you've done swallowed a watermelon seed."

"Oh, Miz Patch, oh, Miz Patch," Eulie moaned.

"Don't give a thought more to it," the woman said. "They's plenty of gals got married in the selfsame predicament."

"It's not true," she confessed sorrowfully. "I lied about it. It's not true."

Miz Patch gave her a long look and then shook her head. "They's a lot of gals got married in that predicament as well."

"I lied about him and forced him to marry me," Eulie told her. "I thought he was lonely and me and the children, we need a place and . . . oh, it was a terrible thing, wasn't it? I should never have done it."

"Well, he would have never wed you otherwise," Miz Patch pointed out. "These Barnes and Collier men aren't real partial to marrying. And he is lonely, though I don't suspect he knows it."

"He said no more kissing and no babies ever," Eulie admitted sadly.

Miz Patch chuckled.

"Don't worry about that, darling," she said, speaking with wry understanding. "A man can get mad enough at you to stay away from your bed for two, maybe three, days. But after that, well . . . truly, it don't matter what you've done, they always find a way to forgive."

Her assurance was comforting. It did not, however, ease Eulie's guilt.

"But it was very wrong, what I did."

"Of course it was," Miz Patch agreed. "Sometime we get to thinking we're cornered, we don't see no other way but the wrong. It's 'cause we're human."

"I should go out there right now," Eulie said. "I should announce the truth and call the whole thing off."

Miz Patch wrapped her arm around Eulie's waist, staying her from any hasty action.

"I don't think that would be a good idea," she said. "You're going to need a husband, and having been up here with him—well, folks would think the worst."

"But we haven't ever . . . I mean, we haven't . . . I haven't . . . been obedient to my husband, ever, I mean."

Eulie buried her face in her hands. She couldn't look the woman in the eye.

Miz Patch, obviously puzzled, tried to make out her words.

"Are you saying you're still a maiden?"

Eulie nodded.

There was a long moment of complete silence before Miz Patch laughed heartily.

"Now don't that beat all," she said. "I wish I'd seen poor Mosco at the wedding yesterday. I bet he was faunching fit for fury."

Eulie couldn't quite see the humor in it.

"He was very mad," she told Miz Patch.

"But he wed you anyway," the woman pointed out.

"There was a shotgun at his back," Eulie said.

"Lots of men would rather be dead than wed," she replied. "And he was sure acting protective of you a few minutes ago."

Eulie couldn't argue with that.

Miz Patch gave her a consoling pat upon the knee

"I think you'd just better make the best of this marriage," she said. "You did promise before God. Moss Collier needs someone like you, almost as much as you need someone like him."

"But Miz Patch, it was so wrong."

She snorted with unconcern.

"There's wrong and there's wrong," she said. "Women have been taking the blame for wrong since the beginning of time. They say Eve brought sin into the world giving Adam that forbidden fruit. But I don't doubt for a minute that it was him, forever whining, 'What's for dinner? What's for dinner?' that drove her to it."

Eulie burst out laughing.

"That's better," Miz Patch said, smiling at her. "Now dry those pretty eyes of yours. You got company outside."

Ransom Toby was astounded to return to Moss Collier's home on Barnes Ridge to find a shindig in progress. Folks from all over were laughing and milling around. Music was playing. Duroc Madison was puffing on the harmonica, and Lem Pierce accompanied him on the squeeze-box. Dancing was not allowed, of course. Dancing was sin, and Preacher Thompson was in attendance. But there were musical games like Skip to My Lou and Chairs that were to Rans's mind just as fun as dancing.

The corner of the porch was piled with the pounding for the new bride and groom. It was the way in the Sweetwood to see that a newlywed couple start out housekeeping with the necessities of life. Everyone was expected to contribute, the poor as well as the prosperous. So people brought what they could spare. A pound of sugar. A pound of coffee. A pound of nails.

The gifts weren't the only thing they'd brought. There were party vittles, which were a great improvement over Eulie's cooking of late. And down next to the river, the Pusser brothers had a jug of corn liquor. Most of the men present made a surreptitious visit in that direction at least once that evening. More often than not, they dragged the bridegroom-host with them.

Rans noticed that Eulie's husband had begun to weave a little bit on his trips back up the slope, and he grinned maliciously. He hoped the man made a fool of himself and fell flat on his face.

Rans thought about getting himself a drink. The Pusser brothers were not the kind of men to worry about the consequences of liquoring up a growing boy. All he needed was a penny to purchase. But he wasn't that interested in drinking. Mr. Leight was here somewhere, he'd seen the gray mule hobbled, and in all honesty, he preferred a long talk with the man over a whole jug of illicit liquor.

Rans was not the kind of fellow who really socialized well. He was uncomfortable in a crowd and he couldn't nod and smile and talk about nothing with people he didn't hardly know. But he made a stab of it tonight, all the while looking for the only man among them that he truly considered his friend.

He spoke to several of the men, but never allowed the conversation to go past the greeting. He did allow the ladies to feed him. Myrtle Browning filled him a dish with ham and greens, a piece of pone as big as a man's hand, a fair amount of pickles, and a slice of vinegar pie. A person couldn't ask more from life from that.

That is, most persons couldn't. He saw Little Minnie sitting on a checked picnic cloth with Mr. and Mrs. Pierce. His sister was talking a mile a minute and both adults appeared endlessly fascinated by what she had to say. As the woman listened, she dampened her hand on a wet rag and rolled Little Minnie's hair around her fingers. The child was already beginning to look as if her head were hung with sausages.

Rans snorted in disbelief and moved on, eating from his plate as he wandered through the farmyard that had this evening, with augmentation of pine-knot torches, turned into the most lively and fascinating spot on earth.

A quartet of young men stood watching the musical games, jawing tobacco and spitting. It appeared to be some kind of contest where the one coming closest to Maylene Samson's feet without hitting her would win. The difficulty was heightened by the fact that Maylene stepped sprightly through the game's movements on the arm of Ned Patchel. Patchel, who was at least ten years older than Maylene, had caught the attention of the fun-loving young lady, much to the dissatisfaction of the fellows her own age. The giggling girl was oblivious to what was going on. Her escort was not. Rans noticed that hitting Patchel's shoes with an ill-aimed jaw of juice was not counting against a contestant.

Rans considered staying close. Clearly there was a fight brewing, and naturally he wanted to be part of it. But he still had his dinner plate, and hunger took precedence over excitement.

He wandered away from the music and over to the twins, who were seated on the porch next to Miz Patch. They were showing her the chair seat that they'd put together that afternoon.

"We cut all the willow strips and put them in the brine to soak," Nora May said.

"And then Uncle Jeptha, that's the old man that lives here, he wove them."

Miz Patch examined the work critically and nodded with appreciation.

"You girls done a real fine job here," she said. "All the strips are really even in size."

The twins grinned proudly at each other.

"Well howdy-do there Ransom Toby," the woman addressed him.

His mouth was so full that speaking was impossible, so he nodded.

"Having a little bite of supper, are ye?" she asked. "That's good. A growing boy needs good vittles and plenty of them."

"Yes ma'am," Rans finally managed, swallowing.

She was looking at the chair seat once more.

"And this is really fine caning," she said. "Who'd a thought that Jeptha Barnes would ever do such painstaking work? As careful and precise with weaving as he is with his words."

"You know Uncle Jeptha?" Cora Fay asked.

"Well, of course I do," Miz Patch answered. "I know everybody in the Sweetwood."

"We'd never seen him till we come here," Nora May said. "He's a hermit. Rans told us so. And he's right cranky and yells sometimes."

"I guess he's mad 'cause he ain't got no legs," her twin suggested.

Miz Patch nodded silently, as if she had come to the same conclusion.

"He was sure patient when he was showing us how to do this," Cora Fay pointed out.

"And he did help us teach the dog about the wheelhoe," Rans said.

Miz Patch raised her eyebrows in surprise.

"What's this about a dog and a wheel-hoe?"

"We found a harness that was the right size for Old Hound and we hooked it up to the wheel-hoe to help us break ground for the new part of the garden," he said eagerly. "It was my idea."

"It was not!" the twins disagreed in chorus.

A small verbal disagreement ensued which mainly consisted of "Did not!" and "Did too!"

Miz Patch finally held up her hands for silence and gracefully changed the subject.

"So where is Jeptha Barnes?" she asked. "I haven't caught sight of him all evening."

"Oh, he's hiding up in the barn," Nora May answered.

"He doesn't care for folks much," Rans explained.

"And he's not putting on a clean shirt for nobody," Cora Fay added.

Miz Patch laughed at that.

"After only one day with the man, you seem to know him pretty well."

Rans sopped up his plate with the last of the corn-pone.

"Have you seen Mr. Leight?" he asked. "I've been looking all over for him."

The twins shook their heads negatively.

"I saw him talking to Mosco Collier," Miz Patch told him. "But that was more than an hour ago, at least. I got no idea where he might be now."

"Well, I'll just keep looking."

He moved on, weaving in and out of the crowd. He returned to the food table to hand in his plate and saw Moss Collier engaged in a serious conversation with Enoch Pierce.

Mrs. Samson, who preferred being called Miss Garda June, pinched his cheek as if he were some baby. He tolerated it, as he always did. His sisters always said that he was prickly and hard to get along with. They never gave him credit for the forbearance he showed among old ladies who treated him like a boy.

He listened for a few minutes to Yeoman Browning tell a story about Old Man George's big sow going lovesick.

And he watched some boys, most of whom were about his age, shooting marbles in a circle beneath one of the torchlights.

Finally he spotted Mr. Leight sitting with his sister Clara on a bench just outside the kitchen. He hurried up to them eagerly.

"Hullo, Mr. Leight!"

He and Clara startled, as if they had been caught doing something. But clearly they had both just been sitting there on the bench staring into space.

"Oh, hello, Rans," Mr. Leight said.

His voice sounded a little bit vague. Rans wondered momentarily if he were ailing.

"Been looking for you all evening," he told the man. "I cain't get a decent spate of conversation from another soul."

Mr. Leight looked up and smiled at him, rather distractedly.

"I was never too good at conversation myself," he admitted, glancing at Rans for only a moment before turning his attention back to Clara.

"Scoot down just a bit," Rans suggested. "They's room for me to sit, too."

That seemed to wake the man up, and he moved

closer to Clara. Clara moved as well, although that was unnecessary. She was already sitting on the very farthest end of the bench.

When everybody was comfortable again, Rans turned to his friend once more, only to find him wearing that strange sappy look again and staring off into space.

"How's your corn crop?" Rans asked him.

"What? Oh, the corn's fine," he answered. "Finished getting it all in the ground yesterday."

"You're ahead of Moss Collier," Rans told him. "He's still plowing."

"Well, he didn't have all the help I did," Mr. Leight said.

Rans flushed with pride and shrugged. But when he glanced over, Mr. Leight wasn't looking at him, but at Clara.

"When a man knows he's got a cheerful home waiting and a fine meal, well, he just naturally works harder and faster."

Rans was dumbfounded at his words.

And Clara's reaction, to his mind, was nothing short of peculiar. She covered her face with her hands as if she couldn't even bear to be seen by the man beside her. And she giggled. There was absolutely nothing funny about what Bug had said, but Clara giggled.

The two were downright peculiar together. But Rans was more or less used to their behavior and chose to ignore it.

He asked a couple more questions. Mr. Leight answered, though he continued to be vague. When he spoke up, his words were directed to Clara.

"I talked to Moss Collier," he told her. "And he's given me permission to call upon you here, if that would suit you, Miss Clara."

His sister placed a hand against her heart as if attempting to slow its beating.

"That'd suit me fine, Mr. Leight," she answered, her voice so scared and small it could scarcely be heard.

The silence on the bench was monumental. Even Rans was intimidated by it. It lingered for several moments. Finally the man bit his bottom lip and then took a deep breath, as if requiring courage, before he spoke.

"It would give me much pleasure, Miss Clara, to have you address me by my given name."

There was a long moment of hesitation and anticipation.

"All right, Bug," she said finally.

Mr. Leight rubbed his palms together and cleared his throat.

"Bug ain't my given name, Miss Clara, it's Manly," he said. "Folks just call me Bug 'cause I got such big eyes."

Clara looked at him then, her expression nothing less than adoring.

"I like your eyes, . . . Manly," she said.

9

Moss Collier was feeling pretty good. He rarely drank and wasn't keen on socializing. But tonight the warmth of corn liquor was sizzling through his veins, and everybody he talked to seemed to be a friend.

In all honesty, he had been annoyed at the sight of company headed his way. He was still smarting from his forced wedding the day before and didn't think that there was a man in the Sweetwood that he would claim for his friend. But yesterday's humiliation seemed to be wiped away, as far as the east is from the west. Today was filled with joyous celebration, pats on the back, foodstuffs and housekeeping essentials in gratifying abundance.

Everyone still believed the worst of him, that he would take advantage of an untried young woman and then do the honorable thing only with a shotgun between his shoulder blades. Rather than condemning his actions as they had yesterday, now that he was a married man, it was almost as if they admired them.

Clifton Knox was typical of the prevailing attitude of the menfolk as he poked Moss playfully in the ribs.

"You sly devil! I had my eye on that little gal for my cousin Ambrose. She's just as sweet and sunny as a pure angel. And then I hear you two have been out scorching grass. You ought to be ashamed."

The man's tone implied pride rather than shame.

As the evening wore on, the liquor flowed more generously and the accolades continued, Moss began to wish that he *had* seduced her.

And if all of that weren't fine enough, he began to see a way out his burden. Oh, not completely out of it, of course. Eulie Toby would be his lawfully wedded wife till death to part, but if he could outlive Uncle Jeptha, he could see the other ones on their way as sure as the world.

It was the middle of the night before the company, bearing the torches they brought with them, headed down the river path, across the ford near the falls, and back to their own places.

Moss watched until they were out of sight and then headed toward the cabin. The slope seemed a bit more uneven than usual, but he managed to traverse it.

He nearly slipped as he made it to the porch and grabbed the corner support to hold him upright. He must have had more liquor than he'd thought. Moss shook his head, attempting to clear it, but that somehow only made things worse. He sucked in a big gulp of cool spring air. That hit him like a fist, and he heard bells, saw stars, and clutched the support beam more earnestly.

He saw Uncle Jeptha wheeling himself up the porch. He had a path up the far side where the ground slope met the porch floor and he could easily move the little cart from one to the other.

"Did you spend the whole evening in the barn?" Moss asked him.

The old man came rolling toward him.

"I sure did," Uncle Jeptha answered. "Got one chair frame completed and two others that's begun. What'd you do, besides consume a whole lot more corn liquor than a fool's allowed?"

"I about got my whole life straightened out," Moss told him with a big, hearty laugh.

"Humph," the older man said and scooted by him into the cabin.

With the assistance of the support beam, Moss, too, headed toward the doorway.

Inside was completely dark and quiet save for the creaking of the wheels on Uncle Jeptha's cart and the moving and shifting of tired bodies.

Moss stood in the doorway, not knowing exactly what to do. He couldn't just start crawling over people until he found the one he wanted. He should just holler out to her, he decided. But then hesitated to use her name. He hadn't called her that yet, and somehow it just didn't seem right to do. But she was going to be his wife. He'd figured that out now, and he supposed a first-name basis was best for happily-ever-afters.

"Yoo-hoo! My bride," he called out in a whisper. "Eulie, where are you?"

He took a step forward. For some inexplicable reason there was a leg sticking out into the middle of where the walkway should be. In his unsteady condition he tripped over it and landed heavily.

"What in the devil are you up to, Moss?" he heard Uncle Jeptha call out.

"I fell," he answered. "Sorry."

"If you're looking for my sister," the owner of the

foot that caused his fall said, "she's out in the kitchen. Ain't that where you sleep?"

"Oh, well, boy, I suspect it is," Moss answered slowly coming to his knees. "Did you get awful tall of late that your legs stick out all the way to here?"

"Guess so," he answered.

Moss carefully stood up and retreated through the door. So she was waiting for him down in the kitchen. That was nice. That was real nice. So nice in fact he began to whistle. He was feeling a little less woozy now and a lot more pleased with himself.

He'd been thinking about her all day. How could a man do anything else? Row after dirt patch row with nothing to look at but the backside of an old mule, a man's mind wandered. And when a man had spent the previous evening hugging and squeezing on some pretty little gal, it was to be expected that she would cross his mind. He remembered the shape of her, the softness of her skin, the scent of her in his arms. And he'd been downright annoyed with himself. He'd said he was not going to touch her. He'd meant it to punish her. But who was it going to punish? She was probably grateful.

But now all that had changed. It was all going to work out much better than he'd imagined, and he could both lawfully and with good conscience be a husband to her.

By the time he reached the door to the kitchen he was singing.

"She climbed upon her maiden's bed,
And took the pillow from 'neath her head,
She tossed the quilts and the blankets, too,
So I crawled right on to her doodle-di-do."

The kitchen was dark save for the remains of the fire. He spotted her, lying in the same cold corner as the night before.

"Eulie," he called out in a whisper. "Hello there, my bride. Are you awake?"

She sat up in her blankets.

"Yes, yes, I'm awake," she assured him in a sleepy voice that suggested that perhaps she hadn't been.

Eagerly and without any thought to neatness or the value of his good shirt, Moss began to disrobe. He dropped his shoes and left them wherever they fell. He hardly had the patience for the buttons on his shirt. And he dropped his trousers and stepped out of them as if he never intended to look back.

Stripped down to his red flannel union suit, he was ready to simply throw himself upon her and her pile of blankets.

He hesitated, wondering uncharacteristically about cleanliness. He'd washed down before the company arrived. Somehow that didn't feel like exactly enough. Barefoot he walked back out the door into the moonlight. He didn't want to go all the way to the river, so he scooped a dipper full of water from the rain barrel and rinsed his face and hands. That sobered him a little, but not enough to distract him from his present course.

"She is my wife," he reminded himself aloud. "When I go west I'll have somebody to cook for me. And the comfort of a woman whenever I feel the need."

With that cheery thought he was whistling again and reentered the darkened kitchen.

She had lain back down again and rolled over, facing the wall. Moss knelt down and crawled in beside her.

"You want to share some of these blankets with me, my bride?" he whispered.

She relinquished his share without an argument, and Moss eased up close to the back. Without one whit of caution or sensibility he reached out for her. The short josey barely covered her backside. He pushed it away and ran his hand over her bare flesh.

That woke her up.

With a screech of shock, she rolled over and faced him. That was even better.

"Hello there, Eulie," he said. "Why don't you give Moss a little kiss."

He didn't wait for her to reply but pulled her snugly into his arms and brought his mouth down upon hers. She was so soft and so sweet and she was his.

He'd never thought to wed, since he'd planned to leave. But now, with absolute clarity, he saw what a good idea it was. A man got a full-time servant who received no wage or even so much as a day off. And at night she turned into his personal whore. Of course, wives were not whores, he reminded himself, and he'd never expect his to be. Wives never did any of the *special* things that whores did. But in his scant experience with whores, he'd never done any of the special things anyway. The regular suited him just fine. And tonight he wanted to do the regular with his very own bride.

"What are you doing?" she asked him, clearly a little nervous.

"It ain't what I'm doing," he answered. "It's what we're doing. It is something important, something that a man . . . and a woman do without their clothes," he said.

"Oh!" Her reply was part surprise and part fright.

He felt the warmth of blush on her skin as he explored her.

"Are you saying you want me to . . . to obey my husband?"

He grasped her shoulders, momentarily taken aback by the thin frailty of her. He pulled her closer, almost protectively. She was not so skinny as you'd think, he decided. Her bosom was a nice firm handful. And he liked the way that her backside sort of pouched out, sort of inviting attention.

"I'm saying I'm accepting you to be my wife in all ways that a woman is a man's wife."

His words silenced her. He continued.

"So that surely gives us something to do on a warm spring night," he told her.

He wrapped his arms around her and forcefully pulled her closer, enjoying the scent of her and the soft way her hollows fit against him.

"We're married, Mrs. Collier," he said. "Married, for better or worse. I've already seen some to the worse, now I want some of the better."

He began pulling up her josey.

Frantically she grabbed at it.

"I can't," she told him with absolute certainty. "I can't just be naked with you."

He'd bent forward to plant tiny kisses on the side of her neck.

"All right," he whispered against her throat. "We'll leave our clothes on."

Eulie sighed, relieved, and released her grasp on the fabric.

"I'll just raise it up to about here," he said, baring

her breasts and tucking the hem of the josey against her collarbone.

It felt so nice to have her in his arms. It felt as warm and comfortable as a soft cotton blanket fresh from the sunshine. And as daring and thrilling as a swift water crossing from a narrow high-perched log.

He eased his hands against the edge of her breasts, but continued to explore the soft flesh of her throat. Moss had not done a lot of kissing. The women with which he had experience were not ones that a fellow might want to kiss. But his new bride was very much a female to be kissed. That's what he'd first wanted from her. A simple kiss. He'd taken it, and he'd had to marry for it. Since he'd already paid the price, it seemed reasonable and right to enjoy it.

"This is very nice," he told her.

She was trembling in his arms.

"There is no need for you to be afraid," he whispered against her skin. "We're not doing anything that lots of other people don't do all the time."

"All right," she answered, her tone stoic and fearful. But the sensation of his lips upon her neck somehow made it difficult to listen to what he was saying.

He blazed a trail up the length of her jaw to the sensitive flesh of her ear and then to her lips. The taste, all heat and excitement, urged him forward in contrast with the leisurely pleasure he wanted to take in it. He wanted to spend a lifetime exploring her body. And he wanted to be buried inside it in the next minute.

He moved his hands along her, confident and sure. One lingered upon her chest exploring the edge of her bosom, but never grasping it. He didn't want to shock her or have her pull away. Uncertainly he eased his hand upon her. It was almost as if he thought he might sneak up on her bosom and she would not notice. Her nipples were tightly raised, as if she had taken sudden chill. The feel of them, tight and taut against his palm, robbed him of caution.

"Do you like this?" he asked her as he gently squeezed the breast she offered. "Do you like having your bosom squeezed?"

"I like it," she answered him in a tiny voice. "I really like it."

"How about this one?" he asked, bringing up his other hand to grasp her other breast. "Do you like this one squeezed as well?"

"Yes," she assured him a little more confidently. "I like it."

He caught her nipples between his thumb and forefinger. "Do you like this, too?"

Eulie gasped. The sound of it went through him like a bolt of lightning, igniting fire in his veins, and settled rigid in the front of his flannels.

"Oh yes, you like that, don't you," he said. "You do like that."

She murmured something unintelligible.

"If my new bride likes to be squeezed, I'm a husband whose going to remember to squeeze her every day."

He kissed her again.

"Open your mouth, Eulie," he whispered close to her.

"What?"

The single word she uttered gave him the access he required. He tilted his head sideways and opened his lips upon hers.

It was exciting and instructive and much more than he thought that a kiss could be. A rush of weakness sped through him that did not extend to his erection, straining against confinement. He ran his hand along it, stiff at full prow as he undid his buttons.

He rolled over upon her, pressing her back against the hard pallet and stretching out on top of her. A groan of pure pleasure emanated from his throat.

Because he was heavy and she seemed so small, he raised himself slightly to be no burden. This had an unexpected but appreciated benefit of wedging his knee firmly between her thighs. They were flesh to flesh. He could feel the warmth and wetness of her against him.

He raised her leg to his waist and they both shivered. It was as if the heat building inside was intense enough to make the outside chill.

Moss brought his lips down upon hers again and now, more sure of herself, she opened eagerly for him. Reveling in the sweet, familiar taste of her, he tugged insistently upon her mouth until she moaned.

"I want to be inside you," he told her, hoping that she understood. "I want to put myself inside you."

Deliberately he pressed against her, wanting her to feel the length of his erection against her belly. He was pretty sure she was a maiden, and though he didn't know it for certain, he'd heard it said that the first time for a woman was difficult and painful. Moss didn't want it to be either. But how that was to be avoided he had no notion. He was desperate to shag down, tight in her. He couldn't allow her to make him stop.

She was anxious, he could tell. Anxious and more than a little bit scared.

He caressed her to comfort her, assure her. He

slipped one hand in between them and stroked her intimately. She startled, but then steeled herself to his touch.

"You're my wife," he stated to her firmly, hoping that she understood that this was her duty. "You are my wife and we will make a life together."

"Yes, that's what I want," she whispered.

"I'll keep you by my side always," he assured her. "Once Uncle Jeptha is passed and your youngers are gone, we'll head west together."

"What?" Her question was unusually loud in the darkness.

He was in no mood to repeat himself. His hand was wet from her. He shifted, positioning himself to enter.

"What do you mean?"

"Easy, Eulie," he told her, as if attempting to gentle her like a skittish mare.

"Wait! Stop!"

She was balking, trying to push away. He didn't think he'd hurt her yet, but his was poised to enter her and he was sure that he would.

"Wait! Stop!"

She slapped at his caress.

"Don't fight me, Eulie," he told her. "The worst will be all over in just a minute."

She continued to struggle. "How many hands have you got?" she complained.

"Just two, Eulie," he answered. "But I got three legs, and the one in the middle is aching like the gout."

"Please! Stop! I need to ask . . ."

He was on the threshold of her body and couldn't wait another moment. He was in no condition for conversation. He covered her mouth with his own. The kiss was his alone; she was writhing and resistant.

Moss wanted to get it over quickly. That would be best, he was certain. Ignore her fear and get the hurtful part behind them. He began thrusting himself inside. Her body was wet and ready, but she was narrow and untried. And she was fighting in earnest.

Her fingernails dug into the side of his neck. Momentarily he relaxed his grip and she got free of him.

"Eulie, sweetheart," he coaxed as he reached for her again.

She jerked away and tried to crawl off the pallet. He grabbed her around the waist and hauled her back into the corner. To his amazement, she began to kick and scratch.

"Easy, darlin'," he soothed her. "Easy, easy."

When he tried to kiss her again, she angled her head to the side and sunk her teeth into his cheek.

Moss screamed loud enough to wake the heavens.

He got to his feet clumsily. He was cold sober now.

From across the silence of the darkness, the two stared at each other.

"Cheese and Christmas, woman, you bit me!"

"You shouldn't curse," she told him.

"Curse!" he hollered. "I ain't even cursed, but if ever I was of a mind to do so, now would be the time. Lord a'mighty, I'm bleeding."

He heard her scrambling to her feet. She was undoubtedly running away. She'd probably go up to the cabin and sleep with her sisters until his temper wore off.

To his amazement, she poked a twig into the coals of the fire and lit some tallow scraps in the reflector bowl. As light filled the room, they faced each other.

Her long hair was wildly tousled and her eyes were wide and scared. Moss didn't know if she was scared of him or of what she'd done.

"How bad is it?" she asked.

He removed his hand down from his face. She gasped. He looked down at his palm and saw it was full of blood.

"The face always bleeds worse than it is," he told her.

"Let me get some witch hazel to put on it," she said, hurrying to the cupboard.

"That'd be good," he agreed. "You're probably rabid."

She quickly gathered up a pile of rags and a pan of water along with the witch hazel. Moss seated himself and checked the placket of his flannels, modestly rebuttoning himself. His erection had disappeared more quickly than dust in a rainstorm. Fortunately, her attention was completely upon his injury.

When she'd cleaned it thoroughly she brought the reflector bowl to the table to get a better look. She didn't seem pleased with what she saw.

The witch hazel stung like blue blazes. Moss put all his concentration into not wincing.

"It might leave a scar," she said her voice trembling nervously.

Moss snorted with unconcern. "I don't reckon I was so pretty before that a scar now would hurt my chances."

"I'm sorry," she told him. "I just . . . what were you talking about? What about my youngers leaving and Uncle Jeptha passing away?"

She put a fresh sousing of witch hazel on the bite. He grimaced.

"Blow on it," he said.

"What?"

"Blow on it. It burns awful."

Moss Collier sat in his ill-lit kitchen in the middle of the night with his stringy-haired bride puffing cooling breaths against his cheek.

"Is that better?" she asked finally.

"That's fine," he said.

She pressed a clean rag to the bite.

"Hold this tight against it," she told him. "It's the only way to get that bleeding stopped."

Moss did as he was bid.

"I knew you wasn't the type to hit a woman," she said.

"What?"

"If you was ever prone to strike me," she said, "I suspect this might well have been the occasion."

"What are you talking about?"

"Preacher Thompson," she answered. "He worried when I came out here that you might take to beating me."

Moss raised an eyebrow. It hurt. He determinedly kept his face still.

"I ain't never beat nobody, and I ain't about to start now," he said. "Although I would like to turn you over my knee, but I'm afraid you'd chew my foot off."

She glanced up sharply as if she thought him serious, then as she looked into his eyes, a smile curved upon her face and she laughed delightedly. He hadn't heard her laugh before. It was a very nice laugh. It was the kind of laugh a man could live with for a very long time.

"I'm really sorry," she said. "I am willing to . . . to do my wifely duty."

"Well, thank you very much," Moss told her. "I truly ain't in the mood no longer."

"What were you saying about my youngers?" she asked.

He ignored her question, patting gently at the injury on his face.

"I think my face is beginning to swell," he told her.

"I'll see if I can find some chervil and make a poultice," she said, turning toward the storage shelf.

"There ain't much in that old herb box," he admitted.

"I know, I looked through it this afternoon."

As she riffled through the contents of the herb box, he watched her. She was still in that short josey, and with her squatted down that way, he could see her knees and a good deal of her exposed thigh. She was pretty in her own way. He'd known that the day at the falls. He'd just not been able to really think about her that way since the wedding. Now tonight, with a little liquor in him, it had been *all* he could think about.

"Here's some," she said delighted. "There ain't a lot of it, but enough to do."

"It's probably older than Methuselah," Moss told her.

"Might as well try it," she said as she hurried back over to him with it in hand.

He watched her dampen the chervil. It wasn't thick enough to make a paste, but she spread in on a piece of cloth thinly enough for it to stick. She laid it directly upon the bite and then wrapped a long strip to wrap around his head and hold it in place. The bandage covered up one eye and forced Moss to use his other one to watch her. Her touch was very gentle and her movements confident and certain. She was accustomed to taking care of people, he thought. She'd probably been taking care of people all her life.

"What did you mean about us going west and about the children?" she asked him.

"Maybe we should talk about it tomorrow," he said.

"No, I think we should talk about it tonight," she assured him. "What is it all about?"

Moss shrugged as he gingerly fingered his injury.

"Marrying you was not something that I ever intended to do," he stated simply.

She looked genuinely troubled, her cheeks stained with blush.

"You surely know that a man, any man, will have made some plans for his life," he said. "My plans didn't include a wife and half dozen kinfolk."

"Only five," she piped in quietly.

"What?"

"Only five," Eulie repeated. "I haven't got a half dozen youngers, only five."

"Oh, only five!" he exclaimed, his tone rife with sarcasm. "Well, I'm working as hard as I can to get that number down to none."

"What do you mean?"

"I mean that I thought that there was not any way to go west now with all of you depending upon me," he said. "But tonight I got it into my head that I could make things work out. That if I could get this family down to a reasonable size, I could still go west."

"Go west?" Her tone suggested that she had never heard of such a thing.

"I'd always thought to go alone," he explained. "I never imagined myself with a wife. But others have done it, I suspect we can, too."

"Go west?" she repeated again stupidly. "Where west? You mean like Cobbly Creek or Three Rivers?"

He turned to look at her as if she were out of her mind.

"Why would I want to go to Cobbly Creek or Three Rivers?" he asked her. "The life there is no different than here. I want to go to Texas."

"Texas?" Eulie looked thoughtful. "I've heard the name of that place. Is that on the other side of Knoxville?"

Moss laughed, regretting it immediately when the movement pulled painfully against his injury.

"Oh yes, Eulie," he told her. "It's a ways farther than the other side of Knoxville."

"Do you have land there?"

"I don't now, but I'm going to get some," he said.

The excitement he'd always felt, the rush to get out there to see a new place and meet new people, swept through him and he wanted to share it. He wanted her to understand it.

"There is land out there, Eulie," he told her. "Land almost for the asking. Grazing land, low rolling hills as far as the eye can see. It's a land for cattle."

"Cattle?"

He nodded.

"If I go out to Texas," he said, "I can graze cattle."

"Why would you want to do that?" she asked him.

"I'm no farmer," he told her. "I never have been, never will be. I hate scratching in the ground. I'm a herdsman, Eulie."

"But everybody around here is farmers," she said.

He nodded in agreement.

"That's what we do in these hills," she continued. "We farm."

He didn't argue that either.

"That's why I want to get away," he told her. "I want to go where there are people like me."

"But *we* are people like you, the folks in the Sweetwood are all like you. And we're farmers, we've always been farmers."

"That's not true," he told her. "Our granddaddies way back as far as Scotland and Wales, they was all herdsmen, cattlemen. They came here to find land to run cattle."

Eulie looked at him skeptically. "I never heard of such a thing," she said.

"But it's true," he assured her. "Nobody would have picked this land for farming."

"They wouldn't?"

He shook his head.

"The ground is too sloped, there are too many rocks. The dirt is too thin for corn and too loamy for cotton. The trees all around sap up the water and give too much shade." He shook his head and tutted with disapproval. "If a man was looking to farm, he could hardly pick a worse spot than these mountains."

"So our folks, our forefathers, they didn't come here to farm," she said.

"No they didn't," he told her. "When the old Scotsman settled here and built this cabin, he never meant to farm. The ground is so poor you couldn't raise a row with a pitchfork. He meant to run cattle."

"How can you know that?" she asked.

"The licks. You've seen the licks," he told her. "You've seen those old hollowed-out salt logs in the woods."

She nodded. "But those were just for their farm animals," she said. "They had to bring salt for a couple of milk cows, maybe, and a litter of hogs."

"If they had kept just milk cows and hogs, they would have left salt for them near the cabin, like we do. They would not have carried it up into the woods where every deer and bear and raccoon on the mountain would take his share."

She still seemed uncertain.

"If they, us, if the people of the Sweetwood were herders before, why aren't they now?"

"Because the hills were too high and the hollows too deep," he told her. "The land is no good for farming. It's equally no good for herding."

"Are you saying the Sweetwood is no good?"

"It's plenty good for hunting and fishing," he admitted. "But if a man wants farming or herding, he'd do better to look elsewhere."

"But we get by," she said. "Year after year we put in a crop. Some make it, some don't, but folks get by."

"I want more than getting by," he said. "I want . . . I want more to show for my labor than what I track in on my shoes. I want more than I even know, Eulie. And I'm just figuring how to get it."

"How's that?"

"By leaving all this behind and starting again in Texas," he said. "I've been saving every nickel I can put by, selling everything I can."

"You're really leaving here?"

He nodded with certainty. "It's been my dream," he

told her. "It's been my lifelong dream. I've been thinking about it since I was a boy. All I've ever wanted was to put this place behind me and never look back."

Eulie's expression was complete astonishment.

"I've only been waiting for Uncle Jeptha's passing," he admitted. "I can't walk out on my responsibility to him. He's held me here a lot of years now. And yesterday I was thinking that you and your youngers were going to hold me here even more. But tonight I realized that a wife wouldn't be such a bad thing to take along. A man should bring things with him that are in short supply–a good horse, a reliable handgun–well, women are in pretty short supply out there as well. I'll just take you with me and we'll settle there together."

Eulie stared at him in thoughtful silence.

"Texas?" she spoke the word finally, almost in disbelief. "I don't want to go to Texas. I don't want to go anywhere without my family."

Moss felt as if she had slugged him in the gut. The pain of the bite on his face was nothing to what he felt at the loss of his dream.

"Don't set your heart against it right away," he pleaded. "Give yourself some time to think about it. We cain't leave any time soon anyway. I've got to see Uncle Jeptha through and your brother and sisters have got to get out and make their way in the world. It's not as if I'm asking you to leave tomorrow."

"No," she told him. "I couldn't leave tomorrow." She considered the idea thoughtfully. "I couldn't leave my family, not never."

She looked over at him. He saw the truth in her eyes.

"But you could leave," she said, her expression

lightening as she became infused with enthusiasm. "You could leave tomorrow."

"What?"

"It's a perfect idea, perfect," she said. "We're your family now, so you won't have to stay here."

"What are you talking about?" Moss asked, totally confused.

Eulie dragged up the other chair and seated herself excitedly.

"You've been waiting here, unable to leave because you have responsibilities," she said. "You are the only kin Jeptha Barnes has in the world."

"That's right."

"But you are not anymore."

"Not anymore what?"

"Not his only family anymore," she said. "We're your family, so he's our kin."

"What are you saying?"

"I was honest with you about why I . . . why I forced you into this marriage," she said. "I needed a place for me and my youngers to be together and I thought that I could work hard to make you happy. And now see how well things have worked out?"

Moss didn't see at all and said so.

Eulie explained. "Us Tobys, we can tend your place, your oh-so-pretty place here by the river. And we can take care of your uncle, provide for him just as you would, while you go west."

Moss looked at her, stunned, not quite believing what he was hearing.

"Everybody gets what they want," she said. "And we'll all live happily ever after."

10

Eulie made her family eat a cold breakfast. She brought the leftover ham and greens from the party. The pone was so hard it crumbled like crackers, but they used it to sop up what they could.

"Nine eggs," Nora May said with a sigh, referring to the morning's gathering.

"And we don't get to eat a one of them," Cora Fay chimed in.

"Those eggs will be just as good for midday or supper and you'll enjoy them just as well."

"I don't see why we cain't go to the kitchen," Rans complained. "Just 'cause your husband's crapulous we got to eat cold vittles."

"Mr. Collier is not crapulous," Eulie said firmly. "He . . . suffered an injury last night."

Rans looked up, stunned and defensive. "I didn't know where he was walking. I had nothing to do with it."

Eulie was puzzled. "What are you talking about?"

He didn't answer.

"What's crapulous?" Little Minnie asked her. Her sausage curls of the night before were still bouncing on the right side of her head. On the left, however, they were completely flat, giving her a strangely off-balance appearance.

Rans answered for her. "Crapulous means he got drunk last night and he's sick this morning."

"That's enough," Uncle Jeptha said firmly. "Your sister is too young to need to know everything you do."

Eulie was surprised that the older man's admonition had the effect it did. Typically anytime Rans was ordered to do something, he commenced immediately to do the opposite. This morning he accepted the set-down with respectful silence.

"Well," Little Minnie said, "if he's sick abed, at least he don't got to eat no cold greens and cornpone."

Eulie expected further protest from her sister. To her surprise the child began to giggle to herself.

"I got a secret. I got a secret," she began in a singsong taunt. "I got a secret. Nobody here knows but me."

"What kind of secret?" Cora Fay asked.

"I cain't tell you," Little Minnie said. "I cain't say nothing at all. Nothing at all, yet."

"You cain't say nothing *yet*?" Nora May asked with heightened curiosity. "What does that mean? That you will say something soon?"

Little Minnie gave her a tight-lipped grin designed to be especially annoying.

"It means I know and you have to wait to find out."

"So when are we gonna find out?" Cora Fay demanded.

Little Minnie ignored the question. "What's my name? Puddin' Tane. Ask me again and I'll tell ye the same."

"You could give us a hint," Cora Fay told her.

Little Minnie thought about that for a minute.

"All right," she said. "The hint is: I won't ever eat cold ham and greens again."

"What kind of hint is that?" Nora May asked complainingly.

"The kind that you'll never guess," her younger sister replied and stuck out her tongue.

"None of that, Minnie June Toby, or I'll be cutting a switch!" Eulie threatened.

"Better not," the child replied. "They's some folks that really wouldn't like that."

Clara touched Eulie's arm and gave a little shake of her head as if to say, *Just ignore her.*

Eulie decided to do just that. She couldn't imagine a brighter, happier day. She'd always heard that a woman's wedding day was the best. For herself, she decided the best was the day she lost a husband and gained a farm.

"Twins, I need you to visit Miz Patch today," she said.

The two girls exchanged a delighted glance.

"We get to see her again today!" Nora May said.

"And we only saw her last night!" her sister chimed in.

"I need you to borrow some chervil," Eulie told them. "I used the last of it. And tell her that the herb box is nearly empty, so I'll take anything she's got abundant to part with."

The twins were clearly pleased and excited, almost too much so to finish their breakfast.

"Maybe you should go with them, Uncle Jeptha," Eulie said. "It would do you good to get away from the cabin. You could get to know the twins a little better."

The man looked at her dumbfounded.

"I never go places," he said.

"Well, that was before. That harness we used to get Old Hound to draw the plow would work just as well with the twins to pull you," Eulie said.

"Of course we can," Nora May assured him. "And the weather's fine and the wildflowers in bloom."

"No," the man said, simply.

"You should get out, see people," Cora Fay said. "Don't you like to go a-visiting?"

"No, I sure don't," Jeptha said with certainty. "There ain't a soul in the world that I want to see."

"That's why you should start with Miz Patch," Nora May told him. "She's real easy to talk to. Folks say she don't never meet a stranger."

"And she ain't even a stranger to you," Cora Fay pointed out. "Miz Patch said last night that she knows you."

"She did, did she?" Jeptha shrugged. "She ain't so much as laid eyes on me in more that twenty years. I don't expect she knows me too well."

"She admired your weaving," Nora May said.

"That's right," her sister agreed. "She said she couldn't believe that Jeptha Barnes could do such painstaking work."

Clearly that statement didn't set well with the man at all. His eyes narrowed angrily. For a moment Eulie feared he would snap at the twins. But his fury was directed elsewhere.

"Then that proves how long it's been since she's seen me," he said. "And if she is thinking me lazy or slothful, then she never did know me at all."

"Oh, I think she was just surprised, Uncle Jeptha,"

Cora Fay said. "It's really fine and tight. I don't suspect she could do no better herself."

"Won't you come with us?" Nora May begged. "We are very strong and we can be real careful with your cart."

"No, girls," Jeptha said. "But I thank ye for the invite. Today I'm going to wheel myself on down by the river and catch me a big old trout."

He turned to Rans. "What about you, boy? It's too wet to hoe that garden today. Want to help me catch us some supper that your sister cain't feed to us cold?"

Eulie watched her brother's face. His expression went from half-sour to nearly ecstatic. It was such a small thing, a polite gesture from one man to another, but it meant so much to him. Eulie didn't really understand her brother. His need for respect and his craving for other people's high opinion was the kind of thing that she'd never wanted for herself. But then, all she'd ever needed was a home of her own and all her family around her.

The men went off together, Uncle Jeptha on the worn-flat pathway propelling the wheeled cart forward with the two wooden oars against the ground, Rans near him at the side of the path. They headed to the storage shed where, Uncle Jeptha assured him, fishing poles hung in the rafters.

The twins finished up their meals hastily and hurried to wash hands and faces and put on their bonnets.

"Do you want us to take Little Minnie with us?" Cora Fay asked.

"I'm not going," their sister stated flatly. "That old woman is always trying to put me to work. I don't have to work. I'm a princess."

Eulie exchanged an exasperated look with Clara, who rolled her eyes.

"You twins go on by yourself," she told them. "I'm sure you'll have more fun without your sister along."

The last she added with a pointed glance toward Little Minnie. But the child was beyond caring what any of her sisters thought. She'd already retrieved the doll that Mrs. Pierce had given her and she was devoting all her attention in that direction.

That was all right with Eulie as long as the child kept herself occupied and out of trouble. She and Clara gathered up all the dishes and piled them into the dishpan. Eulie didn't want to take them into the kitchen for fear that she would awaken the husband-man.

She was so excited about their new life. But still she felt terrible about biting him that way. It all just happened so quickly and she was only half-awake when he'd asked her to obey her husband. He'd told her that he wasn't going to do any of that. Eulie shook her head. Miz Patch must have been right: Menfolk do find a way to forgive.

It hadn't been so dreadful, really. It had hurt some when he'd tried to put his big thing inside her, but not so bad that she would have stopped him if it hadn't been for his words about the youngers.

In a way, though, she regretted stopping him. He was her husband, till death to part. It was kind of sad to think that he'd be leaving for Texas in a day or two and she'd never get to find out for sure what obeying her husband was truly like. Perhaps it was better. What you never have, you never miss, she reminded herself. Already she thought she might miss that kissing and the feel of his hands on her.

She sighed.

"What are you thinking about that has you sounding so melancholy?" Clara asked her.

"Oh, I'm not dreary at all," Eulie answered quickly. "I've never been happier in my life. Really. I've never been happier."

Clara seemed unconvinced, but Eulie didn't even try to persuade her. Her own thoughts kept her occupied.

He had been so sweet about the bite. She didn't know herself if she would have been that kind about it. Preacher Thompson had worried that he might be one of those beating men. If ever such a temperament were tested, it was last night. And except for a few words of near-cursing, he'd been a saint. Just exactly the kind of man that she would have liked to marry if she'd been in a position to marry whomever she liked. But then, she did like him. And they were married. He was leaving. So they'd both be happy. Her thoughts were a little confused.

She shook her head and glanced over at her sister. Clara appeared to be as deeply lost in thought as Eulie had been herself.

"We sure cain't sit here ruminating the morning away," she said.

Clara looked up and blushed, almost embarrassed at getting caught with her mind so far away.

"Let's get started," she agreed.

Working side by side, the two commenced the weekly wash. They laid a fire in the outside pit on the narrow bar of rocky limestone that extended out into edge of the river and began the task of filling the big black cauldron with water. Eulie, the end of her skirts tucked into her apron sash to keep them dry, dipped the wooden bucket and then handed it up to her sister, who poured it in and handed it back. It took better than thirty buckets to fill the wash pot.

Lifting the buckets up out of the river caused considerable strain on Eulie's arms and back. Clara offered to trade places with her when the cauldron was half-full, but she declined.

"I don't mind, truly," Eulie said. "The joy of working with my sister instead of some stranger makes any work seem light."

Clara rolled her eyes skeptically at that remark. But there was no arguing that it was fun for both of them to be together again.

Clara was more shy than her sister. Eulie's forceful personality and sunny disposition had always made her stand out. Clara was the quiet, pretty one, folks said. Most remained unaware of her very dry sense of wit. She rarely told anything that could be considered a funny story. But she knew exactly how to add the right word or the right phrase to an ordinary situation to have those closest to her doubled over in hilarity.

There was a lot of laughter between them this morning.

As the required water heated over the flame, they began to gather up the wash. The day looked sunny and fair, so they decided that anything would have time to dry. And because they had no idea of when the last thorough washing had occurred on the Collier farm, and the evidence suggested it wasn't recently, they determined to wash every stitch of clothing, linen, and bedding they could lay their hands on. With her husband leaving for the West in the next few days, it was paramount that everything be cleaned and ready for him to go.

The women divided the tasks required. Each item was boiled with lye soap for several minutes in the hot cauldron. Clara rapidly punched the clothes with a wooden paddle. Anything with spots, stains, or dirt that resisted this treatment was lifted over to Eulie's washtub, where it was scrubbed on the rub board. Eulie worked methodically. She laid the dirty item on the board, lathered a spot with soap, and gave it a half dozen rapid passes up and down the board before she turned it and lathered up a different place.

After washing, the clothes had to be thoroughly rinsed of soap residue, which tended to irritate the skin and wore out the fabric before its time. The swishing was the easiest part, except for the necessity of standing in the water and the danger of having clothing get away and float out into the river.

The two women wrung out the clothes together, each taking the end of a garment and twisting it in the direction opposite the other. There was no clothesline on the Collier farm, so the women hung what they could on the bushes around the bank and carried the rest of the heavy wet wash up the slope to dry on the garden fence.

The lengths of damp clothes drying in the morning sun grew longer and longer. Eulie smiled with some self-satisfaction. It was important for a woman to keep her family clean. The husband-man had even expressed concern about that yesterday. He would be so very proud of her and Clara this morning. He would be so impressed by how much they'd managed to get done.

"I saw some blackberry in bloom over near the stand of hemlock," Clara told her.

Eulie was delighted. The bushes, eye-catching in bloom, were notoriously hard to spot at berry-picking time, when they became a tangle of overgrowth and vines protectively concealing their fruit.

"We'll go by and mark it," Eulie suggested. "Then we'll know exactly where to head in summer, with our pails in hand and our mouths watering."

Clara giggled at her.

"With all the apple trees and cherry and plums around here," Eulie pointed out, "we are going to live very sweet. There will always be something to savor."

Her sister nodded in agreement and gave her a big hug. "It'll be a lot different than our place on Timber Top," Clara said, referring to their very worst share-crop residence several years earlier.

Eulie laughed and shook her head, recalling the abysmal condition. "I'll never forget Timber Top," she said. "I still can't imagine what Daddy was thinking, taking us to live there. I couldn't decide if we were going to freeze to death or starve first."

Clara tutted at her. "You were always saying how it was not so bad and that we just complained too much," her sister reminded her. "Every single day we lived there you talked about how pretty the view was."

Eulie shrugged. "It was the only nice thing to be said for the place. And if you cain't say something nice . . ."

"Well, now there is something nice to say," Clara told her. "It's nice that none of us have to live there."

Eulie heartily agreed with that. The two women worked side by side, both smiling, lost in thought for several minutes.

"I think we should put up a grape arbor down at the far end of the garden," Eulie told her sister. "There ain't no better eating, and it's such a cool place to sit of an evening."

"It's kind of late to get it started this year," Clara pointed out.

Eulie shook her head. "I wasn't thinking of this year," she agreed. "This year we'll be lucky to get the house in shape and enough food to hold us for the winter. But next year . . ." She let the thought drift off for a couple of moments. "Next year I'll be planting posies around the porch on the first warm day and a grape arbor at the end of the garden and maybe a swing for the youngers, hanging from that old tree over there."

Clara smiled at her. "It sounds nice, Eulie. It sounds real nice."

It did sound nice. It sounded more than nice. It sounded like the life she had always dreamed about. Now, at last it was not only possible, it was happening. And the reality of it was sweeter than she had imagined.

"It's a really pretty place, isn't it?" Eulie said to her sister.

Clara followed the direction of her gaze down the slope, taking in the broad expanse of sun reflecting on the river and the abundance of wood and fields in the distance.

"Yes, it is a lovely place," Clara told her. "But no more than you deserve. I am so happy for you."

Eulie looked at her sister curiously and wrinkled her brow. "What *I* deserve. You're happy for *me*. Sister, this is *our* home. A home for our whole family, together again."

Clara nodded. "And it is wonderful," she assured

Eulie. "But I'll be getting married myself and having my own home."

"Oh, that." Eulie waved the concern away. "We've got years before that happens. It's not near time for you to marry."

Clara looked at her sister intently. "Eulie, maybe I want to marry," she said quietly. "Maybe I think I'm ready."

Eulie could hardly argue that.

"Well, when it happens it will happen," she told Clara instead. "You can never know when the right man will come around."

Clara held her silence for a very long moment.

"Eulie, your husband gave his permission for Mr. Leight to call upon me," she said.

"What?"

"Last night," Clara told her, "Mr. Leight asked if he could formally pay call, and Mr. Collier said yes."

Eulie was nearly fuming with frustration.

"Well, I will set that straight this morning," she said. "I don't care for Bug, it's true. But I see no reason to torture him. You two can never be together, it ain't fair for him to come courting thinking that it can be so."

"What do you mean we can never be together?" Clara asked.

"It was one thing for him to set his sights on you when you were an orphan with your family scattered and no place to call your own," Eulie said. "But now we've got a home. You won't have to marry some man just to have a roof over your head. You can wait for someone to be happy with."

"I think I would be happy with Mr. Leight," Clara declared with conviction.

"Happy with Bug?" Eulie shook her head in disbelief. "Clara, he's so ugly."

"That don't matter a bit to me," Clara told her with matter-of-fact certainty. "I guess I'm pretty enough that our younguns won't frighten the hogs."

"It's not just that," Eulie went on. "The man is so awkward he couldn't lead geese to water with a double rein."

"It's just 'cause he's shy," Clara insisted. "A shy man will get to fidgeting. But once we're married, he'll get used to being around me."

"But Clara, there is just no reason for you to get married."

"I love him, Eulie. And I think he loves me," she said. "I suspect that is reason enough."

Eulie was completely taken aback by her words.

"You haven't said those things to each other?" she asked, horrified.

"No, we haven't said them," Clara admitted. "But they are true just the same."

"Oh, Clara," Eulie almost moaned in disappointment.

"I know you don't like Mr. Leight," she said. "I know that he has never suited you. But he suits me, Eulie. He suits me just fine. And I am the one who would be married to him."

"There is no need to rush things," Eulie told her. "You're still far too young to wed."

"I'm only a year younger than you, and you're married," she pointed out.

"Yes, but I . . ." Eulie had no idea what to say.

"If the courting goes well," Clara told her, "I expect him to propose this summer. We could be married after harvest. And next spring, I'll be putting up grape arbors and planting posies at my own home."

Moss Collier awakened to the sound of women laughing. It was a sound with which he was not very familiar. It was so pleasant, so pleasurable, with his eyes not yet opened for the day, his mouth began to draw into a grin.

The movement rekindled the soreness of his bitten cheek. He moaned painfully and sat up. That was a mistake. The exhausted, whiskey-soaked blood in his head rushed downward, leaving him momentarily faint. He recovered quickly but remained chilled and clammy and nauseated. His head began to pound incessantly. Drinking had never agreed with him.

He fingered the bandage that covered his cheek. It was pretty dry, probably no longer providing any medicinal benefit, and he hated having one eye covered. Gingerly, he removed it. His shaving mirror was up at the cabin, so he had no idea about how he looked.

He did, however, know how he felt. His face seemed bruised and swollen. His bones creaked and his muscles ached. Sleeping on a cold dirt floor wasn't good for a fellow, but this morning he couldn't even complain. He was on his way. At long last he was bound for Texas. It had happened so quickly he could hardly believe it.

"I'll make her a bed," he vowed aloud. "Before I leave, I'll get the shingles on that shed roof, move the grain from the cabin, and make my little bride a nice, comfortable bed all her own.

It didn't seem like too much to give to the person

who had finally given him his freedom. She should have her own bed to sleep in. Especially if she was going to have to sleep in it alone.

He hadn't tried to couple with her again. Getting his cheek bit off had sure taken the urgency off his lust. And it would have been unreasonably cruel to take his pleasure with her, maybe get her with a child, when he was leaving. Of course, it was unfortunate, really, that she would never have children. She would be good with children. She certainly was with her youngers. But she was married to him. So naturally she could never take any other man to her bed. And he would be gone. She'd just live her life chaste.

His brow furrowed as he wondered if this meant that he could never have a woman again. Truthfully, he'd never really thought about having one or needing one. But somehow the thought that it would just be him and his good right arm for the rest of his days didn't offer a lot of comfort.

If he were unfaithful, of course, she would never know. Moss had never really thought about faithfulness or marriage or any of those things. He supposed that he'd simply assumed that marriage was such a fine thing that those suited to try it would always show some respect.

He let that thought swish around in his brain for several minutes to see how it felt. He still wasn't sure. If he had *wanted* to marry her, then they would never be separated. If she wouldn't go with him, then he simply would have stayed here. He'd never intended to wed. But he had. And a marriage was a marriage, no matter how it came about.

Yes, he decided, he would have to be true to his vows.

That was just part of the price that he was required to pay.

And his reputation here in the Sweetwood, he'd have to pay with that as well. His lifelong neighbors had believed the worst of him when Eulie had accused him of something he didn't do. How much worse would they think of him when he actually did run off and leave his whole family to fend for themselves?

"I'm praying for you," Preacher Thompson had assured him last night.

Moss didn't know exactly how he felt about that. Considering the lies and bitterness the match began with, and the extraordinary way they had decided to resolve their problems, he almost hated to draw heaven's attention in their direction.

It seemed as if it was all going to work out much better than he'd thought. His unexpected discussions with Bug Leight and Enoch Pierce has positively buoyed his hopes. But never had he considered leaving while Uncle Jeptha lived. And he always felt badly about waiting for the man to die. Now he could leave the poor legless cripple with his wife and head west. He could head west right away.

This morning, in the clear light of day, he wasn't sure how feasible that plan actually would be. But still the burden he'd felt yesterday was considerably lightened. Eulie Toby had trapped him into marriage and then set him free—more free than he had ever been in his life.

Slowly he rose to his feet. The laughter outside had ended and some sort of serious discussion between the women had begun. He looked around for his trousers. They were missing; only the galluses hung on a peg by the door.

He glanced out the doorway but couldn't see a soul. The yard was deserted, but he could hear the female voices still deep in discussion. Moss edged his way to the corner of the building and peeked around. Sure enough, the two young women were down by the river at the firepit, busily engaged in the task of washday.

Moss grimaced unpleasantly. His trousers were either boiling in that pot or hanging somewhere sopping wet. What the devil was he supposed to put on? He was grateful that he'd been wearing his union suit. The woman might well have left him stranded bare naked.

Uneasily he checked the lower buttons on the placard front of his flannels, assuring himself that the horse was securely in the barn. It was certainly disconcerting to have only a thin piece of well-worn cotton between a man and his modesty. He'd probably shocked the life out of the woman last night. He didn't want to repeat the offense today.

Moss tried to reason what was best to do. He could simply go lie back down on the pallet and wait. Surely she would come eventually to check on him and he could send her to the cabin for his spare trousers. Of course, busy with laundering, it might be hours before she headed this way.

He could call out to her. That would be extremely logical. But he hated to call attention to himself in his current condition. It made him feel so helpless.

He could just brazen it out and walk across the yard like he owned it. It sure wouldn't have been the first time he'd been outside in his underclothes. But somehow he just couldn't do that in front of these two young women. It would be sort of disrespectful, he thought. As if they were not good enough to be treated in a gentlemanly manner. And they were young women deserving of respect. Clara was a quiet, sweet young thing who would make a fine wife for some fellow. And his little bride was a little flighty and too cheerful by half, but she worked hard, took care of her own, and was certainly intent on doing right by him.

He stared across the distance of the yard and imagined himself running across it like the fires of hell were after him. The fires of hell might well be after him, but he would sure look the fool taking off across there.

Frustrated, he began to look for another route. If he headed down the slope toward the river, he could scoot into the tall marshy grass that grew at its edge; then he could follow that into the trees, going up through the woods to behind the barn and then back down the slope to the cabin without ever getting within sight of the firepit. He assessed the route again and glanced at the women washing once more. It would work, he decided. He would get his spare trousers and no one the wiser.

Moss stepped back into the kitchen to get his shoes, grateful that they could not be boiled in the iron pot. He glanced thoughtfully at the bedclothes and momentarily toyed with the idea of wrapping a blanket around himself. But he decided against it. The blanket would be hard to move with in the tall grass.

He went back to the kitchen doorway, edged to the west corner, and peeked around again, making certain the women were still in their place. Sure enough, they continued laundering. Moss's opportunity for escape was at hand.

He walked quietly and close against the wall to the

east corner of the building and hesitated for a long moment. The sprint between the kitchen and the tall grass was probably a distance of twenty yards or better. He would at no time be visible to the women at the firepit, but he would be exposed. With a deep breath and a fateful determination, he took off. Loping down the slippery slope, one foot in front of the other, he was hidden in the tall grass in no time at all.

His heart pounding, his breathing rapid, he squatted down and surveyed his surroundings. There was absolutely no indication that anyone had seen or heard him. He had made it to the secure and modest shelter of cane and cattails. Proud of this accomplishment, he took heart as he pulled the legs of his union suit to above his knees and began to tramp through the swampy wetland toward the woods.

The tall grasses grew in this marshy area next to the river because of the consistent presence of standing water. Walking through was neither pleasant nor easy. Each footstep was taken into at least a couple of inches of brackish water. And a man's footing in mud was never certain. Moss picked his pathway carefully. Just looking at the ground you couldn't tell where it was wetter or drier. He stayed, as best he could, within the stalks of cane and sedge. They tended to grow in less water than reeds or cattail where the depth of the water might be a foot deep. The water lilies, which also grew there in abundance, might be disguising an imperceptible flow of water that was knee-high. The last thing he needed was to get his flannels wet to the waist.

It was also important to keep an eye out for water moccasins. The stout, flatheaded snake was an adept swimmer. It was in the marshes to eat fish and frogs, but the threat of a large human tramping through its territory would definitely lead it to make a venomous bite.

Moss felt a sense of self-congratulation as he approached the rise where the lake met the woods and the marsh ended. This was the worst of his alternative route to the cabin. Once into the woods, he could pick up the pace and be inside and dry and wearing trousers in just a couple more minutes.

He actually had a smile on his face as he stepped out of the thick growth and directly in front of his uncle and brother-in-law.

The two were seated on the point of the bluff woods rise, their cane poles hanging lazily out over the water. Uncle Jeptha was in his cart, his oars set into the ground in front of the wheels to keep him firmly in place on the slope. The boy was right at his side, eyeing Moss with amazed curiosity.

"What happened to you?" Rans asked.

Moss hadn't planned an explanation. It was embarrassing to be caught wearing only his red flannel union suit. It was infinitely more humiliating to admit that he'd been tramping through a wet, snake-infested marsh so his wife wouldn't see him in his underwear. He glanced back the way he'd come, hoping that a feasible falsehood would occur to him.

"I was . . . I was looking at the cattails," he lied with enthusiasm. "We got a lot of people to feed here now. Until we've got something coming up in that garden, we're going to have to find food where we can. Those young shoots, they taste almost like corn and can surely offer a bit of variety from a steady diet of poke salat."

Moss looked up at them hopefully, willing them not to ask him why he hadn't actually picked any cattails while he was there.

"No, I meant your face," the boy said. "What happened to your face?"

Moss drew his hand to the bite on his cheek. It was still sore as the dickens, but he hadn't seen it yet. He had no idea if it was an annoying scratch or a scar for life. Either way, he didn't want the details known.

"Oh, this," he said, attempting to shrug it off casually. "I fell last night."

Jeptha's eyes widened in surprise. The boy visibly paled.

"You did that when you fell last night?" his uncle asked in disbelief.

Moss remembered then that he *had* fallen in the cabin while he was in a tipsy pursuit of his new bride.

"Yes," he answered. "Last night in the cabin. I hit my head on the footboard when I fell."

"Well, Lord a'mighty, Moss, why didn't you say something?" Jeptha scolded. "I thought you might have skinned a shin or bruised a knee, but I never imagined that you were hurt so bad."

"Well . . . ah . . . I was a little worse for liquor last night. And . . . well . . . you know how it is when you get a belly full of corn squeezings. You can dang near break a leg and not feel a thing."

Uncle Jeptha was amazed. The boy was strangely silent.

"Guess I'd best get up to the cabin," Moss said, easing up the rise and into the woods as if he were simply on a leisurely morning stroll.

The two continued to watch him, so he didn't turn

but continued to wave as he backed away from them.

"Good fishing!" he called out to them.

They nodded lamely, still obviously curious.

"Hope you catch us a mess of trout for supper."

As soon as he reached the seclusion of the woods, he began trotting away at a rapid pace and cursing his bad luck under his breath. He felt like a fool and he was pretty sure that he looked like one, running through the woods in his work shoes and red flannels.

When he came to the back of the barn, he crawled over the rail and kept close to the stalls. Red Tex was excited to see him, snorting and stomping. Even the old jenny was curious about his surreptitious behavior.

He spotted Little Minnie playing under the plum near the edge of the clearing. She was faced away from the path he needed to take. But there was surely no guarantee that she wouldn't turn glance around and catch sight of him any minute.

Moss went into the tack room and got Red Tex's saddle blanket. Caution to the wind now, humiliation a surety, he was getting into the cabin to get his spare trousers, no matter what.

The blanket, a brown and tan weave, was stiff and permanently bent into the shape of a horse's back. There was no way that Moss could effectively wrap it around him. He simply held it up, between his chest and thighs on the side that Little Minnie would view if she turned around.

He stepped out in the open yard, but kept his movements quiet and smooth, almost tiptoeing down the path. He watched the back of the child's head, expecting any minute for her to turn around, catch sight of him, and start screaming.

Success was at hand when he set foot on the porch. Unfortunately he still had his eyes on Little Minnie and he tripped over a dishpan of dirty dishes that had been left, for some unknown reason, sitting next to the front door.

As the dishpan tipped over and the noisy tin plates went flying in every direction, Moss dived into the doorway. He was going to get his trousers on, no matter what. He scrambled to his feet and raced to the peg. It was empty. Horrified, he turned to the other pegs, the shelf, the beds. There was not a stitch of clothing, blanket, or linen in the whole cabin.

11

It is one of the hard truths of life, Eulie realized, that a person can do something for a very good and worthy purpose that unwittingly causes an unacceptable inconvenience for someone else.

The sweet-tempered husband-man, who didn't so much as spew a foul name at her for nearly biting his cheek off, was in a terrible fury to discover that she had inadvertently left him with nothing to wear but his union suit.

It was simply an unfortunate mistake. She was to blame. And she admitted that immediately. But somehow that didn't cool his anger. Moss Collier ranted like a mad man. He paced back and forth in the cabin like a caged animal wearing his red flannel union suit, a horse blanket wrapped precariously about his loins.

"So what were you expecting me to do?" he asked her. "Didn't you think that I'd have work to do today?"

"I didn't think at all," she admitted.

"That's common for you, it seems," he pointed out unkindly.

Eulie held her peace, declining to respond to that.

"It's too wet to plow anyway," she pointed out. "Yesterday's rain needs to soak in some."

"But there is plenty of other work to be done," he told her. "There are shingles that need to be cut for that shed roof, repairs to be completed, and a thousand other chores that need doing before I go."

"That's what I was thinking about," she said. "I was thinking about you leaving."

"You were thinking about that?"

She nodded affirmatively "You can't very well leave Tennessee without clean clothes," she said.

"Clean clothes?" he scoffed at her. "I'd venture to say there is not a man in West Texas today wearing clean clothes."

There was no arguing, so Eulie didn't try.

"Maybe you should just take to your bed today and have a nice rest," she suggested. "That's what my daddy used to do. Some days he'd just take to his bed, he said he needed to garner his strength."

"Your daddy was the laziest man that ever lived in the Sweetwood," the husband-man pointed out. "I don't think anyone should use him as the example."

Eulie didn't take offense at his words. They were more than likely true. And after what she had done to him last night, evidenced by the ugly purple bruise on his cheek, she refused to be offended.

As for leaving him near-naked and hollering like a fool, she couldn't even manage to be very sorry. What she felt mostly was amused. It was all she could do to keep from giggling out loud. Here her big proud husband-man, puffing, furious as a wet hen, paced back and forth across the cabin floor wearing red flannel underwear and a horse blanket.

He stopped suddenly and turned to look at her. She bit down on her lip, but it wasn't enough.

"You're laughing at me!" he accused.

"No, oh no," she assured him as one tiny snicker escaped from her throat.

"You are! You are laughing at me."

She did then, full force.

"I can't believe that you are laughing at me!" he exclaimed. "After all you've done to me, all you've put me through, you stand there laughing at me."

Eulie did try to stop, but his tone, a mixture of indignation and incredulity, his puffed-up posturing, considering his current predicament, just struck her as hilarious.

"You just looked so funny," she spurted out in her own defense.

He glared at her, hands on hips, still maintaining his modesty with the horse blanket. She managed to stop for a second, only to burst out once more.

She watched as his expression softened and a wry grin began to curl at the corner of his mouth. Finally, he shrugged, glanced up toward heaven, and then came at her like a wild man.

"If you're going to laugh, I'll give you something to laugh about," he declared in feigned fury.

He grabbed her around the waist, lifted her into the air and began tickling her.

"No! No!" she shrieked.

Her words had no effect upon him. His fingers moved with the skittering movements of a pail full of fishing worms across her rib cage. She screamed, slapped at his hands, pushed him away, but mostly she laughed. She simply laughed. She laughed. She giggled. She shrieked.

And he did, too.

They fell sideways together on the girls' bed. Her feet free now, she attempted to kick at him as well. With little effort he wrapped his legs around her own, effectively trapping her against him.

She wiggled and squirmed to try to get away, but only managed to roll him atop her. Tickling. Tickling. Tickling. She thrashed wildly beneath him, howling with humor.

"I'll teach you to laugh at me!" he vowed, feigning threat.

"Stop! Stop!" she pleaded.

He was laughing himself as he rolled atop her. Joviality dissipated rapidly when she felt that big male thing of his—that part of him that he'd tried to put inside her last night—when she felt it hard against her thigh.

Shocked, she suddenly gasped and stared up into his handsome dark eyes. He gazed back, as if stunned by his own unexpected reaction. He released her immediately.

Abruptly he sat up. Eulie did, too.

He grabbed the horse blanket, which he had carelessly discarded during their roughhousing, and used it to cover his lap.

Nervously, he cleared his throat.

Eulie felt her face flaming. They had been playing, just like children. They obviously were not children.

"Sorry," he said finally, not even daring to glance her way.

"You didn't do nothing," she said.

"And I'd better not," he told her. "We'd better not. I don't want to get you with a baby and then leave you here. They'll be enough bad talk for you to live down without that."

She nodded.

"Besides, it just wouldn't be fair," he said.

"No, I suppose not," she agreed.

They sat together in silence for a long moment.

"It's a good thing then that I stopped you last night," she said. "Even though I am really sorry about the bite. It sure looks bad today."

He shrugged. "It won't amount to much," he said, rubbing the angry-looking bruise on his cheek. "It is probably good that we didn't finish what we started last night. They say a gal cain't get a baby the first time, so you'd have been all right. But it's best if we keep circumspect until I go."

"That's a good idea," Eulie said.

They sat together in an uncomfortable silence. Eulie regretted the unwanted intrusion of his baser nature. And she regretted her reaction to it. She liked having him hold her. It was very pleasant. And having him lie on top of her like that, the warmth and weight of him, that was really nice as well. But he was probably right about the baby. Although she did *like* babies.

Beside her, he chuckled. She turned to glance at him.

"I haven't laughed like that in . . . I don't know when," he told her.

She smiled. "My youngers and me, we laugh like that all the time."

"Do you?"

"Uh-huh," she replied. "I guess with you not having any brothers or sisters you didn't romp and play that much as a boy."

"I was alone most of the time," he admitted. "Mama was so busy taking care of the place, and Uncle Jeptha sickened a lot back then. But I used to pretend I had a friend."

"You mean you just made up somebody to play with."

"Not to *play* with," Moss corrected her, feigning a serious rebuke. "He was a partner to go out West with."

Eulie giggled at him.

He grinned broadly at her, his dark handsome eyes crinkling attractively, the deep tone of his chuckle resonating warmth.

"Did he have a name, your partner?" she asked.

Immediately she noticed his chagrin. He cleared his throat but could not so easily dispense with his discomfiture.

"I just called him Tex," he said, a little too casually.

"Tex? Like the horse?"

Moss Collier blushed vividly. "The horse is *Red* Tex," he stated unequivocally.

Eulie smiled at him and nodded. "Yes, of course, the horse is Red Tex."

They were both silent, contemplative. Then they eyed each other and both commenced laughing once more.

"The day we wed, I worried that you'd never get over your black temper," she teased.

Moss raised an eyebrow. "I had every right to be spitting mad," he pointed out.

"Yes, you did," she agreed. "But life has a way of just working things out. I always trust that somehow things always work out."

He nodded. "That's certainly true in this instance," he said. "I can hardly believe that I'm free to just pick up and go whenever I've got a mind to."

"So when are you thinking to leave?" she asked him.

His expression turned thoughtful. "Well, there are some things I should get done around here," he said. "I want to get that shed roof fixed and that grain moved. I'll do some repairs and some heavy chores. See the crop along a bit. Make certain there's enough meat to get you through this first year."

"That would be mightily appreciated," she said.

"In a few weeks, I could be heading out," he said. "Unless something comes up that you need me."

His words were gentle and sincere. They touched Eulie in an unexpected way, making her suddenly wish that he were not so intent upon leaving.

"You're a good man, Moss Collier," she told him.

"That's not what folks are going to say," he warned her. "They are going to say that I'm lower than a snake for running out on this family."

She waved away his concern. "I'll set them straight right away," she assured him. "I'll never allow a spiteful word to be said about you."

"Maybe you ought to let them think what they will," he said. "It might go better for you if they do."

"What do you mean?"

"I mean that not many people have ever understood why I want to leave the Sweetwood," he explained. "They just say I've got a bad case of the wanderlust and I'll get over it. I don't expect they'd ever understand how you could let me go. It's probably best that they think I upped and left you high and dry."

"That's so unfair," Eulie said. "I'm the one who trapped you into marriage so I could get my family under one roof. They should be told that, so they can place the blame fairly where it belongs and understand why it's reasonable that you should go."

Moss shook his head in disagreement.

"Whatever they think of me, Eulie, I'll be too far away to hear it," he said. "But you'll be right here among them. They need to think well of you, because you're going to need all the goodwill and neighborliness that you can get."

She had to admit there was certainly credence to that.

"I disgraced you so with my lies about a baby," she said. "It just don't seem right to heap more shame upon you."

"You and I will know the truth," he said. "That's all that really matters."

"Yes, we'll know," she agreed. "And Uncle Jeptha and the children."

Moss looked over at her, his expression questioning.

"Do you think we should tell them?" he asked.

Eulie was surprised. "Do you think that we shouldn't?"

He shrugged.

"It's pretty complicated," he said. "A couple marrying for false reasons and living apart so they can both get what they want. They are so young, making them understand it wouldn't be easy."

"That's true," Eulie agreed.

"It's not like they are going to be forlorn or feel abandoned. They don't really even know me," Moss added. "I doubt if my leaving will give them even more than a moment's pause."

Eulie nodded, accepting his decision.

"But at least we'll tell your uncle Jeptha," she said.

Moss shook his head. "I don't know if we should do that either."

"You don't?"

The husband-man wove his fingers together and tucked his chin upon his thumbs.

"I've never really talked to Uncle Jeptha about my dreams," he said. "He knows, of course, that I've always been interested in the West, but my plans have always been for *after* he'd passed on. I've kept them from him because I didn't want to seem like I was waiting around for him to die."

"Oh, no, of course not." Eulie could certainly understand that.

"The old fellow is my only blood relative," he said. "He's a good, decent man. He never asked for what happened to him."

Moss squeezed his lips together as if he found speaking the words difficult.

"I never knew my father," he said. "Uncle Jeptha has always been that to me. Even bad-off as he is, he's always taught me how to work and the right way to behave. He's done whatever he could for me. I guess I'm afraid that if he thought I wanted him to die, he would quit trying to live."

Eulie nodded. "Maybe it would be better if he speculated that your leaving had to do with me, not with him."

"You don't mind?" he asked. "The old man loves me and might think the worst of you for it."

"I'd be honored to take on that guilt," she said.

The two sat together silently for a long moment, contemplating their future.

"It's a lot of lies to be telling," Moss suggested.

Eulie couldn't dispute that.

"Lying is a sin of which I seem to be getting a lot of practice," she said.

The morning was a clear one, and bright. The sun shone through the faint smoky haze that always lingered in the low valleys after a rain, and the sacred blossoms of dogwood were in evidence along the hillside. The company was quiet and congenial and the fish were biting well. Within a couple of hours of their easing those cane poles out over the river, the stringer was nearly full, and Jeptha Barnes felt calm and content with his world.

Young Rans was spirited and pensive at turns, but eager to please. As his companion appeared uneager to converse, the boy kept his silence, sparing the occasional question that simply could not be suppressed.

Jeptha had spent a lot of his life fishing off this point. As a young man he had found it a task most suited to his temperament. His parents had thought him a little bit lazy, not too work-brittle, likely to lollygag the day away. What he'd been, of course, was a little bit sleepy. A common complaint for young fellows who couldn't stay in bed at night.

He and his older brother would sneak out after sunset and run wild in the countryside. They played pranks on men they didn't like, chewed home-cured tobacco, and cursed blue streaks about anything and everything. And they were endlessly on the prowl for the sight of that most elusive and curious of all mountain creatures, the human female.

They would sneak up to the farm where there was some gal they decided was pretty and hide in the bushes half the night waiting for her to feel the call of nature and head to the bushes. Most often these forays were disappointments, although they did once see old Grandma Browning squat and pee not a hundred yards away from them. Unfortunately, the sight had set off a spate of giggling. The old woman heard them and threw a rock in their direction that sent them scurrying away.

The next day she showed up accusing them to their father. He and Nils had immediately confessed to the crime. Pa used his razor strop on their backsides with such good effect that they'd both taken their dinner standing up.

They hadn't learned their lesson, of course. They cheerfully, if more quietly, continued their nightly excursions. The outings had taken on a more formal nature eventually. Nils would be calling on some gal or the other and would make a secret plan to meet her at moonrise at some accessible location for a few minutes of hurried but blissful solitude beyond the watchful eyes of parents or chaperone.

Jeptha had not needed any plan. For Jeptha, there had always been Sary. For him to see Sary, no plan was required. He'd skitter a pebble along the back wall of her daddy's cabin and in two shakes of a lamb's tail she'd come hurrying out. He never knew what excuse she gave her mother, but she always came to him. They would clasp hands and run off in the woods together, not stopping until they were panting, breathless and all alone. Her hair was always so shiny and soft and she smelled as sweet as lilac water.

They would walk together in the moonlight. He would hold her hand and gaze into her eyes. They would talk softly and smile together about the most ordinary of things. He would caress her fingers. And thrill to the hastening beat of pulse at her wrist. There was never anything indecent in their meetings. Even chaste kisses were rare. But none were required They were so much in love every moment shared between them was intimate.

Until that last night together.

"If I never see you again, then I want to be wholly and completely yours this once," she told him. "I could not bear to live without that memory."

Jeptha closed his eyes as he recalled her words. It was almost as if he could not bear to live *with* the memory.

The line jerked sharply, and the cane pole flexed in his hand.

"You got a big one!" the boy called out delighted.

Abruptly Jeptha brought his attention back to the moment at hand. It was a big huge fish at the end of his line. And it was a fighter.

"Get the net," he called out to the boy.

In the early years after he came home from the war, he could only catch small fish. He'd have to let the big ones get away. He couldn't figure a way to drag them onto to the bank to him. He was in no position to get in the water after them. So he'd brought darters and baby bass to the table, half-ashamed not to have thrown them back. But he'd taught himself that when it came to keepers, different men required different standards. He could not bring home what he once had, what a whole man could, but he could put bites of food on his family's table.

Now, after years of experience and a wagon load of

mistakes, he could do a lot better. He could worry a fair-sized fish to the shallows next to the bank, grab the line in his hands, and, if he didn't catch on a rock or root, drag him up to his side. But for a fish as big as this one felt to be, a fellow with a net would be of considerable advantage.

Jeptha worked the pole, easing, pulling, urging the big fish toward the bank. Gently, he had to induce it gently. If he pulled too quick one way and the fish pulled the other, the line would snap.

The boy was wading out into the river, net in hand, eyes trained on the flurry of battle occurring where the water met Jeptha's fishing line.

"Do you see him?" Jeptha asked.

"I do!" Rans cried out. "I do see him. He's a big 'un for sure!"

The excitement in the boy's voice spurred Jeptha's enthusiasm. Ever so carefully he raised and lowered the pole, gradually bringing the struggling, splashing creature in their direction.

Rans was in water up to his hips when he managed to scoop up the fish with the net.

The boy was hollering with delight as he hurried up the bank. The effect of trying to run through the water had his trousers dripping wet all the way up to his waist. He didn't seem to mind, however; he was grinning like a fool. Jeptha couldn't fault him for it; he was grinning pretty broad himself.

The fish was still flapping, flopping, and fighting to get away as Jeptha pulled him out of the net.

"I bet it's a big old crappie," Rans said as they got their first good look at their catch.

Jeptha gave the fish a quick assessment and shook

his head. "No, it's a perch," he told the boy. "But it's a good-sized one for sure."

Rans retrieved the very impressive stringer of fish from its cooling place at the edge of the water. Jeptha, carefully grasping the perch by its open mouth, removed the hook from where it dug tightly into his jaw.

"He's the biggest one we've caught all morning," Rans said.

Jeptha agreed. "And he sure rounds out our stringer. We've got a fine mess of fish for our dinner. I guess we'll have to leave the rest of them for another day."

"Guess so," the boy agreed, laughing.

Jeptha was grateful for the sound of that. There had not been much laughing around this place for a long time, he decided. And this boy was not like his sister, who would find something to smile about in hell itself. Young Rans was a child not given to much merriment. Making him laugh was an accomplishment, indeed.

As they began to gather their things, Jeptha heard a tromping sound in the area behind them that could only be human. He glanced up grinning, expecting to see his nephew come out of the woods, this time perhaps wearing more than his union suit.

The smile froze upon Jeptha's face. It was not Moss Collier.

"Miz Patch!" Rans called out. "You came back with the twins."

The small, delicate woman had weathered the years well; the only lines marring her face, the ones around her eyes, evidenced a life spent smiling. She was neat as a pin, every hair in place, and had an adoring little girl on each hand.

"Thought I'd better check out this mysterious injury of Mosco's," she said. "When we heard all the yelling over this way, we figured you might be needing us, too."

"We caught a big fish," Rans said. "I mean, Uncle Jeptha caught a big fish. It's a perch, but it's nearly as long as an ax handle."

"Did you try to swim out for him?" the woman asked with good humor, noting the soaked condition of the boy's trousers.

Rans chuckled.

"I near would have," he admitted, "if Uncle Jeptha hadn't eased him to the bank as well as he did."

Her smile was bright as a new penny as she turned to look at him. He looked away, unwilling to meet her gaze.

"Good morning, Jeptha," she said.

He acknowledged her with a curt nod.

"Look at all we've caught," Rans said, proudly holding up the weighty stringer.

"That's a fine mess of fish," the woman agreed.

"What you got in your basket?" he asked.

"Some herbs and roots for your sister's medicine box," she answered. "Also, we've been pulling greens as we walked."

"I'm sick of greens," Rans complained. "That's all we've been eating lately. We had them cold for breakfast this morning."

Miz Patch chuckled. "This time a year there ain't much else. All the growing seasons are that way. You think you can't wait for the first ears of sweet corn or a sweet juicy apple and before they are all picked and put away for the winter, they taste like sawdust."

Rans was unconvinced. "A bowl full of sawdust would suit me about as good as cold greens. Right, Uncle Jeptha?"

Jeptha almost missed the question. He was trying to hold himself still. He was trying to hold himself very still. He had the unsettling sensation that the world was tilting and that he would any moment be humiliatingly thrown out of his cart and on to the ground, his leglessness even more obvious than it was now.

He didn't see people. He never saw people. If someone came to the place, he would stay in the shadows of the cabin. He didn't want anyone to see him like this. Anyone. How could he have allowed himself to get caught out in the open like this?

He couldn't look her in the eyes. He couldn't bear to see the revulsion he knew would be there.

"Those fish won't be good for nothing but the hogs if you don't get them cleaned!" he snapped at the boy.

Rans looked up surprised. The fish were in no danger of spoiling, and Jeptha had indicated earlier that he would do his share of the cleaning. But he couldn't explain, he couldn't explain anything now. He just needed for them to go away. He needed for them to leave him alone.

"Get on up to the house and get busy," he said, not quite as unkindly as his previous tone.

Rans was looking at him warily now. The lightness of heart that he'd seen in the boy's face earlier was gone, the mask of cold distrust firmly back in place.

Inwardly Jeptha cursed his own weakness. He liked

the boy, he didn't want to hurt him. But he had to be alone.

No one spoke to him as they left. Silence settled within the shady sanctuary of the point.

Jeptha stared out at the river. He tried not to think. He tried not to remember.

"I love you, Jeptha Barnes," Sary had whispered on that long ago night, their passion spent. "I love your strength and your honor and your humor. I love everything about you. If I never see you again, I will love you to the day I die."

"I love you, too, Sary," he'd answered. "I love you and I'll come back to you. I swear it."

Jeptha felt the sting of bitter tears in his eyes. How young they were. How young and ignorant of the evils of war and the harsh realities of fate.

Jeptha watched the water flowing steadily downstream and momentarily toyed with the idea of rolling himself down into it. Allowing the current to carry him away. To drift slowly and inevitably to a drowning death and an infinite eternity. Giving over and having it all ended once and for all.

His rumination was only an idle pastime. His shook his head wryly.

"With my luck," he said aloud, "I'd get my arms torn off going over the falls, float to the bank, and be rescued to live twenty more years as a burden to my family."

12

THE very aromatic scent of frying fish in cornmeal was wafting through the doorway as Moss, the Toby children, and Miz Patch waited together in the small square of shade beside the kitchen. The seams and waistband of his trousers were still damp and a bit uncomfortable, but at least he was clothed. The older woman had made a poultice and was carefully applying it to the side of his face.

"How did you say you got this bruise?" the woman questioned him, not for the first time.

"I fell," Moss answered with a firm intent to discourage further questions.

The woman looked skeptical.

"A mark this perfectly round is typically a bite," she said.

Moss made no comment and could not look her in the eye. He was not about to discuss his marriage with anyone, even a well-meaning woman like Miz Patch.

She got the bandage secured just as Eulie called them in to eat. Moss felt better with his injury hidden, and he was also very hungry. He didn't wait to be called twice.

"Go get Uncle Jeptha," he ordered the boy.

Rans, who had been talking and laughing with his younger sisters, behaving himself for a change, immediately stiffened his back and hardened his jaw, ready to take offense at being ordered away. And primed to give argument against doing it.

"I suspect you *are* the best one to go get him," Miz Patch interjected. "None of these gals can run as fast as you can. Nobody wants either of you'uns to miss these vittles while they're hot."

Her words seemed to placate the boy somewhat. At least enough that he moved to do as he was bid.

"My wife's brother thinks a little too well of himself," Moss told Miz Patch, by way of explanation and apology.

The woman tutted. "More likely he don't think well enough," the woman said. "Rans ain't like his sister even so much as a bit."

"That's for sure," Moss agreed. "The boy is prickly and disagreeable. Eulie is sweet and tries to please."

They had risen to their feet; the girls had already filed inside eagerly ahead of them. Miz Patch gave him a questioning look.

"Was she just trying to please when she took that hunk out of your face?"

Moss flushed. He'd thought she might suspect, but he hated having anyone actually know.

"I can't tell if she done it in passion or anger," Miz Patch said. "Either way, I'm glad to hear that you don't seem to hold no grudge about it."

"It was my fault," Moss told her quietly.

That raised the woman's eyebrows. She half grinned. "Take your clue from her, Mosco," she said. "You say she's sweet and eager to please. You be that to your new bride and she'll get real willing to give you what you want."

Moss looked at her questioningly. "I thought you'd be saying it's a wife's duty to do what her husband says."

Miz Patch shrugged. "Maybe so," she said. "But I don't think a man gets much joy from a marriage where his wife's just doing her duty."

He chuckled. "To tell you the truth, Miz Patch," he said, "I ain't never heard any man describe marriage as joy."

"You're right, they sure don't say it," she agreed. "But you'd be surprised how many of them feel it."

"They are the lucky ones, I guess," Moss said.

"Luck don't have nothing to do with it," Miz Patch told him. "Like anything in life worth having, hard work is what makes it. Think of marriage like farming, a long-term proposition. You start out with little to work with and a tough challenge every day. You work at it and as time goes by it just naturally gets better. But the harder you work, the faster it comes round to suit you."

Moss chuckled. "I never cared much for farming. I suspect that even if I wanted to make a marriage work, I wouldn't have the resolve to see it through."

The incredulous expression on Miz Patch's face apprised Moss that he'd said too much. He was leaving, and that would be known soon enough. But the less people understood about his reasoning, the better. This was private knowledge. Things between himself and Eulie. Nobody should ever know any of it. It was wrong that anyone should ever even have a hint of what went on between them.

"Miz Patch," he said, firmly. "I don't know for sure what's going to happen with my marriage. But I don't want any gossip being spread around about Eulie."

The woman chuckled. "If you're warning me off," she said, "well, it ain't strictly necessary. I'm fond of children always, and the Tobys especially, 'cause they are in need of it more than most. I ain't about to say a stinging word about any of them."

Moss let out his breath slowly, relieved.

"But if you want to insure no gossip is spread," she continued. "Then you'd best settle into the domestic, get a house full of babies out of that little gal, and keep your eyes focused on the back end of your old mule. The only way to keep gossip away from your family is to not do or say anything for anybody to gossip about."

Moss knew Miz Patch was right. He also knew that leaving to head west was going to set off a whirlwind of gossip that would likely never settle down. People were going to talk, and what could be more gossip-worthy than a man deserting his family.

His family.

The term jolted him somewhat. They were not his family. They were just a bunch of children that were living at his house. Uncle Jeptha was his family. Of course, he was leaving the old man with them. And you only left someone with family. But they weren't his family. Not in any sense of the word. Well, maybe Eulie was. He thought of the softness of her skin and the taste of her lips, the pleasure of laughing with her, and his passionate reaction to her nearness. Yes, he supposed that as family went, his wife was not half-bad.

Miz Patch had stepped through the doorway and at Eulie's order was immediately seated at the table.

Eulie directed the children this way and that, getting things in order. The plates had to be set out, hands had to be washed, food had to be dished out. Moss stood on the threshold and watched his wife bring order to chaos. She did it with a smile upon her face. Eulie could be happy with so little. A little food from a little farm on a little corner of a mountain that was only a tiny speck of the big world. Moss was going to be able to have so much more. He was going to have the whole earth in which to wander. He could hardly wait to get started upon his journey.

"It sure mustn't be easy sitting your whole family at this table," Miz Patch said to him.

Moss stepped inside and took his place.

"No, it's sure not," he agreed.

"All those chairs in the making and no place to scoot them up to," the woman pointed out.

Moss glanced up at Eulie as she set a mess of fried fish in front of him. "I'll be finding us some good long planks and making a new table where everyone can sit around it at the same time."

She smiled at him, clearly pleased. The children shouted with delight. One of the twins threw her arms around his neck.

"Thank you, Uncle Moss," she said.

"He's not our uncle," her sister pointed out.

"Well Uncle Jeptha ain't *our* Uncle Jeptha," she said. "We cain't just keep calling him Eulie's husband."

Moss was taken completely off guard. The children were nothing to him. Why were they wondering what he was to them?

"You'll call him Mr. Collier," Eulie told the girls, only a slight hint of scold in her voice. "And you'll do so with respect. Cora Fay, don't be hanging onto his neck like that. Mr. Collier ain't used to youngers about, you're making him uneasy."

"He needs to get accustomed to having us around," Nora May said.

"He don't need to do nothing," Eulie corrected. "It's his home and while he's here we need to oblige ourselves to him."

"While he's here?"

The question came from Cora Fay. Fortunately at that moment Rans came into the kitchen and right behind him Uncle Jeptha propelled his cart through the doorway.

The older man made his way to the empty chair. Rans leaned against the wall behind him, as if making himself available for assistance.

Moss was somewhat surprised to see his uncle at the table. Jeptha was extremely reticent with company of any kind. He had fully expected the man to hide out until Miz Patch had made her departure.

But he was here, not looking to the left or right, pushing his cart up next to the chair and hoisting himself up in the seat opposite Moss. He didn't say one word of welcome or even glance in the woman's direction.

Clara, with Minnie upon her lap, took the other seat, the twins on either side of her. Eulie stood behind him. It felt good to have her there, Moss thought. It was right somehow. He glanced over at Miz Patch.

The woman's brow was furrowed as she sniffed the air unpleasantly and then glanced beside her. Uncle Jeptha was seated with Rans right behind him.

"Rans," she said with a hint of rebuke in her tone.

weave," she said. "They are good at it, both of them, just naturally real good."

Eulie smiled and gave the two girls a proud glance. "That's wonderful to hear," she said, looking in Moss's direction as if to share the good news with him.

"Yes, it is," he agreed.

Clara, with a twin on either side, gave the two girls a quick hug.

"Miz Patch is the finest weaver in the Sweetwood," she said. "A compliment from her is very special indeed."

"I know you're going to need these two to help around here this summer," Miz Patch said. "But after harvest is in, I'd like them to come work the loom with me."

The twins shared whispered excitement and delighted giggles.

"I'm sure they could learn a lot from you," Eulie said. "But that's a very long walk. They couldn't do it every day. And never in the snow."

"Whenever you could spare them," Miz Patch said. "And of course they are welcome to stay with me, snow or shine. They are delightful little gals to have around."

"Sounds like you are as needful of children as Uncle Jeptha," Little Minnie said with deliberate snideness. The attention centered upon the twins obviously did not set well with her.

Miz Patch gave the child a baleful glance. "I am needful of children," she agreed. "We all are in our way, I suppose."

"Too bad you never had none," Minnie added, her tone nasty and somewhat superior.

"Minnie!" Eulie scolded, between clenched teeth.

Miz Patch ignored the reproof.

"Who told you that I had no children?" she asked.

"Mrs. Pierce," Minnie answered. "She said all the Patchels around here are your stepchildren. That you didn't have none of your own."

Miz Patch calmly continued eating her dinner as she replied. "That's not entirely true."

"It's not?"

Everyone at the table was surprised.

"When I married Mr. Patchel, he had a whole house full of children for me to tend to. But I birthed three children of my own."

Eulie shared a stricken glance with Moss and then admonished the children.

"Eat your fish," she said. "And let Miz Patch eat hers."

Moss nodded agreement, considering the discussion complete.

Little Minnie, however, didn't see it that way.

"Where are they?" Minnie asked. "Where are your children? Do I know them?"

Eulie tried to hush the child. Minnie was demanding and ill-mannered, but she was completely ignorant of the nature of her question and innocent of any motive in asking it.

"It's all right, Eulie," Miz Patch said. The woman turned her attention to Minnie. "My children are buried up on the hill behind my house," she answered. "They've all died and gone to heaven."

"Oh." Minnie spoke the word in a long breathy whisper.

"Pass me some more of those greens, Miz Patch,"

Moss said, hoping to turn the direction of the conversation.

"Were your children boys or girls?" Little Minnie persisted.

Eulie tutted a scold.

Clara whispered, "Enough," in the child's ear.

Miz Patch sat back in her chair for a long minute and then answered.

"I had both," she said. "A son and twin girls."

"Twins!" Cora Fay exclaimed.

"Like us?" Nora May asked.

Miz Patch nodded. "Betty died just hours after she was born," she explained. "Birdie lived almost a month, then we buried her next to her sister. They were both so tiny and frail, they never had a chance of living."

The excitement around the table quieted.

"I thought I wouldn't be able to have another child," she continued. "It was five long years before I was blessed again."

There was no shadow of sadness in Miz Patch's smile.

"We named him Ezra for his father," she said. "But I called him Hickory, 'cause he was as tall and strong as a hickory tree. He was the happiest baby, just laughing all the time. That child never crawled or walked. He took straight to running and jumping and was darting around like a hummingbird, always in motion."

"What happened to him?" Minnie asked.

"He was three when he tripped and fell into the fire," she answered. "We got him out and he lived six days. There was nothing we could do."

No longer hungry, Moss set his spoon beside his

plate. The sound was loud in the silence of the kitchen.

"That's how I got interested in herbs," Miz Patch continued. "I was trying to find something to ease his pain. All the screaming and crying he ever did were in that last week of his life."

The children were wide-eyed and somber, ignoring their dinner. Moss had known Miz Patch all his life and never thought much about her or what her life had been like. He only knew that she'd been a kindly, plainspoken widow ever since he could remember. Her boy would have been nearer Eulie's age than his own, but he couldn't recall the lad. How strange that he should have known Miz Patch and never known something so important about her.

"Is that why you like us so much?" Nora May asked quietly. "'Cause you miss your own twins and your little boy?"

"Do we kind of take the place of them?" Cora Fay added.

Miz Patch looked up at the two girls, startled, and then she laughed. She actually laughed. The warmth of the sound was a sharp contrast to the sadness in the eyes of those around her.

She reached across the table to touch the hand of the twin nearest her. Her eyes were warm and tender, but there was no nonsense in her tone.

"I love you Toby children because you need loving," she stated plainly. "No other reason. You cain't never be my lost children and I wouldn't want you to be."

"You wouldn't even want us to be?" Cora Fay repeated her words as a question.

Miz Patch shook her head. "Not at all. I know where my little ones are. They are up in heaven. And when I die, I'm going to walk through those pearly gates and two angels are going to fly up to me and put a sweet baby girl in each arm. I'm going to hold those tiny bodies against my breast once more and look down into those little faces again. Then I'll hear someone call out 'Mama!' and when I look up, it'll be my little Hickory come running toward me on his fat baby legs."

The woman's obvious certainty and absence of anguish somehow made the story a sweet one instead of sorrowful.

"You can never take the place of my children," she told the twins. "They are in their place and someday I'm going to go there to be with them."

"You don't even seem sad," Nora May said.

The woman shrugged and chuckled. "How could I be sad?" she asked. "I miss them, but I know they are in safekeeping in heaven. And I'm here with you-all, alive and eating a fine fresh-caught perch."

The day had been a long one for Eulie. The laundry had been a heavy, tiresome chore, made easier by the help of her sister. And although company for the noon meal had been welcome, the afternoon spent inventorying the herb box and planning the summer stores with Miz Patch had been busy. The brightest spot in the day had been the laughter and companionship she'd shared with the husband-man.

He and his uncle had spent most of the afternoon splitting cedar shakes for the shed roof. Uncle Jeptha held the ax at the edge of the bolt while Moss swung the big hardwood mallet. Consistently he hit the ax squarely upon the head, slicing off a perfectly grain-cut shingle.

Rans tried to help, even offering to spell Uncle Jeptha who was forced to hold his arms straight out in front of him for long periods of time. But the husband-man didn't let her brother do much. Fetching and stacking were his tasks, but beyond that he clearly thought the job too arduous for a child.

Predictably, Rans had bristled at not being treated equal to a man and ran off to sulk for an hour or so, leaving the twins to help with the shingle-making. Her brother was back by supper, however and complained bitterly about eating cattails, which according to him was a "beggarman's supper" and far inferior to sweet corn.

When Eulie finally got the dishes cleaned up and the fire banked, she gratefully removed her apron and headed up to the cabin porch, where everyone seemed to have gathered. She looked forward to a nice, peaceful evening with her family. All of them together at long last, to catch up with each other and laugh together once more. She didn't mind having the husband-man or Uncle Jeptha with them. Somehow, amazingly, they fit well with the Tobys. It was all working out perfectly. Eulie secretly congratulated herself. Forcing Moss Collier to marry her was the smartest thing she'd ever done.

Eulie's euphoria was to be short-lived, however. What she had not anticipated in her plan for a happy family evening was the arrival of a gentleman caller. It would have been impossible to forget that the husband-man had given permission to Mr. Leight to pay court to Clara. Eulie had assumed that he meant only sitting Sunday, not calling on her in the middle of the week.

But there he was, big-eyed and bug-ugly, sitting on the porch at Clara's side just like he belonged there.

Rans was talking to him a mile a minute. And the other children as well seemed to think of him as their company as much as Clara's.

Politely he rose to his feet when he saw Eulie. He was awkward and obviously ill at ease as he bowed to her like some stilted lowlander and bid her greeting.

"Mrs. Collier, it is surely a pleasure to see you," he said.

Eulie could hardly return that greeting. It was all she could do just to be civil. It wasn't as if she had ever truly disliked the man. He had been a perfectly acceptable neighbor, even a kind and charitable one to take in both her brother and sister and give them work. But when he cast his eyes on Clara, clearly with matrimony in mind, he'd gained Eulie as an enemy forever. She had done all, risked all, to keep her family together. This was the fellow intent on scattering them to the winds. He wanted to take her sister away forever. Eulie was not about to make that happen.

"What are you doing here?" she asked unkindly.

It was such an amazingly rude thing to say that Eulie could barely get her mouth around the words. She was generally tenderhearted and careful of the feelings of other folks. Especially folks who were shunned or despised by others. Bug was that. His ugliness made him forever the butt of jokes and the target of malicious horseplay. Those facts alone should have endeared him to Eulie. But Leight was trying to break up her hard-won home, and she wasn't about to let him do it.

"I hope you aren't neglecting your own place to come visiting over this way," she suggested.

Bug looked downright startled at the suggestion, his bulging eyes seeming even more enormous. "Oh no, ma'am," he assured her. "I got everything done early so I could get away and come see Miss Clara."

He darted a glance in the direction of the young lady mentioned. Clara sat demurely, eyes lowered, a tiny enigmatic smile upon her lips.

"Well, you should have saved yourself the trouble," Eulie told him.

"We'll all of us be taking to our beds soon, so you cain't stay long. You've made a long ride for little purpose."

Bug swallowed nervously. He didn't look at Clara as he spoke, but his words were obviously intended for her.

"I . . . I would walk to the ends of the earth if need be, just for a glimpse of Miss Clara," he said.

Beside him Rans snorted, thinking the sentiment surely some kind of joke.

Eulie didn't laugh, but she was unmoved.

"I don't think the ends of the earth will be necessary," she said. "But if you'd just come as far as yonder hill, you can wave at her and be done with it."

"Eulie!" Clara complained, not at all pleased with her sister's attitude. She glanced at Bug shyly before she continued. "I'm not at all tired," she told him. "And I'm in no hurry to retire. I believe I'll sit a spell."

"Well, even so," Eulie told her. "These children need their sleep."

There was an immediate chorus of dissent, which was ignored.

"I'm worn out myself," Eulie admitted. "Someone must stay up with you if he's here."

Bug appeared ready to apologize for intruding and take an embarrassed leave of the company. Unfortunately, he didn't speak fast enough.

"I don't mind staying here on the porch," Rans said. "Mr. Leight and me were having a fine discussion about farming before you come in. So go on to bed if you're a mind to. You won't bother us a bit."

Eulie could have joyfully boxed her brother's ears at that moment, but she did not. A hand touched her shoulder. She looked up to see the husband-man eyeing her curiously.

"I'm sorry that you are too tired for company, 'cause it looks as if we're getting more."

Eulie glanced in the direction that he indicated, and sure enough, a mule with what looked to be a couple of people upon it was headed in their direction.

"Who in the devil could that be?" Eulie exclaimed.

"Don't curse," Little Minnie chided her.

Eulie looked at the child, thinking to explain to her that "devil" was not cursing, but decided against it. If her lecturing was finally beginning to bear fruit, she didn't want to discourage it.

"Poor Uncle Jeptha," Cora Fay said. "He ain't never going to get to come out of the barn."

"The barn?" Eulie asked.

Nora May nodded. "He's hiding out in there again," she said. "We thought he'd got over his fear of strangers when he come to eat with Miz Patch among us."

"We told him that he shouldn't think of Mr. Leight as a stranger," Cora Fay added. "He is practically family already."

The twin's declaration of near-kinship had Clara looking quite pleased and Bug blushing. Eulie was not in agreement, but managed not to say so. She turned her attention to the arriving visitors.

Eulie looked at her husband accusingly. "Do you have folks coming by here every night?" she asked grumpily.

"Me!" he defended himself. "Why, I go for weeks at a time without seeing another soul. It's you and your youngers that attracts the company."

Eulie could hardly argue that. They stood waiting and watching as the mule came around the crossing and up through the woods toward them.

"Hullo the house!" a man called out to them when they got within shouting distance.

"Who is it?" Eulie asked Moss.

He shook his head unable to answer, but someone else did. Little Minnie jumped to her feet.

"It's Mr. Pierce," she shouted excitedly. "It's Mr. and Mrs. Pierce."

Without another word the little girl went charging down the slope in their direction.

"Hullo and welcome!" Moss called back.

"What are they doing here?" Eulie asked.

"They probably want to discuss their offer," he said.

"Offer? What offer?" she asked.

He turned to her, surprised. "I didn't tell you? I didn't tell you last night?"

"Tell me what?"

"The Pierces want to adopt Little Minnie," he said.

13

THE people on the porch had divided into two sets. Clara and Bug remained within the dim shadows of the roof overhang with Rans and the twins beside them, the latter doing most of the talking.

Moss and Eulie were seated on a bench beneath the bright glow of a waning moon. The Pierces sat in chairs nearby. The appropriate greetings had been exchanged. There had been some small talk about crops and a couple of curious questions about the bandage upon Moss's cheek. That was the extent of the polite discussion. Enoch and Judith Pierce seemed very content to simply sit and listen with avid interest to Little Minnie, who hadn't ceased her chattering nonsense since the moment they had arrived.

"We had tea," the child told them. "We practiced our table manners and pretended that we had real spoons and forks, which we don't have here at all, just old whittled wooden things."

Judith Pierce was smiling at the girl as if she were the most charming conversationalist that she had ever encountered.

"I didn't get my dress dirty, not even a little bit," Minnie went on. "Those twins tried to get me to walk with them through the woods to see Miz Patch. They all gathered field greens, but I didn't and I won't. You can sure get dirty doing that kind of work."

Both the Pierces readily agreed with her. They were dandified people, to Eulie's mind. If the Tobys were the dregs of Sweetwood society, the Pierces were the heights that could be reached. They dressed as fine on Thursday as they did on Sunday. They always appeared clean and slicked-up and ready to head for town. That was Judith's doing. She was a peddler's daughter who'd always had a bit of coin and seen more of the world than most in the Sweetwood. She had high ideas about how to live. And her choice of husband was well-suited to her. Ostensibly, her husband, Enoch, was a farmer. But he was like none other in the Sweetwood. He accumulated land. When someone left or someone died, or a farm completely foundered, he was always there with the cash in hand to buy what they didn't want or couldn't use. What Pierce owned was sharecropped. Poor farmers, failed farmers, young farmers—there were always people who owned no land and knew only farming as a way to work.

Eulie's father had sharecropped several places for Enoch Pierce. Of course, even Eulie had to admit, her daddy's work was no great bargain. When every farmer in the Sweetwood brought in a fine crop, Virgil Toby's would be only middling. And when times were tough, he'd come with no crop at all. Her father had been sick so much. And he'd drunk a good deal, though it was for medicinal purposes, Eulie was certain. In any case, if it hadn't been for the efforts of her mother and the hard scrambling she and the youngers had done, they would have never been able to keep food on the table.

That had been bad for the Tobys, of course. But it was also trouble for Enoch Pierce. He depended upon his sharecroppers to make crop. When they didn't, he lost money. That was not a thing he tolerated easily. Eulie well knew that Enoch Pierce had put up with her father's lackadaisical ways for the sake of the children. The man's kindness ought to put him in Eulie's good favor. But tonight it did not.

"So Heloise, that's what I'm calling my dolly now, Heloise," Minnie continued, "Heloise said that she wasn't going to play with any of those nasty Toby children, just with me. And that I should get some other dollies so that the two of us would have someone to talk to. Neither of us has any interest in those Toby children, especially those silly twins who don't care about anyone but themselves."

"Princess!" Judith scolded, her voice firm but loving. "What is this about 'the nasty Toby children'?"

"She's been saying that," Eulie told her. "Giving herself airs. Telling us that she can't do this or she can't do that."

Eulie heard her own complaints and didn't like the sound of them. Minnie was her sister; problems in the family should be kept in the family. They were never voiced to outsiders.

Judith's brow furrowed with disapproval and she gave Minnie a stern look.

"You mustn't speak of your brother and sisters that way," she told the girl. "You should always be proud that you *are* one of the Toby children."

Eulie couldn't help but feel a hint of joyous justification.

"I won't be one of the Toby children for long," Little Minnie replied with certainty, glancing over at Eulie with a look that was almost victorious.

Judith Pierce gasped, surprised and clearly embarrassed.

Enoch Pierce looked at his wife reproachfully. "I told you that you shouldn't say anything to her," he said.

"I just gave her a tiny hint and she guessed," Judith defended. "It was just such a happy thought I couldn't keep it to myself."

Eulie glanced over accusingly at Moss. She didn't think it a happy thought at all. And she was very angry about being the last to hear of this foolish plan.

Moss was tight-lipped and stern-jawed. Apparently Enoch had spoken to him at the pounding about Minnie returning to their house. He'd promised to discuss it with Eulie, but with everything that had happened in the last twenty-four hours, he just hadn't.

Eulie could hardly fault him for that. He had been reveling in his own plans, his own dream come true. He had likely not given a thought to what the Pierces wanted. And having never had any brothers or sisters, he could probably never know how unreasonable a request it was.

But she was about to make it plain to him, to all of them, that she was not giving up her baby sister, not now, not ever, no matter what.

"Minnie, get on into the cabin and get ready for bed," she told the child sternly.

Her tone, clipped and sharp, clearly indicated that the discussion about to ensue was not going to be fit for a young child's hearing.

Her sister, however, pulled an obstinate pout and clung more tightly to Mrs. Pierce's arm.

"I want to stay with you," she told the woman.

Eulie was mad enough to cut a switch. Fortunately, that was not necessary.

Judith Pierce smiled down at Minnie and then planted a kiss on the top of the child's head. Her words were tender, but brooked no argument. "Go ready yourself for bed, so your fa—so Mr. Pierce and I can speak privately with the Colliers."

"Do I have to?" she whined.

Judith Pierce nodded. "Well-behaved young ladies always do as they are told," she said quietly.

"Should I go ahead and pack my things?" Minnie asked in a whisper that implied some conspiracy.

Mrs. Pierce shook her head slightly to indicate the negative.

Eulie looked mad enough to chew sawdust.

Minnie gave her sister only a passing glance as she laggardly made her way out of earshot. Her distinct preference for the Pierces over her own flesh and blood was perhaps understandable. Their doting attention would be welcomed by any child. And it seemed that the love a sister had to give was different than that of . . . of, well, a parent. A sister loved completely, but could see faults perfectly clear. The vision of a parent was always somewhat clouded.

But Judith and Enoch were not Minnie's parents. They had always been close to her, always been eager to help. But they were not her mother and father. Minnie had not really had any. Ma had died so soon, and Daddy—well, Daddy had just never been himself thereafter. Eulie, Clara and Rans remembered better times, and the twins had always had each other, but Minnie had been left out.

Her young life had been a series of sad crises, punctuated by hard work and responsibility. What the Pierces were offering her was more than food, clothing, and shelter. They were prepared to provide that infinitely sweet and intangible gift, a childhood.

Eulie could understand it. But she couldn't allow it. She turned immediately to Judith. Her words couldn't have been plainer.

"I don't know what song in a million Sundays led you to think that I would give you my little sister, but let me tell you right now, it is not ever going to happen."

The Pierces looked at each other and then at Moss.

"I haven't even had time to talk to her," he complained. "I told you we'd discuss it after Preaching Sunday."

"We just simply couldn't wait," Judith answered. "We love Minnie and we want her with us. I've waited all my life. I could just wait no longer."

Enoch Pierce touched his wife's knee as if to quiet her.

"I'm sorry about this, Collier," he said to Moss. "You told us to give you some time and we should have."

"It wouldn't have mattered," Eulie told them. "He couldn't have changed my mind and you won't either."

Enoch still intended to try.

"I suppose we've gone about this all wrong," he told her. "But please hear us out. We have a proposition that we think will be absolutely the best for everyone concerned."

Eulie didn't even want to hear it. She wanted to simply stand up and walk away. To her surprise, Moss reached over and took her hand. She turned to glance at him. He didn't say a word, but his eyes seemed to will her to take a deep breath, open her heart, and consider what they had to say.

"I'm listening," Eulie told them.

A long moment passed when Enoch seemed to be collecting his thoughts. His wife apparently could not bear the silence.

"I am barren," Judith Pierce stated flatly.

The admission startled all of them, even Mrs. Pierce herself, who then fumbled for her hanky as if fearing her tears would fall. Her husband's complexion was as white as a sheet. Eulie suspected that the word had never before been spoken aloud between them.

Enoch squeezed his wife's hand comfortingly as he attempted to compose himself. He turned his attention to Eulie.

"Mrs. Collier," he began. "I've known you a lot of years, since you were a wee little baby, I reckon. I knew your folks even before then."

"You were our landlord as long as I can remember," Eulie responded. "Ma and Daddy always thought well of you."

He accepted the compliment graciously and hesitated a long moment as if in deference to the memory of her parents.

"Your folks certainly had their trials. Your mother was as hard a worker as any woman I've ever known. And your father . . . well, he sure missed her a lot after she was gone."

It was a generous interpretation.

"People have probably said a lot about your folks.

Poor people got poor ways. But nobody ever said they didn't love their children," Enoch continued. "They set a fine store by young Rans and you girls. They loved you and provided for you as best they were able."

"I am aware of that, Mr. Pierce," Eulie answered.

The man hesitated to continue. "If it was in my power," he began. "If there was something that I could do to bring them back . . ."

His voice drifted off into that wistful place where the hard realities of life must ultimately be faced.

Eulie was in that place as well. Minnie deserved to have a ma and daddy. Eulie deserved it as well. She wished her parents could see her now with a fine man and their own farm. But they were gone and would not know. If they had not been gone, it might have never happened.

"The truth is," Enoch continued, "Judith and I felt very sad for you children, being left alone and all. We felt especially so for Little Minnie. You recall we were there the day she was born."

Eulie nodded.

"When we agreed to take in Minnie, we said it was because we had the room and there seemed like nowhere else for her to go." Pierce glanced at his wife. She was biting down upon her lip, her eyes filled with tears.

"We said we'd give a roof above her and keep her clean and fed. But the truth is, we already loved her."

Enoch gazed briefly at Moss as if willing him to understand before returning his attention to Eulie.

"Your sister has become a . . . a daughter to us," he said. "We've always wanted our own children." He spoke haltingly as if the words were difficult. "We don't know . . . we've just . . . we've just never been blessed."

"Little Minnie is not your daughter," Eulie said firmly.

Enoch nodded. "We know that," he said. "But we love her and we would care for her and we would try to be the kind of father and mother that your own folks were to her."

The man's plea was impassioned, heartfelt. Eulie did not for one moment doubt his sincerity. And as for being good parents, Eulie was certain in her own mind that they would be.

"Minnie doesn't need any new mother and father," Eulie said. "She's got me and my brother and sisters. The Tobys all stick together and now we got a home here at Barnes Ridge farm and cain't nobody never pull us apart again."

The Pierces shared a desperate, stricken glance.

"We love Minnie and she loves us," Enoch said. "She will always be your sister, but that is what she is to you, a sister. You and Mr. Collier will have your own children."

Eulie blushed at his words. "You don't know that we will any more than you know that you won't."

Pierce swallowed, he expression resigned as he pressed his hands together. His wife was biting her lip again, holding back tears once more.

"We've been to every doctor between here and Knoxville," he said solemnly. "We've tried every herb and patent remedy known about, we've taken advice from soothsayers and tea-leaf readers. For the last few years we've just been praying and praying that God would send us a child."

The man looked up. His eyes were full of tears.

"When Minnie came into our lives, we knew at last that our prayers had been answered."

Eulie's own lower lip began to quiver.

"God doesn't answer prayers for one family by tearing apart another," she said finally, with certainty.

"We're not trying to tear your family apart," he said. "We just want to give Minnie a better chance. She is so young and her life has been so full of upheaval."

Eulie knew he spoke the truth, but she deliberately shrugged away his concern.

"Life is hard," she said. "Everybody learns that."

"But must she learn it so soon?" Pierce asked, then answered his own question. "Only if she is a Toby."

It was a harsh, honest statement. One painful enough to make Eulie gasp.

Judith spoke up, her words softening the cruelty of her husband's.

"Minnie has already found out that life can be different elsewhere," she said. "Now she feels left out among you. She's a different temperament than the rest of you children, she hasn't been through as much, she doesn't have so many memories. She's accustomed to us now. She is happy at our home. She hardly has a place in your family and she would be the very center of ours."

"Minnie *has* a place in our family," Eulie insisted forcefully. "She's the baby. She's always been the baby. And she always will be the baby."

Judith's answer was without condemnation and matter-of-fact.

"She's been the baby, a spoiled baby."

Eulie blanched at the truth. She struck back.

"I don't think that's such a great thing that you've done, giving her manners and airs that are above her raising."

"But if she's raised with us," Pierce countered, "there will be nothing above her. Judith is teaching her to read and cipher, as well as the genteel arts. She's very bright and clever. We can send her to school in Jarl. When she's older we might even move to Jonesboro so she can attend the Female Seminary if she is of a mind to go there."

"Minnie doesn't need such foolishness," Eulie told them. "All she needs is to be with her family. We're her family. She needs to be with us."

She turned to Moss.

"Tell them," she demanded.

Moss stared at his bride. His silence spoke volumes.

The Pierces could easily give Minnie the kind of life and care that hardscrabble farming could never offer her. Eulie should be happy for her sister, eager for her to move up in the world. But she was not. Her dream was coming true. They were all going to be together at last. She couldn't just let them take Minnie away.

"The children are in Eulie's care," the husbandman said to them. "If she believes Minnie would be best with her, then that is the way it has to be."

"Minnie loves us," Judith protested. "She wants to be with us."

"She's just a child," Eulie discounted with certainty. "She'll get over that."

In her heart she wasn't so sure.

Rans wanted to spit nails, again. He didn't know how much more of this ill treatment and disrespect he could put up with. Last night had been such a pleasure, sitting on the porch with Mr. Leight for hours as they'd talked about crops and fishing and even the making of cedar shakes. His opinions and observations had been offered, one man to another. Leight had been willing to hear him out, discuss his own take on the subject, even occasionally disagree. It had been a heady experience.

Now, this morning, he was back to the low opinions and low expectations of Eulie's husband. Moss Collier was putting the shingles on the shed roof, the rhythmic sounds of hammer falls ringing across the ridge. Rans should have been right up there beside him, striking blow for blow with him.

"This roof is too steep and dangerous," Collier had told him. "You'll fall and hurt yourself."

Rans puffed up furiously in indignation. He was not about to fall off a roof unless it started kicking or bucking. And even if he did, a fellow was not likely to hurt himself from a ten-foot drop.

Rans despised the way Collier treated him like a child, as if he were eight instead of thirteen. Instead of being up on the roof, he was relegated to moving the heavy sacks of leftover grain, feed, and milled flour and corn from the cabin to the shed. He loaded the sacks three or four at a time into the wheelbarrow and rolled them down to the shed to carry inside. It was not a fit job for a man, Rans thought. If the sacks had not been quite so heavy, even Minnie could have handled the task.

Of course, Minnie wasn't one much for tasking. This morning even less so than usual. The Pierces apparently wanted her to come and live with them permanently. It sounded like a pretty good idea to Rans.

She'd get plenty of good food and nice clothes and be treated like the princess that she thought she was. Eulie was against the idea and told Minnie to just put the notion completely out of her mind.

The little whiner had bawled and sobbed and carried on for half the night. At least it hadn't just been the rest of them to suffer. Eulie had come back to sleep in the cabin last night. From her floor pallet she couldn't have missed one tearful hiccup.

Rans latched the screen open and pulled the wheelbarrow right up into the threshold of the cabin doorway. He would have brought it all the way into the extra room if the entrance had been just a hand's width wider. The sacks were not only heavy but unwieldy. Rans was forced to squat down and hoist the bulky bags up on his knees. Then, half bent over, he carried them out. It was a strain on young arms and a growing back. A full-grown man could have toted them upon his shoulder. But sapling-height and skinny, Rans was far from full-grown.

He was certain, in his distrustful and suspicious knowledge of Moss Collier, that he had been given the job just to remind him that he was not as muscular as other men. Rans intended to show the man that he could do the job quickly and without complaint. But it was hard, thankless work with not one speck of glory or potential for pride. It was little more than housecleaning.

It might have been better if he'd at least have had Uncle Jeptha to converse with. But Eulie had commandeered the man into doing gardening with her. With Old Hound pulling his cart and the twins on either side, he was planting turnips.

Somehow, seeing the older man doing women's work didn't lessen him in Ransom's eyes. Uncle Jeptha was just Uncle Jeptha, and anything and everything he did seemed manly enough. Rans didn't quite understand that. Maybe it was because he was a war hero. He'd lost both of his legs in battle. What more would a man have to prove?

Rans had a lot to prove. Every day of his life he had half a mind to just run off and never be seen or heard from again. But he'd left home so many times now, nobody even looked up anymore. They knew that he couldn't get far; they knew that he'd be back.

With three bushel sacks loaded, each easily tallying in at better than fifty pounds, Rans grasped the handles on the wheelbarrow and began making his way perilously off the pouch, to the path, around the cabin and down the steep slope to the shed. It was a struggle. At any minute he could overbalance and have the entire haul spilled out on the ground. He was determined not to do that.

The cessation of hammer blows indicated that Collier was watching him. It was extremely difficult to appear unburdened and unconcerned while hefting a load that weighed more than he did.

He reached the shed entrance without incident and gratefully set the wheelbarrow down on its back legs. The morning was still cool, but his small, sturdy body was slick with sweat. He managed, just barely, not to sigh with relief. But he did take a deep breath before attempting to carry the sacks into the shed.

Moss Collier called out to him from the roof. "If that's too much for you," he said, "get Clara or Eulie to help you, or wait until I'm finished here."

Rans didn't even dignify the suggestion with a response. He would not wait and he would never ask for help. With his jaw set tightly and anger pulsing through his veins, he half lifted, half slid the first sack onto the shed's dirt floor, then dragged it across the room into place. He hated the insufferable clod that was Eulie's husband. He completely hated him, Rans decided. He wasn't about to be treated this way much longer.

His fury made the work go faster. In just a couple of minutes he'd stacked the grain in the far corner and was headed back up the slope to the cabin.

Someday, he swore to himself, someday he'd run away for good. Someday he'd run away and never, ever look back. That's what he wanted, he decided. He wanted to go to a place so far away that no one would know his name or his father's. Someplace where they would have never heard of the Sweetwood. Somewhere he could be the man that he knew he could be, that he must be. Moss Collier didn't believe he could be a man. Moss Collier didn't respect him. Well, he'd be dad-blasted if he was going to respect Moss Collier.

Why was he even working for the man? There was no law that said he had to. He could leave today. Mr. Leight would take him in. Mr. Leight would give him work and treat him with respect. And Moss Collier wouldn't even care. Of course, Eulie would. But he was practically grown. It was past the time for him to take his orders from his older sister.

That thought was in his mind as he entered the cabin for another load. His eyes were drawn to the strongbox beneath the corner of the bed on the far side of the room.

Rans glanced back guiltily toward the doorway. He was only looking. There could hardly be any harm in looking.

He dropped to his knees and pulled the box out from its hiding place. The name carved into the top of the box declared without question that it was someone's personal property. He undid the latch and carefully opened the lid.

On top lay a frayed, yellowed pamphlet that he pushed aside with unconcern. Beneath it, shiny and well oiled, was the blued nickel .44 Frontier Colt. The sight of it alone was enough to take a boy's breath away.

Reverently he picked up the heavy gun, the cold metal a sharp contrast to his sweaty palm. He had never held a handgun before. He hunted with his father's old Spencer. And he'd fired a Winchester a time or two. But before this moment, no revolver or pistol had ever crossed his path. He snapped open the loading gate and spun the cylinder, assuring himself that it was not loaded. Closing it up once more, he held it in his right hand and balanced it on his left arm as he squeezed one eye shut and aimed the piece at the fireplace, lining up a particular chipped hearthstone in the sights. With his thumb he pulled back the hammer until it cocked. He curled his forefinger around the trigger and slowly pulled it tight. The hammer snapped with a loud click.

"Bam!" Rans said aloud.

It was, in its own way, a very satisfying sound.

Rans held the gun admiringly, stroking the shiny finish and imagining himself carrying the same. He glanced down into the strongbox once more. There was a small blue and white box. Rans lifted it out, knowing what it was. He wasn't much for reading, but he recognized the name Winchester on the top and the number 1873. Inside, one hundred cartridges waited to be loaded into the six chambers in the cylinder. He fished one out, opened the loading gate again and slid it into place. He snapped the cylinder back and aimed at the hearth once more. This time, however, he neither cocked nor fired. The knowledge that he could seemed powerful enough.

"Bam! Bam! Bambam! Bam!"

He pointed at different objects and pretended to be firing around the room. He was gleeful and almost giddy. When he finally got out of this place, he decided, the first thing he would get for himself was a gun just like this one.

He glanced guiltily at the doorway once more. It sure wouldn't do to be caught. Momentarily, he imagined Moss Collier, his dreaded enemy, stepping into the cabin. Rans would turn, aim straight for his chest, and put a bullet right through his black heart.

The thought was a sobering one. He didn't like Collier, but he was Eulie's husband. His thoughts were wicked. But he didn't mean them, of course, he reminded himself. He would never hurt anybody. He'd never use a gun against a man unless it was self-defense.

More subdued, he removed the cartridge from the gun and returned it to the box. Reluctantly, he put the Frontier .44 inside as well.

It clinked against the contents of a small canvas bag. Curious, Rans reached for the sack. It was a money pouch and very heavy. He set it upon his lap and undid the drawstrings to open it up.

Rans glanced inside and gave a long whistle. There was more money in there than he'd ever seen in his life. He dug his hand inside, running his fingers through the coins as if they were cool water. Moss Collier was rich! The thought was both thrilling and disconcerting. Why would anyone need so much cash money? How could a farmer ever accumulate such a sum?

It was a puzzle, for certain, but not one he need spend time ruminating about. Rans was tempted to pour it out on the floor and examine it, but he was afraid that a stray coin might roll under the bed and get away from him. There was so much money that one would think that a coin or two wouldn't matter, but Rans was pretty sure that a man like Moss Collier would know the count of it to the penny.

Rans put the money sack back into the box and pushed it back under the bed.

He rose to his feet. The day suddenly seemed brighter and work more of an adventure. Dutifully, he began loading the grain sacks upon the wheelbarrow once more.

14

EULIE deliberately put a spring in her step and a smile on her face. Her life was perfect, wonderful, everything she'd always wanted. She was determined to enjoy it, no matter how miserable she was.

Now that the shed had a new roof and the grain and feed were stored down there, she had moved every stick, stone, and whatisit in the cabin out into the yard. Her sleeves rolled up and her hair wild, she was scrubbing down the old place from ceiling beams to floor joists.

The past three weeks in the new home had been trying, to say the least. She had, for so very long, tried to reunite her brother and sisters. Now it had finally happened, and her ungrateful siblings no longer cared. It was like trying to keep a family together with boss ball thread.

Clara was so calf-eyed and stupid over that ugly Bug that she was hardly even tolerable as a companion. He showed up now nearly every night, and the two would sit together on the porch, rarely speaking, while they mooned over each other and Rans talked their ears off. She had always been such a good worker. Now she forgot nearly everything she was told. That very morning she'd scorched the husband-man's good shirt so badly he'd never be able to take his jacket off in public again.

Eulie dipped her brush in the bucket of lye water and continued her scrubbing. She suspected that the last time the corners were cleaned out of this house was when Moss's mother had done the job. Ten years of bachelor living really showed—and smelled.

So Clara wanted to marry. She wanted to up and leave the home that Eulie had finally gotten for her. And she wasn't the only one. The twins were so excited about working with Miz Patch again, it was almost as if they were trying to wish the summer away so that it would be fall. The way those two were talking, as soon as the garden was in and the grain shocked they'd be going over to the widow's place to weave until spring.

Eulie shook her head. Learning the loom and patterns from Miz Patch was an honor. Having a fine weaver was a great asset to a family, even to a community. Although most women could work the loom in some form of fashion, most of it plain-weave tabby. The secrets, shortcuts, and superior skills of weaving were lessons usually passed from mother to daughter. Therefore, the finest weavers, those most prized and respected, tended to run in families. To have the Toby family acquire such knowledge would be a boon today as well as a dozen generations down the line. But not having the twins underfoot every day would make it feel like the family was not together anymore.

Eulie was scrubbing down the corner where Uncle Jeptha's bed usually sat. She sniffed the air and frowned. Even with all the furniture and bedding gone from the room, she could still smell the man. The stench of his unwashed body had apparently permeated the very walls of the cabin. Eulie tutted to herself. That just couldn't go on indefinitely.

With Clara gone and married and the twins working with Miz Patch, the winter would be a long one for her and Rans and Minnie.

The thought of Minnie gave her a long pause and a pang of frustration. What had that foolish Judith Pierce been thinking? Eulie wasn't so upset about her wanting Minnie. For all that the little girl was laggard and lazy, she was sweet and cute and lovable. Of course a childless woman would be eager to have her. Eulie didn't fault her for that. But telling her the plans before she was certain that they would not go awry was more than foolish, it was cruel. Little Minnie got set upon the idea and now her girlish heart was near-broken.

"She'll get over it," Eulie told herself aloud, hoping for the hundredth time that it was true. Living was full of disappointments, even tragedies, and the youngest always seemed to adapt to them easiest. But Eulie knew from her own life that adapting was not the same as dismissing. Hurts could mark a child, often more strongly and permanently than her elders. No one wanted to see Little Minnie hurt.

The crying and whining didn't bother Eulie much. She was accustomed to her sister using both tactics to get her way. But watching the child as she played or worked or talked, Eulie could see that the sparkle had unmistakably gone out of her eyes and a near-melancholy had settled about her like a cloak.

Eulie had no idea how to change that. At long last the Toby family was able to offer security. But to keep it would require constant vigilance, hard work, and a share of good luck. The daughter of Enoch Pierce would never want for anything in life and would have no care from whence her good fortune sprang. Eulie couldn't give her the pretty dresses and dolls that the Pierces could. She couldn't offer an acquaintance with town or an education of any kind. Minnie would not grow up with two parents devoted to her. Eulie was only her sister, and she couldn't in all honesty say that she'd done such a fine job of raising Minnie so far. Once Moss went west, they would be on their own again. And any resemblance to a typical family would disappear. She couldn't even make Minnie the center of attention. In a large household the focus was always shifting.

In every way that people would normally judge such things, the Pierces offered a better life for Minnie than she would get on Barnes Ridge. But she wouldn't be with her family. And that was the most important thing.

At least, it was the most important thing to Eulie.

She was thoughtful as she continued scrubbing down the walls, stripping years of grime and chimney smoke from the weathered wood.

Not everybody thought the way Eulie did about things. That was not a completely new idea for her. She'd always tried to see the best in the world. Rans was always expecting the worse. Eulie realized that he looked at things differently than she did, but she'd just always believed that he was wrong.

That's what she'd thought of Moss Collier as well. Because he had wanted to leave, he had planned not to marry. Eulie had simply thought that his being alone was wrong, and she had forced him into wedlock.

But she was beginning to change her way of thinking about things now. It was like Moss talking about his Texas, flat plains of grass and shrub as far as the eye could see. It was so unlike the coves and balds of the mountains around her. But it wasn't that the other land should be seen as good or not good. It was just different.

When Eulie looked at this farm on Barnes Ridge, she saw home and hearth, a place where she could be safe and fed and warm with those she loved. Moss Collier saw hardscrabble, poor soil and a life of drudgery he wanted to get away from. He'd called it a prison.

When Eulie looked at the people of the Sweetwood, she saw friends and neighbors and folks who cared about her. Her brother, Rans, saw gossips and backbiters and a herd of his betters set upon putting him in his place at every opportunity. There was as much truth in her brother's outlook on the world as there was in her own.

If Moss could think different and not be wrong, and Rans could think different and not be wrong, then, what Minnie thought about her life and her family might not be wrong either.

It was not a comforting realization.

"She'll grow out of it," Eulie told herself once more, but her conviction in the statement was definitely shaken.

Eulie stepped back from the wall and wiped the sweat from her brow as she surveyed her work. It looked much better than it had, but for all the effort she was putting in, it would have been easier to whitewash. Of course, whitewash would never have taken the smell out.

It was going to look a whole lot better and be a whole lot better. She'd get the cabin and the kitchen and the garden in shape. The husband-man was turning his hand to every other task on the place. It seemed that now that he'd decided to go, he wanted to take care of all the chores that would be difficult for her after he left. He worked in the field all day long and then at sundown he barely paused for dinner before coming up with some other job to be done. He was fence-mending, porch-patching, table-making and ditch-digging pretty much all the time. He never seemed to rest, not day or night. He must be very anxious indeed to get out West. But then again, he was not.

"I'm going to stay until we get the crop in," he told her one evening as they watched from a trustful distance as Bug and Clara sat on the porch together.

Moss was repairing a lug strap on the mule harness, his heavily gloved hands pushing the four-inch needle in and out of the dark, worn leather.

Eulie had looked at him, surprised. "Wouldn't it be easier for you to do your traveling when the weather is good?" she asked.

He'd shrugged. "A couple of months won't make any difference for me," he told her. "There is a lot of hard, tough work on this farm that Jeptha just ain't able to do. And that brother of yours is no bigger than a minute, though I have to admit he's a sturdy little fellow and you can't never fault him for not trying. I swear he'd attempt to throw an anvil across the river if I suggested that it ought to be done."

Eulie chuckled at the truth of his words.

"He curries your good favor," Eulie told him. "He wants you to think well of him."

"I do," Moss admitted. "But I don't think your brother cares all that much. Did you know he asked Bug if he could come back and work for him?"

"What?"

"I heard him myself offering, almost begging, to go back," Moss said.

"Well, I'll soon put a stop to that," Eulie declared.

"There is nothing to stop," he said.

She looked at her husband-man gratefully. "Thank you," she said. "I'm beholden to you for taking things in hand."

"Not me," Moss told her. "I didn't say a word." He gestured toward the porch. "It was Bug that set the boy straight. Told him that his first duty was to family. And that his family was here on Barnes Ridge."

Eulie glanced over at the young couple on the porch. As usual, they sat in comfortable silence together. Those two would never be described as big talkers. Clara was so pretty, like her mother before hard work and a bad marriage faded all her bloom. Bug was . . . Bug was not anyone Eulie would have chosen for her sister. Her sister deserved a finer, more handsome, more fun-loving fellow with lots of heart and a giving nature. Eulie would have chosen someone . . . someone like Moss.

She turned to the man beside her.

"Thank you for being so good to my family," she said. "I know it ain't been that easy to care for us, especially my brother."

Moss chuckled and shook his head.

"You Tobys aren't so bad," he assured her. "Even Rans is fairly tolerable, except for shooting off his mouth and being so dadblamed belligerent."

"Don't curse," Eulie scolded.

The husband-man rolled his eyes and shook his head before grinning at her. "That's the one thing I'm not going to miss about you, Mrs. Collier. When I get out West, I'm going to cuss a blue streak every morning, just so I don't forget what to say."

Eulie's heart gave a little flutter unexpectedly.

"You're going to miss me?" she asked him.

Moss became suddenly flushed and jittery. He accidentally jabbed himself in the thumb with the leather needle. He cursed again, this time so loudly the lovebirds on the porch even looked over.

Eulie smiled now, remembering it. The warm, fluttery feeling inside was back again. She reveled in it. Despite all that she had done to him, the husband-man obviously liked her. He'd liked her when he'd kissed her that day by the falls. And he liked her now that she was his wedded wife.

He liked her now that he was leaving.

That thought did not cheer her. Just a few weeks ago she'd hardly known the man. Now she had grown so accustomed to having him around, to talking with him, to laughing together. She was going to miss him when he was gone. It was as if he had become family. But then, that was what marriages did, she reminded herself. They added people to families.

The rattle of wheels against the porch boards caught her attention and she turned to the doorway. Uncle Jeptha sat there, his brow furrowed, a worn, yellowed pamphlet in his hand.

"What's this doing among my things?" he asked her.

"I found it on the floor," she answered. "It was so

old and faded, but kept so nice I thought it must be some of your war papers."

He shook his head.

"No, it belongs to Moss," he told her.

"Oh, I didn't know," Eulie said.

"Any of you Toby children read?" he asked.

"No," Eulie told him, shaking her head. "Judith Pierce says that Minnie can, but I never seen it."

Uncle Jeptha continued to look at the mysterious paper thoughtfully.

"Is something wrong?" she asked.

He was quiet for a moment and then shook his head.

"No, no, it's nothing," he said. "Moss keeps it in his strongbox. I'll put it back there."

He turned around and wheeled himself back off the porch and among the household goods that were spread everywhere around the yard.

Eulie followed him, chatting aimlessly about the cabin and the cleaning. Jeptha found the carved hardwood strongbox. As he opened it, he looked up at Eulie.

"Did you know that Moss keeps a gun and his money in here?" he asked.

Eulie was surprised, but not particularly curious. She had other things upon her mind.

"You should keep this under the edge of the bed," Jeptha continued. "And not let those children play in it or nothing."

She nodded, vaguely listening. Her youngers were not prone to rifle through other people's private property.

"There ain't nothing in here that's of interest to children," he continued.

"Uncle Jeptha," she interrupted, "I have a favor to ask of you."

The man looked up at her, puzzled.

"What is it?" he asked.

Eulie hesitated, screwing up her courage. It was not the kind of thing that a person generally asked of another.

"Uncle Jeptha," she said, "would you please take a bath?"

•

The kitchen was closed, warm, private. But that didn't make him any less jittery. It wasn't everyday that a man got buck-naked in front of two other people. Especially a man that had only ugly useless stumps where his legs were supposed to be.

The big pine washtub sat steaming with hot water, more of the same was heating on the hearth.

"I don't know why the boy has to be there," Jeptha had complained to Moss. "He's awful young to see the kind of sight he's likely to see."

"Eulie thinks that he needs to know how to help you," Moss answered. "After I'm . . . in case I'm not here, he needs to learn what to do."

Jeptha supposed that was right. Although he didn't see it as very important. If Moss was not there, Jeptha could just wait until he got back. Surely the woman didn't think that he'd need to bathe that often.

He didn't know what she thought or what she expected or what she wanted. All he knew was that two women whose opinions mattered to him had told him that he had a vile stench. Obviously that necessitated some course of action.

Moss poured a near cup full of powders in the

water and sloshed it around to make it dissolve.

"What's that?" Jeptha asked him.

"Poke root," he answered. "Eulie says that it's good for itch and will get rid of anything that pesters you—chiggers, mites."

"I ain't got no lice," he assured his nephew. "Except maybe for a few nits in my hair and beard."

"She sent sassafras oil for that," Moss told him. "And a fine-tooth comb."

Jeptha nodded. Reluctantly, self-consciously he began to remove his clothes. Carefully he folded his shirt.

"Just leave your clothes in a pile," Moss said. "Eulie's got the laundry fire going and she's going to boil them good and give them a wash as well."

"Then what am I going to put on when I get out?"

"She's got one of my work shirts here for you," Moss answered. "And my old trousers that were so much patched at the knees, she's just cut them off and seamed them together at the end. She's made you some underwear, too. Cotton flannels, they're real soft."

Jeptha glanced over at his new wardrobe, feeling a little threatened. Getting clean and dressing in fresh clothes seemed almost too big a step for one day. He'd rather face gunfire. But he'd promised to do it.

Shirtless, he fidgeted with the buttons on the front of his trousers. Rocking left to right, he eased them down over his hips and beyond the stumps of his legs. He was naked.

"All right," he said.

"Rans, squat down and let him put his arm around you," Moss said.

The boy did as he was told. Moss offered his own shoulder on the right. They lifted him up and lowered him slowly into the bath.

Jeptha gasped as his flesh came into contact with the hot water. It was startling at first, but it felt good. It felt very, very good.

The washtub was just deep enough for him to sit with the water shoulder-high. As a young man, his legs would have hung uncomfortably over the side. That was no longer a problem.

"You want one over the top?" Moss asked, holding a full bucket in his hand.

Jeptha nodded. A half minute later a gallon of water splashed down upon his head, drenching his hair, face, and beard. He wiped the excess out of his eyes.

Moss moved a chair up next to the tub.

"Here's your soap and brush and the sassafras oil," he told him. "Eulie said that once your hair is clean rub it in real thorough and then drag the comb through it until every nit and tangle is out. Let it set for a while before you rinse it."

"I can do that," Jeptha agreed.

"Do you want my razor?" Moss asked.

Jeptha fingered his beard. It was thick and coarse, and wet it hung down near his belly button.

"I don't want to have to start shaving again," he answered. "Why don't you just bring me some shears and I'll trim it short."

Moss nodded and reached down to pick up the dirty clothes.

"We'll leave you to your solitude, then," he said.

He walked toward the door. The boy hesitated.

"You think we should leave him alone like that?" Rans whispered. "What if he tips over and cain't get back up?"

"He's sitting down," Moss answered, his tone impatient and superior. "He's no more likely to tip over in the tub than he is in his cart."

Jeptha glanced over at young Rans. His cheeks were bright red with the humiliation of the setdown.

"I'm pretty steady here," Jeptha told him, more kindly. "If I get into trouble, I'll holler so loud they'll be able to hear me down at the meetinghouse."

Rans acknowledged his words and left with Moss.

Jeptha picked up the dark yellow soap and started rubbing his head. The cake must have had a good measure of rosin, because it lathered up better than he expected. He dug his fingers into his thinning hair, scrubbing his scalp with rough, determined motions. He slid down in the tub to rinse the soap out. He was surprised at how whole he felt. The buoyancy of the water gave him more stability, not less. It felt almost as if he had legs once more.

The sassafras oil smelled slightly sweet as he furrowed it through his hair. It was pleasant and almost comforting. The fine-tooth comb, however, was not. Jeptha pulled and worked at the mats and tangles, wishing he had the shears already. He'd just cut himself bald-headed.

Finally, when the comb would pass unhindered through every lock of hair on his head, he eased back with his neck against the edge of the washtub and relaxed. Eulie said the oil needed to soak in. He was willing to allow it to do so. And rest up a minute before he washed.

He'd missed this, he realized. He'd missed this very innocent pleasure of being clean and alive. He remembered a different sense of it from the war. The field hospital may have known nothing about saving gangrenous limbs, but they sure had a bent toward cleanliness. Soap and water was their main cure for everything. Perhaps that was why he had given it up without a fuss. It was tied to too many bad memories.

But there were good memories as well. He closed his eyes lazily and, contented, he allowed his thoughts to wander. Saturday nights when he was a boy, he and all his brothers washed in the river. Truly it was more swimming than washing, and more horseplay than anything else. He and Nils frequently ganged up on Zack with the intent of drowning the pesky baby brother. They never had, but they had sure had him come up sputtering a time or two, mad enough to chew splinters.

A slight chuckle escaped Jeptha's throat. The sound of it was so rare and unexpected. He tried never to conjure up the past in waking hours. It was horrible enough to live it in sleep. But by avoiding the bad memories, he had let go of the good ones as well. And he missed them. He missed the recollections almost as much as he missed his family.

One single tear escaped from his eye and coursed its way down his cheek.

"Sary," he whispered aloud. And saw her in his mind as she was then, fresh-faced and bright-eyed.

He'd said good-bye to her a dozen times, each one more impassioned than the last. But in the wee hours of that morning he'd meant to leave he'd sneaked over to her father's farm to see her again one more time.

He'd tossed a handful of gravel against the back wall, and five minutes later she was in his arms.

The night had a slight chill, but Sary had come to him in her josey. Her legs and arms bare, he was forced to embrace her to keep her warm.

"Where is your wrapper?" he'd asked her. "The air is cold."

"The world is cold," she answered. "And it will be every night and every day that you are gone from my arms."

He hadn't meant to make love to her. He had thought to wait until he returned, until he could offer her marriage. If he didn't come back—and that thought had occurred to him—he didn't want her to be ruined. He didn't want her to be forced to explain on her wedding night why she came to her husband no virgin. He wanted her to live happy, to be happy, even if it could never be with him.

He supposed that she had been. Sary had found happiness with another man. She had married elsewhere and undoubtedly she had managed to explain to her husband on her wedding night why she had not been chaste, why he was not her first.

Jeptha had never had to explain himself to anyone, ever. That one woman, that one night, was all he had ever known of life's sexual pleasures. It was the only carnal knowledge he possessed. But it had been enough to sustain his love for her for more than twenty years.

He sighed and sank lower in the washtub as he recalled the glow of her fair skin in the moonlight, her hair tousled and spread out upon the ground around her like a halo of passion. She sighed and whimpered and pleaded for his touch as she declared her love for him. He answered her in word and in deed.

Her breasts were small, barely a handful, but they were high, well-formed and topped with hard pink nipples. He toyed with them and tasted them and relished their texture against his tongue. Her young, firm body was beautifully exposed to him as he tucked the thin longcloth josey around her collar.

Just lying atop her, feeling her flesh against his flesh, that alone was enough almost. Almost.

He parted her thighs with near-reverence, marveling at the softness of her skin and the enticing redolence of her desire.

"I don't want to hurt you, Sary," he told her, as he hesitated upon her threshold.

She was beyond caring.

"Love me, Jeptha," she whispered. "Love me now, tonight, for all time."

She grasped his buttocks, her gentle hands urging him forward, her fingernails digging greedily into his flesh. The sensation nearly unmanned him as he pressed himself inside the hot, narrow opening of her body.

It was like nothing that he had imagined on sleepless summer nights. Then he had thought lovemaking to be only physical, sensual. He discovered it was spiritual as well. The joining of man and woman, two as one, just as heaven intended it to be. He had to bite his own lip to keep from crying out in the intensity of it, emotion, sensation.

He confronted the last impediment of her body to his own. He struggled against his need, his imperative to press on. Rigid with self-control, he tried to ease through slowly, gently, to minimize the pain.

Sary would have none of it. She wrapped her legs around his waist, impelling him forward. She gasped when he tore through the barrier, but she did not flinch from him or draw back. She urged him on until he was buried full measure inside her.

"I love you, Sary," he had whispered to her then. "I love you this minute and I will love you until the day I die."

He began to move then. At first just barely rocking, trying to be careful, considerate. Then he moved in long, slow strokes in and out, in and out, gathering speed and response as their passion spiraled. Her movements beneath him were driven by need, unschooled, and shadowed by the lingering discomfort of her newly opened body. Together they were awkward at first, impatient, two bodies craving separately and unsatisfied. Then, as they found their commensurate rhythm, they moved together in a harmony that edged them further and further toward all that was human and earthly. Two people, they became one. Striving, struggling, moving, they spoke words of love, of desire, of ageless, timeless, indestructible yearning. And they spoke not at all.

As they approached the summit, the heat between them sparked a blaze that became an inferno, a pyre upon which all former understanding of what it meant to be man, woman, and human was incinerated to ash.

As Jeptha felt the essence of him, his line, his name, his future, gush from him in a hot flood of total fulfillment, absolute completion, he cried out her name.

"Sary!"

The door to the kitchen opened and the boy, Rans,

came charging in carrying shears and a shaving mirror.

Jeptha jerked upright in the washtub, but could do nothing to hide the huge, throbbing erection that had risen with the enticement of ardent memory and now hung, thick and aching, between the stubs of his legs. He could not allow the boy to see such a thing, but the murky bathwater was not sufficient to hide the spectacle.

Unable to come up with any other quick course of action, Jeptha lashed out.

"Dangnation!" he hollered. "Cain't a man even bathe in private in this household anymore?"

Rans froze in place, cut short by the angry venom in Jeptha's voice.

"I just brought you the things that you asked for," the boy answered defensively.

"Well, leave them on the chair and get out," Jeptha said a little less harshly as he used one arm in an attempt to cover himself.

"Fine," Rans said as he slammed the articles upon the chair with enough force to crack the glass in the nickel-framed shaving mirror. "If you need anything else, get it yourself."

The boy stormed out and Jeptha glanced after him, inwardly cursing. He was a selfish, bitter, legless cripple. Young Rans was, in his way, as wounded as Jeptha himself. He saw slights where none existed and took too seriously the ones that did. The boy had his own pain; he didn't need Jeptha's. Nobody needed Jeptha's. Not even Jeptha himself.

"I've been such a fool," he said aloud, the admission hard-won.

15

PREACHER Thompson's four-week circuit kept him away from the Sweetwood for three Sundays a month. Services were conducted without him, of course, led by his wife or one of the deacons. But the fact was, most people didn't show up except when the preacher did. And that made the monthly Preaching Sunday a very special occasion.

The morning was cool and fragrant and heavy with dew. Eulie was unflappably cheerful and very excited. She was running around like a chicken with its head cut off trying to get everyone ready to go.

"It's our first time to attend church as a family," she said. Then, momentarily puzzled at her own statement, she changed her wording. "Well, our first time as a new family," she tried. But that didn't suit her either. "Well, it is the first time we've gone with you, Moss Collier," she declared finally.

Moss grinned at her tolerantly. He didn't really want to go. He had never been much of a churchgoer, and although the pounding had taken most of the sting out of the shotgun wedding, he was still a little embarrassed. Especially since he knew that soon he'd be leaving.

But it appeared to be so important to her that he washed and shaved and put on his good shirt, which now sported a big scorch mark on the back, and his dress coat.

The youngers stood in a line in front of the cabin awaiting inspection. Dressed in their go-to-meeting clothes, Clara and Rans carried their shoes and stockings, unwilling to waste the precious leather on the hard-packed trail between the ridge and the meetinghouse. The twins had none, but were content to be barefoot. Little Minnie wore her fancy kid boots as if the world held an infinite supply of footwear for her.

Eulie did the traditional motherly check of hands and necks and ears. But she also gave reminders about smiles and noise and the use of *yes, ma'ams* and *no, sirs*.

Clara was as eager to attend the meeting as her sister. Undoubtedly she was expecting Bug to request permission to walk her home. Moss couldn't see how he would deny such a request, especially since the man had made his honorable intentions perfectly clear. But just the same, Eulie wouldn't like it.

The twins were clean and shined and identical, as usual.

Rans was typically surly.

Little Minnie was gussied up fancier than plain potatoes at a box supper. Eulie had taken a good deal of time with the girl. She had twisted the little girl's hair into a dozen big sausage curls and tied ribbons upon her at nearly every location. Still, Minnie was pouting, and there seemed no help for it.

"I want everyone on their best behavior," Eulie said to them. "And try not to get dirty."

The prospect was doubtful. It was to be a very long

day. And there were far too many potential disasters.

Red Tex was groomed and saddled and ready to ride, but he was also a little skittish of the big burlap sack tied to him that contained the clattering dinner plates and eating utensils of seven people. Nor did he like the three-quart stove pot that was suspended by a rope from his saddle horn. It contained the food, field peas with fatback, that they were taking as their part of the noon meal. It was obvious that Eulie did not like getting close to the big horse; still, she checked the lid on the pot a half dozen times to make certain it was secure. Preaching Sunday always included dinner-on-the-ground, a sort of picnic after the service. It gave opportunity to relax, to visit with neighbors, and to eat cooking that was not one's own.

"I wish I was bringing something from the garden," Eulie said to Moss. "Field peas seems like such a poor offering."

In truth, the easily grown legume was produced in great abundance and often shocked as animal feed. But they were perfectly good for human eating. Moss actually preferred them over tired old brown beans.

He waved away her concern. "If some people think themselves too high in the pecking order to eat plain," he said, "then it leaves more for the rest of us."

She laughed at his little joke.

"Everyone is about in the same shape," he continued. "The gardens are all up and going but not producing enough yet to make a difference on the table."

"But you know that someone will have gotten a real early start and will be coming with something grown fresh," she said.

Moss nodded. "Of course, there are always those

folks. They must plant their seedling by the fireplace in midwinter. They'll be serving summer squash before the rest of the Sweetwood gardens have spinach."

Eulie smiled at him and nodded in agreement. "And they always act like they are so surprised that no one else has anything coming up yet. As if they're producing early simply because they are living right."

Moss grinned at her. "Next month everything will be coming up and we'll eat fresh vegetables until our bellies ache."

It crossed his mind that he might not be here next month. He could be gone to Texas already. He could leave tomorrow if he set his mind to it.

No, he decided, he'd get the crop in and maybe wait until apple picking. There was really no hurry. He didn't want to leave Eulie in a lurch.

"All right," she asked in general. "Is everybody ready?"

There were nods all around.

"Then we'll—" Her words were cut off in midsentence.

"I'm ready."

They all turned to see Uncle Jeptha rolling his cart out of the cabin and across the porch. He was clean and dressed in his new clothes. His hair was cut and his beard trimmed. He looked to be almost a different person. Since Eulie had insisted upon his bathing, he'd kept himself neat and tidy. It was very curious, but Moss knew better than to say anything. The man was very touchy about it.

That first evening when he'd come to the supper table, the whole family was stunned into silence.

"Uncle Jeptha, you look wonderful," Eulie blurted

out finally. "You look so . . . so healthy and so . . . so much younger."

He prickled as if he'd been insulted.

"I'm forty-two years of age," he said snarling. "Just exactly how old did you think that I was?"

He'd continued to keep clean and be well-kept, but his disposition hadn't improved.

"You're going with us to the preaching?" Moss asked him. He tried to keep the stunned disbelief out of his question. In all his life, Uncle Jeptha had kept strictly to the homeplace. The furthermost he'd venture was the summit ridge or the fishing hole. And he avoided people almost entirely. To show up at Preaching Sunday was to put himself in the way of nearly every soul in the Sweetwood. And his opinion of God, religion, and churching in general, was not high.

"If I'm cleaned up and dressed up, I might as well go," Uncle Jeptha answered. "Besides, I want to see if that fool hound could really pull this cart down the mountain without killing me."

There was no reason to argue. Rans went for the harness, and the twins whistled for the dog. Within a few moments he was all hooked up and ready to go.

Moss mounted his horse. He loved the sense of height and power the animal gave him. There was also that exhilarating sensation of freedom. On Red Tex a man could travel to the ends of the earth.

The twins led the way on either side of the harnessed hound. Clara and Rans followed after them, Clara with her head in the clouds. Rans was unable to stick to the path, wandering into the weeds along the edges.

Moss slipped his heel out of the stirrup and offered his hand to Eulie.

"You can ride with me," he said.

She looked up at him, wide-eyed and dumbfounded.

"I didn't think Red Tex rode double," she said.

He felt sheepish and shrugged. "He's a big horse and you're a small woman. I don't think you'll break his back."

Eulie continued to look uncertain. She turned to her sister.

"Little Minnie," she said, "would you like to ride on the horse?"

The difficult child didn't even so much as lower her stubborn chin, but she marched right over to Red Tex, confident in her natural right to be the one to ride.

Eulie had to lift her up so that she could get her foot in the stirrup. Easily Moss put the child up behind him. Red Tex stirred, not liking it one bit. Moss wasn't fond of the arrangement either. It wasn't as if he required company, and he had never allowed anyone else to sit upon the valuable horse. But he'd wanted Eulie up beside him. In the month since their marriage, he had grown more than accustomed to her, he'd grown fond. He liked talking to her and laughing with her. The cheerfulness that he had found so disagreeable at first was now a welcome addition to a hardworking day.

He was also honest enough to admit to himself that he missed her nearness. Little Minnie's thin, girlish arms around him held no allure. But when he imagined Eulie up behind him, embracing him, her body close to his own, his heart beat a good deal faster.

For the good of their separate futures and Moss's own peace of mind, Eulie now shared the new bed he'd built with Minnie. Moss took his lonely nightly repose upon a floor pallet. But he remembered all too vividly the feel of his bride in his arms.

It wasn't that he wished to change their arrangement. He was leaving. It would not be right to put a child inside her. But he still longed for her nearness and the warmth of her touch.

Like most men who lived alone, he was plagued frequently with carnal desires. He had always managed to keep himself in control. He felt less in control in the last few weeks than he had in his entire life. Eulie had invaded his thoughts by day and his dreams by night. His body responded to that like a stallion penned up with a mare at breeding time.

He couldn't, shouldn't, do anything about it. But it was awfully nice just to be close to her.

He motioned her over. She approached carefully, clearly not pleased at the prospect of walking next to the big horse.

"I'm thinking to build you a root cellar," Moss said.

"A root cellar?" She seemed astounded at the suggestion. "We've always just buried our vegetables in a ditch. If you get them just under the ground, they don't usually freeze and they keep real well."

He nodded. Ditching the excess garden crop was as common a practice for putting by winter stores as canning, salting or smoking.

"But a root cellar would be better," he contended.

She couldn't deny it.

"The Knoxes have one," she told him. "Why they've got potatoes and yams in there that look as good as the day they were pulled from the ground."

"Then it's settled," Moss said. "I'll dig you a root cellar to keep your plenishments."

Eulie appeared both delighted and nonplussed.

"But that's so much work," she told him. Casting a surreptitious glance toward Minnie, she apparently deduced that the young girl wasn't paying any attention. "You've done so much already. I know that you must be anxious to . . . be doing what you've dreamed about."

He dismissed her objection.

"I've already got some timbers cut," he told her. "I can get Jeptha and your brother to help me with the boards. We can carve it out of the side of the ridge. It will mean a lot less digging and you'll be able to walk straight into it with no stairs to lug things up and down."

Her expression was filled with such open adoration that it almost made Moss uncomfortable. He didn't need to please her and needn't court her favorable opinion. He shouldn't be making her like him and depend upon him. But somehow he couldn't seem to help himself.

Her opinion was important to him. She was important to him.

Suddenly, Moss's eyes were drawn to the trail up ahead of them. A speckled fawn scrambled out of the brush. It was hard to say who was more startled, the young deer or the group of humans. The lanky little animal stared at them for one frightened moment before scampering away. She did not fail, however, to capture the attention of Old Hound, who, with a howl of thrilled announcement, took off after her.

Uncle Jeptha jerked valiantly upon the reins and managed to get the dog halted, but not before he tipped the cart, throwing Jeptha to the ground.

Moss dismounted off Red Tex in a rush and handed the horse's reins to Eulie as he hurried forward.

Jeptha lay on his back, looking up at the sky. He was still grasping the harness lines.

The children were gathered all around him. Moss knelt by his side with concern.

"Are you all right?" he asked.

Wearily, Jeptha pushed himself up into a sitting position.

"I wondered if that old hound would try to kill me," he said. "I guess it's a lot to expect of a hunting dog not to hunt."

"Maybe I should buy another goat," Moss said. "They are a lot easier to bridle."

Jeptha tutted and shook his head. "I don't want no dang goat around the place, eating the clothes off the line and climbing up on the roof. I'll teach the dog to take me, or I'll stay at home like I always have."

Moss righted the cart and Jeptha, unassisted, put his palms on the ground and raised himself up, hand-walking back to the trail. He struggled a little getting inside, but he managed all right.

It was a hard thing to watch, so Moss didn't. Uncle Jeptha's pride was monumental and his appetite for sympathy nonexistent. They never talked about what had happened. They had never discussed his missing legs, not even when Moss was a boy. He'd always known somehow that it was best just not to mention it.

The children seemed to understand the same thing. They neither gawked at him or tried to help. It was as if in the short time they had lived on Barnes Ridge they had come to understand the bitter, wounded man as well as Moss did himself.

Except for the boy, of course, who thought he was grown-up and knew everything there was to know and just blurted out whatever came to his mind.

"You know," Rans said to Jeptha as he gave him the lines. "We could make some straps for this cart, so if the dog took to running, at least you wouldn't fall out."

Moss rolled his eyes impatiently. He didn't bother to give time for Jeptha to answer.

"That's the most stupid idea I've ever heard," he told the boy too harshly. "If Uncle Jeptha were strapped into the cart he couldn't get out and the dog could drag him, might even kill him."

Rans looked up at him, his chin raised high and his eyes narrowed. Without a word he turned and ran down the path as fast as his feet would carry him.

Jeptha sighed loudly and looked up at Moss. There was more than a hint of censure in his expression.

"I didn't think the idea of being strapped in was all that bad," he said.

Moss felt the full force of his mistake. With Rans out of sight, there was no one to accept his apology but those gathered around him.

"I didn't mean to get onto the boy so," he admitted. "He's a good fellow and works hard and he tries to please. But he's got a chip on his shoulder as big as a boulder. Sometimes he just annoys me so much I act like a fool."

Jeptha nodded. "He annoys ye so much, Moss," he said, "because he's so much like ye."

The meetinghouse was filled, every bench occupied and a dozen young men standing in the back. Preacher

Thompson was waxing eloquent about the Hebrew children in the fiery furnace.

The preacher wrote his sermons on the days he was home and then delivered them on his circuit. By the time he returned to the Sweetwood he had given his exhortation three times and had honed each word and turn of phrase to its maximum effect.

The congregation could therefore personally discern the steely determination of Shadrach, Meshach, and Abednego willing to face the flames rather than deny their faith. They could also shiver in their own boots as King Nebuchadnezzar looked down into that furnace and spied, not three, but four men walking unburned in the flames.

Eulie paid only tacit attention to the message. She couldn't have been happier about just being there. This is what she had always dreamed about. Her family, one unit, conjoined and inseparable.

It was important to be together in this place, where her parents and grandparents once sang and worshiped as she did now. Where some day, far in the future, her own children would do the same.

That idea caught her up short. She wouldn't be having any children of her own, she recalled. Moss was leaving and she would live like a maiden lady all her life.

But she would have nieces and nephews, she reminded herself. The Tobys were obviously good breeders. For certain there would be nieces and nephews. She determinedly took comfort in that thought.

Her family, all neat and tidy, sat beside her on the bench. It hadn't been easy. The twins had asked to sit with Miz Patch, but took Eulie's refusal to allow it good-heartedly. The same could not be said for Little Minnie, who had gone running into Judith Pierce's arms the moment they arrived. Both the woman and the child tearfully begged to share the service from the Pierces' pew. Eulie would not even consider it and turned a cold heart to their pleas. Her family would sit together today, each and every one of them.

Even Rans, whom she feared was off on another snit, was hunched over, chin in hand, at the end of the bench. Uncle Jeptha was beside him, his cart in the aisle.

The man's appearance had caused considerable astonishment and speculation among the congregation. The rush of whispers began even as he pulled his cart up by the door and unhitched Old Hound. No one even spoke to him. Eulie thought that surely a man who had lived in the Sweetwood all his life would have someone come up to talk to him. But he looked neither to the left nor to the right, as if determined not to catch anybody's eye.

Rans and Moss lifted him in his cart up the meetinghouse steps. Eulie noticed that people took extravagant efforts to move around him at some distance, as if his incapacity were somehow contagious.

Even Preacher Thompson kept a goodly distance between them as he offered a greeting.

"Jeptha Barnes," he said. "It's good to see you in church. I hope this means that you've begun to contemplate where you will spend eternity."

Uncle Jeptha had to raise his chin high to look the man square in the face.

"I'm not contemplating it any more than usual," he answered.

Eulie leaned over to quietly question Moss in the seat beside her. He had been listening avidly to the message from the pulpit, and Eulie felt a twinge of guilt for distracting him.

"Could you believe Uncle Jeptha decided to come with us?" she asked.

Moss's widened his eyes to express his disbelief and he shook his head. Clearly he could not.

Eulie attempted to turn her attention back to the preaching, but couldn't manage it fully. This was what she had wanted. This is what she had prayed for and schemed for. And it had all come to pass.

Eulie's heart was filled with delighted gratitude. Her whole family living under one roof and attending church together at long last. She didn't add any extra joy for the presence of Moss and Uncle Jeptha. They were part of her family as well. She felt that without any sense of strangeness or uncertainty. They were her family, and it was as important to her to have them with her as one of the children.

The sermon ended, and the congregation noisily came to its feet as the hymn of invitation began:

"God is calling the prodigal,

Come without delay.

Hear his loving voice calling still."

Beside her, Eulie discovered that Moss had a fine baritone voice that blended beautifully. It was wonderful to stand beside his long lean masculine body. Just to be close to him. Close to the width of his shoulders and the strength of his hands, just to be close made her feel safe, protected, and somehow feminine. It was a heady sensation. Unexpected. And surprisingly bittersweet.

As Preacher Thompson gave the benediction, Eulie

slipped her palm into her husband's. It was probably not a good idea, but she just wanted the touch.

As the preacher pronounced the *Amen*, Moss gave her hand a slight squeeze. Eulie opened her eyes and looked up at him. They shared a quick smile. It was, she realized, one of those glances that married people share all the time and take no thought of. One that said merely, *I'm here. I'm here with you.*

The contact broke. The moment passed. The crowd began leaving. Jeptha waited to be last, as person after person stepped around him. Finally it was just them, just Eulie's family left in the church. And they began to make their way out.

Preacher Thompson stood in the doorway, shaking hands and asking questions about crops, fishing, Aunt Dinah's ague, or the price of corn.

He took Eulie's hand and leaned forward, quietly asking if she was satisfied with her marriage.

"Oh yes, very much," she insisted, feeling the heat of blush rise to her cheeks.

The preacher turned to Moss, who was right behind her.

"You look happier already," he said. "I promise you, Collier, once that baby comes into the world, you'll be glad you did the right thing."

Eulie felt an immediate overwhelming need to set the record straight. To confess all and explain how guiltless and victimized Moss Collier had been.

The husband-man, correctly sensing what was about to occur, herded her away from the doorway at near breakneck speed.

"I was just—" she began, but he cut her off.

"It's nobody's business but ours," he told her.

She could hardly fight the wisdom of that.

He left her at the bottom of the steps to go back and help Uncle Jeptha.

On either side of her for the next twenty feet stood lines of young men. The gauntlet, a tradition seemingly as old as the hills themselves, was the major source of love and marriage on the mountain. In a community with homesteads dotted miles apart and enough work to keep every pair of hands busy from morning to night, young folks had little time for meeting and getting to know potential mates. The gauntlet was a courting device, set up to remedy that.

All the single men in the congregation, from pimply-faced youths who'd yet to receive their full growth to aging bachelors not set upon a bride of their own, formed a narrow corridor through which every soul leaving church was forced to walk. The closeness made it possible to verbalize to even the most elusive of Sweetwood females the question of the day.

"May I see you home this evening?"

Because courting was basically a Sunday activity, this was, for most of the unmarried, the only contact with the opposite gender. After a few harmless walks on Preaching Sunday, a fellow might ask to sit other Sundays on her porch, usually with her entire family present. If her father got to know him and like him, he would eventually be allowed to pay court to the female of his choice. But it was no easy road. A young man had to be determined and brave to speak to a girl right in front of her father, who was more than likely looking daggers at some wet-behind-the-ears, worthless whippersnapper who had the audacity to speak up to his daughter.

And often, the fellows had to be persistent in the face of repeated rejection. Even if a girl had set her cap for a certain fellow, it was considered very smart among the young ladies to feign complete deafness for several weeks. An ardent, anxious, stammering farmer wearing his heart upon his sleeve couldn't tell whether the gal of his dreams was ignoring him because she didn't like him or ignoring him because she did.

Eulie had always gotten her share of invitations, although no one had ever pursued her consistently. Today there was not one word spoken to her. She walked through unmolested. She was a married woman now, no longer of any interest to gauntlet participants. It was a strange feeling, almost a rite of passage. The man she loved would never call out her name here. But then, Moss Collier had never once stood in the gauntlet. He had never sought a wife.

Up ahead of her, Bug had stopped Clara and spoken his invitation. Eulie watched her sister blush, appearing even prettier than usual as she agreed that indeed she would have no one else but Bug to walk her home.

Eulie wanted to roll her eyes in disgust. But somehow she could not. The two were shyly smiling at each other, beautiful Clara and ugly Bug. As he offered his arm and she took it, they appeared perfectly content and happy together.

They shared a quick glance into each other's eyes. Eulie was momentarily startled by the intensity of it. Clearly, these two people were in love with each other—a reality that was, for Eulie, difficult to fathom.

"They sure make a perfect couple, don't they?"

The words were spoken by Miz Patch, who came up

beside her. She had been waiting for the twins at the end of the gauntlet.

Eulie raised an eyebrow in surprise.

"A perfect couple?" Her tone was incredulous. "How can you think that? She's so pretty and he . . . he looks like a bug."

Miz Patch chuckled lightly and shook her head.

"Oh, I suspect it will even out as the years go by," she said. "Life is a long time. People change, especially on the outside. If you don't love the core of the person, the source of their soul that remains constant, then anything that happens can likely destroy your feelings. And some terrible things can happen in a life."

"You sound as if you speak from experience," Eulie said.

Miz Patch didn't reply.

"You must have loved your husband very much," Eulie continued.

Miz Patch glanced over at her, and her shiny brown eyes, normally so full of laughter, were somber and serious.

"Ezra Patchel was a fine, good man," she said. "I was honored that he allowed me to share his life and comfort him in his old age. Like you, I had done some things that many men would have found impossible to forgive."

Eulie was startled. Had Miz Patch lied publicly? Had she humiliated her husband? Had she trapped him as Eulie had? She couldn't imagine the dear woman doing any of those things and was intending to say so, but she saw that Miz Patch's attention was now focused upon the church door.

Eulie turned in that direction as well to see Rans

and Moss carrying Uncle Jeptha in his goat cart down the steps.

Everybody in the church yard was watching. But as soon as he was set safely upon the ground, each and every one of them turned away, unwilling to look.

"Why is everyone acting so strange to him?" Eulie asked.

"Because he is like a stranger to them," Miz Patch answered. "He purposely kept himself away, kept himself alone for twenty years. No one knows him."

"But surely he must have old friends here," she said. "People who knew him before."

Miz Patch shook her head negatively. "We pretty much lost everybody in the war," she replied. "Look around you. There are no men of middle years here, there are only old fellows and their grandsons.

Eulie's glance quickly swept the clearing and she realized that Miz Patch was right. It was as if a whole generation had been wiped away clean.

"Lem Pierce was too crippled up to go," Miz Patch continued. "Preacher Thompson was a chaplain and returned unharmed. The rest are all dead and buried long ago. We women are here, of course. Lots of spinsters in our group. And those of us who did wed, well, we married the fathers of the boys who stood in our gauntlet."

It was a melancholy realization that brought an unexpected tear to Eulie's eyes.

Miz Patch must have sensed her sorrow and turned to her. The woman's own expression changed immediately from wistful to matter-of-fact.

"Don't get all weepy on me now," she said. "It'll just give folks more cause for speculation."

Miz Patch was right, and so Eulie wiped her eyes and deliberately firmed the quivering of her lower lip.

"We've got to get this dinner set up before the young folks start chewing on the fence posts," she said.

16

THE dinner had been a big success. Eulie had yet to eat one bite, but every man and child had been adequately fed. The former were now ensconced together in little groups, talking hunting and crops or telling fish tales and outlandish stories. Those inclined to smoke or jaw or dip moved to the far edges of the clearing. Preacher Thompson did not approve of tobacco, and anything he did not make allowances for during the week, he doubly didn't on Sunday. The men with the habit didn't allow the preacher's opinion to even slow them down, but just to save themselves from a potential lecture, they did move out of the pastor's immediate line of vision.

The older children, eternally full of energy, scampered in and out of the men's discussions and tore through the edge of the woods with great noise and plenty of laughter. Their younger counterparts, with bellies pleasantly full, napped upon quilt pallets laid out in a dozen locations throughout the yard.

"You'd best get yourself something to eat," Myrtle Browning said to her. "Before the food gets so cold it freezes up completely."

Eulie smiled at the little joke and could have suggested the same to Mrs. Browning, though apparently even among the married women there was a careful hierarchy of who ate first. Or rather, who ate last. The most important woman among them would always be saved the dregs.

Eulie, having been responsible for her family from girlhood, had always thought herself to be an equal among the women. It was a surprise, and not wholly a pleasant one, to discover that as an unmarried female, she been kept apart. She had, in some sense, been isolated from the inner circle. Now she was unexpectedly welcomed with open arms. Her sister, Clara, had been handed her plate of food and shooed on her way, but Eulie was now expected to sit among the marrieds as one of them. It was a strange and heady feeling to be a part at last.

Eulie filled her plate and took her place on the ground. There were several empty chairs around, but she correctly ignored them. The eldest were still standing. A young woman, like Eulie, couldn't think about a chair until they were all seated. The exception to this was Lulu Patchel, who was sat in a ladderback rocker with her new baby at her breast. The shapeless Mother Hubbard she wore had hidden button plackets in the side seams to allow her to bare her breast without any excess of fleshly exposure.

The baby was barely six weeks of age, and this was the first time most had seen him. He was almost perfectly bald, except for one straw-colored swirl at the crown of his head.

"What's his name?" Eulie asked.

Lulu shrugged. "He ain't got one yet, I reckon," she answered. "I'm just calling him 'the baby' for now."

"For mercy sakes, Lulu," Miz Patch said as she popped a bite of bread in the young woman's mouth. "It's time to put your mind to it. The other children will get used to calling him Baby and then he'll be thirty years old and shamefaced to hear his family holler for him."

"It ain't that easy," Lulu declared with a full mouth. "The first one you got a name all picked out 'cause you've been waiting all your life. The second one, well, that one you name after his daddy. My third one was a girl, so I was happy to pick out something pretty. But now here's another boy. They ain't hardly nothing left to call him."

"Did you look through the Good Book, like I told you?"

Lulu nodded. "I did. And I even found a name I thought was real high-sounding, but Jonah didn't like it."

"What was it?" Miz Patch asked.

"Verily," she answered. "Jonah said it sounded like a girl's name. But I told him that Jesus was talking with his disciples and said, 'Verily I say unto you.' There weren't no women disciples, so Verily had to be the name of one of the men."

There was no arguing that.

"I swear my back is near broke," Gertie Samson complained as she seated herself across from Eulie. "My bones are so sore I can hardly get up and down."

"What you been doing, Gertie?" Dora Pusser asked. "It's too early to chop cotton."

"Chopping cotton would be a treat," Gertie answered her. "I been switching that Dudley from morning to night. I'm plumb wore out from the effort."

"Young Dudley ain't a-minding ye?" Garda June, Gertie's mother-in-law, asked in surprise as she, too, sat down to eat.

"Not minding me don't even commence to tell it," Gertie exclaimed. "That boy's mouth has turned so fresh, it's all I can do not to slap it off his face. I don't know what's wrong with him."

"How old is Dudley now?" Myrtle Browning asked as she brought her plate to join them.

"He's just turned twelve," the boy's mother answered.

"Well, that's what's wrong with him," Myrtle told her.

A titter of knowing laughter filtered among the older women.

"I think Myrtle's got the right of it," Miz Patch said. "It a pure misery for a boy trying to turn into a man. And if he's going to suffer, he's sure to want his mama and daddy to suffer right along with him."

"He's always been such a good boy," Dudley's grandmother defended, looking accusingly at her daughter-in-law. "I've never had a lick of trouble with him."

The women ignored Garda June's observation. Grandparents could only rarely be counted upon for a realistic appraisal of their descendants.

"He'll get past this," Mrs. Thompson, the preacher's wife, assured her. "You just have to keep steadfast and be patient."

"How long is it going to last?" Gertie asked.

"About ten years, give or take a month or two," Dora answered.

Mrs. Pusser's words brought howls of laughter from the women. Her two boys were the wildest in the Sweetwood. In their middle twenties already, neither showed any evidence of straightening up or settling down.

"So what am I going to do in the meantime?" Gertie asked them. "I can't go on switching the tar out of him. He's getting so big, he don't even mind it. And considering the condition of my back, I think it actually does hurt me more than it hurts him."

"Keep a bucket of cold water at the ready," Myrtle suggested. "When he starts acting up, you just give him a good dousing."

"Do you think that'll work?" Gertie asked.

"My mama used to swear by cold water on my brothers," she told her. "And it sure never done my own boys no harm, as far as I could tell."

Gradually more women joined the circle until nearly every family in the Sweetwood was represented.

"I think he's et his fill," Lulu said finally. "Mother Samson, you want to burp him for me?"

Garda June moved to put down her plate, but Miz Patch stayed her hand.

"Let Eulie do it," Miz Patch said. "She ain't held the baby yet."

Eulie was startled at the suggestion, but dutifully put down her plate and held out her arms for the small, sleepy child.

She lay the baby high upon her left shoulder and rhythmically patted him on his tiny back. The little body pressed close to her own was amazingly warm and sweet. Eulie felt a jolt in her heart for this child. Moss was leaving, and there would never be one of her own. She had not thought about what joy she'd be giving up. It came home to her now in the soft sweetness of a tiny human form.

"It's said to bring good luck," Miz Patch said to her. "You and Moss are going to want a family. They say if you hold another woman's baby you'll have one of your own within a year's time."

Mrs. Thompson looked up startled. "But isn't she . . . I mean . . . I understood that you were already on the nest."

Eulie felt two spots of color flame up on her cheeks. Was it confession time? Must she tell all?

The decision was taken out of her hands as Miz Patch spoke.

"It seems that our Eulie was mistaken about that," she said. "And we have none but ourselves to blame."

The news was greeted with general astonishment, and Miz Patch's accusation even more so.

"How are we to blame?" Garda June asked.

Miz Patch had risen to her feet and was lording over them imposingly.

"Eulie, here, was motherless among us," she said. "Who would tell her how the mare gets a foal? Or how a happy rooster keeps the hens a-laying? With her mother buried in the ground, it was our duty to explain it to her, but not a one of us did. The poor ignorant girl mistook what a little sparking and spooning could do to a gal's figure."

Wishing that the earth would open up and swallow her, Eulie kept her eyes to the ground as Miz Patch continued to berate the women for not taking better care of her education.

"I've spoken to Clara, myself," Miz Patch announced. "But we all need to remember to see to the twins and Little Minnie when the time comes."

"Do you mean to tell me," Mrs. Thompson said

incredulously, "that all the time Moss Collier was swearing that he hadn't, he really hadn't."

"Eulie?" Miz Patch asked.

She raised her eyes. All the women were looking at her. She couldn't quite believe, awaiting her reply. Miz Patch was making it easy. She'd blurred the truth, taken on Eulie's lie and made it almost too easy.

"He hadn't," she said finally.

She almost corrected her answer to "He hasn't," which was the full truth, but Miz Patch spoke up too quickly.

"It surely shows the truth that the Lord moves in mysterious ways," she quoted. "If we'd talked to Eulie like we should, she'd never had accused Moss Collier. And with that wanderlust of his, he'd have never taken a bride."

"It's hard to believe it to be a misunderstanding," Mrs. Thompson reflected.

"He must have been madder than a thousand furies," Garda June stated with near-disbelief.

"But he sure seems pretty pleased with himself now," Miz Patch pointed out. "I do think it might be good to mention the truth to the menfolk in private. The story is bound to come out one way or another."

There were nods of agreement.

"So it all turned out for the best," Lulu said in a dreamy, almost wistful tone.

"It certainly seems so," Myrtle said, looking at Eulie almost accusingly. "Though how a woman could make such a foolish mistake is what I don't know."

"I wouldn't worry too much about babies the first year," Miz Patch told her, cleverly turning the subject of the conversation. "Moss Collier will get one on you soon enough."

"She could be carrying already," Dora Pusser pointed out. "They've been married a month."

"You think you might be?" Garda June asked.

"Oh no," Eulie answered. Then realized immediately that she had answered far too quickly. Obviously it was a question whose answer required some consideration.

The only thing she knew about . . . shagging . . . or being obedient to her husband was the desire she felt in her husband's arms and what she'd been told. She racked her brains for something to say, some explanation of why she was so certain. She knew animals had certain seasons. But people seem to have their children at all times of the year. A woman could be barren, like Judith Pierce, but that wasn't a thing that could be known so early. Eulie thought and thought and thought and finally came up with one fact she'd heard spoken by her Moss Collier.

"I can't be carrying. My husband-man told me that a woman can't get a baby the first time," she announced.

Her words, rather than hushing the women's questions, sent the group into a gaggle of disbelief.

Miz Patch widened her eyes expressively as if to warn Eulie that she'd made a mistake. Eulie had no idea how to fix it. Fortunately, Miz Patch came to the rescue.

"Well, that story is an old wives' tale," she said, a bit more loudly that was rightly necessary. "I don't know why young people persist in believing it. But you're just as likely to get a baby the first time as the hundred and first. Ain't that right, Garda June? Didn't you get with child on your wedding night?"

Garda June was whispering too avidly to have even heard the question. And the subject simply would not be turned.

"Do you mean," Gertie questioned, "that in a whole month of marriage you two have only been together as man and wife one time?"

The woman's incredulity was equally discernible on the faces of the others present. Eulie had gotten it wrong. She had made it worse. She had never been good at lying and it was getting her in trouble again. But somehow she couldn't force the truth from her lips. It was private, between the two of them. She could not, should not, share it. If she told part of it, she might tell all of it. And Moss didn't want her to do that.

"Oh!" Eulie feigned surprise. "I thought he meant the first time each night."

Miz Patch gasped, but gamely covered it with a cough.

Fortunately, Eulie was saved from the need of making further explanation by the very loud and satisfied belch that emanated from the tiny baby.

All the women made congratulatory *ooohs* and *ahhhs*, as if the child's ability to burp were the most amazing feat they had ever witnessed.

Every female present was looking at the baby, except one. Judith Pierce sat silently at the far end of the circle. She had obviously just finished her meal and was wiping her mouth with a dainty handkerchief.

Eulie, wishing desperately to turn the attention away from herself, and also still smarting a good deal from Mrs. Pierce's unwanted intrusion into her family, seized upon the opportunity presented.

"If holding a new baby can get you with child, shouldn't Judith Pierce hold the baby?" she said.

Around her the women looked surprised, perhaps even embarrassed. It seemed that they, too, had given up on the Pierces' ever producing a child.

Judith's face was pale and perfectly blank, almost as if she had no feelings on the matter at all.

"Of course Judith should hold the baby," Miz Patch said.

She took the child from Eulie and carried him across the circle to lay him in Mrs. Pierce's arms.

Judith looked down at the child. He was looking up at her, blue eyes wide open, little fists flailing, his tiny rosebud mouth making the sweetest baby sounds.

Mrs. Pierce was stone-faced.

Eulie was very surprised and curious at her behavior. Everybody who held the baby cooed and smiled at him. Judith was supposed to be so wild for a child of her own, yet, she just gazed at him with no expression at all.

"He's been a real good baby," Lulu told them. "I have to give him that. He's a lot more placid than my others have been. And he's not had so much as a night of colic."

Judith continued to silently hold the child.

"Well, you've simply got to give the child a name," Garda June told her. "It doesn't have to be a perfect name, just something to call the boy."

Lulu hesitated thoughtfully.

"Well, you know, I admire your husband's name, Mrs. Pierce," the young woman said. "Maybe I should call him Little Enoch."

Judith looked up then. Her countenance almost

gray, Eulie watched in horror as her composure was swept away in a torrent of sorrow that was near-frightening to behold.

She bent forward across the baby's body. A howl of grief emanated from her that was like the cry of a wounded animal.

All around her the women jumped to their feet. The baby was quickly snatched away and handed back to his mother. Garda June and Dora Pusser stood like a wall between Judith and the rest of the people in the clearing, hiding the sight of anguish from curious gawkers.

Judith slipped from her chair to the ground on her knees. Miz Patch and Gertie Samson held her in their arms as wrenching sobs broke from her. Her tears were like shards of glass cutting and wounding all those around her.

"Why me? Why me?" she asked over and over. "I have tried to do right all my life. Why is God punishing me?"

"He's not, Judith," Miz Patch told her. "I promise you that he's not."

"What's happening?"

The little familiar voice caught Eulie's ear even above the din.

"What's happening?"

"Little Minnie, get away from here!" Eulie ordered.

The girl ignored her and pushed her way into the circle of women.

"Are you all right? Mama? What's wrong? Are you all right?"

As soon as she heard Little Minnie's questions, Judith raised her eyes and struggled for control.

"Don't cry, Mama," Little Minnie said. "Please

don't cry. I love you, Mama. Don't cry. We are such pretty girls. Pretty girls ought never to cry."

Judith embraced the child as if she were a lifeline.

"I love you, Mama," Little Minnie repeated. "I love you."

A pain twisted inside Eulie. A pain that was wholly new and yet all too familiar. She thought she might be sick.

Moss had a full belly and a contented heart. He'd come to Preaching Sunday just to please Eulie, but he had thoroughly enjoyed himself. It was actually pleasant, he discovered, to socialize. He had seen people that he hadn't laid eyes on in years. And he'd talked to folks that he saw more often about things that never came up. It was warm and fun and somehow familiar.

Moss wondered what his life might have been like if his childhood—well, if he had had a childhood.

He wandered along the edges of the crowd speaking to first one person and then another. He kept pretty close to Uncle Jeptha, who pushed his goat cart around one group after another. He spoke to no one and no one spoke to him. It was uneasy and uncomfortable.

Moss tried to make up for it by feigning a friendliness that he didn't wholly feel. The response to his overtures were surprisingly positive and open. And the conversations they precipitated were frequently entertaining and occasionally informative.

"You're Young Collier's boy?"

The question came, a bit too loudly, from old Grandpa Madison. The man was ancient and frail. He didn't hear too well or see too well, and it took a cane in each hand for him to stand. But there was nothing wrong with his mind or memory.

"Yes, I'm Collier," he answered.

"What's yer given?" the old man asked. "I cain't recall."

"Mosco," Moss answered. "Mosco DeWitt Collier."

The old man nodded sagely. "The DeWitts were your kin up in Virginy," he said.

Moss was surprised. He'd never heard of the DeWitts, nor had he any inkling where he'd gotten the name, except from his father.

"I got your farm," the old man continued.

"What?"

"I got your farm," he repeated. "Your mama sold it to me when Young Collier died in the war."

"Oh."

"There ain't much there to speak of these days," he said. "There's a well covered up and some flower bushes where the cabin used to be. But you're welcome to come and look the place over anytime. It's always good to remember where ye come from."

"Yes, I'm sure it is," Moss replied politely.

"You are the last Collier on this mountain," the old man told him with a disbelieving shake of the head. "Colliers used to be as thick as thieves in the Sweetwood. And there ain't no Barneses left, neither. Except Jeptha here."

Grandpa Madison squinted, trying to take in the full vision of the man in the goat cart.

"Ain't seen you in quite a spell, boy," the old man said. "You been keeping to yourself?"

Uncle Jeptha didn't even answer. But the old man didn't seem to take offense.

"No, I ain't seen you in quite a spell," he repeated. "Do you recall the time I caught you and yer brother snitching my watermelons?"

"I remember everything," Jeptha said. "I didn't lose my mind in the war, just my legs."

Grandpa Madison nodded sagely and then spoke to Moss once more. "We used to call him Jigging Jeptha Barnes," he said. "Jigging Jeptha Barnes, the dancing fool."

The silence gathered around them. Moss had no idea what to say. He'd never really thought about Uncle Jeptha's life before he lost his legs. He figured that Uncle Jeptha never thought about it either. It must be so hurtful for him to recall it all.

"I heard you're newly wed, Collier," Grandpa Madison went on, clearly unconcerned that he might have said anything amiss.

"Yes, sir," Moss answered. "I've been married a month."

"Well, you best get busy," he said. "Ain't no new Colliers or Barneses being born in the Sweetwood. The names will die out as if they never was, except if you see they don't."

As they moved away, Moss looked down at his proud, silent uncle in the cart.

"Are you all right?" he asked, concerned.

"I should not have come," he stated unequivocally.

Moss had no idea what to say to that.

"You go have yourself a fine afternoon," Uncle Jeptha said. "See to your wife. I'm going to make myself scarce and wait until time to go home."

Moss nodded, wishing he had a better idea, but he didn't. Jigging Jeptha Barnes. Moss tried to imagine his uncle with legs, upright and dancing among this crowd. Somehow he just could not.

"I'll talk to Eulie. There's no call for us whiling away the whole afternoon," Moss told him.

Uncle Jeptha shook his head.

"Don't ask her to leave early," he said. "She's so looked forward to this. I don't want to spoil it."

Moss didn't want to either, but he hated to see Uncle Jeptha so uncomfortable and on display.

"Your Eulie, she's a good girl," Jeptha said unexpectedly. "I'm not sorry that you married her. And I'm not sorry she brought all those children to my house." He hesitated a long moment. "But I am sorry that I was foolish enough to come here today."

Moss watched as Uncle Jeptha propelled himself off into the seclusion and privacy of the woods.

He turned and began scanning the crowd in search of his wife. Moss didn't see her anywhere. After the big hubbub among the women, he'd caught sight of her heading alone down toward the river. He suspected that she might still be there and followed in that direction.

Moss felt strangely unsettled and yet calm and peaceful as well. It was as if two parts of him were seeing through his eyes at the same time and coming up with different conclusions. The leaving part of him, the wanderlust, which was most familiar, chafed at the need to see these people in this place, all so familiar and ordinary. But there was another part of him, a part that was somehow new and to which he was unaccustomed that almost longed for the continuity of it. He was the last Collier in the Sweetwood. He knew nothing of the Colliers. He hadn't even known that his father had had a farm of his own. He only knew how much his mother had loved her husband. Who would know that when he was gone from here? Who would know Uncle Jeptha? Who would know the sacrifice he'd made? Who would remember that he had been a dancing fool?

"Eulie," he muttered to himself. He must ask Eulie to try to remember everything.

He found her sitting on a big sandstone boulder at the river's edge. She had her elbow upon her knee and her forehead in her hand. The hair upon the sides of her head had come loose from the neatly braided twist on the back of her head and hid her face like a veil.

"Hello," he greeted her.

She looked up, startled. Her eyes were red and she hastily wiped away the remnants of tears.

A wave of protectiveness swept through him like a summer storm.

"What happened? Did somebody do something? Did somebody say something?"

She nodded.

"Me, I said something. I said something mean and petty to Judith Pierce and it hurt her and it hurt Little Minnie."

Moss sat down on the rock beside her and quite naturally wrapped a comforting arm around her. It was a friendly gesture, he assured himself. Nothing more.

Eulie leaned her head against his shoulder, as if she couldn't hold it up any longer. Moss almost sighed aloud. She was warm and sweet-smelling beside him. And that blonde hair of hers was so soft and silky against his neck.

"She calls Mrs. Pierce mama," Eulie said quietly.

"Ahhh," Moss commented noncommittally.

"You should have seen them together," she continued. "Judith was holding on to Minnie as if her life depended upon it. And the both of them crying like their hearts were broken."

Moss was silent for a long moment. To his thinking, the Pierces offered a wonderful chance for Little Minnie. They were good people, and they obviously loved and cared about the child. But Eulie's youngers were her concern, not his. Any decision she made about them would always be made with an abundance of love and the very best of intentions.

"You didn't break their hearts, Eulie," he told her quietly.

"You should have seen them, heard them," she insisted.

"I'm not saying their hearts aren't broken," Moss told her. "I'm saying that you did not do it. Minnie can't be blamed so much, she's just a girl, and a mixed-up, confused one at that. But Judith Pierce is a grown woman. She should never have allowed the child to call her mama, to believe that she could live there with her forever, without making certain that was exactly how it was going to happen."

Eulie sighed and nodded. "I couldn't believe she told Minnie they were going to adopt her before she'd even asked me about it."

"She was in the wrong," Moss stated flatly. "It hurt Minnie. Minnie blames you for that, but it was truly Judith's fault."

"I suppose she was mighty desperate," Eulie said. "She would do anything to make what she's longed for come to pass."

"And that's all good and well unless it hurts someone else," Moss said. "She was hurt, but she also hurt you and Minnie."

Eulie looked up at him, her brow furrowed thoughtfully.

"So you think that Judith would not be a good mother?" she asked. "I was right to turn them away."

"I didn't say that," Moss corrected. "I said that a lot of Judith's pain here, she brought on herself. Desperate people ofttimes behave foolishly. Don't hold it against her. But don't be blaming yourself for any of this. Everything you've done, including marrying me and taking on Uncle Jeptha, you've done to try to better the lives of your family. I admire you for that."

Eulie raised her head up and looked in his eyes, her own filled with wonder.

"You admire me?" she asked.

Moss nodded. "Oh yes, I admire you," he told her with certainty. "From that first day at the falls when I glimpsed those long legs of yours and wanted to kiss you, until this very moment when I see a glimpse of your gentle heart. I admire you."

They sat looking at each other, the bond between them forging forward, growing stronger, the sound of the fast-running river the only intrusion into their private communion. The intensity of it was almost more than Moss could bear.

Drowning, he grabbed for a joke.

"Who could not admire the woman who got Uncle Jeptha to bathe?" he said.

The spell was broken. She giggled delightedly.

He hugged her tightly, pressing her body against

his own. It was a teasing, friendly gesture but one that he managed to enjoy very much.

"Hey, you two!" a voice called out to them. "We're getting up a game of Wink-em. You want to play?"

They turned to see stripling young Tyre Dickson.

"You don't want us," Moss answered. "We're old married folks."

The fellow's answer was toned with teasing challenge.

"Well, if you're afraid you'll lose her, Collier, then for sure you'd better stay out of the game," he said.

Moss glanced over at Eulie. Her sad mood gone now, she was her usual bright-eyed, cheerful self.

"You want to?" he asked.

Laughing, she nodded.

"Then let's go," he said.

He hurried to his feet and hollered out to Dickson. "Any extra girls I get, I'm going to keep."

"Don't start chopping till you've treed the coon," the fellow hollered back. "You'll be lucky to keep the one you got. And you'll only keep her 'cause you've already tied the knot."

"He makes it sound like a pretty dangerous game," Moss said to Eulie.

Still seated on the rock, she was grinning up at him.

"Perhaps there is something about me that you really should know," she said.

Moss folded his arms across his chest and gave her a stern look of feigned consternation.

"I have a feeling you're not about to give me any good news," he said. "All right, Mrs. Collier, I'm waiting for a complete and full confession."

Her eyes shone up at him, teasing and full of joy.

"Well the truth is," she began and then hesitated dramatically, "I am the fastest Wink-em player in the Sweetwood."

Moss shook his head and laughed out loud.

"You would be," he told her. "And I suppose you'll try your very best to make me look the fool."

Her eyes were wide with teasing innocence. "It wouldn't be fair any other way," she said.

Moss, pretending disgust, offered his hand to help her up. As she came to her feet, he didn't immediately let it go. They walked hand and hand away from the river.

This is how it would have been if he had courted her, he thought to himself. But of course, he would have never courted her. He'd never intended to court. He intended to leave. Somehow he wasn't sorry about all that had happened. He wasn't sorry that he'd been forced to marry her.

If a man was going to leave a place behind, the very least he should hope to carry with him was not the fine saddle horse or the versatile side arm, it was fond memories of the place he'd left behind. Eulie was helping him create those fond memories.

How could he help but love her for that?

When they reached the clearing, they saw that the game was almost ready to begin. A half dozen chairs were grouped in a circle. Several young ladies were already seated. Their gentleman friends, or at least the fellow who was getting the attention today, stood behind them.

Bug and Clara were in the group. Eulie's sister looked very pretty, animated and blushing. Bug stood at her back, looking puffed up and proud, his grin almost wide enough to offset the size of his bulging eyes.

Maylene Samson was laughing and giggling in that a-little-bit-loud, a-little-bit-less-than-proper manner that she was infamous for. She was the current belle of Sweetwood society, collecting beaux the way some young girls collect hair ribbons. She was a pretty girl, there was no denying that. But *pretty* was not what made Maylene so sought after. In truth, Moss thought, Clara Toby was a good deal prettier and his Eulie had finer features and a better hair color, even if he did say so himself.

No, it was not Maylene's looks that made her so popular. It was the teasing, flirty, almost suggestive way she treated every male in trousers. From young striplings like her cousin Dudley Samson, who was staring calf-eyed across from her now, to the old grandpas so blind they couldn't tell the sixteen from the sixty-year-old, except by feel, they were all taken with her.

Today she was sitting in front of Ned Patchel. Patchel, one of Miz Patch's stepsons, was even older than Moss. More than a decade undoubtedly separated him from little Maylene.

Moss gave heaven a quick thank-you that if he was going to be foolish enough to get himself trapped into marriage, he was glad it had been to Eulie and not Maylene. If he'd wed Maylene or some gal like her, his life wouldn't be worth living.

Yes, Moss decided as his wife took a seat in the chair in front of him, the day he'd kissed Eulie Toby up at the falls might well have been the luckiest day of his life.

"All right," Tyre Dickson said. "Is everybody ready to begin?"

Nobody protested.

"Then, fellows, start winking," he announced.

Around the circle, the young women sat perched on the edge of their seats. There were three chairs, however, that were empty. The boys standing behind them had no girls. It was the object of the game for these young men to "steal" girls from the ones that had them.

A boy with an empty chair could wink at the girl of his choice. If she got out of her chair before the fellow behind her could stop her, then she went to sit with him.

Most of the attention was directed at Maylene. Clara got her share as well, but she seemed very slow to move. Her deliberate indolence allowed Bug to catch her every time.

Moss knew that Eulie would never make it easy for him. She moved quickly when she set her mind to it. And she was faunching at the bit for a fun time this afternoon.

Moss played the game with the same kind of determination he put to everything else in his life. It wasn't difficult for a man to keep his eyes on winkers he suspected of being interested in his girl. It was the ones you didn't expect who caught you off guard and always managed to rob you.

Delbert Pusser unsuccessfully winked at Maylene three times and at Clara once before casting an eye at Eulie.

Moss reached for her as quick as lightning, but it was not fast enough. She was out of the chair and gone. He spent the rest of the game trying to get her back. Tyre Dickson managed to steal her while Delbert was watching Moss. And Delbert's brother, Donald, got her away from Dickson.

When Moss finally got her back he was so excited he grabbed her by the shoulders, pulled her to him and kissed her on the mouth.

Moss wasn't sure who he surprised most, Eulie or himself. With hoots and catcalls all around, the two shared a secret, private moment where faraway places and personal responsibilities could never intrude.

17

In the small clearing in the woods, the fertile scent of the loamy forest floor so close beneath his cart was familiar and comforting. It was like leaning against the breast of Mother Earth herself. He heard someone approaching, but he didn't turn toward the sound. With any luck at all, Jeptha thought, whoever it was would spot him and walk away. That's what he wanted. No casual conversation, no people surreptitiously looking in his direction.

The afternoon sunlight dappled through the trees, laying long dark shadows like prison bars across the ground.

He'd been a fool to come. He knew, of course, exactly why he had. A taste of the sweet forbidden always whetted the appetite for more. For more than twenty years he'd purposely, correctly, kept his distance. But just a few minutes, just a very few minutes, and all his long-held resolve had shattered.

The person stomping along the path was getting closer. At any moment now he would be spotted. He was not a praying man, but he wished desperately in his heart for a moment of privacy. His emotions were far too raw for another encounter.

The footsteps ceased. He was no longer alone in the clearing. He didn't turn. He made no effort to greet or acknowledge. He still held hopes that the unwelcome intruder would simply go away.

"So, Jeptha Barnes, have you come here to hide?"

The woman's voice was familiar, too familiar, and too insistent to be ignored. Reluctantly he turned to look at her.

"Well if it ain't *Miz Patch.*" His tone was snide, the emphasis on her name unkindly. "Have you come to gawk at the freak in the cart or to make more comments about my bathing habits?"

She did not cower at his words or cast her glance away from him. She looked him over calmly, without any hint of hesitation, undaunted by the close-up sight of his legless body.

"Obviously my words did some good," she said. "You look quite a bit cleaner than last time we spoke."

He raised his chin defiantly, his eyes narrow. "Eulie asked me to clean up. I did it for her," he said. "Don't you be thinking I did it for you."

Miz Patch chuckled, but there was no humor in the sound.

"I would never think that in anything you do, I would ever be a consideration."

He didn't know what to say to that. He didn't know what to say at all. He'd wanted to be alone, to stay hidden until it was time to go back to the homeplace. He silently swore to himself that if he ever got to his cabin, he'd never leave again. He had determined to do that once before and had kept his resolve for more than two decades.

"I should never have come," he muttered to himself.

"Did you think that they wouldn't look at you?" she asked him. "Did you think they wouldn't be curious or stare or feel ill at ease?"

"No," he answered. "I knew they would. I knew it and avoided it for twenty years."

She huffed disapprovingly and shook her head.

"As if that made it better instead of worse," she said. "A war wounded veteran catches attention and sympathy. A war wounded veteran who has, for a generation, hid himself like a hermit, is a folktale told over a campfire on spooky nights, a marvel to be seen in the flesh at long last."

"I just want to be left alone," he said. "I don't need their sympathy or want their attention."

"If they'd seen you once a month for the last twenty years, no one would even bat an eye by now," she said. "They would have grown accustomed to the sight of you long ago. But you hid out then, like you're hiding now."

"What business is it of yours?" he asked angrily, hating the fiber of truth in her words.

"It's no business of mine, Jeptha Barnes," she answered. "It's no business of mine at all. You've already wallowed half your life away in self-pity, you might as well throw the rest of it away, too."

"My life? You think I've thrown away my life?" he asked furiously. "I didn't throw it away. It was stolen from me. Stolen from me in the first blush of youth."

She shook her head, refusing to agree.

"Nobody robbed you," she insisted. "You have your life. Maybe it is changed, maybe it is harsher than you imagined it would be, but it is here."

He looked down at the stumps of his legs and gave a humorless chuckle of snide derision.

"This is no life," he said. "It's a life sentence."

"Because you've made it one," she said. "You lived through the war, Jeptha. You lived to come home."

"Well, maybe that's not the great prize that some would think it to be," he told her.

She blew out a sigh of frustration and raised her hands as if she were giving up. "There is just no talking to you, is there?"

But she had not yet finished speaking her piece.

"Do you think you are the only human on earth to drink from the bitter cup?" she asked him.

The question caused him to sit up straighter, but he didn't answer.

"I have buried a fine, caring husband and three of the most blessed children ever put on this earth," she said. "I was abandoned by the only man I ever loved. And became an old woman before I was twenty. I've seen pain and misery, disease and hopelessness until I was sick myself just from the stench of it."

The words were ripped from her heart.

"You are so prideful in your misery, Jeptha Barnes. As if your suffering were so unique. As if your sorrows were the greatest ever borne. There is not a thing in the world that you can tell me about grief or loss or anger at God that I haven't felt."

Her hands were clenched tightly, her own anguish and despair visible in her eyes.

"Of all of them, you were given a chance to go on," she said. "And you've thrown away that opportunity as if it were nothing. Would you have wanted Nils to do that? Or Zack? Or DeWitt? What about Tom or

Judd or Claude? Is this what you would have wanted them to do if they had been given this chance instead of you? The war is over, Jeptha. You dishonor the memory of those we lost with your failure to move beyond it."

"I have no legs," he told her.

"You have your life," she answered.

She spun away from him, clearly intent upon walking away. Somehow he could not let her do that.

"Sary!" he called after her. "Sary, come back here."

Slowly she turned to face him.

"You're calling me?" she asked. "You're calling me to come to you?"

"I . . . I have to explain," Jeptha said.

In truth he had no idea of what he wanted to say or why he didn't just let her go. It would be so much better if she would go. He could hide once more.

"There are . . . there are things I have to explain," he said.

"Explain?" she questioned. "You think you have things to explain? Why don't you start with the six long months that I came to your cabin every day. The six long months that I waited and waited upon that porch. The six long months when you refused to see me, when you told your sister to send me away. The six long months that I cried and begged and pleaded to be by your side and was turned away."

"I . . . I thought I was going to die," he said. "I didn't want you to see me like that. I wanted you to remember me as I had been."

"You wanted me to remember you as a foolish, wild-eyed young boy instead of the man I loved?"

"It was that boy you knew," he said. "It was that boy

that you loved. The one who held you close that night in the woods."

She shook her head. The anger had gone out of her now. She was hurt. He could see that. He had known that. But he'd never had to see it before.

"I was *in love* with the boy that night in the woods," she admitted. "I was just a girl myself. But I *loved* the man who wrote me letters from the war. Letters about great things and small, letters about the future as well as the past. I *loved* that man whose heart was so very close to my own."

Jeptha swallowed thoughtfully.

"I had forgotten about the letters," he said. "They were the only thing that kept me going through those hard, horrifying days. Knowing that when lights were low, I could share it all with you."

"I still have them."

"What?"

"I still have the letters," she said. "Ezra asked me once to get rid of them. He rarely asked me for much and I tried always to do as he liked. But in this one thing I refused him. I kept those letters. I treasure every single word."

There was a silence between them.

"Patchel was good to you, then?" he asked finally, more quietly.

Sary nodded.

"Did you . . . did you tell him about me?"

She chuckled lightly and shook her head. "I didn't have to," she answered. "Everybody in the Sweetwood knew that I loved you. They all knew that I went to your cabin every day. They all knew that I begged to see you. They all knew that you'd broken my heart."

"I worried," Jeptha said. "When I heard you'd married, I worried that he wouldn't treat you well."

"But not worried enough to come and try to stop the wedding," she said.

"What?"

"That's what I dreamed about," she told him. "That's what I hoped. That you would come charging down the mountain and ride right up to the church and claim me for your own."

Jeptha's brow furrowed, he couldn't quite believe her words.

"That was more than two years after I returned," he said. "Surely you weren't still pining after me for more than two years."

"Two years?" her question was incredulous. "Oh no, I didn't pine after you for two years–more like twenty-two."

Her declaration momentarily knocked the breath out of him.

"But you married, you had a family," he said.

"I cared for Ezra," she answered. "I was a good wife to him and mothered his children the best I knew how. But I never loved him. I knew that. And he knew that. I loved you, Jeptha. I loved you and I love you and nothing you can do now nor ever can make me stop. I've tried to make the best of my life. I tried to live it full and with purpose. But I never had to stop loving you and I never will."

Her words almost unmanned him. Jeptha felt the sting of tears in his eyes and he ground his teeth together, forcefully pushing them back.

"I never stopped loving you, Sary," he told her.

Her eyes widened and her anger was back.

"You never loved me at all," she accused him. "You could not have loved me and sent me away like you did."

"I sent you away because I did love you," he insisted. "I sent you away because I wanted the best for you."

"Being with the man I love would have been best for me," Sary said.

"I didn't even think I would live," he told her once more. "I didn't want to shackle you with a dying man."

"Don't you think I should have been given a choice about that?" she asked him. "Don't you think I should have had something to say about it?"

"You would have stayed with me out of pity," he said. "And I could never have stood that."

"I would have stayed with you out of love," she said. "Whether it had been a day or a month or ten years or a lifetime, I would have been exactly where I wanted to be."

"But that wasn't the life I wanted for you," he said.

"It was the life I wanted for myself," she said. "I wanted to be your wife. I wanted to be by your side. For better and worse and sickness and health and everything."

"You deserved more."

"And since when in life do we get what we deserve?" she asked him.

His heart was pounding furiously. He had to somehow make her understand.

"Look at me, Sary," he said. "Look at me. Do you see what the surgeons left of me? Do you see that I will never be whole?"

"I see that you will never walk," she answered. "I see that you will never dance a jig or run with me to the woods. But I also see the man I love and I wish that he had loved me enough to make me his wife."

"Sary, I have no legs!" he told her, angrily slapping the remnants of his limbs. "I could not have offered myself as a husband for you."

She raised an eyebrow. Her tone was haughty and unmoved by his declaration.

"Oh, my mistake," she said, facetiously. "I didn't realize they'd cut off that part of you as well."

Rans had not allowed the slights and injustice of the morning to ruin his whole day. He managed not to run off and waste Preaching Sunday. But he made a point to steer clear of Moss Collier. He didn't like the man and the man didn't like him. Well, maybe Moss liked him well enough, but he thought he was a child. Rans was certain that he was a man in practically every way, except perhaps his height. He deserved to be treated like a man.

With that thought in mind, after finishing his food, he avoided the children's games and sought out older boys who gathered within the seclusion of the edge of the woods. Beneath the tall cool shade of the towering hemlocks they were able to see without being seen.

Joe Browning was there and Stuart Madison. Rans had a powerful admiration for both young men. Conrad Samson was also there. Rans had had run-ins with him a time or two and didn't care for him much. His younger cousin, Dudley, was there also. But Dudley was not even as old as Rans and therefore of little account in his eyes.

Having already discarded his coat and footwear,

Rans leaned his back against the scratchy bark of a tree trunk and gazed at the other fellows over the tops of his knees.

Stuart had filched a pipe somewhere. It wasn't much, just something whittled out of an old corncob, but it was much-used and mellowed by time and temperature. He packed the narrow blackened bowl with tobacco and carefully lit it. He puffed enthusiastically to get it going. Smoke billowed out in great scented clouds around them. It was wonderful.

Stu passed the pipe to Joe and he began to smoke it as well.

"Look what I got," Dudley said, eagerly emptying his pocket.

Rans looked at the boy's face and almost felt sorry for him. He was trying so hard to please. But he was just a kid still, so it didn't matter.

From the farthest depths of his trouser pocket, Dudley brought forth a small rectangular box and held it out for inspection. Joe, Stuart, and Conrad all sat up immediately.

"Is that what I think it is?" Joe asked.

Dudley nodded. "It's a deck of playing cards."

Stuart whistled appreciatively.

"Where'd you get those?" Conrad asked.

The boy shrugged. "I got 'em," he answered simply.

It was almost possible to see the respect for Dudley grow in their eyes.

Joe passed the pipe to Conrad and held out his hand for the cards.

Dudley blithely handed them over as if they mattered to him almost not at all.

Joe slid the flat wooden lid out of its grooves and

then upended the contents of the box in his hand.

They were old and worn, yellowed, with corners frayed, but they were playing cards. Rans had never seen any close up. Of course, he was not about to say so.

"Are they all there?" Conrad asked. "It looks like a short deck to me."

Dudley puffed up angrily, taking offense at his cousin's suggestion. "They are all there," he said. "Do you want to count 'em?"

Conrad's face immediately turned beet red. It was well known that he was extremely poor at ciphering. He just could never quite get a handle on the logic that if you had two bushel baskets on one side of the fence and two on the other, that you actually had four bushels. Dudley, being family, would naturally pick up on the weakness in a way that outsiders would be too polite to do.

Conrad took another couple of puffs on the pipe and handed it over to Rans.

He was not totally unfamiliar with tobacco. But his experience was not particularly positive. He'd made himself absolutely green on several occasions and had once burned his throat so badly he could hardly speak.

Gamely, he took a long draw and managed to let the smoke out slowly, suppressing a strong desire to cough. He glanced up confidently, only to discover that no one was paying his success any attention. They were completely focused upon the cards.

Rans tamped down his disappointment. That was the way it should be, he decided. Men didn't watch other men to see if they could smoke. It was understood that they did or did not by preference.

"Do you play much poker?" Joe asked Dudley.

"Sure," Dudley answered with the enthusiasm of feigned confidence that so often accompanied lying.

"Oh, he don't know the first thing about it," Conrad told them snidely.

"I do so!" Dudley insisted.

"Oh yeah?" Conrad taunted. "Then you tell us: What's an inside straight?"

Dudley hesitated, his big ears and the back of his neck both beginning to color up floridly.

Rans felt a sudden strong sense of protectiveness for Dudley. The boy was younger and therefore of little importance, but Rans understood how keenly a boy could need respect at his age. Rans himself was considerably wiser and more experienced. Having on occasion been the target of Conrad's ridicule, he responded to a deep inner need to defend those he perceived as younger or weaker. He had no idea what an inside straight might be either, but he was pretty sure what it wasn't. Like the cavalry coming in for the rescue, Rans lazily sat up and gave the older Samson boy a dismissive glance.

"We know what you think it is, Conrad," he said. "You think it's getting the cards all back in the box neatly."

Howls of laughter erupted from the boys around him. Rans himself didn't even smile. He knew it would be necessary to stare down Conrad, who would undoubtedly want to start something.

The portly older boy was head and shoulders taller than Rans and probably weighed more than double. But with his prickly pride and quick temper, Rans had of necessity become quite a scrapper. He had complete confidence in his ability to fight Conrad Samson. He might not win, but Rans knew he could show himself well, take whatever the bigger fellow dished out, and that's all that really counted for a man.

Conrad was apparently not as sure of himself and after a long, assessing look at Rans, decided to take the better part of valor. He pretended that it was a joke and chose to laugh rather than take offense.

When he did, Rans wisely laughed with him and the moment passed as a complete victory for the younger boy.

Stuart was shuffling the playing cards and began explaining the intricacies of poker.

"You bet that what you hold in your hand is what is better than what is in everybody else's," he said.

"What do we bet?" Dudley asked.

"Money," Stu answered.

He looked around the group. Every one of them was shaking his head shamefaced. Rans momentarily wished he had back the penny he put in the collection plate.

"Dudley, go gather some acorns," Joe said.

"Acorns? What do you think I am? A squirrel?"

"We can use the acorns as if they were money," Stu told him.

Reluctantly the boy headed for a nearby oak tree.

"The fellow with the cards is called the dealer." The instruction went on. "Everybody gets dealt five cards. You can keep all five or throw any or all of them away and get more."

Rans listened intently, trying to understand the gist of flushes, straights, and three of a kind. Poker was a man's game. He wanted to be able to play it.

When Dudley returned with his shirttail loaded

with acorns, Joe divvied them up evenly and they began to play.

At first Rans was unsure of what was better than what and made a lot of mistakes. He threw away cards he should have kept and kept those that he shouldn't have. But slowly he began to get a feel for the game and discovered, to the surprise of himself and the rest of them, that he had amazing good luck.

He won hand after hand until his pile of acorns became a small mountain. Poor Dudley had to go back to the oak tree for more, while Rans continued to win. It was the most fun he could remember having in his whole life. Laughing, happy, he was delighted as deal after deal produced three aces or four deuces or his inside straight of four, five, six, seven, and eight.

It was not surprising that the other fellows didn't find losing the game to be nearly as entertaining. When Delbert and Donald Pusser showed up, they gladly gave it up altogether.

To have the Pusser brothers in their presence was a great honor for the younger fellows. They were completely grown-up men, out in the world, running wild, drinking whiskey, up to no good most all the time. They were the undisputed envy of every boy between the ages of nine and nineteen. Amazingly, at least to Ransom's thinking, they were not particularly admired among men of their own age.

"Don't quit your game 'cause of us," Donald told them.

"Oh, it ain't no fun, nohow," Dudley complained. "Rans has done won all the acorns."

His brother, Delbert, eyed Rans shrewdly. "So you're a poker player, Toby?"

Rans shrugged.

"I enjoy betting on a card or two," he answered with studied nonchalance.

He was thoroughly delighted to be singled out for attention by Delbert Pusser, but thought it best to act as if he really didn't care.

"We saw you playing Wink-em with the girls," Joe said, changing the subject.

Delbert shrugged. "Well, we'd a rather played shag-em," he said. "But none of these Preaching Sunday gals ever want to play."

The risqué comment brought great guffaws from all within hearing. Dirty talk was just one of the many things young fellows found to admire about the Pussers.

"No sirree," Joe Browning stated in worldly-wise tone. "There ain't much shagging getting done here in the Sweetwood."

"Except by married folks," Conrad pointed out.

"It ain't shagging if they's married," Stu told him.

"It's the same thing," Conrad insisted. "It's the same exact thing."

Donald snorted. "Tell that to one of these men around here that's been married ten years."

More hoots of laughter ensued.

"I heared that you've been shagging that old whore down in Jarl," Stu said.

"Where'd you hear a thing like that?" Delbert asked.

"Around, I just heared it, around," Stu said.

"Round," Donald piped in, teasing. "Why that's the kindy heels that old whore has got. Round ones, easy to tip her on her back."

The boys were all laughing once more.

"I heared you got the syphilis from her," Stu continued.

His words brought an immediate hush. The young boys didn't know that much about what venereal disease might be, but they had all been warned of the dangers of it.

"Not me," Delbert answered. "I ain't got syphilis. It's Donald that's got it."

Donald raised his chin with an expression that was almost prideful.

"She gave it to me," he joked. "Didn't make no sense to give it back."

The boys chuckled again, but this time a little less heartily.

"It ain't much trouble," he assured them. "I just get a little twinge with it now and again. And once you got it, you don't need to worry no longer about getting it."

That made sense to Rans. He knew that a man got syphilis from consorting with loose women. And consorting with loose women was something men did. Well, at least it was something that some men did. Certainly Mr. Leight never ran around with any round-heeled gals. And Rans had a powerful admiration for Mr. Leight.

Still, it seemed like fast living and fast women were a part of being a man. Rans didn't want to bypass any aspect of manhood. He wasn't that interested in gals at the moment. But he made a mental note to add them to his list of things he needed to know about.

Perhaps someday, he ruminated to himself proudly, he could sit around the group of men and brag that he had syphilis himself.

Donald turned to fix his gaze directly upon Rans.

"I bet you've been seeing, or at least hearing, some shagging around your place," he said.

Rans was momentarily startled by the question. Almost immediately the image of what he'd seen as he happened upon Eulie and Moss that night in the kitchen came to his mind.

"Look at him, he's blushing," Conrad said nastily.

Rans couldn't control the flush in his cheeks. But he could bridle his tongue.

"That Collier has always been downright finicky fellow when it comes to females," Delbert added. "With as little shag-timing as he's had, he's probably wild having a woman within grabbing distance the clock around."

His words brought more laughter from those around him.

"I bet they're poking like a pair of rabbits," Donald agreed.

Rans knew that it was all said in fun, but somehow it didn't feel very amusing to him.

"That's my sister you are talking about," he said finally, sternly, with no less than a hint of implied threat in his tone.

In the eerie silence that followed every eye was upon him. Most stared in startled disbelief.

"You going to take on the Pusser brothers?"

Conrad's question was both incredulous and taunting.

Rans had no words to answer. Starting something with the Pusser brothers was not at all like taking on Conrad Samson. Even if he lost a fight with Conrad, he'd be able to get in a few good blows and take only a minor beating. The Pusser brothers, however, could easily squash him like a summer mosquito. Still, he had the right of it. They shouldn't be talking about Eulie that way. He had the right of it and he was required as a man to uphold the right.

"You'd best keep my sister's name out of your mouth," he said.

Donald's brow was furrowed, as if he didn't quite understand what was happening. Delbert, however, was watching Rans with some interest. Fortunately, he did not look ready or eager to throw a punch.

"Rans here is right," he said. "It is his sister and she's married up fair and square. Even if its true that she got her baby before she got her vows."

Rans didn't know what to say about that. Eulie had made people believe that of her. He was in no position to try to proclaim the truth.

"Moss Collier and Eulie Toby," Delbert said the names together as if he couldn't quite believe it. "It's hard to imagine them two as man and wife."

"Maybe 'cause you fancied Eulie for yourself," Donald suggested.

Delbert looked at his brother as if the man had lost his mind. "I never fancied Eulie," he said. "I had my eye on that Clara. She's some looker. But if she prefers old bug-eyed Bug to me, well, I suspect she weren't my sort at all."

It was Rans's turn to look incredulous. He could not imagine a fellow like Delbert Pusser giving his sister Clara so much as a second glance. Of course, Clara was pretty. But she was no fun-and-frolic gal, that was for certain.

"You know why I cain't imagine them two as married?" Delbert said.

"Why not?"

"'Cause they didn't get no shivaree."

"How come they didn't get one?" Joe asked.

"The preacher was against it," Donald answered. "'Cause Collier was in such a temper, he was afraid that a shivaree would make it worse."

"They got a pounding," Rans pointed out.

"It ain't the same," Delbert said. "It ain't the same at all."

"It don't seem much like a wedding without a shivaree," Conrad agreed.

"Weddings are just so girlish," Delbert said. "A shivaree is a man's custom. It's a tradition. No pair should get down the road with nothing to look back on but a few vows and a handful of posies."

The wisdom of that spoke for itself. There were nods of agreement all around.

"We could still give them a shivaree," Joe Browning said.

Every eye turned to look at him. Every head considered his words.

"You're right," Stu agreed. "There ain't no time limit that says it's got to be the first night."

"No, they sure ain't," Donald said with certainty.

"They'll have been wed four weeks tomorrow," Conrad put in. "It'll be kind of a remembrance or something."

"Let's do it," Joe said. "Let's do it today. Give them a shivaree here, this afternoon."

The enthusiasm for the idea was unanimous. Now all that needed to be settled was what direction the event should take.

"We could tie him to that horse of his and make her lead him around," Dudley suggested.

"Or we could tie them both to the horse backwards and send them on a wild ride."

"Or we could . . ."

Delbert turned to his brother. "I knew there was a good reason why we brought the boat," he said.

18

Eulie was surprised at the pleasant turn of the afternoon. She had certainly looked forward to having her family together. She had dreamed with great longing what Preaching Sunday would be like with the Tobys reunited. But she had not, in all her schemings and imaginings, thought about how delightful, pleasant and just plain fun it could be to be a new bride—a new bride with a doting husband-man beside her.

Playing Wink-em had been a joy. They'd laughed and laughed. Moss Collier had a wonderful, deep-throated laugh. The sound went through her in some curious way and warmed her heart. From his own admission, Moss did not laugh a lot. Eulie decided that it was her mission, for the few more weeks that he was here, to see that he laughed every day.

After the game was over, she fully expected him to go on about his business. He would stand around jawing with the other men and she would wander around to check on the children and then settle herself among one of the small circles of women to do handwork and make idle chatter.

But that was clearly not to be. The husband-man took her arm and they strolled among the crowd together. It was wonderful to walk next to him, to have him tall, broad-shouldered and so masculine, at her side.

He was probably uncomfortable, she told herself. Although he did know nearly every person who was there, he had never been a frequent attendee of Sunday service. Undoubtedly he was ill at ease and required her presence to relax. However, that was not at all how he behaved. One would get the impression from watching and listening to him that he actually preferred her company to anyone else's. Surely that could not be true.

They talked with Lathe Dickson about fall molasses making. Moss didn't own his own mill and typically transported his sorghum to the Dicksons', where he traded a day's labor for the pressing. To her amazement, Moss discussed the matter as if he fully intended to still be in the Sweetwood when the time came. That would be September at the very earliest, and in lots of years, the seed tassels on the cane wouldn't brown up until well into October. She supposed that he was striking a bargain on behalf of her and the children.

When they stepped away, Eulie asked him about it.

"It seems almost unfair to hope that Mr. Dickson would accept a day of my labor or the children's as equal to that of yours," she said.

Moss appeared startled. It was as if he'd forgotten that he was leaving.

"We'll work something out," he assured her.

They stopped and chatted with Yeoman Browning for several minutes. Eulie felt very much as if she were in the way. It wasn't just that the talk was of wood traces and tracking. Yeoman, who had been an acquaintance of hers for years, was now suddenly embarrassed to be around her. It was, of course, easily attributable to her terrible scheme to trap the husband-man. Yeoman was a friend of Moss's. And he'd been forced to be a part of a wedding that Moss clearly had not wanted.

Eulie tried more than once to simply step away and let the men talk in private, but the husband-man slipped his arm around her waist and kept her firmly at his side. Eulie didn't understand his reasoning, but suspected that he wanted to get all the uneasiness over with. So she stood there, smiling as serenely as possible, as the two men discussed hunting.

"I saw a big rub up on Spider Bald," Yeoman told him. "It's that same brown, I'm sure of it."

"The one you've been trailing all summer?" Moss asked.

Yeoman nodded. "I don't have no time to go after him between now and the end of the season, but I was thinking that once my crop is in, I might just run him to ground."

"If you can catch him just before he settles in for winter, he'll be sluggish and easier to bring down," Moss pointed out.

Yeoman nodded. "Sounds like a good plan," he said. "You want to go with me? He's plenty big enough to share."

"It's mighty tempting," Moss admitted. "If I can get everything caught up around the place, maybe I could take a day or two."

"A nice, juicy bear steak sure would go down easy this winter," his friend said.

Moss nodded. "And there is no finer eating in this

world than a big hunk of fresh, light bread sopping up bear grease."

"Mmmm," Yeoman agreed.

"You men," Eulie teased. "It's hardly halfway to suppertime and you're already making hunger noises."

The two laughed.

"Do you think there is any of that cobbler left?" Moss asked her. "Maybe they'd let me have another piece."

As they moved in that direction, Eulie questioned him. "So bear is one of your favorite foods?"

He nodded.

"It's such a sweet meat and not a bit gamy," he said.

Eulie couldn't help but agree. "Mr. Pierce killed a bear and brought us a fine haunch of it the autumn when Mama was sick," she said. "It sure tasted mighty good."

Moss smiled down at her. "Well, maybe Yeoman and I will bring him down."

"I hope so," she said.

Obviously he was going to stay long enough to go bear hunting as well as getting the crop in, building a root cellar, and making molasses. With all that he was planning, Moss was going to be lucky to get headed toward Texas by midwinter.

"Do you think they have bears in Texas?" she asked.

Moss was surprised at the question, and his brow furrowed thoughtfully.

"I don't know," he said. "I never thought about it. Every place has bears, doesn't it?"

Eulie shrugged. "I couldn't say. I've never been anyplace but here," she reminded him.

"They must have some kind of bears," he said.

"If it's all grass and no trees," Eulie pointed out, "I don't know where the bears would hide."

Moss considered that for a long moment.

"Maybe they hide behind the buffalo," he said.

Eulie giggled delightedly. "Are buffalo that big?" she asked.

Moss shook his head. "You've seen as many of them as I have," he told her, laughing.

It was at that moment that her attention was captured by a movement across the clearing. The Pusser brothers were hurrying toward them with a trail of young boys following in their wake.

The oddness of the moment was such that Eulie was momentarily frightened. Perhaps something had happened to one of the children.

"What is it?" Moss asked.

Before she could answer, he'd turned to see for himself.

The little group of men and boys were running toward them now. One of the Pusser brothers was carrying a rope.

"Shivaree!" someone cried out.

There was hardly enough time for it to be considered a warning. Almost immediately, somebody grabbed Moss. They held his wrists and pulled his arms behind his back.

"What are you doing?" Eulie protested. "What are you doing?"

"Shivaree!" somebody shouted again, as if that answered everything.

Moss was struggling, kicking and fighting, a half dozen men and boys trying to hold on to him. Eulie took her cue from that. Throwing herself at Donald

Pusser's back, she began flailing at the man with all her might. With one hand he dusted her off of him as if she were a pesky gnat. She landed on the ground with a thud, but immediately she was on her feet.

She saw Rans in the crowd and her heart lightened. "Help me," she called out to him.

It was at that moment that she realized that her brother was actually a part of the horde that had set upon them.

Eulie glanced around, looking for aid. Every person in the clearing was on their feet. Everyone was watching. Some had expressions of concern, but for the most part they were grinning or laughing. This was a shivaree. This was a mountain tradition for newlyweds. This was supposed to be fun.

Moss was yelling, cursing, threatening them, so they gagged him with a worn pocket handkerchief. They tied him tighter than a hog ready for the scalding tank, his wrists and ankles snugly bound so that he could make very little movement at all.

"Let's go," Delbert said. "We got him now. Stretch him out and raise him up."

The band of attackers raised him up lengthwise to their shoulders. Moss had given up struggling, apparently deciding that allowing them to take him where they'd planned might be better than wiggling out of their grasp and being dropped upon the ground.

Eulie followed them, protesting one minute and pleading for assistance the next. No one came to her aid.

The chant of "Shivaree, shivaree," seemed to ward off any concern the folks around them had for Moss Collier's safety. They paraded him through the clearing to give all the folks in the Sweetwood a close look at what was happening. The fact that they did not come forward or offer assistance made them tacitly part of the event, which was far older than anyone in attendance.

The shivaree was the community's way of helping to forge a strong, lasting bond between a couple just wed. Nothing could do that quicker than setting up a situation of mock danger and forcing the newlyweds to face mutual enemies. It was a time-honored way to teach two individuals accustomed in life to thinking of themselves as *me* and *you* into seeing the world as *us* and *them*.

They began heading for the river laughing, chanting, suggesting that they intended to see if he could swim.

Eulie's heart flew to her throat. If they threw him in the water tied up that way, he would very likely drown.

"Let him go," she pleaded. "Don't hurt him. We've been married a month. We don't need a shivaree."

Her words fell on deaf ears. When they reached the river, Eulie saw a small, flat-bottomed boat waiting at the water's edge.

They cast him into the boat. He squirmed into a sitting position immediately and began struggling against his bonds once more.

Eulie hurried forward to help him.

It was with some surprise that Eulie felt Delbert Pusser grab her. She expected that she'd probably be kept from helping Moss, but she hadn't anticipated actually being held. Delbert pulled her wrists behind her back, and she cried out.

"Where's the other rope?" Delbert called out to someone behind them.

Eulie felt the rough scratch of braided cord tighten against her wrists.

"What are you doing? Stop this! Stop it!"

Desperately she kicked at her captors as the other end of the rope was wrapped around her ankles. She caught young Joe Browning right in the mouth and felled him like a tree.

"She busted my lip," he complained.

The other fellows laughed heartily.

"No wonder Collier got the wedding night before the wedding," Donald Pusser said. "She's one feisty little spitfire."

She saw Moss, struggling in the boat, jerking at his bonds as she screamed her protests.

A moment later, a big, work-muscled arm stayed Pusser's hand.

"Let her go."

Bug stood in the midst of them, his voice so low and cold the threat was unmistakable "You don't harm the bride," he said. "Shivarees don't harm the bride."

"We're not about to harm anyone," Delbert assured him. "We're just going to drop them at the island for a delayed honeymoon."

Bug considered Pusser's words for a long minute.

"I'll tie her," he said finally.

"All right!" Pusser cheered him.

Bug lightly looped the rope upon Eulie's wrists and then scooped her up as if she weighed nothing and carried her to the boat. He set her gently beside her husband before pulling the rag out of Moss's mouth.

"If you don't get home tonight, I'll bring a boat to fetch you first thing in the morning," he promised.

"Thanks," Moss told him.

Donald waded out to the back of the boat and climbed in, taking up the paddle. Delbert pushed the bow off into the water and jumped aboard. They were out in the middle of the stream in no time and were able to allow the current to carry them downstream with only the token use of paddles.

"You just sit there nice and still now, Collier. No fast moves," Delbert said to Moss by way of warning. "You may not give a whit about drenching you and me, but this little gal of yours will sure have a tough time swimming to the bank all bound and hobbled like she is."

Moss kept still.

"If anything happens to her, Pusser," the husbandman said, "if she even so much as gets a bruise, I'll beat you to within an inch of your life."

"Whewee! Did you hear that, Donald?" Pusser answered, with high humor. "Collier's done got himself lovestruck here. He's going to pummel me if she so much as gets a bruise."

"That sounds like pussy-trailing to me," his brother replied. "I kind of like to see a little black and blue on my women. It's like marks of ownership."

Moss twisted sideways to look over his shoulder at Donald. "You touch my wife and you're dead," he told the loudmouth with stone-cold certainty.

Donald jerked the paddle out of the water, and for a moment, Eulie thought he was going to hit Moss with it.

Delbert's laughter forestalled him. "He is just full of threats, ain't he? Don't pay him no mind." As Donald eased his paddle back into the water, Delbert spoke to Moss. "This is a shivaree, Collier, not a kidnapping.

We ain't about to hurt you or your little gal."

The island, a small stretch of land in the wide, lazy part of the river just above Big Fork, was little more of a sandbar with a stand of oaks and willows. But it figured frequently in tall tales and ghost stories told to younger children. Eulie had never been there, but she wasn't frightened about going. As long as she was with Moss, somehow everything would be fine.

"I'm sorry," he said to her, as if he should have been able to prevent the Pusser brothers from undertaking the shivaree.

"I'll be fine," she assured him. And she knew it was true. At his side, she would not be afraid to go anywhere.

The boat traveled downstream as she and Moss tried to talk them out of their plan.

"We can't just go off together on some shivaree," Eulie told them. "We've got a family. Five youngers that depend upon us. And Uncle Jeptha, too. He's a war veteran."

"You've already had your fun," Moss pointed out. "And everybody saw you get the best of me. It really won't make any difference whether you leave us on the island or let us off on the yonder bank."

The brothers were not interested in any of their arguments. It seemed that nothing would dissuade them from following through with their chosen course of action. As the island came within sight, Eulie glanced over at Moss. He seemed to be surveying the distances to both the east and west banks, apparently gauging the likelihood of the two of them swimming to shore.

The afternoon was growing later and the sun was already low in the sky, skimming light across the water.

"How long are you going to leave us here?" Moss asked.

Delbert chuckled. "Well, let's just say you'll have plenty of time to get frisky with the missus."

That struck Donald as hilarious, and he laughed uproariously.

When the prow scraped up against the sand, the Pusser brothers jumped out and dragged the boat halfway ashore. It took both of them to carry Moss out. As they slipped into the dark shadows of the trees, Eulie found that she was frightened for the first time. She did not like being alone out here at all.

The solitude only lasted a moment before Delbert reappeared. She was hoisted up over his shoulder and carried on to the island. He put her down within a short distance of Moss, who was once again struggling against the rope that held him.

"At least untie us," Moss entreated. "There could be a bobcat or a panther around here. With my hands tied, I could never protect her."

"Cats ain't that fond of swimming," Delbert told him, dismissively.

"It's going to be night soon," Moss tried again.

"And morning after that," Donald piped in.

"Let's go," Delbert said. "We'll leave the mated pair to their own company."

They started to go, but Donald hesitated.

"We don't have to put the two of them so far apart, I don't suppose," he said.

He walked over to Eulie. Jerking her up easily, he carried her over to Moss.

"I believe this belongs to you, Collier," Donald said as he dropped Eulie directly on top of him.

"Ummphh!"

The breath was momentarily knocked out of them both.

"You two have a big time, ya hear?" Delbert called out to them laughing as he and his brother walked away.

Donald hooted along with him as they pushed their boat back out into the river and disappeared from sight.

"Are they gone?" Moss asked her.

His voice blew upon the side of her neck, all warm and ticklish. She turned her head to look down at him, so close beneath her.

"They're gone," she told him.

"Well, at least we can be grateful for that," he said. "Are you all right?"

"I'm fine," she said. "My arms feel kind of cramped, but I'm not hurting at all."

He wiggled a little bit as he lay beneath her.

"They really got me trussed up like the Christmas goose," Moss said. "I don't think I can get loose. What about you?"

He was so close, so very, very close. She had missed this. She had missed the warmth of being next to him.

Eulie began to pull against her wrists. To her surprise, she easily managed to get her thumb loose. Without any examination of her reasoning, she did not then simply slide the rope off her hands. She ceased struggling.

"I can't get undone either," she said.

His face was only inches from her own. She gazed down into the eyes that had become so familiar, the eyes that she so admired.

"Kiss me," he whispered so softly that perhaps he hoped that she would not hear.

She angled her head and brought her mouth down upon his own. They could share a kiss. The contact, sweet and sensual, swept her away. It was just a kiss, she told herself. Just one kiss. There was nothing too dangerous about it. One kiss, but it was like a hundred kisses, a thousand, as his warm lips lingered upon hers, toying and testing and teaching. A month ago one kiss had gotten them married. Today it made them instantaneously intimate. There was no shyness in either of them. They wanted the touch, the taste of each other. They wanted the incredible closeness of it.

With hands bound behind them, there was no embrace, no caress, only the joining of two mouths.

"Mmmmm," he moaned deep in his throat, as if finding her delicious.

Their lips separated, but it was not at all enough. He nipped and teased at her mouth, unwilling to let her go completely, unwilling to allow the precious intimacy to slip away. He caught her lower lip between his teeth and tugged ever so gently, willing her nearer.

He began struggling beneath her once more, pulling frantically at the cords that held him fast.

"I want to hold you," he told her. "I have to hold you."

His ineffective movement had the untended consequence of rubbing his body lasciviously against her own.

Eulie gasped, both from the unfamiliar pleasure of his lengthening erection against her thigh and the startling jolt of pure carnal desire that rushed through her veins.

Their mouths were once more locked together in a sweet exploration of lips and teeth and tongues. He raised himself to a half-sitting position, pressing toward her. It was not a commensurate substitute, but it was his only alternative.

With his hands useless behind him, he used his mouth to stroke and caress where his fingers might have. He eased her to his side and then rolled partway over her, giving him more control over his movements and exposing more of her to his view.

He inched a path along her throat with a thousand tiny prickling love bites. When he reached her ear, his tongue snaked out to lash it. He captured the lobe between his teeth, treating it with the reverence one would accord a hard-won trophy. His panting breath skittered along her flesh like hot grease in a skillet. Eulie heard a curious, mewling sound with which she was unfamiliar. She realized with surprise that it was coming from her own throat.

His lips were back on her own once more, tasting, osculating, suckling, until in her passion and impatience, Eulie could bear it no more. She slipped her hands free of her bonds and embraced her lover, burying her fingers in his hair.

It was through a lust-tinged haze that Moss first realized that there was something different. In the last few minutes of desperate desire, something, somehow, was changed. But with blood pounding in his ears, the duet of labored breathing, and the indecipherable moans of two healthy humans following the inclinations of nature, he did not immediately care what had happened. As long as his bride continued to kiss him so ardently and he could rub the throbbing erection in the front of his trousers against her firm young thighs, the entire world could crumble around him and he would not take note of it. She was all and everything that he had ever craved or longed for in his life. She was every bit of it. And she was wholly more than that. More than he had ever dreamed or imagined a woman could be to him.

His lips, which sought to nuzzle and kiss every part of her that they could reach, found the long slender fingers of her hand and the delicate underside of her wrist. Such beautiful hands, he thought. Such beautiful hands. So work worn and callused, yet so capable of tender caress.

Hands.

"You're untied!" he told her.

She seemed startled, as if she had only just noticed it herself.

"Yes . . . I . . . I must have gotten loose," she muttered.

Her gaze was still dewy-eyed and her mouth still pouting prettily from his kiss.

"Free me," he told her. "Get me out of these ropes."

"Oh! Oh . . . of course."

He rolled away from her, presenting his back. She pulled and jerked at the bonds for a moment before unscrambling the complicated knot. When the tie gave way, he sat up immediately and rubbed his wrists for a moment before going to work on the binding at his ankles. It was not all that easy, made more difficult by his need to keep his right arm lying lengthwise across his erection.

He'd allowed himself to get out of control again.

He had always thought himself a man very capable of keeping his appetites in check. Obviously, that was in the days before he acquired a stringy-haired bride. He didn't really mind for himself. He would suffer the consequences of unspent passion as a duly earned penance, he already ached with it. But it was so unfair to Eulie. She was a generous and giving person. She responded to his sexual overtures with all the warmth and enthusiasm that she brought to life in general. He could kiss her until she was breathless with desire and she would kindly forgive him for leaving her unfulfilled. He didn't deserve her good nature.

Having untangled the rope at his feet, Moss stood up immediately.

He glanced down at Eulie. He thought to offer his hand, to pull her into his arms, but decided against it. He was still as randy as a billy goat. Distance was undoubtedly the best idea.

He walked out to the water's edge and stared across the expanse to the far bank and the mountain view beyond. The sun was near to setting behind the high peaks behind him and the shadows were long. It gave the terrain an aura of beauty that was almost otherworldly. And at the same time there was a familiarity about it that was somehow comforting. His mother, his father, his grandparents—all the generations, even back to the old Scotsman—had gazed up at these hills the way he had. It was almost as if changelessness, continuity, became an end of its own.

Deliberately he closed his eyes and waited for the emotion to pass. He waited for the inevitable sensation of choking confinement, that hopelessly hemmed-in feeling that had been the spur that induced his wanderlust from boyhood. He waited. Amazingly, there was nothing.

He opened his eyes, thoughtful. What had happened to his thinking? Where was that grievous yearning to get away? Perhaps the freedom to leave had somehow relieved him of the desperation to go.

Eulie stepped up behind him and wrapped her arms around his waist.

"You'd best not touch me," he told her. "I'm still hotter than a two-dollar pistol."

She didn't move safely away from him. On the contrary, she held him even more tightly and lay her head against his back. He felt the touch of her lips between his shoulder blades. The gesture was so tender, so loving, that tears welled up in his eyes. He blinked them back impatiently, startled at the strange rush of his emotions.

He reached down and grabbed her hands at his waist and released himself from her grasp.

"We'd best not be playing with fire, Eulie," he told her. "We aren't getting off this island tonight. In daylight we might have tried to swim. But it's just too dangerous in the dusk."

"So we'll be here till morning?" she asked.

He nodded.

"Leight will show up bright and early. He's a good man, Eulie, one that a person can always count on," he said.

Eulie nodded. She remembered how Bug had discouraged Rans from leaving Barnes Ridge to work for him. He had intervened against the shivaree gang, unwilling to allow her to be hurt. And he had tied her bonds so very loosely. For the first time, she was thinking more kindly of Clara's unattractive beau.

"So we are stuck here together all night," she said.

"It seems so," he answered.

"And we can't play with fire while we're here?"

Her words were flirty, teasing.

He turned to look at her. He couldn't help smiling. She was sweet and pretty. Just as he'd thought her to be that day at the falls, now so long ago. She'd brought such happiness to the farm, into Uncle Jeptha's life, into his own life. She'd taught him to smile again, to laugh. That was a gift she'd given him of her own free will. Nothing he had asked for or even deserved. He owed her so much. He could not use or misuse her.

"We've already talked about this, Eulie," he said. "I am leaving and I can't leave you carrying a baby. It wouldn't be fair."

The truth of that quieted her. They stood thoughtfully apart, both staring out at the darkening of the distant horizon.

"We could do it once," he heard her say quietly.

"What?"

He turned to look at her.

"Once," she repeated. "You said that the first time I can't get with a baby. So we could do it once."

His mind put up a thousand barriers to the suggestion. The front of his trousers, however, seemed to like the idea very much.

"We could do it this one time," she said. "We're here and with no one else around and nothing else to do. It would be safe because it's our first time."

There was something strange and unusual about her tone. It was high-pitched, and she was talking very fast. She was not looking him in the eye.

Moss put it down to nervousness. The poor girl, he thought. It couldn't be easy to suggest something to a man. Even one that you were tacitly married to.

"I don't know, Eulie," he said. "I'm not sure that would be very smart."

"Why not?" she asked.

At that moment Moss honestly could recall no good reason.

"You're my husband, but you're going away," she said. "If we don't . . . if we don't, well, then I will never know what it's all about. I'd really like to know."

Moss would really like to know as well. He wanted to know the warmth between her thighs, he wanted to feel the smoothness inside of her. He wanted to spill the hot seed boiling up in him into the depths of her body.

He swallowed the tremendous lump that had formed in his throat. The lump in his trousers was not so easily dispensed with.

"But we could only do it once," he told her. "That would be the only way to be certain that there is no child. And the first time is usually not very good."

She was looking directly at him now, her voice a more typical tone, her demeanor unfailingly cheerful.

"Well, if it isn't very good," she assured him sunnily, "then at least I won't miss it and long for it when you're gone."

The thought that she *might* miss him, might long for him after he was gone, was almost too excruciating to bear.

"Do you really think you want to?"

She walked over to him. Easily she was in arm's reach. She bit her lip nervously.

"I want to . . . if you want to."

"Oh, Eulie, you can't even know how much I want to," he said. "But I'm just afraid that if—"

She raised her index finger to touch his lips, silencing him.

"I'm afraid, too," she told him.

His heart was racing. His blood was pounding. His palms were sweating.

"Are you sure?" he asked her.

"I'm sure," she answered.

He didn't know quite what to do next. Surely he should grab her or kiss her or . . . His thoughts trailed off in unexpected directions.

"I've never been with a woman who hadn't been with someone else," he admitted. "I may disappoint you."

"If I've never been with anybody, how will I know if I should be disappointed?"

Her question caught him off guard and he glanced up to see his bride looking at him with eyes lit with mischief.

Moss found himself grinning back at her. It was just them. Just the two of them. What they found together would be their own. And it would be as much hers as his. They would make the best of it. Better or worse, they would make the best of it.

19

"LET'S go fix us a place to be man and wife, Mrs. Collier," he said.

She blushed prettily. It made him feel protective. Hand in hand they walked back into the woods. They tramped around for several moments looking for the perfect spot to bed down.

Moss finally found it on the high point at the north end of the island. The trees were thin and the moon was visible on the rise. Tall grass grew thickly, rising thigh-high. With his knife, Moss cut and stacked it like hay for a cozy bed.

He slipped his galluses down over his shoulders, allowing them to hang ineffectually at his hips as he removed his good shirt. It would probably be forever grass-stained, but it was already scorch-marked and he was far from being able to regret it. He was still decently covered by his red flannels. They would take the disrobing slowly, he decided. He didn't want to shock or offend her any more than would be absolutely necessary.

"Here, put this down, too," Eulie said.

Moss turned to her and she handed him her dress. His mouth went dry. She was standing in the silvery gray light of evening, looking proud and pretty somehow in her worn, homespun undergarments. Her legs were sheathed in black cotton stockings. He followed the length of them until they disappeared under the hem of her white josey. Moss remembered with great clarity, that beneath that thin covering, she was baby-smooth and bare naked.

He swallowed determinedly. He would not just grab her and bury himself inside, he reminded himself. If they were only to have one night, one coupling, one experience to remember all life long, he would not waste it being selfish and greedy.

He spread her dress out neatly atop the bed of grass before turning to look at her once more.

Moss knew that he should rise to his feet and take her in his arms. But somehow his knees had turned into jelly. All the strength and power and muscle in his body seemed to have centered in one low-lying area and he was not sure if he could stand. So he did not. He sat on the edge of their bridal bower, gazing up at her.

"Take your stockings off," he said to her.

Eulie nodded gamely, though he could see once more that she was nervous. She bent forward to undo the ties on her shoe.

Moss leaned slightly sideways to catch a glimpse of a pale, rounded backside beneath the tail of her josey.

She glanced up and caught him looking. They both straightened, flustered, and she pulled modestly at the hem behind her.

"Did you see anything?" she asked him.

"A little," Moss answered honestly. "Not as much as I wanted."

Her expression changed. Any sense of shame or discomfiture dissipated. His words endowed her with a power. An age-old power that women always held with men.

Eulie gazed at Moss thoughtfully for a long moment before she leaned down to unlace the other shoe.

"Look all you want," she told him casually.

This time her movements were exaggerated. She actually bent lower than was necessary and thrust out her buttocks in a manner that was both provocative and more revealing.

Moss stretched out on his side, bracing his elbow on the ground. From this vantage point he could see so much his throat went dry.

She straightened slowly, giving him ample time to survey her fully.

"Did you see everything?" she asked him.

Moss cleared his throat, hoping to ensure that his answer did not come from his voice box in startling soprano.

"I saw a lot that I liked," he told her. "But to see everything, you'd have to be naked."

Eulie took his statement as the challenge that it was. She grasped the hem of her josey and slowly raised it.

Moss saw the tops of the black cotton stockings and then the pale flesh of her thighs above them. She revealed the thin covering of pale blonde hair that covered her mons, the rounded curve to her waist, a tiny, sculpted belly button, a delicately feminine rib cage, and a pair of high upswept breasts with hard pink nipples.

Pulling the josey over her head, she cast it down on their makeshift bed. She raised her arms over her head and removed the pins from her hair, allowing the baby-fine tresses to hang loosely at her shoulders. She stood above him, proud, exposed.

Moss could not imagine any woman looking more desirable, more enticing. He glanced at her face and saw her lower lip trembling. She was not as sure of herself as she pretended to be.

"You are beautiful," he told her and opened his arms in invitation.

She dropped to her knees beside him and fell into his embrace. Eagerly he ran his hands across her naked flesh. She was unbelievably soft and he felt incredibly hard.

He ran his hands down the long length of her back. She shivered.

"Are you cold?" he asked her, pulling her more tightly into him.

She gave him a little half-embarrassed chuckle.

"*Cold* is not what I am at all," she told him.

He laughed, too. Then he kissed her. That was something that they had gotten good at. It had been so enticing when their hands had been tied, only able to express their feelings with lips and tongue. They had learned a lot about each other from that. Now they put that experience together with eager caresses and lustful curiosity.

They lay together side by side as he stroked her buttocks and thighs. The expanse of flesh between her waist and her stocking tops was extremely alluring. He ran his hands over it again and again.

"You never did take your stockings off," he pointed out between kisses.

"You should leave me some modesty," she answered.

"Modesty?"

He made the word a question as he rolled her on to her back and spread her legs with his own.

"I don't see anything modest about your choice of clothing," he said.

"That's because you still have on everything but your shirt."

"Well, I am not the one who looks so well without clothes."

She smiled up at him, pleased with his compliment. But he was speaking the truth. His bride had a nice, tight little figure that showed off better naked than dressed up. It was a secret about his woman that no other man would ever know.

Moss raised himself on knees and elbows, admiring her beneath him. He lowered his mouth to her breast, sucking and teasing until she began to squirm. He moved to the other breast giving it the same treatment. Her pleasure was evident. And in all her wiggling, she began to rub the juncture of her thighs up against his knee.

From the moan that escaped her, it was clear that the movement gave her a lot of pleasure.

Moss slid his hand down to where she pressed herself so eagerly against him. She was hot and wet and slick, and he easily lodged a finger inside of her.

"Oh! Oh my!" she said as she rocked her pelvis eagerly against his hand.

"This is where I'm headed," he told her. "This is where I want to be inside you. But I want to take my time getting there. Can you wait?"

"Oh, I . . . I don't know . . . I . . . oh, I feel so strange."

Moss dragged his thumb across the stiff little nub

that poked impudently out of her thicket of thin blonde curls.

She gasped and jerked at the contact.

He enjoyed her reaction so much, he did it once more just to watch her again.

"You're very sensitive down here," he told her.

"Yes," she admitted breathlessly as she continued to squirm against the action of his hand.

"Do you ever touch yourself down here?"

"What?"

"Alone in bed?" he asked. "Or maybe when you're at your bath, do you ever touch yourself down here."

He leaned down close to her, nipping her throat before he spoke again.

"Answer me," he demanded softly. "And do not lie."

"Sometimes," she confessed. "Sometimes I touch myself."

"And does it feel good when you do it?" he asked.

"Not this good," she answered.

As a reward for her honesty, he set his thumb directly on top of her and began to move it in a rotating fashion.

Eulie was whimpering with need. He was big as a fence post and throbbing with desire. But if they were only going to get once, he wanted it to be the very best that could be had.

She raised her knees up beside his hips, opening herself more fully to him. He was nipping and tasting his way across her bosom and down her stomach.

Her sighs and pleadings were louder now. Her hips were bucking and undulating rhythmically against his hand.

She cried out, desolate when he removed his thumb.

That cry turned into a scream of pleasure as he lowered his mouth over her and took the passion-swelled nub-bin between his teeth.

Her climax was loud and shattering. Her whole body outside went straight and stiff. Inside, her muscles clenched and spasmed against his fingers.

Moss had never done this with a woman. He had never touched one in this manner. But he'd enjoyed it. He'd enjoyed making it happen for her, watching it happen for her. If not for his own raging, now painful erection, he might have been content with just the pleasure of giving her pleasure.

He lay down beside her, wrapping her in his embrace, and continued to stroke and caress her as she relaxed and her breathing quieted. She snuggled against him, so warm and satisfied. It felt wonderful. It also felt as if he didn't get some relief soon, he would shatter into a million pieces.

"That was wonderful," she whispered to him. "I just feel so warm and content, just too lazy to ever move again. I've never . . . I never imagined it was like that. And I didn't know a man could do that with his hand and . . . and his mouth."

Moss felt proud enough to crow like a rooster but managed to restrain himself.

"Well, Eulie," he told her. "My hand and my mouth feel just marvelous. But I got other places that are achy and neglected."

Her brow furrowed curiously, and he drew her palm down the stiffness of his erection.

"My goodness," she said. "Is it always that big? I don't know how you carry such a thing around in your trousers."

"It's not always this big," he assured her.

"Well, it seems to be like that any time I have anything to do with it," she told him.

A little explosion of laughter erupted from him.

"I think you have that effect upon it," he told her.

Holding her hand, he showed her how to stroke him. He lay back, eyes closed, moaning as he held himself in control.

When she suddenly ceased, he raised his head. Her nimble fingers were working at his trouser buttons.

"I think it's time to get you out of these clothes," she told him. "I can't be the only one sitting out here in the open air, naked."

"I let you keep your stockings," he told her.

As she tugged his trousers down over his hips, she grinned at him.

"I don't intend to be nearly as generous," she said.

She wouldn't allow him to so much as raise a hand in assistance as she disrobed him. Dispensing with his boots, socks, and trousers was actually pleasant enough. But when she slowly released the buttons on his union suit, pausing to run her hands inside along his bare flesh, he became increasingly excited.

Moss put his hands behind his head, partly to relax in comfort and partly to keep him from simply grabbing her and rutting away.

She slipped his arms out of the sleeves and dragged the fabric down to his waist without much trouble. When she released the straining buttons below, his erection sprang forth in a way that was almost comical and momentarily startled her.

"Oh my!" she said and then determinedly looked away as if the sight of him fully engorged was too vulgar for her to look upon. But as she continued to ease the union suit down his legs, Moss caught her taking a couple of surreptitious glances.

When he was completely naked he sat up, and she came eagerly into his arms. It was wonderful to be skin to skin, naked to naked with her.

Tentatively, she reached out to touch him intimately.

"It's so smooth," she said with genuine surprise. "I never expected it to be so smooth."

He pulled her hand away.

"I don't think you'd better do that," he said.

"You don't like it?"

"I do like it," he told her. "I like it very much. But I want to be inside you. I don't want to hurt you, but I want to be inside you."

"I want it, too," she said. "I'm not afraid any more. You made me feel so good, I know that nothing with you could feel bad."

Moss was not sure if she was right, but he hoped she was.

He urged her to lie back in the tousled grass and he lay on top of her.

Her hair was spread out like a moonlit halo around her head. And he thought to himself that no angel had ever been so lovely.

Moss struggled to control himself. He had overcome her fears and shown her pleasure. He didn't want to ruin that now with haste or clumsiness. He kissed her and stroked her as he eased into position. Ever so gently he pressed himself forward into the narrow opening of her body.

She was so hot and so tight, he bit his lip against

the intensity of it. He wanted to push on inside. But there was a barrier to be breached. Pain to be inflicted.

"Easy, easy now." He controlled himself as he would a skittish horse. "Let's take it very easy." Calm words as his heartbeat roared in his ears.

Slowly he pressed forward. Don't hurt her, he warned himself. Just don't hurt her.

His own need urged him, but he gritted his teeth and held control. He tilted his hips ever so slightly, moving within her at a snail's pace. Gently, oh so gently filling her. Giving her time to become accustomed to him. Forcing himself to prove just how unselfish he could be.

When he reached the restriction of her maidenhead, he stopped completely, waiting, breathing, struggling with the animal appetites that compelled him to please himself, to get satisfaction, fighting the urge to relieve the desires of his own flesh.

Determinedly he held fast to his concern for her. And fate rewarded him. The thin veil of flesh gave way without resistance and he slid full entry, like a hot knife though butter.

He was inside her, and her body stretched and adjusted to accommodate him. But it was not solely physicality that held them in awe. The unanticipated intensity of their union, the incredible completeness of two people becoming one was almost overwhelming.

She was relaxed beneath him, as if all her emptiness, both flesh and spirit, was, at last, full. He felt a surge of pure tenderness for her. He wanted to care for her, shield her, protect her from everything that might hurt her in the world. Including himself.

"Are you all right?" he asked.

"Oh yes," she answered.

"That's the worst part," he promised. "The rest will be better."

He began to move within her, withdrawing and then pressing forward once more. The snug fit inside her was infinitely pleasurable. He had to clamp down tightly on his jaw to keep from losing control.

She lay docile beneath him, allowing him to do his will for perhaps a minute or more. Then she raised her knees, opening herself more fully to him. With more room, he was able to intensify his thrust, almost pulling out and then pressing fully within once more. With her feet beneath her on the ground, she gained a little leverage, and she began to meet his rhythmic movements with her own.

It was smoother, hotter, finer than anything he had ever felt. No woman, ever, had so filled his senses and thrilled his body this way.

His blood was pounding. His body aching. His seed screaming for release. He was not going to be able to hold off. He was going to spend himself early and then it would be over. There could only be one time and in another moment, it would be ended.

Determinedly he took his mind elsewhere. If he allowed himself to think of the hot, wetness, the tightness of her surrounding him, it would be all over. He had to think of something else. He had to think of somewhere else.

Moss took his heart to the place he'd always taken it. To that mystical haven that had always offered sanctuary from the cares of his day, the sorrows of his past, the pain of the present.

Deliberately he dreamed of Texas.

In his mind's eye he saw the vast rolling prairie, with native bluestem high as the horse's flank as he rode through it. Above him the sky was endless and unclouded. He could feel the warmth of the west wind against his face and hear the call of meadowlarks. Evidence of abundant game, both large and small, was all around him. Cattle grazed in the distance, sleek and healthy. The ground was fresh and new beneath the horse's hooves, unsullied by scythe or plow.

He was there. He was there at last. And it was everything that he had ever imagined it to be. New visions. Unfamiliar vistas. A new earth, wholly his own and of his own making.

It was boldness, perfection. It was life at all its finest. And it was her. Eulie. The woman beneath him. The woman whose body now joined with his own. She was all. She was everything. She was his Texas.

The hot flood of dream and desire and the destiny of the human race shot from him in spurts so powerful they were akin to pain.

"I love you!" he cried out to her.

He could only hope that in her passion she hadn't heard his words.

20

HE needed to leave. It was time to go. If he was ever to get away, it was now. Forget the crop and the sorghum, the apple picking and the root cellar. If he did not leave for Texas very soon, he might never get away at all.

Such were the thoughts of Moss Collier less than a week later as he walked in from the fields, sweat-soaked and aching. He worked hard, punishingly hard, attempting to exhaust himself. He hadn't had a decent night of sleep since he'd held her in his arms out on the island. He would have thought that getting a fine measure of sexual relief would have made everything easier. But it was worse. It was much worse. His appetite was whetted, and it seemed that now that he knew what it was like to hold her, caress her, put himself inside her, he could no longer live without that satisfaction.

Beside him young Rans, leading the hitched jenny, was tight-lipped and sullen. Still angry, Moss suspected. He wasn't quite sure what was the last thing they'd argued about, but for certain Moss had been as testy as a bear with his butt in a briar bush for days. He almost felt sorry for the fellow. Except, of course, it was almost impossible to feel sorry for anyone as prickly and hardheaded as Eulie's little brother. When he left, the bulk of the crop work would fall to the boy. That would be a tremendous job for one so young. But he had to leave it to him. He had to get away.

Eulie had not been herself for the last week either. Moss's mood was bad, but he'd always been rough-spoken and grouchy. Eulie—endlessly, hopelessly, annoyingly cheerful Eulie—had turned into a fitful, unhappy complainer. She was sniping and grousing at everybody in earshot from daylight until dark. Nothing that anybody said or did seem to suit her. She wasn't sleeping very much either. And it showed in the heaviness of her step and the dark circles under her eyes.

The Colliers were, Moss conceded, a decidedly miserable pair. The uneasy truce of two people selfishly seeking separate goals had been shattered by a consummation that had been more than physical communion. They, two souls, had become one flesh, and such a confluence was not so easily dissipated.

"Moss! Moss!"

He heard her calling his name and looked up. She was running up the ridge toward them at a frantic pace, her eyes wide and frightened.

Fear leaping into his heart, Moss raced toward her.

"What is it? What's happened?" he called out.

The next moment she was in his arms and too breathless at first to even speak.

"Minnie," she finally managed to get out.

Moss glanced up looking around, frantically surveying the distance as far as he could see. He saw nothing amiss and did not see Eulie's little sister anywhere.

"What's happened to Minnie?" he asked.

She was shaking her head now, tears in her eyes. Moss continued to hold her in his arms. She was shaking.

"I can't find her," Eulie said. "I can't find her anywhere."

"She has to be somewhere."

"I noticed that she was gone," Eulie said. "I started looking and I started calling. I've searched everywhere. She's not anywhere. Oh, Moss, I don't know if she's wandered into the woods or fallen into the river."

Neither choice was a good one. A little girl in a heavy dress, even one who was a good swimmer, which Minnie was not, would be rapidly sucked downstream and over the falls. The sharp, jagged rocks might not be fatal, but drowning would be likely. The woods were little better, laced with the traps and snares of hunters. Bears and panthers were more rare these days, but snakes, even bees could prove a danger to a young child lost.

"When did you last see her?" Moss asked. "What was she doing?"

"I . . . I don't know. I . . . I saw her at breakfast and then after, I suppose. I was working in the garden. The twins were there. I thought she was there, but . . ."

She gave him a look of helpless anxiety.

"We've been calling and calling and she doesn't answer," she told him.

"Where is everyone else?"

"I sent Clara up to the bald point at the top of the ridge to see if she could spot her. The twins are tramping the edge of the river in either direction and Uncle Jeptha is searching the trees at the far side of the cabin."

His heart pounding, Moss deliberately remained calm.

"Be easy, sweetheart," he told Eulie. "You won't make it better by losing your head. We'll find her."

She nodded as if she believed him, but her face was still stricken with fear.

"Find who?" Rans asked.

"Minnie is missing," Eulie answered and then turned to Moss. "Should we send Rans down the mountain to gather more people to help us search?"

Before he could reply, the boy piped in with a chuckle. "Why don't I just go down the mountain and tell her to come home," he said. "She's at the Pierces'."

"What?" Eulie's question was incredulous.

"I saw her getting her things together this morning," Rans explained. "I asked her where she was going and she said 'home.' I think that probably means she is with Mr. and Mrs. Pierce."

"Minnie told you that she was going to run away from home and you didn't try to stop her?"

"Why should I?" Rans asked. "I run away all the time and nobody ever tries to stop me."

Eulie was exasperated. "That's totally different," she said.

"How?"

"Well you are a lot older and know your way around the woods and . . ."

"Minnie surely knows her way to the Pierces'," Rans said. "That's not the difference. The difference is that Minnie has someplace to go and I never do."

"You don't know what you are talking about."

"I know exactly what I'm talking about," he answered, his voice now raised in anger. "Minnie has someplace to go. She's got a home. One where she is happy. One that she stumbled into on her on. And you just can't stand that, can you. If it wasn't Eulie's idea, if it wasn't what Eulie wanted, then it can't be good, it can't be right."

"Daddy told me to take care of all of you," she insisted.

"Oh, Daddy," he said, feigning respect. "You mean the miserable, lazy souse who spawned us? I don't think you should take anything he said too much to heart. He never cared a whole lot about us when he was alive, I'm sure he cares even less as he rots in hell."

The argument had gotten louder and had drawn the attention of the rest of the family, who were hurrying up the ridge toward them.

"Don't talk about Daddy that way!" Eulie scolded him.

"Why not? Because it's not true?" Rans was in a fine fury. "You know that it is. Virgil Toby was as low-down and worthless a man as ever walked this earth. He never cared for us or Mama or anything else. All he wanted was his bottle of whiskey and as long as he had that, nothing else in the world mattered to him."

"He loved us," Eulie insisted. "In his way, he loved us."

"Well, I don't love him," Rans answered. "I'm ashamed that he was my father. I am ashamed to bear his name. In the Sweetwood being a Toby means being poor, laggard, drunken, and useless. That stain on who we are is the only thing dear Daddy has left us. And it'll take a lifetime to wipe it out."

"Is that what you think?" Eulie yelled at him.

"Yes, it is," Rans answered. "And I think that if Minnie has a chance to start over, begin clean, to leave the 'nasty Toby children' behind her forever, then I say let her do it. I wish the rest of us had such a chance."

Eulie hauled back her hand and slapped her brother hard across the mouth. The contact stunned him. It stunned all of them. The whole family stood frozen in place, not believing what had happened.

"I am sick to death of your miserable complaints and bad temper," Eulie hollered at him. "I'm trying to do what is best for this family, for all of us. You only ever think about yourself. Daddy was sick and miserable and unhappy, but you never feel sorry for him, mourn for him. You just think about you and how everything that happened, no matter what happened, it happened to you. You blame Daddy for every slight and wrong and miserable moment that you've ever lived. Well, it's high time that you take some of that responsibility onto yourself. If people don't like you, maybe it's because you are sour, quick-tempered, and disagreeable, not that you are Virgil Toby's son."

Hands on hips, she stood nose-to-nose with her brother, steaming with fury. He tried to step around her, and she grabbed his arm.

"Running away?" she taunted him. "Isn't that what you always do? When things get tough, Rans Toby runs way. Every time things don't go like he wants, he runs away."

"Leave me alone," he growled out.

"Well, do us all a favor," Eulie said furiously. "Next time just keep on running. If you don't want to be in our family, then we don't want you around, either."

He jerked away from her then, stiff with anger and injured pride. He began a brisk pace toward the cabin.

Eulie didn't even glance back in his direction. She focused her attention on Moss.

"Can you take me to the Pierces' on your horse?" she asked.

He nodded. "If that's what you want," he said.

"I'm bringing my sister back home where she belongs, whether she likes it or not."

The clearing around the cabin was quiet and peaceful for a change. Jeptha should have been grateful for it. The noise and constant upheaval of a passel of young-uns was a little wearying for a man of his age and disposition. But somehow this afternoon the quiet was disturbing. It was almost too quiet.

Moss and Eulie had headed off to fetch Little Minnie more than an hour ago. Clara and the twins had been so stunned at her strange behavior and worried that she might get into an equally unkind argument with Minnie that they decided to go down the ridge to the Pierces' themselves. Jeptha had no idea what help they could possibly be, but he hadn't tried to dissuade them. He had his own worries to consider. His own thoughts to plague him.

Seeing Sary again, talking with her at long last, had been both heaven and hell. To hear that she had loved him, that she loved him still, had been a sweet balm to the wounds of his heart. But her inability to see his side, to understand that he rejected her out of love for her, that was a very bitter pill. She doubted his motivations. And she'd made him doubt them himself.

He *had* done it for her. He was certain of that. Or at least he had been. He'd not wanted to shackle her with a man who was only half a man.

Working in the quiet solitude of the garden, he allowed himself to dwell at length on what she'd said, what he'd said, and all the things that he wished had been said.

He knew that she was partly right as well. He had hidden out, hoping that he would die, hoping that he would never have to face his life, or what was left of it. He chose not to face Sary, for fear that he would see her horror, her rejection. It was easier to be noble and set her free than to try to make a life with her, when he didn't have the courage to live.

But of course, all that was before, he thought. It was before . . . before what, he didn't know. Somehow in the last few weeks everything had changed for him. Having Eulie and the children here had affected him in a way he'd not anticipated. It was as if seeing himself as part of a family again had made his leglessness seem more an inconvenience than an incapacity.

Of course, nothing was really different. He still had no legs. He still pushed himself around in a cart. He would never dance again or run in the woods. But for all the things he couldn't do, there were still a good many that he could.

Oh, my mistake, Sary had said to him, facetiously. *I didn't realize they'd cut off that part of you as well.*

That part of him was still in perfect working order. And a plaguey inconvenience it was. It seemed almost unfair that if a man was never to have sex again that he should retain the will and the means to do so. It might have been easier if that cannonball had gelded him when he was gimped. Idly, he began to wonder if a man with no legs could make love to a woman. There didn't seem to be any reason why not. It might require a bit of imagination and modification. Lust, however, was a great innovator. A man trying to fulfill his passions, or those of a woman he cared about, always found a way. But would a woman even want that? Wouldn't she be repulsed by him?

It wasn't *a* woman that concerned him, as if any other ever entered his mind. It was only Sary.

I loved you, Jeptha, she had said. *I loved you and I love you and nothing you can do now nor ever can make me stop.*

Surely she couldn't have meant that. Yet he knew that Sary would never lie to him.

In some deeply buried place in his heart, a little flame of hope had ignited.

He thought about the letters. It was amazing that he'd forgotten about them. He would have sworn that he knew every word in them by heart. They had, in some way, been the making of him. When he'd walked away from the Sweetwood, he'd been little more than a wild-eyed kid, full of vinegar . . . and confusion.

The war had changed that. It was as if he'd had opportunity for a close-up look at all that was real and valuable in life. Men facing battle laughed and joked together in the hours beforehand, unwilling to allow the fears and finality to ruin what little time they had left.

He'd learned the priorities of human existence. Warmth was more important than food. But food more than comfort. The camaraderie of other men was very basic. And the memory of those back home who loved you and missed you was not as far down on the list as he might have imagined.

The letters had been his adulthood. That was how he thought of them. They were the life he'd had between childhood and amputation.

Jeptha rarely thought about that time. Of course, he tried not to think of the past at all, but even when he did, it was the hazy, nostalgic vision of youth. He thought now of the sober, thoughtful, considered man that he had become in that time. He was so glad that he'd shared that time with Sary. It had been his best time. It had been a time he could look back upon with some pride. It was surprising that he never did.

Perhaps it was because he was not so changed.

The thought came to him almost in passing. But it was one of monumental import. The things he had learned to care about, to value, to hold dear, those were what made a man who he was. That remained constant from the war to now. His code of ethics and honor had not transformed. Even his need for the personal satisfaction of a job well done continued on, long after the job he could do well had dramatically changed.

All of those important parts of who he was and what his life was about were the same as always. He had not left everything on a dew-dampened field in Virginia. Somehow he had thought Jeptha Barnes, the man he was, lost forever. But truly, the only thing lost was a pair of legs.

He thought about Nils and Zack. He thought about Moss's father, DeWitt. The world would never know what they had learned from war, what kind of men it had made them. They lived on only in the memory of those that loved them. Sary was right about that. Because he lived, he owed something to those that had not.

A surgeon and a cannonball had cut off his legs. But he had cut himself off from the lives around him. That was a far worse amputation.

Jeptha finished weeding the last row and surveyed the garden critically. It had suffered a late start, too much rain followed by too little, and a rabbit-crazed dog ripping through it in full harness. But it was growing, still providing for their table, its scars and injuries hardly visible to anyone unaware of their existence.

He turned his cart and rolled it across the clearing and up the path toward the cabin. He'd spent many long afternoons within the confines of its four walls. Now he wanted to get the makings to weave another cane seat. There was no telling when the family might expect company for dinner.

Somehow the gray fog that had surrounded his heart had lifted a little. Just enough for a peek at what was outside him, what was beyond the confines of his prison. Could he live out there? he wondered. Was he man enough to have a life that was full and complete?

It would be a life without legs. But it didn't need to be a life without purpose or meaning . . . or even love.

Jeptha propelled his cart across the porch. He opened the screen and went through the door of the cabin. It was cool and dark inside and seemed inordinately empty. He wheeled himself over toward the bed, his thoughts far away. In the dim light of the interior he rolled over something with one of his wheels.

He snorted impatiently. Eulie was a very conscientious housewife and tried to keep the place neat and picked up. But with a whole houseful of younguns, it was near to impossible.

Jeptha retrieved the item and gazed at it curiously. It was the little yellowed pamphlet on Texas. He screwed his mouth up in disapproval. Apparently the children had been in Moss's strongbox again. They really should not be allowed to rifle through someone else's things. Especially so if they could not seem to manage to get things back in order.

He pushed himself over to the other bed and pulled out the box beneath it with the intent of dropping the papers inside. Perhaps it was the ease in which he was able to drag the box toward him or some sixth sense that warned him that something was amiss. But in the shadowy darkness of the cabin, he reached his hand inside the box. It was empty. The sack of money that represented his nephew's life savings and the fine side arm with its box of ammunition were gone.

A sick wave of dread filled Jeptha's throat. He wanted to vomit.

21

RANS regretted his hasty behavior almost immediately. But he was leaving for good this time. Eulie had as much as said that he should go. He was sick of her and of Moss Collier and of everyone and everything in the Sweetwood. But if he were going away for good, he needed money for provisions. And the gun—well, the world outside was a dangerous place. He needed the gun for protection.

He was heading downriver, never to return. He raised his chin high. Rans Toby was going to make his own place in the world. To be his own man at long last. He would never be treated with condescension or disrespect again.

Just the thought of that bright future had him whistling to himself as he walked and made the stealing of the gun and the money seem less wicked. Once he'd established himself out in the world, he'd have lots of money to send home. He could easily pay back what he'd stolen, and more.

He was about a half a mile past the falls when he spotted the Pusser brothers out in their boat. Rans hurried to the bank of the river and hailed them.

"Where you headed?" he called out.

"Jarl," one of the brothers yelled back.

"Do you got room for a passenger?"

Rans watched as a short discussion took place between the two men. A couple of moments later they began to paddle the boat out of the downstream current and into his direction.

When they got within talking range, Delbert shot out a question.

"Where you off to?"

"Downriver," Rans answered. "I . . . I got business downriver."

Delbert raised an eyebrow at that, but didn't say anything. Rans was glad. He did not want to explain himself. And he wasn't about to say that he was leaving home. They'd think he was some little boy running away.

The Pussers eased the boat up against the shore. Rans grabbed the prow and made way to hop in. He threw his sack of needments on board, against a row of corked jugs covered by brown gunnysacks. It landed with the distinctive jangle of coins. The sound caught the attention of both brothers.

"What you got in your poke?" Delbert asked. "Nails?"

Rans nearly sighed aloud with relief as he hurried to seat himself in the boat. It was probably not a good idea for anyone to know that he was carrying a stash of money. It was the plain truth that he had robbed Moss Collier, even if he did intend to pay him back. The law might not take such an eventuality into account.

"Horseshoes," Rans answered, very pleased with his own brilliant deceit. "I've been collecting lost and worn horseshoes and muleshoes. I can trade the iron to the blacksmith in Jarl."

Donald gave him an inquisitive look.

"Most usually he trades for labor," the man said. "You ain't got no animal to have shod."

That was an unfortunate weakness in the lie Rans told.

"Moss is going to ride his horse down later," he mumbled hurriedly.

"You mean you're going to use horseshoes that you found to help out Collier?" Delbert said. "You must be a mighty fine brother-in-law."

"We're a family," Rans said, echoing the kind of words his sister would use. "What we do for one another is the same as doing it for ourself."

The Pusser brothers didn't dispute his words. They probably understood family as well as he did. Or as well as perhaps he should have. Eulie's words were never his own. He had never felt that strong sense of them being bonded together that she had always talked about. He supposed that he'd never had to. No matter what the circumstances and how far apart they were, Eulie kept the family together as one. That's why she didn't want Clara to marry. Why she found it so hard to let Minnie live with the Pierces. And that's why she would always blame herself for today, the day that he actually left home forever.

The trip was mainly uneventful—except, of course, for Rans it was a tremendous adventure. Riding in a boat was a rare treat. And he had only been down the river a handful of times in his life. There was very little talking going on. The Pusser brothers, like himself, seemed to be content with their own thoughts.

However, as they neared the dock at Jarl, Delbert

struck up a conversation about poker. After his success with the game at Preaching Sunday, it was easy for Rans to warm up to the subject.

"The men in the saloon in Jarl," Delbert told him. "Now they are real poker players."

"Oh yeah?"

Delbert nodded. "There ain't nothing these town men likes better than whiling away the afternoon with a glass of beer and a deck of cards."

"Preacher Thompson sure wouldn't approve of that," Rans said, chuckling.

"The preacher!" Delbert laughed. "That man wouldn't darken the saloon door. He knows by a damn sight that he ain't welcome."

The cursing momentarily caught Rans off guard. Eulie didn't allow anything even close to cuss words. A genuine "hellfire" was rare in his experience.

"That's for d-d-damn sure." Rans answered, momentarily stuttering over the word. "For real damn sure," he declared again, emphatically.

"That's what Donald and I are hoping to do this afternoon," Delbert said. "We're going to the saloon and play some poker. You could come with us . . . ah . . . no, I guess you'd better not. These men don't play poker for acorns. If you don't got money, them fellows would just think you was a kid."

"Who says I ain't got money?" Rans said.

"You got money?" Donald asked, apparently surprised.

Rans remembered too late that he didn't want anybody to know. "I . . . got a little," he answered. He turned back to face Delbert. "I got a little . . . ah . . . traveling money. I suspect I've got enough to sit in for a hand or two. And the way I win, I'll probably be playing poker all afternoon."

Slowly, rather slowly, Delbert smiled.

"Then you just come with us, Rans Toby, and we men will have us a fine time."

Rans wanted to pinch himself to see if he was dreaming. Here he was, already in Jarl, a companion to two of the most admirably disreputable fellows he'd ever heard of, and fixing to spend the afternoon playing poker. Why, he might even win enough extra money that he could send Moss Collier's to him on the Pusser brother's return trip. If he'd known it was going to be this easy, he'd have left home years ago.

They docked the boat and unloaded the jugs. The gunnysacks were unwieldy and, with three gallons in each one, very heavy. But Rans toted one all the same, wanting to be of help to the Pusser brothers in any way he knew how.

Fortunately, they did not have to go far. The unsavory establishments of the small community were all down near the riverside. As one continued away from the water, the establishments got cleaner, nicer, more wholesome in appearance. Rans didn't bother to venture that far. He followed the Pusser brothers down a smelly back alley brimming with rotting garbage and the even more odorous and loathsome contents of chamber pots.

Rans made a face and held his nose. Donald pointed at him and laughed.

Delbert was more sympathetic.

"You'll get used to it," he told Rans. "The honey wagon don't get down here that often."

"The honey wagon?"

Donald laughed again delightedly. "Maybe we can get you a nice ride on the honey wagon. Would you like that?"

"Stop teasing my friend," Delbert scolded his brother. "The honey wagon is what they load the dung around here into."

"They load up the dung?"

"It's too close to the river to dig outhouses, so they load it up and haul it out north of town to bury it," Delbert said. "If you're ever looking for work, the honey wagon hires a lot of shoveling boys."

Rans repressed a gag. He was no orphaned waif forced to take any job available. He had money in his pocket. His future employment would be something entirely different.

They went into a seedy-looking bar at the far end of the alley. The lurid yellow paint on its swinging doors was cracked and chipping. The doors creaked loudly as they passed through.

The inside of the place was no finer than its outward appearance. It smelled mostly of stale beer, with occasionally unpleasant whiffs of acrid vomit. Rans glanced around the place. There were several old men in differing states of inebriation, a couple of down-at-the heels drifters at the bar, and the most amazing-looking woman that Rans had ever seen. Her face was painted white as a bedsheet. She had a spot of bright color on each cheek and the biggest, reddest lips that were ever on the earth.

"That Ida, she's quite a gal," Donald whispered into his ear.

"Is she the one that gave you the syphilis?" Rans asked.

"Nah, she ain't the one that gived it to me," Donald answered. Then he leaned closer. "So I gived it to her."

Donald thought that was a great joke and hooted with laughter. Rans was not quite sure why it was funny, but joined in nonetheless, just to be sociable.

Delbert gave the proprietor behind the bar the liquor jugs. In turn, the man counted out the payment on the bar. When the transaction was complete, Delbert stashed the money in the inside pocket of his jacket.

"Where's all the poker players this afternoon, Sam?" he asked the bartender.

The man gave him a strange sort of look and then muttered something about expecting them later.

"Now that we've got some money," Delbert said, "we thought we'd play a hand or two. Can we borrow your cards?"

The man immediately reached below the counter.

"I want that little blue deck in the fancy case," Delbert said. "It'll do us just fine."

The bartender's face had no expression at all, but he nodded. The little blue deck was not under the counter, but in the cashbox next to the wall.

"Here you are," the man said, handing the cards to Delbert.

Pusser turned and smiled broadly at Rans.

"Why don't we play a couple of hands, just the three of us, until some of the other fellows arrive."

"That sounds good," Rans agreed.

The three of them took a table in the corner of the room, next to the front window. There was a lantern hanging over the center of the table, but it was the sunlight through the window that illuminated the game.

Rans set his pokesack right next to his foot and leaned down to carefully get a few coins out of the money bag. He wouldn't need much, he thought. Delbert and Donald, having just got paid, had plenty for him to win, so he could play against the other men when they arrived.

The fancy deck of cards didn't appear all that fancy to Rans. They looked just like the deck that Dudley Samson carried. Except some of the cards seemed to be very much used.

The bartender brought them glasses of beer. The last thing Rans wanted to admit was that he had never tasted the stuff. So he drank the sudsy brew as if such consumption were an everyday occurrence. He didn't like the taste of it much. But he drank it anyway.

Delbert shuffled with great dexterity and Rans was favorably impressed. He anted up and the cards were dealt.

It was just as it had been that Preaching Sunday. Rans was lucky enough to get really good cards and he played them with great skill.

He won hand after hand. Donald took the pot twice, but Delbert was forced to fold again and again. And when he did go the distance, he never had more than a middling pair.

The pile of money in front of Rans grew. The Pusser brothers, trying desperately to get back some of their losses, urged the stakes higher and higher. That was all right with Rans. The higher the stakes, the more money he won. There seemed to be no chance that his luck would change.

But it did.

Delbert won a couple of hands. Rans was actually

glad for him. He hated to take all the man's money. As Delbert's cards came up better, he wagered a little bit recklessly, Rans thought. But amazingly, his bets came through for him.

When Rans threw in the last coin he had on the table, he'd had enough. He didn't care about seeing the other men anymore. He was ready to get out of the ill-smelling, seedy saloon.

Surprisingly, Delbert folded on that hand, and Rans easily beat Donald's pair of fours. With new winnings in hand, Rans was revitalized. He could play this game all night long.

And they did.

As night fell, there were more and more men showing up at the saloon. Not one of them even hinted at any interest in participating, but a small crowd gathered around to watch. They were called sweaters, Delbert told him. Men who liked the excitement of the game, but didn't have their own money to bet. Sweaters was a good name for them, Rans thought. With all the people standing around, they could get no benefit from the opened window. A veil of tobacco smoke hung like a cloud over the table. It was getting unbearably hot. Fortunately, the bartender kept a cool glass of beer at Rans's elbow all evening. It didn't really taste that bad once you got used to it.

Rans had to reach back into his pokesack a half dozen times to keep in the game. His luck was bound to turn any minute. And it did.

He picked up the card dealt him, neatened them into a pile, and slowly fanned them out as he held them before his eyes. Jack of hearts, king of clubs, king of diamonds, seven of clubs, king of spades.

Rans wanted to scream aloud to the heavens. What a hand! Three kings and he hadn't even taken a draw. With as much nonchalance as he could manage, Rans laid his cards down on the table. His pile of silver had dwindled considerably, and he reached into the poke-sack at his feet to get a fresh supply from the money bag. To his surprise, he found only a handful of coins left. His heart began pounding, and he felt a wave of nausea that was almost paralyzing.

He had the sudden panicked feeling that he should grab his handful of coins and run from this place as fast as his legs would carry him. But he'd already anted in, and he was holding three kings.

This would be the last hand, he decided. He'd win back as much money as he could with his kings and then he'd leave this place. He placed his bet.

"I'll see yours," Donald said. "And raise."

Delbert took a quick glance at his cards. "How much do I need to stay in?" he asked, as if he hadn't really been paying attention to the game.

Rans told him, and he threw his money in casually before turning his attention back to the painted-faced Ida. The woman was leaning forward on Delbert's chair. Her spangly red dress was cut very low and from his position directly across from Delbert, Rans had a perfect line of sight down the front of the woman's dress. The view more amazed Rans than excited him. The woman's teats were big enough to be cow udders.

Rans discarded the seven and the jack and added his new cards to his hand.

Six of spades, no help.

King of hearts.

His own leaped in his chest. Four kings would be

very hard to beat. If he played it right, he could get all his money back and more. But Rans couldn't give any hint of his joy. If the Pusser brothers suspected he had such a hand, they would drop out and not bet. Rans needed to win and he needed to win big.

Delbert drew three cards. Donald one.

The betting recommenced.

The pot grew bigger and bigger as the wagering went higher and higher. In disgust, Donald folded. By the time Delbert called, everything that Rans had was sitting in the middle of the table.

With repressed excitement and a goodly portion of nerve, Rans laid his cards on the table. The four handsome kings staring up at him proudly.

The crowd made a whistling sound. They were impressed.

Delbert eyed the cards as well.

"That's a pretty good hand, Rans," he said.

Rans couldn't help grinning ear to ear, he was so pleased with himself.

"Unfortunately," Delbert continued. "Tonight, it's not quite good enough."

Pusser laid down his own cards.

"Straight flush," he said. "Four, five, six, seven, and eight. All diamonds."

A shout went through the crowd. Rans was looking directly into Delbert Pusser's cool blue eyes. He could hear the jubilation around him, but it was as if it were very far away.

The man raked his winnings toward his side of the table.

"You want to try to win some of this back?" he asked Rans.

"I don't have any more money," Rans answered. He was surprised at the sound of his own words. They were so dispassionate.

"Maybe you could sell your horseshoes," Delbert said.

The way that he said it, the tone of his voice, and the look on his face said to Rans distinctly that Delbert had known all along that there were no horseshoes. He'd known that the pokesack contained money. And he'd deliberately set out to win it.

"Can I buy you another beer?" he asked.

Rans shook his head. He picked up his pokesack and rose to his feet.

Delbert announced loudly that he was buying a round of drinks.

Without fanfare, Rans quietly slipped through the swinging doors. He walked to the corner of the building and just stood there for a long moment, trying very hard not to think. But the enormity of his loss overwhelmed him and he bent over and vomited in the alley.

He had lost it. He had lost every penny of it. He'd stolen money to help him get away and he'd lost it in a poker game.

He'd have to stay in Jarl. There was no way he could travel farther. And this close to home, Moss Collier would surely find him and demand his money back. Rans would have to take a job. What kind of job he could get, he did not know. The memory of Delbert's advice about the honey wagon filled him with disgust and dread.

Once more he threw up. The beer did not sit well on his stomach, especially when mixed with the tension and terror of losing so much.

"Are you all right, young fella?"

Rans glanced up to see an old grayed and bewhiskered stranger beside him. He'd been one of the sweaters at the game.

"I'm fine," Rans choked out. "Just had too much to drink, I guess."

The man nodded. "A little boy your age shouldn't be drinking at all. You should be home with your mam and pap."

"I ain't no little boy," Rans told him angrily. With the disgrace he had been through that day, the last thing he was willing to put up with was condescension.

The man raised an eyebrow.

"I didn't intend no insult," the man said. "I just knew that you had to be really young or really stupid to play poker with a deck of cards as crimped as that one."

"What?"

The man chuckled lightly but there was no humor in it.

"All the face cards had ragged edges," he said. "And the aces had the corners shaved. That old deck has cleaned more rubes than a crossroads bathhouse."

Rans stood there, stunned to silence.

"Let it be a lesson, boy," he said. "It's a hard way to learn, but a sure cure for ignorance."

The man walked on. Rans continued to stand there. The waves of sickness he'd felt were boiling now into anger. He hadn't just lost the money, he'd been cheated out of it. He'd been cheated. The Pusser brothers had cheated him.

He would get his money back. He would demand

that Delbert Pusser hand over the winnings. They were got unfairly. Rans would make him give them back. How would he make them do that? he asked himself. The Pusser brothers were grown men. Rans was only thirteen. How could he make them do anything?

The answer came to him. Rans squatted down and opened the pokesack. He withdrew the handsome blued nickel side arm. The sight of it would certainly make the Pusser brothers sit up and take notice. He fished through the sack until he came up with the cartridge box. Quickly Rans opened the loading gate and slid six shots into the barrel. He snapped it back in place and rose to his feet.

Fury putting steel in his backbone, Rans marched back into the saloon. Donald was halfway up the stairs with the painted woman, Ida, on his arm. Delbert was standing at the bar, laughing. The laughing fueled the anger inside Rans. Delbert had pretended to be his friend, cheated him out of his money, and now stood happy and laughing as he guzzled another glass of beer.

Rans walked right up to him and raised the gun.

"You cheated me. I want my money back."

There was a rash of startled movement and nervous expletives as those around quickly moved out of the way. Silence followed.

"You cheated me," Rans repeated. "I want my money back."

"Cheated?" Delbert looked as cool as if he were discussing the weather. "You lost fair and square, Rans. Why on earth would you think I cheated?"

"The deck was marked," Rans said.

"You didn't make any objection to the deck."

"I'm making objection now," he said. "That deck was marked."

Delbert turned to the bartender. "Get us the deck, Sam," he said. "Let's see if it's marked."

The man leaned under the counter and brought out a deck of cards in a fancy case.

"Show us the cards," Delbert said.

Sam opened the case and spread the deck out on the bar.

"Which ones are marked?" Delbert asked.

Rans glanced down at the cards. They were the same style and the same color, but they were not the same cards. They were perfect and pristine. Not a worn or frayed one among them.

"That's not the same deck," Rans said. "It's the deck you keep in the cashbox."

"Do you have a deck of cards in your cashbox, Sam?" Delbert asked.

The bartender shook his head. "I keep all the cards under the counter," he answered as he opened the cashbox and showed it to Rans. There was nothing in it but money and papers.

The marked deck was long gone. But Rans was unwilling to give up.

"You cheated me, Delbert Pusser," he said. "You cheated me and I want my money. I want my money now."

"Well, you're not about to get it," Delbert told him calmly. "Go home, Rans."

"I'm not going anywhere without what is mine," he said. Rans drew back the hammer on the gun until it cocked. "Give me my money or I'll shoot you."

He stood facing Delbert Pusser. The man's expression was cool, but Rans could see beyond it. A line of sweat had formed on his forehead. His lips were pale, almost bloodless as he stared down the .44 Colt that was an arm's length away. At this distance, Rans couldn't miss.

Suddenly he saw a movement out of the corner of his eye. Rans hardly had an instant to glance in that direction before he saw Donald Pusser lunging at him.

He turned.

He shot.

And shot.

And shot.

And shot.

And shot.

And shot.

22

RANS was a thirteen-year-old boy who wanted to be treated like a man. Eulie couldn't imagine anyplace in the whole world where that was more likely to happen than the Caulfield County Jail in Jarl, Tennessee.

She sat with her husband, nervous and fidgety, waiting for the sheriff. Waiting to find out what was going to happen. Waiting to learn if she could see her brother.

Moss held her hand in his own. The firm clasp imbued her with much needed strength and comfort. Her eyes were still puffy from last night's tears. Moss had come to her, carrying her from her bed to the front porch, where he dried her eyes, listened to her outpouring of fear and regret and held her all night long.

They were just leaving the Pierce home when Uncle Jeptha caught up with them. Minnie was wailing pitifully, but that was a vast improvement over the kicking and screaming that accompanied her initial refusal to go with them. The man in the dog-drawn goat cart had come charging down from the ridge like the demons of hell were after him. The look on Jeptha's face raised such alarm even Minnie hushed immediately.

"What's happened? What is it?" Moss asked.

"Rans is gone," he said.

Eulie shrugged it off. "He leaves after every argument," she told him. "He'll show up again in a few hours."

"I don't think so," Jeptha answered. He turned to Moss. "The boy's been in your strongbox. He's taken the money and your gun."

Eulie clamped her hand over her mouth in disbelief.

"He didn't. He couldn't."

But he did and he had.

The long night of wait and worry had ended at dawn. Yeoman Browning had ridden up to the ridge to give them the news that had come up river. Rans Toby had been arrested in Jarl for shooting the Pusser brothers.

Eulie was dumbstruck with disbelief.

"Is anybody dead?" Moss had asked.

"Not so far as I know," he'd answered.

Eulie could hardly remember what occurred in the next few minutes. She recalled the girls' crying. And Uncle Jeptha's offering solemn advice to Moss as he saddled the horse.

Then they were off, riding double down the mountain. Eulie couldn't recall asking to go or even having anyone inquire if she wanted to. Women rarely had any dealings in town. And certainly never with jails or lawmen. But Moss had simply known she needed to see her brother and hadn't for a moment allowed the conventions of womanhood to stand in the way of what was best for his wife. Her fear of the big red horse had been paltry when measured against her need to get to her brother's side, to offer him what aid and assistance she could.

Now Moss sat beside her in the jail as she waited to hear her brother's fate.

"I'm going to let Minnie live with the Pierces," she said abruptly.

"What?"

She turned to glance up at him, so strong and handsome and steady beside her.

"I'm going to let them adopt her," Eulie said. "I . . . I made a deal with God. I'll let Minnie have what she wants and He'll see that nothing bad happens to Rans."

Moss looked at her, his sad eyes worried. "I'm not sure that God is in the business of making deals," he told her. "If you are going to let Minnie go with the Pierces, you should do it because it is the best thing for Minnie, not because you want to help Rans."

She nodded, knowing that he spoke the truth. It had been her dream, her ambition, to keep her family together. It was part of her obligation to take care of her youngers and do what was best for them. It had just not entered her mind that her dream might run counter to her obligation. She'd thought that uniting the family was an absolute, something that was always the right thing to do in every situation. Eulie knew now that wasn't so. Heaven had set out a number of absolutes in life. But most things had to be worked out through trial and error and compromise.

"It *is* the best thing for her, isn't it?"

Moss didn't answer.

"They love her and care for her," Eulie told him. "They can provide for her. They've already been more like parents to her than Ma and Daddy ever were."

"They are good people," Moss agreed.

Eulie was silent for a long moment and then sighed.

"It's settled, then," she said. "Our Little Minnie will become Minnie Pierce. She never wanted to be 'one of those nasty Toby children.'" She could almost smile at the use of the abhorrent phrase. "Clara will marry Bug. The twins will spend the winter learning weaving from Miz Patch. And Rans . . ." She turned to Moss, biting down on her lip to hold back tears. "Help me keep this vow," she said. "If . . . or when . . . Rans gets to come back to us. I will give him his freedom. I will allow him to go and do and be whatever he wants. He is Rans Toby, a person himself, not merely my younger brother."

Moss patted her hand. "I won't have to help you keep it," he told her. "I know full well that you will."

She looked up into her husband-man's eyes. He believed in her. He trusted her. If he could do so after all that she'd done to him, surely she could believe and trust in herself.

The door opened and the sheriff walked in.

Eulie's backbone stiffened with apprehension. Moss rose to his feet and offered the man his hand.

"I'm Moss Collier," he said. "From up in the Sweetwood. This is my wife, who is sister to Ransom Toby."

The sheriff nodded at her and shook Moss's hand. The two men sat down.

He was big and sandy-haired with a pompous air about him. Eulie could sense that there was not one stitch of sympathy or understanding in his heart. He was the kind of fellow that never admitted to a mistake and had no tolerance for those who made them.

From inside the desk drawer he retrieved a gun.

"Is this yours?" he asked Moss.

The husband-man answered yes and reached for it. The sheriff shook his head.

"Sorry, the gun is evidence and must be confiscated," he said. The man hesitated for a long moment before adding, "that means we can't give it back to you."

The explanation was somewhat snide and very condescending.

"I know what confiscated means," Moss said evenly.

"Good," the sheriff commented, pleased. "Some of these folks from up in the mountains are none too bright and ignorant to boot. They don't understand the first thing about the law or the courts or even the state of Tennessee."

He snorted with derision and shook his head.

"You take them no-good Pusser brothers," he said. "They're from up your way, ain't they? That Delbert, he's more sly than he is smart. And his brother, Donald, I swear a man would get more intelligent conversation talking to a fence post."

"We heard Rans shot the Pusser brothers," Eulie said. "Are they . . . are they all right?"

The sheriff nodded. "Oh, they're right enough, I suppose," he said. "Donald was shot in the armpit. Doc Turner fished the slug out last night. He's likely to recover just fine. A bullet grazed Delbert's cheek. He ain't quite as handsome as he was, but he weren't all that handsome to begin with."

"Thank God," Eulie whispered.

"Witnesses say that the Pussers cheated the boy out of his money," the sheriff continued. "They say he only fired when Donald lunged at him."

"Then it was self-defense," Moss said.

"You do know a bit of the law," the sheriff answered.

"But no, it's pretty hard to claim self-defense with a gun against two unarmed men."

That statement brought an unhappy silence to the room.

"The truth is," the sheriff continued, "I don't really care too much about them Pusser brothers. They are cheats and criminals and got no worse than they deserve."

He paused for emphasis and looked Moss square in the eye.

"But Sam Wainthrop, he's the owner of that saloon. It ain't much, but it's Sam's livelihood. Your boy done shot up the place something fierce. There ain't hardly an unbroken piece of glass in the place."

"How many shots did he fire?"

"Oh, he emptied the gun," the sheriff said. "It's a wonder there weren't a lot more people with bullets in them."

Moss let his breath out slowly.

"If you could see your way clear to make some reparation on Sam's damage," the man continued. "I'd drop the charges down to a misdemeanor and let you take the boy home."

Eulie's mouth opened and her eyes lightened with hope. They could take him home. It would be a misdemeanor and they could take him home.

"How much would this reparation cost?" Moss asked.

The sheriff considered thoughtfully.

"Oh, I imagine twenty dollars would probably cover it," he said.

Eulie swallowed her buoyant expectation. Twenty dollars. That was a near-fortune.

She heard Moss clear his throat. It was a nervous sound.

"The money the boy was playing poker with," he told the sheriff. "That was my life savings. I don't have any more."

The sheriff nodded, understanding. "Too bad," he commented.

"Could I sign a paper?" Moss suggested. "Agree to pay it in the future? As soon as my crop comes in I'd have some of it."

The man shook his head. "I don't think Sam would go for that," he said. "But you could go to the bank here in town. Maybe they'd take a mortgage on your farm. It wouldn't hurt to ask."

"The land isn't mine," Moss said. "It's my uncle's and it's all that he has."

"Ahhh," the sheriff said. It was all he could say.

The three sat in silence for a very long minute. There were no words. Nothing to express. There was no way to raise twenty dollars.

"What will happen to Rans?" Eulie asked.

"That's up to the judge," the sheriff answered. "He'll be in town week after next and hear the case then. I'm sure he'll take the boy's youth and the evidence of cheating into account."

"Will he go to jail?" Moss asked.

"Not for long," he assured them. "Maybe a couple of years."

"Two years!" Eulie nearly screamed out the words.

"Maybe just one," the sheriff suggested quickly. "And he could get out a few months early if he minds his manners and does what he's told."

Eulie endeavored to compose herself. Screaming

and crying would do no one any good. Where was her cheerful ability to look on the bright side?

Deliberately, she forced herself to think of all the good things. At first, she was at a loss, but eventually her mind adjusted to the idea.

Rans wasn't hurt, and he didn't injure any innocent bystanders.

The Pusser brothers might have cheated him, but he had stolen Moss's money. So everything that had happened to him was his own fault. Going to jail was a reasonable consequence for his actions.

Folks always said that adversity builds character. Jail could end up being the making of Rans Toby.

If all that was true, why was her heart breaking? One of the problems of always believing that things will work out for the best is that when they don't, a person has nothing to fall back on.

"Can we see him?" Moss asked.

"Sure," the sheriff replied, rising to his feet. "He was pretty shook up at first. That graze across the face that Delbert took bled a lot and I think the boy believed that he had killed him. It'll do him good to see somebody from home."

The inside of the jail was dank and dark. Moss followed Eulie, who was wide-eyed and clearly frightened. There was only one bar-enclosed cell. Within it, three men waited for the next visit of the circuit judge.

Rans looked up when they walked in and hurried to greet them.

"You came!" he said. "I can't believe that you came!"

"Of course we did," Eulie told him. "The minute that we heard."

The reality of the situation overrode his joy and he glanced guiltily over at Moss.

"Then I suppose that you've heard everything," he said.

"We've heard everything but why," Eulie told him.

The boy lowered his eyes guiltily. When he raised them again honesty and sincerity shown through.

"I don't have any reason," he said. "I don't have any excuse."

They were words of truth, the kind that were always so very difficult to admit.

"I stole from your husband," he continued, "who gave us all a home together." He turned toward Moss and looked him in the eye, his voice softened with sincerity. "And I know how that really came about."

Moss took the words for what they were, a late apology, and gave the boy a nod of acceptance.

"I stole from him," Rans went on. "And lost the money. Then I used a gun to try to get it back."

"Oh, Rans," Eulie said, her words only a little above a whisper. She'd grasped the bars, the cold metal against her palms. The boy wrapped his own hands around hers in a protective gesture peculiar to little brothers.

"You know, Eulie, that I've always blamed Daddy for everything," he said. "I've always blamed him for my life. Blamed him for what people thought of me."

"Daddy had a lot of faults," Eulie conceded.

"He did," Rans agreed. "But in all the days that he lived, Virgil Toby never so much as stole a loaf of bread, he never gambled away anything, and he never raised a gun at another soul."

Rans lowered his head, full of regret.

"Daddy made his mistakes," he said. "And he had cause to be ashamed of them. But at least now it's certain that I won't never be one of the folks in the world in position to throw stones at him."

Rans and Eulie continued to talk. She explained to him about waiting for the judge's visit. She told him that he would probably go to jail.

The boy's confession and his bravery in the face of his fear impressed Moss. Rans was obviously near to quaking in his boots. But he pretended calm and control. And he tried to comfort his sister with those.

When he turned his attention to Moss, the boy's demeanor was both respectful and regretful.

"I won't belittle the wrong I've done you by promising that you'll get all your money back," Ran said. "I consider that debt my primary obligation, but it could be years before I can even begin to make good on it. And a life savings lost can take a lifetime to replace."

Moss nodded. He was surprised that the boy understood that. Perhaps Rans knew more of being a man than he had given him credit for.

"And I'm sorry I won't be there to help you get the crop in," he said. "At least when I get back from prison, I'll be bigger and stronger."

His words were determinedly cheerful and positive.

"Now you are beginning to sound like your sister," Moss told him. "Trying to see the silver lining in every dark cloud."

The boy nodded.

"I suspect it's a pretty fair way to live," he said. "Especially in a world that can be full of rain."

Eulie began to speak to her brother again, and Moss excused himself. He went back into the outer office and spoke to the sheriff once more.

"Where is this Sam Wainthrop's saloon?" he asked. "I thought I'd might go over and talk to the man."

The sheriff eyed him warily. "You ain't about to start something, are you?" he asked. "I know how you hill people can be about feuding and such."

Moss took the comment in stride. He was itching to point out to the disparaging sheriff that Jarl, Tennessee, was not exactly a high-toned flatland city, but he managed to restrain himself. Denials were a waste of breath. Strangers to the Sweetwood liked to believe that it was populated by ignorant, inferior people. They were often treated that way when they came down from the mountains. It was no wonder that most folks were so content to stay home.

"I'm not about to start anything," he assured the sheriff. "I want to talk to the man about those reparations."

That satisfied the man and Moss was given directions. Outside, he untied Red Tex from the hitching post and mounted up.

Moss rode through the little town in the direction of the river. He thought about the Sweetwood. He thought about Eulie. He thought about grazing cattle and the wild vast Texas prairie that he had never seen.

And he thought about Rans Toby.

He annoys ye so much, Jeptha had said, *because he's so much like ye.*

Moss had been uncertain what the man was talking about at the time. He was not at all like Rans. He never looked for trouble. He didn't have a hot temper. And he had nothing to prove to anybody.

But the two of them did share a common misconception. They both believed that life would be better if they could get away from the Sweetwood. Every time things got bad or feelings were hurt, Rans headed out, he ran away. Moss had never run. But just like the boy, the minute difficulties came his way, Moss was, in his mind, gone to Texas. He'd never settled into his life, never tried to improve his lot. He'd just dreamed about getting away.

Moss had had more years to think about it, and he'd managed to focus his hopes on a specific place, a faraway haven. Young Rans had just determinedly wanted to get away from the familiar, to get away from the life he knew and the troubles he had.

As he turned Red Tex's head toward the direction of the river, he wondered if either of them would have found out differently.

Truly, Moss believed that Sweetwood farming was not the finest choice of livelihood. He was certain that cattle grazing was a far superior way of life. But not every person got all the choices. A place couldn't make anyone happy and satisfied with life. Those things came from inside the heart. And they were as likely to be found in a hellhole as in paradise.

Red Tex drew a lot of admiring looks from passersby as they got closer to the water. The streets and alleyways got poorer, dirtier. Wainthrop's saloon was obviously not one patronized by the more upstanding of Jarl's citizens. When he located the place with the distinctive swinging yellow doors, he was even more convinced of that fact. It was a desperate place, catering to the tastes of desperate folk.

Moss almost hated to leave the horse tied at the hitch. The area around Wainthrop's bar was the kind of mean-living place where a man might rob his own grandmother in broad daylight for the penny in her garter stocking. A fine animal like Red Tex might well prompt a petty criminal to become a horse thief.

Moss patted the animal's neck affectionately as if encouraging the horse to take care of himself. Then he walked up to the building and stepped through the swinging doors.

In the clear light of day, the place was awful. It was as dirty and ill-kept as the handful of patrons sitting around guzzling pale, sudsy beer.

Moss surveyed the room for damage. The mirror behind the bar had caught a bullet. And from the point of entry a web of cracks fanned out in every direction. Clearly it was damaged beyond repair, but who would want to see themselves in a place such as this? The glassware was stored on shelves behind the bar. There were a lot of shelves and not very many glasses. It was quite probable that many of them had been victims of the shoot-out.

Moss walked along the length of the bar until he came to a place where the wood was gouged cleanly with a hole about as big around as his little finger. Moss surveyed the room carefully, looking for other damage. He didn't see any.

"Twenty dollars," he mumbled to himself. "I wouldn't give twenty dollars for the whole place."

"What can I get for you?" the bartender asked him.

"I'm looking for Sam Wainthrop." Moss answered.

The man looked immediately defensive. "What do you want him for?"

"A little matter of business," Moss said. "Are you Wainthrop?"

The man hesitated for a minute.

"Yeah, what of it?" he said finally.

Moss offered his hand. "My name's Collier," he told the man. "I come from up in the Sweetwood."

Wainthrop had accepted the handshake, but his expression got wary at the mention of the Sweetwood.

"You here about the shoot-out?" he asked.

Moss nodded. "The boy was my wife's brother."

The bartender looked him over uneasily as if assessing whether or not he was in physical danger.

"I didn't have nothing to do with nothing," he declared forcefully. "That boy came in here with those no-account Pusser brothers. He was ripe for plucking and they plucked him. I didn't have no part in it, nor profit neither."

"I didn't believe that you had," Moss told him. "I'm sure the Pussers didn't have no trouble getting the upper hand on a child of thirteen."

"That's the truth," Wainthrop agreed.

"Of course," Moss continued, "you didn't make any effort to put a stop to it, either."

"What could I have done?" the man asked, as a protest of innocence.

"Well, maybe you could have kept that marked deck out of their hands," he suggested.

Wainthrop swallowed nervously.

It was a nearly two hours later when Moss walked into the lockup section of the jail once more. The sheriff had kindly allowed Rans out of the cell, and he was seated with Eulie on a small bench at the end of the room. They were talking as perhaps they had never talked before, at times solemnly saying the words that brothers and sisters rarely voiced, but also remembering together the childhood memories that none but siblings could ever share.

"Where have you been?" Eulie asked when she glanced up and saw him. "You were gone so long, I was beginning to worry."

Moss grinned at her, pleased.

"Well, that's good, don't you think, Rans?" he said jokingly. "Wives are supposed to worry about their husbands. Especially when they are in town on their own for an hour or more."

His teasing was light and cheerful. He knew it contrasted with the dark, dank gloom of the jail. But he just couldn't keep the sunniness inside himself. He was a happy man.

Moss sat down in the narrow space next to Eulie and draped his arm around her back. Ostensibly this was to make more room on the bench, but in truth, Moss did it because he just simply wanted to hold her.

She smiled up at him and he grinned back.

"What is it?" she asked him.

Rans echoed her question. "You look like a cat that just fell in a crock of cream."

Moss didn't get time to answer. The door to the office opened, and the sheriff stood on the threshold.

"All right," the man said. "The paperwork is all signed and recorded. The charges are dropped. Toby, you're free to go."

"What?"

The question came from Rans and Eulie almost simultaneously.

"You're free to go," the sheriff repeated.

The brother and sister sat stunned. Moss rose to his feet. They turned to stare at him.

"Let's get on out of here before the man changes his mind," he suggested.

That was what they did. The sheriff returned Rans's shoes and galluses. And the boy tucked his pitiful sack of needments under his arm as they headed for the street.

"I can't believe it," Eulie said. "He don't even have to come back for the trial?"

"There is not going to be a trial," Moss told her. "The sheriff ruled it a fair fight. The Pussers can't complain unless they want to defend themselves as gambling cheats. And I don't think they'll want to do that."

From his pocket Moss withdrew at handsome wooden box and handed it to Rans.

The boy's eyes were wide as he pulled it open.

"It's the marked deck," he said.

Moss nodded. "I thought you might want it as a remembrance of your adventure in town."

"How did you—"

Moss held up a hand to silence him.

"Never mind about all of that," he said. "It's over. We're all tired. Why don't we go home?"

Eulie was smiling broadly, but her eyes were bright with unshed tears.

"I just can't believe it," she told him.

He shrugged. "I don't know why not," he said. "Aren't you the one who's always telling me how things work out for the best?"

He turned to Rans.

"Do you know how to get to the dock from here?" he asked.

The boy looked around for a minute to get his bearings. "I think it's a turn to the right at the next corner and then straight down the hill."

Moss nodded.

"Why don't you run on down there and ask the boatmen if anybody's headed up river this late in the day," he said. "If we can get partway by boat, maybe we'll be home by midnight or so."

"Yes, sir," Rans answered. "If there is any boat headed that way, I'll find it."

The boy took off at a dead run. It was as if freedom had by itself made his feet fly across the ground.

Moss turned to offer Eulie his arm.

She stood stock-still, staring at him.

"Aren't you going to take my arm?" he asked her. "It's not every day that a Sweetwood man gets to escort his bride through town."

"Where is Red Tex?" she asked him.

Moss scratched his head for a moment, looking thoughtful.

"You know your brother was right about that horse," he said. "A farmer just can't have an animal around the place that doesn't earn its own way."

"You sold your horse?" Her words were an incredulous whisper.

"I bought a bunch of broken beer glasses, some wood repairs, and a cracked mirror," he said. "And I got three dollars in my pocket and a deck of marked cards to boot."

"But Red Tex was so important to you," she said, her eyes searching his for answers. "He was part of your dream."

"Red Tex is a horse," Moss told her. "Your brother is family."

"How will you get to Texas?" she asked him.

"Well, I was kind of thinking I wouldn't go this year anyway," he said. "With all the things that need doing around the place and all, it seems like I'm not going to have all that much time to cater to my wanderlust."

He looked down into her eyes. He saw her love for him reflected there. He saw how much she cared.

"Texas will still be there next year," he assured her. "It will be there next year or in ten years, or even long after I'm gone."

"It's what you've always wanted," she reminded him.

Moss shrugged. "I don't seem to want it so much anymore," he said. "Besides, I'm planning on having you spend the rest of your life making it up to me."

"Making it up? How?" she asked.

Moss chuckled softly.

"Oh, some burnt dinners, a few scorched shirts, some mornings with nothing to put on over my underwear."

He took her hands in his own.

"A pat on the back at the end of a hard day, a kiss in the moonlight from time to time, a warm body beside me in bed at night. In due time, maybe a youngun or two."

"Oh, Moss."

"I love you," he told her. "It wasn't something that I intended to happen. It was never what I'd planned for my life. But the things we plan are not always what would make us happy. Travel and adventure, even cattle, seem a paltry substitute for the love of a good woman, a home, a hearth, a family."

Her eyes were misted with tears as she gazed up at him.

"You are my wife," he said to her. "There is nowhere in this world that could matter to me without you there. And when you are there, it no longer matters where in the world it is."

She wrapped her arms around his chest and held him so tightly, it was as if she would never let him go.

"Moss Collier, you are the most wonderful husband-man a gal ever trapped into marriage," she said.

23

IT was barely three weeks later, on the next Preaching Sunday, when, after a heartfelt sermon on the forgiveness of the woman at the well, Rans Toby slipped out of his place on the pew and made his way down to the front of the church to be saved. He manfully confessed his wrong to heaven and humbly asked to be forgiven.

"Jesus told the woman to 'go and sin no more,'" Rans stated before the congregation. "I believe he's saying the same to me. So from this day forward, I swear off gambling and drinking and . . . and, well, other sinful vices that I don't even know about yet."

There was a chorus of hearty *amens* from all around the building. Even the Pusser brothers, having taken their usual seat in the back of the church, looked a bit uncomfortable and sheepish as the young fellow took full blame for everything that had happened that day in town.

The people of the Sweetwood hadn't felt that way, and it had already been very strongly suggested that the two men, as soon as they were able-bodied once more, put in a goodly amount of time assisting Moss Collier until their debt was paid off.

Sitting proudly beside her husband-man in the

pew, Eulie squeezed Moss's hand, her eyes misting as she watched her little brother take his place of respect among the men of the Sweetwood congregation.

The service ended and there were hugs and handshakes all around. People congratulated Eulie as if she were the proud parent of Rans. She understood full well that her brother had taught her as much as she'd been able to teach him.

"The boy is going to do real fine," Miz Patch told her as the two walked out of the church together. "He ain't going to be perfect. And this ain't going to end all his troubles, but he's going to do real fine. We're all going to help him."

Eulie hugged the older woman joyfully. "I feel like I ought to pinch myself," she confessed. "Moss and I are so happy together. Clara and Bug are planning their wedding. The twins have a good future ahead of them learning to be weavers. And did you see how proudly Little Minnie sat on the Pierces' pew with her new mama and daddy?"

Miz Patch smiled at her and nodded.

"I always believe that somehow everything will work out for the best," Eulie told her. "But you know, when it does it's almost more scary than the messes I get myself into."

The older woman laughed, understanding.

They stopped and stood together in the meetinghouse doorway, gazing out onto the beauty of the misty mountains and the verdant green of summer. All around the clearing, friends, family, and neighbors were gathered together. They were talking, laughing, living everyday lives that in this one space of time were well and good.

The two reached the bottom of the church steps and began the walk through the long row of men and boys on either side of them.

"The joys and sorrows of life always have a way of balancing out," Miz Patch said. "Nobody lives happily ever after. But there is, ever after, plenty of happiness to go around. There are still going to be days to come when you are lower than a well digger. And times of such contentment and bliss they will make this moment pale by comparison."

Eulie shook her head in near-disbelief. "I can't imagine anything that could happen to make me happier than I am at this moment," she said.

They reached the end of the courting gauntlet. To Eulie's complete surprise, Uncle Jeptha had wheeled his cart up to the line.

"Sary Patchel," he called out. "May I see you home this evening?"

Epilogue

TYPICALLY, the fine gray saddle horse danced nervously as the twins, with the help of their current beaux, Stu Madison and Joe Browning, draped the banner upon the animals rump.

O.T. OR BUST, it read.

The horse was headed for the Oklahoma Territory. Land was being given away. All a person had to do was run in there and stake a claim. The animal was being readied to do just that. He was packed with great care, saddlebag evenly weighted on either side, a bedroll tightly stowed against the back of the seat, a rifle in the scabbard. The only unnecessary item was a wooden box with the name COLLIER etched into the top. It carried not essentials in the strictest sense of the word, but rather souvenirs of this place, these people, those things that he might never lay eyes upon again.

Once the sign was tied on to their satisfaction, the young people stood back to admire their handiwork and then turned to solicit an unbiased opinion.

"What do you think, Mr. Barnes?" Stu asked the neatly dressed, clean-shaven man in the goat cart.

Since his marriage six years ago to Miz Patch, Jeptha Barnes had become a common sight in the

Sweetwood, one that no longer drew stares or overt sympathy. Jeptha Barnes was merely Jeptha Barnes, a lucky fellow who had survived the war.

"It looks well enough," he told the young folks. "But that high-strung horse ain't going to stand for that sign across his backside very long. He's likely to toss off both his rider and all his gear just to get rid of it."

It was sage advice and undoubtedly true.

"Well, we'll let him take it down before he rides off," Cora Fay said.

"Just so he sees it and knows we did it," Nora May agreed.

Miz Patch came out from the kitchen building, two little scampering children at her heels. She carried a pokesack, which she handed to Browning.

"Tie this to the saddle horn," she said. "A fellow is bound to get hungry on the trail."

The young man did as she bid.

"Virgilia Collier!" she said sharply. "You get away from that horse's hooves. He'd as soon kick you as look at you."

Eulie's five-year-old daughter was an adventurous little soul, curious in the extreme and in trouble more often than out.

Her brother, young DeWitt, ignored the horse completely as he toddled on his fat baby legs toward his favorite place in the whole world. His arms outstretched, he hurried eagerly to plant a juicy baby kiss on Uncle Jeptha's cheek before settling himself comfortably in the front of the goat cart. The man, grinning ear to ear, hugged the narrow little shoulders to him.

"Where's Eulie?" Miz Patch asked.

The twins shared a glance before they replied.

"She was in the root cellar," Cora Fay said.

"She's crying and she doesn't want him to see it," her sister added.

Miz Patch nodded. "It's so hard for her to let him go."

"But she didn't say one word to make him stay," Nora May pointed out.

"That's 'cause it ain't her place," Miz Patch said. "He's a man and got it in his mind to go. She's got to let him."

The truth was accepted with nods all around.

"Looks like the Pierces coming up the hill," Jeptha said.

Everyone turned to look.

"Minnie!" the twins called out in unison and began running in her direction.

The beautiful young woman in the fashionable walking gown hurried toward them, her hand carefully holding down the elegantly dressed, wide-brimmed hat upon her head. The three met about midway up the slope and embraced joyously. They saw each other only on Preaching Sundays and special occasions, but they were now fast friends as well as former siblings. Hand in hand the girls walked together up to the group, where hugs and kisses were exchanged all around.

They were joined by the rest of the Pierce family. Little Enoch, who was three months older than Virgilia and never let her forget it, made a beeline for his playmate. Toby, who was a little bit shy, clung to his big sister's skirts until Minnie leaned down and picked him up. She was devoted to her little brothers and a great help to her mother in the care of them. She credited Eulie Collier as the person who taught her what a big sister ought to be.

Enoch and Judith brought up the rear of the procession, she, obviously in expectation of yet another child, leaning a bit heavily upon her husband's arm.

"We're so glad you came," Miz Patch said.

"We couldn't miss it," Judith assured her. "He's family to us. We have to say good-bye."

Miz Patch nodded and glanced toward her husband, who appeared to be in full agreement.

Enoch, forever a farmer and businessman, was surveying the area of the Barnes Ridge farm with some appreciation.

"This place looks better every time I see it," he said to Jeptha. "And I'm not talking about all the flowers and folderol Eulie's got growing about the place. That new barn is as pretty a sight as any on the mountain."

Jeptha beamed with pride.

"It's sure good and sturdy," he said. "It ought to last this place another hundred years."

"For a man who claims to hate farming," Enoch said, "Moss Collier has sure begun to shine when he turned his hand to it."

Moss's uncle couldn't have agreed more.

"Look! It's Clara coming on that old mule," Cora Fay said.

As one they turned to glance and wave in that direction.

"Why is she by herself?" Nora May asked. "I wonder where Uncle Bug and the boys are?"

They had to wait for the answer from the woman herself. She made her way along the side of the hill and then up the slope toward them. Sitting tall and proud upon the old mule, Clara was one of the most highly respected matrons in the Sweetwood. With her helping hand always extended to those in need, folks in hard times or trouble knew they would never be turned from her door.

She dismounted eagerly to hug her sisters, Miz Patch, Judith Pierce, and whichever children she could catch.

"Where's your family?" Minnie asked. "Surely they didn't want you coming here alone."

Clara shook her head.

"Haywood and Raywood have come down with the chicken pox," she announced.

There was a collective moan among the parents.

"I guess that means they'll all get it," Judith said, glancing toward her boys.

"You've already had it, though?" Miz Patch's statement was presented as a question.

Clara nodded. "Oh yes, I remember it as the summer of scratching and whining. We all got it, except Rans. And Minnie, she wasn't born yet."

The young girl moaned in distress.

"I hope I don't get it. I don't want any ugly pock marks on my complexion," she said.

Enoch chuckled lightly. "I wouldn't be that opposed to it," he said. "It might help thin out all those moon-eyed lollygaggers who hang around our front porch. I have to beat them off the place with a stick."

"Oh, Papa!" Minnie complained.

There was good-hearted laughter all around.

"Where Eulie?" Clara asked.

"She's in the root cellar," Miz Patch said. "She's taking it hard."

"I'll go talk to her."

The conversation resumed as Clara went to comfort her sister. Virgilia and Little Enoch were running like wild Indians through the posies that grew around the porch. Cora Fay and Nora May discussed the latest dress fashions with Minnie as their gentleman friends looked on, bored.

Inside the cabin, two men were discussing business.

Moss Collier, a little older and a little wiser, was still the dark-eyed, handsome man that Eulie had tricked into marriage, although he was beginning to fill out some in the middle, evidence of good living and contented pleasure. Beside him, Ransom Toby was now a hairsbreadth taller than Moss himself, long-legged and slim. His face still carried that testy, suspicious, dissatisfied expression that had sat so ill upon him as a boy.

Women found this irresistible. At nineteen, he was the undisputed heartthrob of the Sweetwood. The young ladies would have gladly set up their own courting gauntlet for him to walk through.

"This is the last of it," Rans said as he laid out a stack of coins upon the table.

Moss counted the coins as he picked them up.

"Your obligations are definitely paid in full," he told the younger man. "The stolen money, the gun, even old Red Tex has been accounted for."

"You've been good to me, Moss," Rans said. "I wouldn't want us to part with me still owing you anything but my friendship."

Collier accepted the words and the payment gracefully.

The two men clasped hands. They were equals now, brothers. There was a mutual respect born of long grueling hours working together for a common goal. And the unquenchable love of the family they shared.

"The land that's going to be in the run," Moss said, "a lot of it is farming land, but the opportunities for grazing are tremendous, and it's so much closer to the railhead than most of Texas."

Rans nodded in agreement.

"And you still think cattle to be more profitable than farming?"

"No question about it," Moss answered, giving Rans a hearty pat upon the back. "And grazing is so much more pleasant than farming. It's the kind of life a man could really take pleasure in."

"We'd better get out there," Rans told him, glancing toward the door.

Moss was in full agreement.

"The good-byes will take a coon's age," he said. "And there's a lot of ground to be covered before dark."

"I just wanted to . . . I wanted to thank you," Rans said. "You've done so much for our family. I know how you and my sister came to be married. She told me all those long years ago. There aren't many men who would have taken us all on with such a glad heart."

Moss chuckled. "Truthfully, I wasn't that glad about it at first," he said. "But it's all worked out for the best."

"You sound like Eulie," Rans pointed out.

"That happens when you marry," Moss said. "You begin to take on the qualities you most admire in your mate. One of these days you'll find that out for yourself."

"I hope not very soon," Rans told him with a chuckle of honesty.

The two men stepped out onto the porch, and a cheer erupted from the family and friends gathered. Eulie and Clara came around the corner from the direction of the root cellar. Both were tearful, but smiling, determined to see only the silver lining of the nearest dark cloud.

The good-byes were heartfelt and effusive. With the Oklahoma Territory so far away and so many dangers between here and there, it was unlikely that they would ever see him again. There had to be enough plain speaking and sentiment to last a lifetime. Handshakes and hugs were offered all around. Most everyone was dry-eyed for his sake, but here and there the unmistakable evidence of tears could be seen. The sorrow of farewells must be allowed to run their course.

Finally, he stood beside the saddle horse as it stomped uneasily, eager to be gone. Eulie met him there. Her nose was a little red and her eyes a little puffy, but she smiled up at him with love. He grinned back. She wrapped her arms around his neck, holding him close to her for a long moment.

"I'll think about you every day and pray for you every night," she told him.

"I'm counting on it," he said.

They were close, these two. As close as a brother and sister could be.

Rans mounted up and raised an arm in salute before turning the horse toward the downward slope.

"I'll send word as soon as I get settled," he promised.

They followed him a little way, calling out last-minute advice and cheering him on. One by one they dropped out of the parade until only the children pursued him.

Eulie stood watching him go. When he reached the bottom of the hill, she would call the children back. She wished that she could call him back as well, but she could not. Her family was not something that she owned, something that she could control. Even her own children were not. They were lent to her to enrich her life, but ultimately their own choices would have to take precedence over what she wanted for them.

A pair of warm, strong arms wrapped around her shoulders. She looked up into the face of her husband-man.

"Did he pay you the rest of the money he owed?" she asked him.

Moss nodded.

"Yes ma'am, he sure did," he replied. "And I managed to sneak it into his saddlebags while he was saying his good-byes. He's going to need it a lot more than we will."

She turned in his arms and gazed up into her husband's eyes, so in love, so fulfilled.

"Are you jealous?" she asked him. "Do you wish it was you heading off on the trail?"

He grinned at her. "I would sure look a sight with you and these little youngers following after me."

It wasn't really an answer, so she held her ground, waiting for one.

"There is a part of me that envies him," Moss admitted. "I envy his youth, his freedom. I envy the sense of adventure."

Eulie nodded, appreciating his honesty.

"But," Moss continued, "if he knew how happy and contented I am with my little farm, my little children, with my wife, he would envy me. Youth is not as pleasant as it should be. And a man craves freedom only when he doesn't have it."

"What about adventure?" she asked him.

He pulled upon a lock of pale blonde hair that had escaped from the coil at the back of her head and gave an exaggerated, long-suffering sigh.

"Being married to you is more adventure than most men could take—even under threat of a shotgun."